By His Grace & Favor

BOOK ONE
LORD DERE'S DEPENDENTS

CHRISTINA DUDLEY

PROLOGUE

In the agitation of their thoughts, and much discours of things hear aboute, at length they began to incline to this conclusion, of remoovall to some other place.
—Wm Bradford, *History of Plymouth Plantation* (c.1620)

If Mrs. Markham Dere had any regrets in her uniformly pleasant life, it was that she had no one to tell her how well she had done for herself. For with nothing but lavish beauty, grace, plentiful fortune, an enterprising mother, and impeccable connections, she had succeeded in capturing the heart of Mr. Markham Dere, heir to the Dere barony. And while this fortunate union lasted only until Mr. Dere's premature death seven years later from a suppuration formed in consequence of pneumonia, it was quite long enough to be blessed with a son and for Mrs. Markham Dere to have become thoroughly familiar with her husband's foibles. Flaws which, once he was departed, she could bury in forgetfulness and sentiment.

And to all these marks of providential favor was added yet one more: Mrs. Markham Dere became mistress of Perryfield without being required to await the current baron's decease.

"It is too bad the rector has three or four boys already boarding with him and cannot take on another," she sighed to this current baron, one Lord

Ranulph Dere, on one of her regular calls at the great house. "And too bad moreover that it would not be appropriate for a tutor to live with Peter and me at the cottage."

After a hesitation the baron replied in his soft voice, "I suppose the tutor might lodge here at Perryfield and teach Peter in the old schoolroom."

"Do you think?" she brightened, looking much like the handsome Miss Ingles she had once been. "That is so good of you to offer, Uncle! And it would be *so* convenient for Peter. The walk from Iffley to Perryfield and back five times per week will not be so very bad for a small boy like him, except on those inclement days when I daresay I could hire the cart from the inn to bring him."

Lord Dere regarded in puzzlement his great-nephew Peter, who was not so very small, and whom the peer would have called a healthy, roaring boy—just see how he swung his restless limbs as he sat, the heels of his boots thwacking satisfactorily against the mahogany chair legs! But perhaps Mrs. Dere could not help her concern, after the lung ailment which carried off her husband.

"You both might consider removing here to Perryfield, now that my nephew is no more," Lord Dere mused, helpfully inserting his foot in the trap. "When Markham was alive, of course, he liked to have his own roof, as any young man would, but now..."

"Now that he is gone," whispered Mrs. Dere, applying her handkerchief to the corners of her eyes. "Things are so altered!"

"Yes. I am sorry for it, my dear. He ought to have long outlived me. But again, now that Markham is gone and Peter is heir to Perryfield, perhaps it makes sense for you both to remove here."

His niece by marriage showed just the proper amount of reluctance, raising possible objections only to yield quickly, asking to be taken through the rooms that very day, and, indeed, almost before Lord Dere could say Jack Robinson, Mrs. Markham Dere and Peter were installed in his home.

A brief tussle followed between the new mistress and Mrs. Robson, the housekeeper of twenty years, but Mrs. Dere prevailed in this as well, as she did in all things.

Not a month later she sat at the Perryfield breakfast table, bathed in triumph and mild summer sunshine, running an approving eye over the new paint and plaster of the room (truly, the paper chosen by Lord Dere's mother had been so hideously old-fashioned!).

"Post, madam," announced the footman Wood, marching straight past Lord Dere's outstretched hand to deposit the stack at Mrs. Dere's place.

"Ah," she purred. "Answers to my advertisement."

"Which advertisement?" asked Lord Dere. He was not unhappy with the recent changes to life at Perryfield, but he was sorry Wood did not hand him the post.

Mrs. Dere shuffled through the letters. "For Peter's tutor, naturally."

"Did the rector have no one to suggest? One might shoot an arrow over Oxford and bring down a flock of tutors."

"I think it always best to consider every possibility," she answered. "Where has Wood gone? Here is one letter for you, sir. Peter, pass this to Lord Dere."

Always eager for movement, the boy sprang up, tipping his plate when he pushed off the table and sending his toast butter-downward on the cloth. His mother clicked her tongue but did not look up, and the next moment Lord Dere's letter was delivered, now bearing several greasy fingerprints.

After Mrs. Dere sorted the candidates into two piles, she began to re-read the promising replies, that she might further winnow the chaff from the wheat. Absorbing work, which was why she did not notice Lord Dere's murmurings until Peter cried, "Who, sir? Who will have the Iffley cottage?"

Lord Dere raised his pale blue eyes, still clear despite his eight-and-fifty years. "Mrs. Barstow, my boy."

"Mrs. *Barstow*?" repeated Mrs. Dere. "My good sir, what are you talking about?"

"I daresay you have never heard of her," he answered gently. "She would have been Markham's cousin—first cousin, once removed, or second cousin? At any rate, my own aunt's youngest child, so *my* cousin Camilla, whom I have not seen, oh, for years and years. But I remember her as a sweet, shy person. She married a clergyman. And perhaps I met her oldest child once as an infant? Yes, I do believe I did—bright brown eyes, which is a curious thing, isn't it? Brown eyes are usually described as 'warm,' not 'bright'—"

"But sir," interrupted Mrs. Dere, "what of this Mrs. Barstow? What did Peter say about the Iffley cottage?"

"It was *I* who was saying it. That, now that you and Peter have removed to Perryfield, I may offer the Iffley cottage to the Barstows."

"But—but—you say Barstows in the plural? Who are these Barstows?"

"Heavens, Mrs. Dere, I just explained to you. My cousin Mrs. Barstow—Camilla—and her one, two, three..." He consulted the letter again, frowning and then tapping his fingertip on the table to count—heaven forfend!—each additional Barstow!

Mrs. Dere's hand fluttered to her bosom, all the tutorial candidates forgotten. "Lord Dere, what can you be thinking? Peter and I have only just quit the cottage! And while I was as careful a mistress of it as any in England, you will remember Peter is an active boy, so it would benefit from new paint and—and—carpets—"

"Draw up a list, Mrs. Dere, and it will all be done, though in that case I had better write to this...*Miss* Barstow (the eldest daughter) and tell her their removal must wait until after harvest home, or there will be nobody to do the work. Perhaps they may come in another month."

"But who precisely is 'they'?"

His smooth brow furrowed as he pondered the grammar of her question, but upon deciding it was correct though odd-sounding, he said, "Mrs. Barstow and her four daughters, one son, and one widowed daughter-in-law with infant, poor creature."

Mrs. Dere swayed in the face of this astonishing assembly of unmarried ladies and fatherless children springing up *ex nihilo*, and she stared at him, utterly confounded. Her son Peter dropped the marmalade spoon on the cloth, however, and shouted, "A son? The Barstows have a son? How old is he, sir?"

"Let me see...seven. Gordon Barstow is seven. Why, you and he might share this new tutor! Mrs. Dere, in your calculations, you will have to determine if any of these young men would be amenable to *two* pupils, rather than just the one. But—oh, dear—if it was too much to expect Peter here to walk from the Iffley cottage to Perryfield for lessons, perhaps it will also be too much for this Gordon."

"Yes," Mrs. Dere struck in, recovering her wind and rising to face this new eight-headed peril. Who *were* these Barstows, that they thought nothing of draping their eight selves about the neck of a distant relation and demanding he save them? What was the world coming to? Oh, how disagreeable to have the baron's compassion so easily played upon!

"Too far for Gordon indeed," she resumed. "He had better be sent to school in Oxford. Magdalen College School or Nixon's."

"No, Mama!" protested Peter, going unheeded.

"Or perhaps these persons would do better to remain where they are. So many children! Why should they all uproot themselves?"

Lord Dere sighed, shaking his distinguished, silver-haired head. "But they must go somewhere, Mrs. Dere. For they have been overcome by misfortune. In the last year, both my cousin Camilla's husband and her older son have died! The son first, from injuries sustained in a naval action, and Mr. Barstow more recently of a fever. The new priest kindly did not expel them at once from the parsonage, though he would have been within his rights, but Mrs. Barstow says they cannot stay and stay."

"But—but—*eight* people, Lord Dere! The cottage could not hold *five* in any comfort!"

"You are right to say it will be a squeeze. Perhaps—if the walk for Gordon will be burdensome—perhaps some of them should join us at Perryfield? Though they may not like to be separated after so much loss."

He could not have more swiftly silenced all Mrs. Dere's objections if he had meditated on the matter for a fortnight. The mere mention of this potential danger, of having to invite any of this *swarm* of poor relations to share the roof and possibly the rule of Perryfield, took her breath away. Lord—better to stuff eight penniless, luckless, hapless dependents in Iffley Cottage than to welcome any (or all!) to Perryfield! Suppose this Mrs. Barstow or any of her hundred daughters or the daughter-in-law should be a cunning, enterprising baggage? Insupportable! But one could not gather so many females without at least *one* of them turning out to be a minx. Ah, Mrs. Dere mourned anticipatively, it was the ruin of everything. Absolutely everything. For what would become of her own golden life, which she had arranged exactly how she wanted it?

She was too new to Perryfield and to managing Lord Dere to insist on her own way and too wise a woman to act rashly. Therefore she beat a decorous retreat.

"You are right, Lord Dere. They will not like to be separated. I am certain room can be found at the cottage. It is likely the children were already sharing bedchambers at their rectory and would prefer to continue. And if the son is but seven, the others cannot be much older."

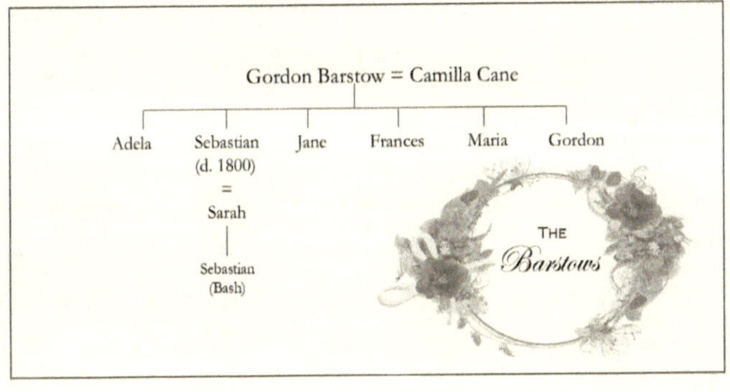

Gordon Barstow = Camilla Cane

Adela   Sebastian   Jane   Frances   Maria   Gordon
          (d. 1800)
             =
          Sarah

          Sebastian
          (Bash)

THE
Barstows

CHAPTER 1

He must needes go, whom the dyvel dryveth.
—Thomas More, *The confutacyon of Tyndales answere*
(1532)

It was her sister's elopement which finally broke her.

Miss Barstow, eldest child of the Reverend and Mrs. Gordon Barstow, had managed to survive the successive deaths within a twelve-month of her ailing father and her beloved brother, as well as the defection of the young curate she thought to marry. She had survived, as well, the impending loss of their home to the new parson and had even succeeded in securing a new roof to shelter them by appealing to her mother's cousin, whom no one but her mother even remembered. And lastly she had not only survived, but had *organized*, the visits of the bailiff to make his inventory, and the remover, to pack up what little remained.

All these things Adela Barstow had done. With tears, yes, but tears she managed to hide from the rest of the family.

But on the morning when the Barstows were to climb into the diligence which would take them from Twyford to Henley on the first leg of their journey, Adela found Jane and her portmanteau gone, with only a note pinned to her pillow.

"'Dear Della,'" read the hasty scribble, "'you will never forgive me, and yet I beg you to. I have gone with Roger. I love him, you understand, and if I were to accompany you all into Oxfordshire, I would never see him again. I know Papa did not approve of him, thinking him too wild, but my Roger promises me he has only been adrift because he had nothing to anchor him in life. When we return from Scotland, he plans to throw himself on his aunt's mercy and see if she will not purchase him an army commission. Do not fear for me, Adela, and tell my mother what you can to comfort her. Who knows? Perhaps if fortune smiles upon Roger and me, I may one day have something to give in support of our poor family. In the meantime this will spare you the expense of keeping me. I know you will be their rock, Della. And only think how much better seven will fit in Iffley Cottage than eight! All my love. Your sister, Jane.'"

Adela fainted.

Fortunately she had been sitting on their shared bed at the time, so that, when she returned to consciousness and saw the familiar beamed ceiling, her first thought was, "Thank heavens! It was only a dream."

But it was no dream. First she noticed that the beams were running crosswise to her usual morning view. And then that she lay atop the coverlet, not beneath it.

"No," she moaned, sitting up. "No, no, no. She cannot have done this." But there was the note, fallen from her hand, and there was Jane's announcement in black and white.

She was gone. With the rakish Roger Merritt.

The next thing Adela knew, the tears she had held back for weeks and months welled up. Brimmed. And then overflowed with such force she did not know if she could ever stop them again. Nor were they silent. They were accompanied by wails she could not stifle to save her life. Wails which began somewhere in her stomach and swelled and spiraled, bursting forth at last with alarming loudness. It felt and sounded like the end of the world, and Adela might have gone on crying until such time if, in one of the gaps between her racking sobs, her ear had not caught shuffling and whispering and hushing.

Jamming a ruthless fist against her mouth, she screwed her eyelids tight, and, with shoulders shaking from the effort, gradually choked herself into silence, listening again. And though she heard nothing this time, she *felt* them there.

At last, with a sigh, she rolled onto her side and cast bleary eyes at the doorway, where every last remaining member of the Barstow family crammed, regarding her in dismay. Her mother Mrs. Barstow, soft blue eyes wide, hands to her lips. Her sister-in-law Sarah, brow furrowed, jogging baby Bash in her arms. Adela's second sister Frances peering over the shoulders of the two widows, while youngest sister Maria tried to poke her head between. Even Adela's younger brother Gordon was trying to wriggle his way into the room, the white lapdog Poppet clutched to him.

"Let me, Mama," insisted Gordon. "Poppet will comfort her."

"But Della, you *never* cry," nine-year-old Maria declared.

With a squirm and a yelp, Poppet writhed his way to freedom and bounded forward to paw at Adela's slippered foot, followed by the rest of them. It was like the first crack in the dike before the whole structure collapsed, Adela thought later, for her own tears were lost in the floods of the others'. After some minutes of this collective mourning, even Poppet began to whimper in sympathy, but his contribution recalled them to themselves enough that they smiled ruefully at each other, rubbing at their faces and digging for handkerchiefs.

"Della, darling," her mother sighed, "you have been so strong for us all! I am almost glad to see you weep at last. For what family was ever asked to bear so much in so little time? First Sebastian and then—your father—and now to leave Twyford—to go—"

"It is not only that, as if all that were not enough," hiccuped Adela, her voice breaking again. "Mama, you must brace yourself because I am afraid—I am afraid there is yet one thing more to bear."

"One thing more?" gasped Mrs. Barstow. "Has something come from Lord Dere? May we no longer have Iffley Cottage?"

Adela shook her head at this, dashing a hand at her eyes. But she could not—*could not*—bear to share the thunderbolt herself and therefore thrust Jane's note at her brother's widow. With trepidation, Sarah hitched Bash on her hip and read.

"What is it, Sarah?" Mrs. Barstow breathed.

Her daughter-in-law sank to the bed, her stricken gaze meeting Adela's. Then, with what gentleness she could, she imparted the shocking news of Jane's elopement.

Sarah was at once swallowed in a tide of questions and exclamations from Frances, Maria, and Gordon, but Mrs. Barstow only went very, very white. So white that it effected an immediate, if temporary cure on Adela, who sat up to gather her mother in her arms.

"Sit, Mama."

"She is ruined," whispered Mrs. Barstow.

"I hope not," Adela replied. "I think Mr. Merritt *will* marry her." And again, when her mother shook her head, wordless and shocked: "He *will*, Mama. He *must* marry her. He could not treat a gentleman's daughter so."

"But there is no longer any gentleman to protect her." Mrs. Barstow choked. With an effort she raised a shaking hand to grasp Adela's shoulder. "But even if he does marry her, what will become of them, having only the two hundred pounds a year from his aunt? Suppose the aunt is so angry she cuts him off entirely?"

"I don't know. She wouldn't, would she? The elopement is scandalous, but Jane is a good girl. Jane will win her, Mama."

"I hope so, darling. Heaven help us! Heaven help my poor Jane. I am glad her father is not here to see this. Nor Sebastian. Sebastian would be compelled to pursue them and—and—" she broke off, but each younger Barstow remembered Sebastian's high courage and protectiveness and shuddered. Yes, better that Sebastian never knew about this either.

"Della, do you think we ought to write to Lord Dere to inform him?" her mother asked.

"What could Lord Dere do for us?" returned Adela.

"Nothing in the way of help," Mrs. Barstow answered. "I only meant, is it right of us to come, when this has happened? Would we still be welcome, with this scandal now hanging over us?"

"I—I don't know."

And she didn't. But how could they even consider telling Lord Dere and risk the possibility of him rescinding his offer? What would become of them then?

"It is too late," Adela made excuses. "We go today. He expects us. It is too late for thunderbolts. If—if he asks us to leave when he learns the truth, then we will have to face it, but perhaps he will take pity on us. It is always more difficult to—be heartless—face to face."

There were a thousand other questions. A hundred thousand! All of them to be raised and fretted over and despaired of, but none to be answered. Not that they did not try. Even without Jane, the Barstows were so numerous that, for several portions of their journey into Oxfordshire, the other passengers chose outside seats. And on those occasions, whenever the younger children happened to doze, Mrs. Barstow and Adela and Sarah whispered and whispered.

In the best of all possible worlds, Roger Merritt and Jane Barstow would make all haste to Gretna Green and be married by week's end. They would then proceed into Shropshire where Mr. Merritt's aunt (whose name the Barstows did not even know) would greet the match with unexpected joy, perhaps inviting them to take up residence with her in her modest home and telling her nephew and niece that they must consider all she had as their own. Jane would then write to them of how Mr. Merritt had metamorphosed into a quiet man who enjoyed quiet pleasures, and, after some years, there would be two children and no more, so that they might always live within their means.

But when they thought of Roger Merritt, dashing and reckless, full of jests and fond of sport, such an outcome seemed unlikely, if not altogether impossible.

"He loves her, however," Sarah tried to comfort them. "I'm sure of it. They will marry. You know how...lively my own Sebastian was before we wed."

Mrs. Barstow seconded this, though her dear son had not been a thing like Roger Merritt, except perhaps in his enjoyment of riding and shooting, and Sebastian's years in the navy gave him a discipline Roger Merritt utterly lacked. Thus the two widows reassured each other, however, for remembering Sebastian Barstow was a more pleasant activity, though bittersweet, than dwelling on Jane's folly.

It was left to Adela through the long hours to consider what, if anything could be done. How very vulnerable they were, with no male relative to champion them! No one to pursue the couple in hopes of discovering Jane, or to take her away before it was too late. No one to demand that Merritt do what was proper, or to punish the man if he refused.

No one.

The Barstow ladies were fatherless, husbandless, brotherless. And the only two Barstow gentlemen left to them were ages seven and six months, respectively.

The idea first came to her in Henley, when they transferred from the Twyford coach to the Oxford-bound one, this diligence quite jammed with passengers, including clergymen and fellows of the colleges, making private conversation impossible.

At first Adela wondered if this cousin of her mother's, this Lord Ranulph Dere, might be enlisted to aid them. If they managed to keep Jane's elopement secret until they proved what good tenants and respectable people they were, might he not then be trusted with the information? Trusted not to expel them and even to help them find the couple? And if Jane and Merritt were not yet married, surely a baron could exert his influence, even one as old as Adela's mother guessed. A baron was a baron, after all.

If the Barstows could win Lord Dere, flatter him, ingratiate themselves, could he be brought to bestir himself on their behalf?

From there it was but a short step to her next conclusion: if Lord Dere could somehow be bound by a nearer tie than mere "distant cousin" or the still chillier "benefactor," his charity toward them would accordingly metamorphose into *obligation*. If he became, say, a husband or father to them, charity would become Duty.

Adela scrutinized her mother under her lashes. Mrs. Barstow had dozed at last, her head fallen against Sarah's shoulder. Could it be done? Could Mrs. Barstow save them? They had not reached Nettlebed, however, before Adela regretfully discarded the possibility. Her mother would never.

It was not that Mrs. Barstow boasted no lingering charms. Her stature was elegant, her features regular, her hair only sprinkled with silver. But her widowhood was too recent, and she had been devoted to her husband. Adela could not imagine even suggesting the idea to her without shattering her mother's careful composure like glass.

Still less could it be asked of the second Barstow widow Sarah. Beg Sarah to forget her young, dashing naval husband for a man of nearly sixty, in order to secure the welfare of her many, many in-laws? Poor Sarah was already sharing her tiny pension with them, though by rights she should be saving it for herself and Bash. No. Sarah could not save them either.

Then I *must do it*, Adela thought.

Something clutched her about the midsection at the realization, making it difficult to breathe and driving her heart into her throat.

Marry a strange lord old enough to be her father? Older, even, for Mr. Barstow had been but four and fifty at his death.

I must. How can we go on, otherwise? It was not just Jane's elopement—that was simply another nail in the coffin. The largest and most final nail, perhaps, but heaven knew there had been plenty of nails to begin with. Adela was grateful already to Lord Dere for the offer of the Iffley cottage. It was smaller than the rambling Twyford parsonage, but of necessity would fit them, and the baron charged a rent which would hardly cover its maintenance. He also had found two servants for them, relations of those at Perryfield, and offered to pay the manservant's wages, that he might assign him additional tasks required to keep the cottage in good repair. To these gifts was added another equally precious: Gordon might share his great-nephew's tutor! Adela had been lying awake nights wondering how her younger brother might be educated—he might study hard enough to win a scholarship, but even if he succeeded, after losing both Mr. Barstow and Sebastian, how could the Barstow women bear to send Gordon away to school?

So far Lord Dere has been generous and kind-hearted. If not for these boons, who knows what would become of us, with only Mama's little legacy and Sarah's widow's pension? As it was, they must watch and count and scrape every penny.

Yes, Lord Dere looked to be kind and generous and—and wasn't that what mattered in a husband? Not youth or looks or dash. Only see how such things had turned Jane's head and led her to disaster! Not only her, but all of them, if Jane's misadventure became known.

But Jane must have thought of that, Adela realized—Jane must have known that her family's instant departure from Twyford guaranteed that the scandal could be dampened, if not altogether kept secret. Who in Oxfordshire would note Jane's absence (besides Lord Dere), the Barstows being complete strangers to the place? They would appear in the community, all in some degree of mourning and all *female*, save Gordon and baby Bash, and perhaps one young lady more or less would not even be noticed.

But Lord Dere would know one of them was missing...Lord Dere and the niece living with him. Adela recalled uneasily a line from the baron's last letter: "No need to mention the terms of the lease nor the servants' wages to my niece Mrs. Markham Dere. Having lived at the cottage herself, she will have strong opinions as to the 'proper way of doing things.'"

Frowning, Adela ran a gloved finger along a crack in the leather-covered bench of the diligence. How could she have forgotten the opinionated niece? A person who felt strongly about the "proper way of doing things" would most certainly deem elopements reprehensible. And elopements which might or might not end in actual *marriage* even worse. Mrs. Dere might even persuade the baron that he must put utmost distance between scandal and their own exalted family. Suppose Mrs. Markham Dere refused to associate with the Barstows, or insisted they be driven from Iffley? Oh, heaven!

Even if the Barstows succeeded in keeping their secret, such a person as Mrs. Dere would certainly object to any upstart dependent trying to worm her way into Lord Dere's heart, and Adela could hardly blame her. Such a May-December affair would not only reflect poorly on the baron, but it would threaten the inheritance of Mrs. Dere's own son.

Oh, my, my, my. How complicated things grew. Clearly Mrs. Markham Dere must be added to the task list for Adela. Such a person would need to be blinded or won over, or at least distracted from what was happening under her nose.

Her heart beating faster as anguish pressed upon her, Adela gave a desperate shake of her head and mentally pushed aside Mrs. Markham Dere for later consideration. Later, later. The baron was enough to deal with, for the present.

Adela tried to imagine him. Would he be heavy, old, gouty? Or wizened and gnome-like? Would she have to woo him through an ear trumpet? If so, she could hardly hope to do so without Mrs. Dere noticing.

Adela was young enough that she had never had to ask such questions before. Mr. Liddell the curate may not have been dashing, but he was youthful and sufficiently attractive, and Adela had thought she could well learn to love him. But he had chosen instead a bride who brought with her the promise of his very own living, and that had been that.

By the time they reached Shillingford, where they drank overpriced tea while waiting for the horses to be changed, Adela had formed her resolve. If she could at all manage it, she would marry Lord Dere.

"What is there to smile about?" demanded fifteen-year-old Frances crossly, rolling her shoulders and trying to stretch her back. "Between the jolts of the cart ruts and sitting between Gordy and Bash, it's impossible to know a moment's peace. At least you have some cushion where you sit. You ought to take a turn in my place."

Adela made a face at her. "I will, then. And you may sit beside the matron who smells of gingerbread and complains if anyone opens the window so much as a whisker." But she made an effort thereafter to school her features, lest she have to answer any questions. This must be her own secret, for everyone would try to talk her out of it, and then what would become of them?

Besides, in the face of such long odds, her smile had been more rueful than amused, for she had been thinking how curious it would be, to be Lady Dere, the wife of a baron!

CHAPTER 2

**They were then only passengers in a common vehicle.
—Edmund Burke, *Two Letters addressed to a Member of the
Present Parliament* (1796)**

The Henley Coach rattled into the busy yard of the Angel Inn in the early evening and discharged its burden of the exhausted, dusty and disheartened.

A young man seated in the coffee room glanced up, as he had at each new vehicle to turn from the High Street into the yard. On the three previous occasions he soon returned to his newspaper, but this time his attention was caught and held by a large party of ladies and children, all dressed in varying degrees of black or black trim despite the warmth of the day.

Curiosity piqued, he had not long to wait before, in the constant comings and goings at the busy inn doors, a firm but sweet voice reached his ears. "—Of carriages ordered by Lord Dere of Perryfield?"

"You too, miss? Not yet, I'm afeared," answered the innkeeper. "But if you care to wait within, there is another gentleman in the coffee room also on the watch for his lordship's coach."

The next instant a small young lady with dark hair appeared beside the host, her gaze following the man's pointing finger and surprising the watching young man before he could look away. For a lingering moment they studied each other, fascinated. Her rosy lips parted in uncertainty, but before he could nod or otherwise acknowledge her, the bell of the door jingled, and she turned away.

Adela (for it was she) found herself a little breathless. She should not have stared. The man was undeniably attractive, with his waving red-brown hair, intent look, and well-formed person. She had not noticed at first the shabby state of his clothing or how his coat pulled at his shoulders as if tailored for a narrower man. Whoever he was, whether Lord Dere's steward or lawyer or man of business, she had no intention of thrusting an acquaintance on him, nor of waiting awkwardly in the same coffee room. But before she could slip out, every other Barstow crowded through the door, pushing her further and further within. The clamor of voices grew, but Adela replied first to her mother. "No. No carriage yet, madam, but doubtless it will be along shortly. We had better wait in the yard, there being so many of us—" (Not to mention, if they remained in the coffee room, Maria and Gordy would surely beg that something be purchased in the way of refreshment, and they had already spent too much at Shillingford.)

"Della," cried Gordon now, winding a coaxing arm about her and lifting round green eyes, "there is a man outside with a box of kittens. Hadn't we better take one as a friend for Poppet?"

"We ourselves are Poppet's friends, Gordy."

"But a *small* friend! And suppose Iffley Cottage is overrun by mice."

From the way her mother put her hands on the boy's shoulders, Adela knew Mrs. Barstow had already told him he might choose one if Adela said he might. And indeed, little Gordon's winning looks and manner usually secured him everything he asked for from the women of his family, even more so with the recent loss of the older Barstow men.

"Suppose there is already a housecat at the cottage," Adela persisted. "Wouldn't seven new tenants and a dog be difficult enough for him and the servants, without adding a new cat?"

"But Della, you told us before we left Twyford that new places and new sights and new acquaintances made life an adventure, and that surprises were half the fun of it."

Adela lifted dubious brows. If she had said such a thing to her younger siblings (and she likely had), of them all, the absconded Jane had been the one to understand her most literally. Wherever she was, Jane's life was now nothing *but* new places and new sights and new acquaintances.

"Only do come see, Adela!" urged her youngest sister, appearing on the other side of Gordon and clasping pleading hands. "There is the most cunning one with a little mask of black and brown spots."

Sighing in defeat, Adela followed her siblings out to the innyard, finding her mother's arm wound through hers.

"Thank you, darling," Mrs. Barstow murmured. "I think the gambols of a kitten might cheer us, and it will cost us nothing. We can feed it scraps." Adela noted with sadness that her mother appeared to have aged in the two days since Jane's disappearance, but perhaps the same could be said of herself, for the fatigues of the journey had not profited any of them.

The kitten was exactly as Maria described, and it regarded Adela with impossibly round eyes. Irresistible. When Maria and Gordon could not agree on a name, Frances christened it Outlaw, "Because her mask makes her look like the most adorable little robber!" and her younger siblings agreed to it, if only because they need not then yield to each other.

Outlaw purred and blinked in Gordon's arms and all was well until the boy unlatched Poppet's wicker basket to perform introductions. The white lapdog sprang up eagerly, expecting a treat, only to be confronted with a hissing, arching ball of golden fur. Poppet's tender little black nose was swiped at, provoking yelps more of astonishment than pain, and when Gordon leaned forward to reassure him, Outlaw gave a yowl of her own, frantically wriggling from Gordy's grip and tumbling to the ground. Maria and Frances lunged for the kitten, knocking each other's bonnets awry, but

Outlaw eluded them both and scrambled to safety up the nearest buttress, which happened to be the leg of the young man emerging from the inn.

With an oath, the involuntary prop danced and spun in a circle, uncertain what manner of clawed demon had ambushed him. The kitten screeched and clung on, climbing higher and drawing additional vivid exclamations from the young man while the witnesses struggled to smother horrified laughter.

Perhaps three long seconds later, Adela roused herself to hurry over, apologies bubbling to her lips. "Sir! We beg your pardon," she gasped, seizing Outlaw by her tiny scruff to lift her off. But the kitten's scratchy little claws were firmly embedded, obliging Adela to give a mighty tug. While this effort successfully detached Outlaw from her victim, the kitten's claws took with them the hem of the gentleman's neckcloth, unwinding several of the neat folds.

"Dear me," Adela muttered, seeing the now dangling ends of the neckcloth and the bareness of the man's throat. "I do, do apologize." Without thinking, and almost dazed with panic, she made matters worse by snatching at the loose material and attempting to stuff it back in the remaining knots and folds.

"Stop—do stop—" he commanded, raising an elbow to prevent her flustered hand from chopping him in the Adam's apple.

Adela obeyed at once, scarlet with mortification, her guilty hand falling back to her side while the other clutched Outlaw so tightly even the kitten's squeal could not escape.

"Lord Dere's coach!" bellowed the ostler.

Without a second look at the stricken Adela, the young man left her, striding to meet the handsome vehicle and flicking his fingers at one of the jack-boys to fetch his valise. To the footman hopping down he said, "To Perryfield?"

"Perryfield?" echoed the footman, "oh, aye, after we unload you all at Iffley Cottage."

"But I don't want to go to Iffley Cottage."

"Did you say Iffley Cottage?" piped up Adela, scurrying over. "That's us. The Barstows. His lordship wrote that he would send his coach to meet us and convey us to Iffley Cottage. Will this be the only vehicle? There are seven of us, you see, though of course the baby and my brother may sit upon our laps, and my youngest sister as well, if need be."

Gordon began to protest this babyish treatment, but she waved him to silence.

"Then in you go," said the footman, opening the door and unfolding the steps while another bustled to take up the luggage Adela indicated. But when the first servant assisted Mrs. Barstow and Sarah to climb in and turned back for Frances, he noticed the young man still standing like a post in the yard and frowned at him, perplexed. "Are you certain you aren't with these ones, sir?"

"Of course I'm certain! I'm not a member of their party—we don't even know each other."

"But who are you, then, if you aren't with them that are going to Iffley?" the footman persisted, for all the world as if the young man would change his mind, if he only gave it careful thought.

"I'm Weatherill. Gerard Weatherill. The new tutor at Perryfield. Is another carriage being sent to fetch me, then?"

The footman's mouth popped open. He glanced at his counterpart, who stared back, equally perplexed. "Mr. Weatherill the new tutor? But—his lordship said you were coming tomorrow."

"And yet here I am," answered Mr. Weatherill dryly. "There's clearly been some miscommunication."

"That's right." The first footman consulted the second. "Anyone say anything to you, Ogle, about the tutor coming today?"

"Not a word, Harker. And Mrs. Markham Dere said tomorrow. She told Mrs. Robson this morning that the schoolroom and tutor's bedchamber had to be ready by end of today, against Mr. Weatherill's arrival tomor—"

"Nevertheless, *here I am*," Weatherill interrupted, with some asperity, though his impatience fought with a temptation to laugh. First the ferocious kitten, followed by the interfering young lady's ministrations, and now this? "Seeing as you cannot do otherwise than return to Perryfield once you have conveyed this—other family—to Iffley, and seeing as I am, in fact, standing before you, would it be possible for me to ride up with the coachman?"

But a tutor to the heir of Perryfield being higher in rank than the coachman Fishwick, Harker's eyes widened at this potential *lèse-majesté*, and again the interfering young lady interfered.

"Pardon me again, sir," said Adela, her hand on the coach door, every other Barstow having situated himself within, "you would be welcome to share this coach—to sit inside with us, that is—if you would not mind the detour to Iffley. We are not introduced, but I daresay we would have been very shortly, even if not for this muddle. The coach muddle, I mean, not the kitten muddle. Because if you are indeed the new tutor at Perryfield, I believe my brother here—Master Gordon Barstow—will be the second of your pupils."

Hearing his name, Gordy poked his head out the open door. "What was that, Della?"

"This gentleman, Gordy," she replied. "Mr. Gerard Weatherill, was it? He will tutor you and Lord Dere's great-nephew Peter at Perryfield. Please, Mr. Weatherill, won't you accept a ride with us? I do feel very badly about your neckcloth and Outlaw's—the kitten's, that is—inexcusable conduct."

After a hesitation, he nodded, earning a wide smile from her before she took Harker's hand to climb in.

Despite the elegance and fine features of the coach—with its japanned and silver-trimmed exterior, the baron's coat of arms and crests picked out beautifully in red and white, and its Wilton carpets, Morocco leather, mahogany blinds, and spring curtains within—it was made to hold six passengers at most, and as they crowded in, Weatherill had to stuff down another urge to laugh.

"We're like a drift of young pigs being brought to market," Miss Barstow said, as if she read his thoughts. "Though pigs never traveled in such style. Frances, you put Poppet's basket on your lap, and Maria, you had better hold Outlaw so Gordon can sit on me. There, Mr. Weatherill—you may squeeze beside my mother Mrs. Barstow. And this is my sister-in-law Mrs. Sebastian Barstow, my sisters Miss Frances and Miss Maria—Frances has our dog Poppet in that basket—and Gordon you know. And I," she finished, settling her little brother more comfortably, "am Miss Barstow."

"A pleasure," Weatherill murmured, nodding to each in turn as the coach jerked into motion. And he found he meant his words. Upon closer inspection these Barstows were a fine, healthy family, the grown ladies uncommonly handsome. He wondered whom they were mourning but had to content himself with saying, "Have you traveled far, Mrs. Barstow?"

"Some thirty miles as the crow flies, but longer by the coaches. We set out early this morning from Twyford in Berkshire."

"Twyford to Reading, Reading to Henley, Henley to Shillingford, Shillingford to Oxford," said Frances, regarding him over the dog's basket. She was a colt-like girl of perhaps fifteen who was all arms and legs and eyes.

"Don't forget Nettlebed," spoke up Maria, leaning around her mother to peep at him. She had brown eyes like her oldest sister, and Weatherill guessed her to be less than ten. "Henley to Nettlebed to Shillingford to Oxford."

"But we didn't change coaches after Henley, we only made stops," put in Gordon from his sister's lap as he fiddled with the Venetian blind. "So really it was Twyford to Reading, Reading to Henley, Henley to Oxford."

"Stops do signify," countered Frances, "because once one climbs down, does it really matter whether one climbs back into the same coach or a different one?"

"What about you, sir?" Adela asked, to cut short their bickering. She removed Gordy's hand from the blind and gave him a furtive poke to make him sit still.

To her surprise, a shadow crossed the tutor's features and the leather squeaked as he sat back. He busied himself with tucking in the ruined ends of his neckcloth. "London. I come from—that is, I came from London."

Her candid brow knit. Was there a difference? She supposed there was. If he hailed from London, then he had also come from there. But if he merely came to Oxford *by way of* London, why then he might have come from nearly anywhere in the kingdom, as countless coaches converged on the capital and dispersed from there.

In any case, his reticence discouraged further questions on the matter, and they would have been back at the starting point, if not for Gordon.

"Were you a tutor there, in London?" the boy asked, then looking over his shoulder and adding unhelpfully, "What?" when Adela poked him again.

"Don't *pry*," Maria scolded, also unhelpfully. But she sat in the corner opposite Adela and could not be got at.

"Not a tutor," Weatherill answered. "A—an assistant schoolmaster of sorts. At a—charity school."

His guarded tone (and Adela's physical reproofs) must have penetrated even Gordon's boyish unawareness because he did not follow this response with more questions, and a little silence fell, unbroken for some minutes until Frances opened the blind on her side and Mrs. Barstow said, "I wonder how much farther to Iffley. It has been so long since I was in Oxfordshire that I can't recall, though I believe Perryfield lies just outside the village."

As they were all newcomers to the place, no one had information to offer, but his mother's remark jogged Gordon into speech again.

"Have you met your other pupil Peter Dere already, sir? Because I haven't. None of us have. He's a year younger than I, Della says."

"I have not yet had that pleasure," Mr. Weatherill replied. He had got hold of himself by this point and banished the shadow from his countenance.

"We were trying to determine what relation he is to me," the boy continued. "For Lord Dere is Mama's cousin—first cousin—and he is Peter Dere's great-uncle. So would he be my second cousin or third?"

Weatherill considered, one of his fingers tapping a bar of the silver-plated trim. "Let me see...well, Peter Dere's grandfather, as a brother of Lord Dere, would have been a first cousin of Mrs. Barstow as well. His son, Peter Dere's father and Lord Dere's nephew, would have been her first cousin once removed, which makes Peter Dere her first cousin twice removed."

"But what does that make me and Peter?" Gordon insisted.

The corner of the tutor's mouth twitched. "I haven't the faintest idea."

There was a pause, and then his audience burst out laughing, as much from amusement as relief, to see his peculiar mood pass.

"And you call yourself a tutor!" teased Adela when their mirth died away.

"I'm afraid I do, though my proficiency only extends to the usual subjects. Greek, Latin, geography, mathematics, and so forth. Genealogy is not in my line."

"Mr. Weatherill," began Mrs. Barstow in her soft voice, "allow me to say how glad I am you will be teaching Gordon. His father, my late husband, planned to begin his instruction last year, but his failing health prevented it."

"You mean Mr. Barstow intended on teaching Gordon himself?" asked Weatherill, noting, *Ah ha, the mourning is for the father, then.*

"Oh, yes. My husband was a clergyman and used to take on pupils, as well as teaching my older son Sebastian before he went to sea." A little sigh escaped her.

"Allow me to offer my condolences," he said politely. Then, thinking to spare the older woman further scrutiny, he nodded to Mrs. Sebastian Barstow on the opposite seat. "These can be wearing times, for families of naval men." To his alarm and discomfiture, however, Mrs. Sebastian Barstow flushed scarlet and hung her head, pressing her cheek to the child in her arms.

"What...have I said?" he wondered. "I should not have mentioned anxiety, perhaps."

Knowing precisely what Sarah was undergoing because her own throat had tightened, Adela blurted, "It is not that. It is—unfortunately—my brother Sebastian was mortally wounded in the Action of 31 March off Malta. He—is no more." It had been early May before the family learned of it, and all that time that he was dead, all those days, they had been nursing Mr. Barstow through his final decline and taking comfort in how Baby Bash grew in strength and delightfulness.

"I am very sorry for it. And sorry for—touching—twice—upon such a tender spot." His words were barely audible, and if in his mortification he could have hurled himself from the moving coach without adding to the party's inconvenience, he would gladly have done it.

"You could not have known," Adela excused him at once. "And—and we had better grow used to discussing it, for we will have to say as much, over and over, to all we meet here." In saying this she looked at each family member in turn, speaking more to them than to him, but he was glad to be pardoned in any case.

And not a moment too soon, for the appearance of the Tree Inn's great elm marked the beginning of Church Way, from which lanes branched downward toward the river.

Welcoming the distraction, the Barstows leaned to peer through the slats of the blinds, Mrs. Barstow murmuring to Maria, "Take a firm hold of Outlaw, darling, for we are nearly there. Lord Dere said in his letter that Iffley Cottage stands very near the parsonage."

CHAPTER 3

Behold now, the place where we dwell with thee
is too strait for us.
—2 Kings 6:1, *The Authorized Version* (1611)

Iffley Cottage was separated from the road by only a square courtyard planted with grass and flower borders and enclosed by a low stone wall. The home itself was modest and square, two storeys built of rubble, with a half-tile, half-slate roof and window shutters painted a charming dark blue. On the south and west faces roses climbed, though this late in the summer only one variety still bloomed. When compared to the humbler, low rubble-and-thatch cottages they had passed, Iffley Cottage looked positively elegant, and Sarah touched Adela's arm, smiling. "The charming yard! We may sit outside on fine days."

It was on the tip of Adela's tongue to reply, "And how Jane will love the roses!" but she caught herself.

After Harker assisted them to alight, Mrs. Barstow clasped her hands together, eyes welling in silent gratitude, and Adela was scarcely less moved. The home might be too small for so many; it might be theirs on sufferance; it might only hold them until scandal broke; but it was charming.

Harker observed their response with satisfaction while Ogle fetched their portmanteaux. "You'll find it as tidy and trim inside as out," he declared. "Lord Dere gave orders that it be so, and he sent men over to meet the removers when they came and will send them again if everything isn't placed to your liking."

"Thank you," Adela replied, seeing her mother still unable to speak. "The baron is too kind. Please send to him our thanks and compliments on his health."

"Is Perryfield far from here?" asked Mr. Weatherill.

Adela started, to find him over her shoulder, ruined neckcloth and all, but it was not continued remorse over Outlaw's depredations which made her take a tiny step away. It was—she didn't know. Perhaps...embarrassment? Now that they stood before the very real and solid Iffley Cottage and their meeting with Lord Dere loomed, her intended campaign to win the baron's heart was no longer simply theoretical. It would begin as soon as the next day when they called. And for such an undertaking, surely the fewer spectators the better. In fact, Adela had only considered the scrutiny (and possible disapproval) of her family and the Deres, but now it occurred to her that Lord Dere would have a whole household of onlookers with opinions. And beyond these there would be his friends and acquaintances and even the larger community where he was the *grand seigneur*. Heavens! Adela's wooing of him would take place not in isolation but before a great cloud of witnesses, as it were. A great, great cloud of witnesses.

She put out a hand to steady herself on Frances' bony shoulder.

Harker was pointing. "'Bout three-quarters of a mile east, sir, if you follow the Upper Field and Tree Lane, just before it crosses Wallingford Way. There was a glimpse of the Perryfield park as we came." He looked measuringly at Gordon. "Nice dry ground, not marshy like by the river. A boy like you could run it in under ten minutes, and on a frosty day it might be a fifteen-minute walk, with plenty of time for stopping to look at anything interesting along the way."

"Let me try now!" cried the boy. "Has anyone got a watch?"

"It had better wait, Gordy," said Adela. "Mama will have to accompany all of us, the first time, for we do not even know Lord Dere, to look at him. Besides, don't you want to see what the cottage looks like inside?"

Robbed of his footrace to inspect rooms filled with the same furniture he had seen all his life, Gordon's shoulders drooped a fraction, but Mr. Weatherill said, "Speaking of not knowing Lord Dere to look at him, Gordon, imagine the baron's response when I am deposited on his doorstep in a few minutes, a day earlier than anyone expects. *One* perfect stranger appearing without warning is distressing enough, but *two* would be—"

"Yes, I suppose you're right, sir," Gordon agreed, and Adela threw the tutor a grateful glance.

After a hesitation (in which he realized he was just standing there gazing at her), Weatherill made a hasty bow and backed toward the waiting coach. "Well, good day to you all. We will meet soon enough again at Perryfield."

"Yes, and—Mr. Weatherill—again, our apologies for Outlaw and—the damage to your neckcloth," answered Adela. She would have added that they would be glad to mend it for him but decided the offer would be awkward. Surely one of the maids at Perryfield could be of assistance.

The tutor made another bow before climbing back into the coach, Harker neatly folding the steps behind him and hopping to his place.

And the Barstows were left to their new life.

Mrs. Barstow took Adela's hand. "Do you think a letter from Jane will be waiting?"

The same thought had crossed Adela's mind, but she answered, as much to herself as to her mother, "We had better not count on it. She will not have reached Scotland yet."

If Jane and Roger Merritt ever made it to Scotland. Though she did not voice this last thought aloud, she knew it was on her mother's mind, and Adela gave herself a shake. "Come on, then, Barstows! Let us see inside."

With a whoop, Maria thrust Outlaw at Frances, and she and Gordon raced for the door, poor Poppet swinging in his basket and the others not far behind them.

When they had trooped all through it, led by the maid Reed, with manservant Irving bringing up the rear, they returned to the sitting room off the entry, one of only two rooms which might hold everyone comfortably. But even here the sofa and armchairs and escritoire and tables from Twyford left little unoccupied space.

"Goodness," said Adela, with a helpless laugh. "What a mercy we sold the pianoforte."

"And that Jane didn't come—" began Frances, breaking off abruptly when Adela shot her a sharp look and Sarah succumbed to violent coughing. "Oh—er—that is—"

"Mrs. Markham Dere had a great deal fewer things in here, and *she* had a pianoforte," spoke up Reed. Though the Barstows had only known the maid-of-all-work a scant hour, they were already daunted by her: tall, stern, prominent of nose, firm of opinion, and commanding of voice. "Irving and I had our hands full with the removers and arranging what we could."

Adela imagined it was Reed who had her hands full, for Irving was thankfully a smaller, quieter man who bowed a great deal and spoke hardly a word except when someone addressed him.

"Yes, it must have been trying," Adela said to soothe her. "Now that we are here, I daresay a few more things might go, to make space. But for now, Reed, Irving, if you would excuse us...? We must decide who will have which bedchamber, and I fear there might be unseemly squabbling."

When the servants were gone and the door shut, Mrs. Barstow sighed. "They will know about Jane soon enough, I suppose. Even if they have not already wondered, we must explain to Lord Dere, and the Perryfield servants will talk."

"Well, a few more hours of peace is nothing to sniff at," Adela said, "and at least we might be spared what Mrs. Markham Dere's opinion on the matter would have been."

The others laughed, for there had indeed been a great deal of "this is where Mrs. Markham Dere stored the linens" and "Mrs. Markham Dere did not use this room as a bedchamber but as her dressing room" and "Mrs. Markham Dere preferred the curtains on this window to be shut at all times."

"Besides," Adela continued, "it's true enough that we might squabble over the bedrooms. They are not overlarge. Even Mrs. Markham Dere's dressing room! She must be a slender person, if she managed to dress there."

"May I have the dressing room?" asked Gordon, bouncing on his chair. "Bash can share it with me when he's older."

"Only if Bash stays the size he is now forever," scoffed Frances. She caught up Poppet and wagged a finger in the dog's face. "Poppet, Outlaw, I am sorry to tell you, but Mrs. Markham Dere did not approve of lapdogs or other pets. She said there were animals enough abroad."

"I don't like Mrs. Markham Dere," frowned little Maria.

"Hush, darling. We don't yet know her, and she might be perfectly amiable," Mrs. Barstow said.

"Yes," agreed Adela. "All that talk of her might just be Reed expressing her own notions. And certainly we too will have our decided opinions about how we will live in Iffley Cottage, now that we are mistresses here. Mrs. Gordon Barstow, for one, heartily approves of lapdogs and other pets."

"So I do," smiled her mother.

"But the bedrooms!" Gordon reminded them. "Mrs. Markham Dere's dressing room is like a secret cupboard."

"That it is," Adela meditated. "But I think it more sensible if Sarah takes the room beside the cupboard because of the door between. Bash might sleep in the cupboard."

"But Bash and I cannot occupy two entire rooms!" protested Sarah. "That would leave the five of you to cram into the two remaining."

"Perhaps Gordy should take the cupboard for now," Mrs. Barstow said. "And Sarah and Bash the room adjoining. Then, when Bash is older, the boys might have the bigger room, and either Sarah or I would exchange for the cupboard."

"That could work, Mama," Adela took this up. "And in the meantime, you shall take the little room with the blue paper, and Frances, Maria and I will take the front bedroom with the green."

"Three of you in one room! No, Adela, you had better take the blue room, then. I think it's a little bigger."

But Sarah was shaking her head. "I suspect they are the same size. Adela, suppose you shared with me and Bash? He rarely, rarely wakes up at night now, and you saw how they placed the beds: one in each of the rooms. If you shared with Frances and Maria, a second bed would need to be stuffed into either the blue or green bedrooms, and I hardly believe it possible."

Adela hardly believed it possible either, upon consideration. What *would* they have done, if Jane had not eloped? Then one of them—probably Adela herself—would have had to share a bed with Mrs. Barstow. She was not the only one to suppress a sigh and put on a good face. Iffley Cottage might have served a family of three well, but for seven...

Better than the workhouse! she reminded herself dryly. Far better.

They later discovered that the two smaller mattresses which could not be made to fit in the cottage were stacked upright in a shed, alongside surplus miscellany (such as Frances' workbasket and Maria's bookcase), Irving's garden tools, and Reed's cheesemaking apparatus.

The rest of the day was spent in arranging their belongings and getting in each other's way, before sitting down to a cold meal generously sent from Perryfield, and finally collapsing upon their (mostly) shared beds. And after such a long, long, distressing day, not even the thought of Jane or the fear of meeting Lord Dere on the morrow could keep Adela awake, and she fell at once into a deep sleep.

Some five minutes away by road, Gerard Weatherill leaned from the open casement of his bedchamber at Perryfield, coat brushed and hung, mangled neckcloth repaired as best he could—oh, yes, he knew basic sewing—shirt open at the neck to catch any breeze.

He had done it.

He had escaped.

For what other word could be used to describe slipping the bonds which had held him throughout his youth and early manhood? Though for years he had dreamed of leaving, he had remained for his younger sister's sake. *Next year,* he had told himself. And then, when the time was gone—*next year will be soon enough.* Until the refrain became, *When Susanna is of age, then nothing will prevent us going.*

But her health, always delicate, suffered in the frigid winter of '98-99, failing to recover in the months of dank grey and constant rain which followed. And then at last, as the calendar turned and the new century lay before them, the old woman whom Weatherill paid to sit with Susanna in his absence summoned him from his teaching duties to his sister's side.

"You must go, Gerard," Susanna urged hoarsely, her hand almost weightless in his. "Promise me. You have wasted too many years already, waiting for me and hoping Father would change. Now you will be free."

His brows drew together as he shook his head. "No. No, Susanna. Together. We will go together."

"...Better this way. I would have...been a burden."

"*No.*"

"I...could not have...worked."

"Please, Susanna. You were never a burden." How could she be? Though she was ten years younger, she had been his faithful companion. The only one who understood what it meant to be a child of Rioting Rob.

No, indeed. Gerard knew the truth of the verse that two were better than one, "for if they fall, the one will lift up his fellow."

But before he could swallow his tears to remind her of this, she was gone.

Rioting Rob was exactly where Gerard knew he would be—where he always was—on the second gallery, in the large room above the chapel where the billiard table was found. When his son appeared, Rob Weatherill took one look at his face and threw his cue down.

"Aaarh," the respected sire grunted. He swayed, his mouth working, before scraping both hands through his silvering hair and shambling toward the door. When they were alone in the passage he asked, "Did Susie have any last words for her pappy?"

"I'm—afraid she was gone before they could be spoken," replied his son.

"She was a good girl. Like her mother. Better than I deserved."

There was nothing to say to this, but Gerard nodded. Yes. Susanna Weatherill had been a good girl. Like her mother. And neither one had deserved a father or husband as shiftless and imprudent as Robert Weatherill.

"You'll be going then," his father said. It was a declaration, rather than a question. His gaze was unnaturally penetrating as he studied his son.

"I hope to," answered Gerard.

At the other end of the passage familiar faces appeared, and they were soon calling to the popular Rob, who lifted a hand like a king greeting his subjects.

"Might we discuss this in your chamber—sir?" Gerard asked.

After seven years in the Fleet Prison, Rob Weatherill had worked his way into one of the larger rooms in the wings, this one over the coffee-room in the hall gallery. Though the rent paid to the tapster for it was higher, and though he no longer had any family members sharing the space with him, he considered the eight shillings paid per week a consequence of his consequence, as it were. Rioting Rob must be seen to live like Rioting Rob, however little that left to pay his long-suffering creditors or to support his ailing daughter.

"Not going to my chamber," his father replied, a note of defiance rising in his voice. "I'll be in the tap-room." The tap-room, where he reigned supreme. He started down the passage, leaving Gerard no choice but to follow.

"I'll be advertising, sir," he announced to his father's retreating back. "For a position at a school or as a tutor."

Robert Weatherill stopped so abruptly that Gerard almost ran him down. "This is Keele's doing, I'll be bound. So you aim to pass yourself off as a pedant? What will you call yourself?" he jeered. "'Gerard Weatherill, fellow of Fleet College'? 'The Scholar of Shoe Lane,' perhaps?"

"Mr. Keele says he has taught me all he knows," Gerard said, the muscle along his jaw beginning to stand out. "And he, at least, is an Oxford graduate."

Weatherill Senior's upper lip curled, but Gerard was old enough now to understand the poison of his father's barbs drew its potency from his own shame and disappointment with life. "Oxford graduate, fiddlestick," he railed. "What is Keele now but a sham schoolmaster—a worthless, hopeless debtor—propping himself up by teaching worthless, hopeless debtors' spawn in the Liberty of the Fleet? Well, go on, then. You're of age. No sense in you rotting here any longer. Go as far as you can. Change your name, if you like. I'll have no more to do with you."

"I will write to you, Father."

"As you please." Rob Weatherill thrust a hand in the inner pocket of his coat and came up with a half-crown. With a flick of his thumb, he tossed it at his son. "Here. To pay for Susie's—for whoever the parish sends to—prepare her." A telltale break in his voice seemed to infuriate him, for without another word or backward glance, he swept away from his only remaining child.

So here Gerard was in Oxfordshire, for no other reason than that Mrs. Markham Dere's letter was the sole response to his advertisement. Her own notice had yielded several candidates, but most of these she dismissed because, as she put it in her reply, "I would like my son Peter to be educated by someone who will not only shape his mind, but also impart to him some London polish." That is, surrounded by Oxford dons, their perceived sameness and familiarity repelled her. Gerard Weatherill could only hope his new employer never discovered exactly how exceedingly worldly and *un*polished his London background was. He had hoped, of course, to remove somewhere much, much further from London, but beggars could be no choosers.

Lord Dere, thankfully, was not the sort of baron who removed in state to the capital for each legislative season (Mrs. Markham Dere had explained with a sigh), and the quiet life of Perryfield, isolated even from the bustle of Oxford, promised further welcome obscurity. Here Weatherill could live quietly and teach for a year or two, and then perhaps sue for a new post in one of the more anonymous industrial towns to the north.

Weatherill pulled the casement shut and turned to regard the room assigned to him. On the second floor, neither family bedchamber nor servant quarter, it might be appropriate for a visiting poor relation. Older, mismatched furniture; a view to the side of the house rather than the park; a smaller fireplace enclosed by a plain mantel devoid of knick-knacks. And yet it was the largest and most elegant room he had ever occupied. *As large as Rioting Rob's over the coffee-room,* he thought dryly. *An eight-shilling-a-week room, if ever there was one. If only Susanna could have seen this!*

But Susanna was right. If she had lived, he would never have left her, and if he had taken her with him, he would not have been given this position.

When he put out the candle and settled himself in the vast bed, however, his last thought before sleep was neither of Susanna nor of his father. It was of an overcrowded coach and a young lady whose lively brown eyes peeped at him around the active young boy on her lap.

The Angel Inn

High Street, Oxford

Iffley Cottage

Perryfield

The Fleet

London

CHAPTER 4

I'll look to like, if looking liking move.
—Shakespeare, *Romeo and Juliet*, I.iii.482 (1597)

As if it were a Sunday, the next day found the Barstows dressed and neat, even Maria, who needed egg wiped from her mouth, and Gordon, who went exploring with Poppet before breakfast. Frances dripped blood on her black-and-white striped muslin when Outlaw climbed her arm, but that was remedied as well before they set out for Perryfield.

"Don't run, Gordy, at least this first time," admonished Adela as her younger brother did just that. "It wouldn't do to arrive perspiring and disheveled."

"If only we had a carriage of our own," Frances sighed. "I don't see why Lord Dere didn't send his coach again."

"But how could he know when we might like to call?" her sister asked reasonably. "I suppose if we had sent Irving to *demand* it, Lord Dere would have been willing enough—he has in every other way tried to be welcoming and considerate." She blushed as she said it, thinking that later everyone might say, *Oh, yes, Adela was predisposed to like the baron. She came* determined *to like him.*

As the footman Harker promised, the walk to Perryfield took them beside the Upper Field, now harvested, though along its edge burgundy and purple blooms of great burnet and knapweed encroached from the marshier Iffley Meadow to the other side, where cows now grazed. The churchway gave onto Tree Lane, the former "sheep way" in medieval times, which led in the direction of Wallingford Way, the road which had brought them from Oxford.

"That must be it!" cried Gordon, hopping and pointing to a pair of chimneys visible over a long stone wall taller than their heads. They were obligated to follow this wall for some distance, but it was punctuated by an arch, enclosing what appeared to be the stone frame and traceries of a lovely window, only there was no glass. Crowding to peer through, they saw a spreading, square lawn, enclosed by the same wall and bordered by flower beds. At the far end of the greenery stood the great ivy-bearded house: symmetrical and constructed of the same glowing stone, mullioned windows marching the length of each of the three storeys like playing cards laid upon a table.

"Very elegant," murmured Sarah, shifting Bash from one hip to the other.

"And ten times as large as our cottage," Frances observed. "Do you think Lord Dere might trade with us? There are seven of us and only three of them."

"Plus servants," Adela reminded her. "Running a large house requires many more servants. Nor did you count Mr. Weatherill the tutor."

"Four, then, plus servants," amended Frances. "Though Mr. Weatherill is somewhere between family and servant. But if we traded houses, Lord Dere and Mrs. Markham Dere and the Peter boy would leave all those servants at Perryfield, so it would *still* make more sense..."

"Come, come," prompted Mrs. Barstow. "Let us make our call. There is no use in debating impossibilities, and my cousin has already been exceptionally generous."

Adela's heart thumped faster and threatened to take flight when the footman admitted them and led the way to the drawing room, a light-filled, white-plastered space, as spacious as the sitting room at Iffley Cottage was cramped. Across the vast carpet were grouped light Sheraton chairs and sofas of sycamore inlaid with Satinwood, each arrangement attended by matching pedestal tables. The pianoforte held pride of place in a corner, while marquetry bookcases flanked the fireplace, one enclosing a cylinder-desk so cunningly made Adela would have wept to write letters at it.

But these were things she noticed later.

"Mrs. Gordon Barstow, Mrs. Sebastian Barstow, Miss Barstow, Miss Frances Barstow, Miss Maria Barstow, Master Gordon Barstow, and—er—Master Sebastian Barstow," declared the footman Wood in his best colorless tone, but really he was counting the chairs to ensure there were enough.

One part of Adela's mind did the same thing—the Barstows were always such a *crowd* wherever they went, even without Jane—while the other part panicked. *There he is! Lord Dere!*

Not a heavy, gouty old man at all. In fact, he was rather slender, with silver hair and pale blue eyes and a smooth brow. Kindly in appearance. When he straightened from his bow, his lips parted to greet them, but Mrs. Markham Dere beat him to it.

"You are most welcome to Perryfield," she smiled coolly, extending her shapely arms (and displaying to advantage her sheer muslin shawl with its fine leaf embroidery. She was a handsome woman, all gleaming golden hair and classical proportions, and it was plain she was used to exciting admiration. "And I do hope Iffley Cottage is to your liking. How many happy years Mr. Dere and I spent there. You must meet my son Peter, as well, if Wood will summon him. He might be with his tutor Mr. Weatherill, whom I hear you have already met."

"Thank you, Mrs. Dere," said Mrs. Barstow as the footman retreated and they all chose seats, she taking Maria beside her and Adela raising an eyebrow to remind Gordon of his manners. "We did indeed meet Mr. Weatherill. But allow me to express at once our family's heartfelt gratitude for the offer of Iffley Cottage—" She would have addressed Lord Dere alone and called it "*your* cottage," but Mrs. Markham Dere's putting herself forward had thrown Mrs. Barstow into confusion, and she ended in looking from one to the other.

His brow knitting, Lord Dere raised a hand to deflect Mrs. Barstow's thankfulness, but before he could speak his niece-in-law took charge again. "I hope you will be happy there," she replied. "While I was mistress of it, Mr. Dere and I took the utmost care of it and were frequently complimented on improvements we made, though I daresay if our family had been as large as yours, Mrs. Barstow, we would undoubtedly have built an addition to it." Her keen eyes narrowed slightly as her gaze swept once moreover the little assembly. "But—am I mistaken? Is there not one more Barstow? I do believe Miss Barstow wrote that you were eight altogether. Was—pardon me for not being able to rattle off all your names on the spur of the moment—was oneof you too knocked up by the journey to come today?"

So soon the moment was upon them! Mrs. Barstow turned helpless eyes upon Adela, and her oldest daughter rushed to meet the challenge.

"It is Miss Jane Barstow you are thinking of, madam," Adela answered. "My next younger sister. We were indeed eight in number when I wrote to the baron, but—it happens that—Jane will not be joining us in Oxfordshire because—because she is to be married." She could have bitten her tongue after this last phrase—she should have said Jane was already married, to forestall further awkward questions.

But it might not be true.

"Oh, but how delightful!" rejoined Mrs. Markham Dere, sincerely relieved to have the number of penurious dependents reduced by one. "To whom, pray? And did Miss Jane not wish to be married from Iffley Cottage with you all beside her?"

Adela swallowed, her face hot. Unable to sustain Mrs. Dere's gaze, she favored the woman with a vague smile and shifted in her seat to include Lord Dere. "Certainly we tried to persuade Jane to...delay a little and accompany us, but her—suitor—a Mr. Roger Merritt—was so insistent that she—let herself be persuaded." The laugh she forced at this point emerged a little high, but since neither of their new acquaintances knew what her laugh ought to sound like, Adela hoped it escaped notice. "Jane would have loved the climbing roses at the cottage, in any event," she hurried on. "Perhaps she and—Mr. Merritt—will visit sometime soon. Though, as you observed, Mrs. Dere, guests will be a squeeze."

"The Merritts would be welcome to stay at Perryfield," spoke up Lord Dere at last, as his niece was drawing breath. "As would any other guests you at Iffley Cottage care to invite."

Mrs. Dere's eyes went round as horrified buttons at the issuing of this *carte blanche*, but Adela regarded him with genuine appreciation. "Really, my lord? While we are not expecting anyone, we thank you for this further proof of your kindness."

Her words brought a wave of color to his own countenance, and he muttered, "Please—among family I would rather not be 'my lord.' Let it be 'sir' or 'Lord Dere,' if you must, but let us not have any 'my lord' or 'your lordship.'"

The Barstows made various sounds of acquiescence, Adela catching Sarah's eye. *He truly does not like to draw attention to himself,* her look said, and her sister-in-law raised wondering brows in return. It was not as if their acquaintance in Twyford included dozens of peers, but the one grandee in their sphere had insisted on every inch of his title and privilege.

Perhaps wooing him—and marrying him—will not be horrible, Adela thought. A kind, generous, modest man. Though doubtless Mrs. Markham Dere would be harder to get past than any watchdog. Despite hearing of Mrs. Dere's manifold opinions from the maidservant Reed, Adela had still cherished hopes of a sweet, retiring creature like Sarah, rather than this...masterful woman. This woman with her eyes and airs would not be at all eager to see the baron take a young bride and would certainly view such a person as an usurper!

As Mrs. Markham Dere and Mrs. Barstow made polite conversation, Adela studied the Deres beneath her lashes and considered.

She could not charm Lord Dere without first charming (and lulling) his watchdog. But the methods which might best charm the watchdog could very well repel the one held prisoner by it. For no matter how modest Lord Dere might be, Adela did not suppose any baron in the realm would enjoy being under the thumb of a niece by marriage.

It had always been the case since Adela Barstow was a very young girl, that if some unpleasant task loomed in her future, say, a loose tooth to be pulled or a cross old parishioner to be called upon, she could not rest until it was behind her. And if completing the task at once was not a possibility, she at least preferred to make a beginning.

If I am to make my family secure from disgrace and destitution, she ruminated, *Lord Dere's heart—or at least his hand—must be won, Mrs. Markham Dere or no Mrs. Markham Dere. I know neither one well enough to form a plan of attack, but the wooing must commence nonetheless.*

Waiting for a suitable pause in the talk around her, she turned to address their hostess. "What a lovely instrument that is! You must be a musician, Mrs. Dere. We hope you will play for us sometime because we Barstows are quite fond of music."

"Oh, I don't know about that," Mrs. Dere demurred, the corners of her mouth curling in a deprecating smile. But when both Adela and Mrs.

Barstow added cajoling murmurs, she soon yielded. "Certainly, certainly, then, when there is an occasion."

"Let it be today," spoke up Lord Dere. "You all must stay to dinner, and then Mrs. Dere may perform afterward."

"Dinner?" echoed Mrs. Dere, blinking. "My dear sir, that will not be for hours, and perhaps the Barstows did not plan on staying so long. Though we live in the country, we nonetheless seldom dine before three, and I am sure, having just arrived, they must have much to arrange at Iffley Cottage..."

"Oh, yes," Adela agreed quickly. "Thankyou, sir, but we could not possibly today, despite the excellent progress we made yesterday. It helped immeasurably, to have the furniture already arranged, and Reed was so good as to pass on some of your ways of doing things, madam." Having petted Mrs. Dere, she looked appealingly at the baron. "But if you had leisure, sir, perhaps we might wander the grounds?"

"I will show you all over them myself," Lord Dere said. "I know Mrs. Dere is not fond of walking out of doors."

But Mrs. Dere had no intention of being left behind. Who knew what other rash promises the man might make? "Nonsense," she returned. "This would be a special occasion. But do you not think, sir, we should begin with the house? That will give Peter time to find us. I am certain he will be sorry if he does not meet Gordon at least. What *can* be taking Wood so long? Unless Peter has gone to the moon, surely he might have been found by now."

"Might they be in the schoolroom?" Adela ventured. She hoped not. Surely Mr. Weatherill would not have begun instruction without waiting for Gordy.

Gordon himself did not look particularly alarmed at this possibility, but Mrs. Dere swelled at Adela's suggestion. "If Wood hadn't the wit to seek him there—!"

"The schoolroom *is* on the second floor," interposed the baron in defense of his servant, "and as lessons have not yet begun, I suspect Wood would not go there first. Come, Mrs. Dere. The boy will turn up. Let us begin with the long gallery."

Like all galleries, this impressive space was hung with portraits of past family members and took a long time to go through. It was followed by multiple parlors, a morning room, a dining room, a library, Lord Dere's steward's office, and so on. Before long, Bash fell asleep in his mother's arms, and Sarah elected to wait for them in one of the parlors, Frances offering to keep her company.

That left four Barstows to troop after the Deres to the first floor, where they were shown a number of bedchambers with very fine views (Mrs. Markham Dere inhabiting the loveliest, overlooking the park and rose garden), and where both Gordy and Maria began to show signs of impatience, skipping and running up the passage and hurtling to any windows to look out.

On one side of her, Mrs. Barstow pressed her daughter's arm and, on the other, Mrs. Dere's lips tightened.

"Shall we proceed outside?" Adela proposed. "Mama and I would be glad to linger, but perhaps touring houses would try the patience of a saint, if he happened to be under the age of ten."

Lord Dere was digging in his coat pocket and soon brought out a little tin, which he opened to reveal ginger candies. "From the apothecary," he explained to the children. "When you get old like I do, they soothe the throat. And once your throat is soothed, you imagine it scratchy, that you might have more."

Delighted, Maria and Gordon each took one, as did the baron. Mrs. Barstow and Adela refused the treats with a smile and Mrs. Dere with a shudder, but harmony was restored.

I like him, Adela thought. *Not to marry, but simply as a kind old gentleman.*

Her complacency did not last long, however, for Mrs. Dere's fair brow creased in annoyance. "Where *can* Peter be? I daresay, Mrs. Barstow, you will not mind taking a minute to see the schoolroom where Gordon will be taught? It is only one more set of stairs, and then we might at least rule that out."

Of course no one made objections, though Adela's skin prickled. There was no more reason for Mr. Weatherill to be found in the schoolroom than Peter, if lessons had not yet begun, she told herself. But suppose they had? *You can hardly avoid Mr. Weatherill if you intend to be much at Perryfield.* And she *must* be much at Perryfield.

Following the others, Adela absently worried at her lip. She noted that the baron neither shuffled nor stooped, and he had no difficulty in climbing the stairs to the second floor, though these were narrower and steeper than the grand staircase from the ground floor to the first, but no sooner did she make these observations than they became bound up in her growing uneasiness. *What* am *I thinking? Am I out of my mind? A girl my age should be dreaming of dashing young men who evoke heart flutterings, not congratulating herself that her chosen one's rheumatism is not too far advanced!*

Perhaps, instead of marrying him, she should simply confess Jane's misadventure and throw the Barstows on his further mercy. She felt certain already that he would not expel them, though he might regret having been so generous. He might suffer them as a blot upon the family and *wish* them gone, even as they clung on. Certainly Mrs. Markham Dere would be at him day and night to send them away, and any hope of marriage portions or little independences or allowances to Adela's younger siblings would have to be abandoned altogether.

No, no, no. Adela steeled herself once more. Needs must go when the devil drives. Her plan must go forward, and fie upon all heart flutterings and dashing young men!

CHAPTER 5

Whence commest thou in these Pitiful rusty cloaths?
—Gordon Burnell, translation of Aristophanes' *The World's*
***Idol,* sig.B2 (1659)**

The schoolroom here to the left is the largest room on this floor," Mrs. Dere gestured when she reached the landing. "It is a suite of three rooms, actually, with the door you will see leading to the tutor's personal quarters. As for the rest,"—pointing down the passage—"these are the servants' bedchambers."

The door to the schoolroom stood ajar, and the next moment it was thrown wide when Peter Dere peeked out. "Mama, come see! Mr. Weatherill and I are preparing the schoolroom." He stopped to stare at Gordon Barstow, and the two boys took each other's measure.

Gordy being older, his mother and sister were relieved to find he was also an inch taller. Already at a disadvantage as the poor relations, it would have gone hard with them if Peter Dere been a great, strapping, handsome boy, in addition to being Lord Dere's heir. But, no, Peter's appearance was in all respects typical, and Gordon's larger size (and the self-consequence he drew from imagining himself the man of the Barstow family) effectively counterbalanced Peter's superiority in fortune and connection.

"Come in," the tutor called to them, sending a *frisson* through Adela, and the man himself appeared the next moment. He was dressed as shabbily as the day before, though his neckcloth was repaired. The late summer sunlight filtering through the window made both his red-brown hair and the rusty patches of his clothing shine, so that one was torn between admiring his handsomeness and lamenting his condition. At least, Adela was. The charity school which formerly employed him must have taught the lowliest of pupils, if they paid their teachers so poorly! She rather wondered that Mrs. Markham Dere had not changed her mind on the spot about hiring him to instruct the heir to Perryfield.

A glance at the woman almost made Adela giggle, for it was plain the mistress of Perryfield was asking herself exactly that question. Perhaps she had assumed his worn appearance the previous day derived from the arduousness of travel.

And perhaps Adela was not the only one to read Mrs. Dere's mind, for she saw the tutor flush as he made his bow. But his chin lifted, a muscle twitching in his jaw. "Peter was helping me arrange things. You see the desks and appurtenances all in order."

"I've chosen this one," Peter told Gordon, placing a hand on the square deal desk nearer the window. His eyes narrowed as he spoke, as if he expected Gordon to argue, but Gordon thought haggling over such trifles with a younger boy beneath him, and he merely gave a nod.

"I thought we might begin Monday of next week at ten o'clock," continued Mr. Weatherill. "Would that hour give you enough time for your breakfast and the walk over, Gordon?"

"I could send the chariot for you, lad," suggested Lord Dere. "The weather is not always this fine. Harker could fetch you and Ogle return you every day."

Adela saw Gordon's eyes light at this proposal, and she knew he was picturing being allowed to drive himself, once the servants were won over, but even if she had not doubted the wisdom of this scheme, she had reasons of her own for interposing. "We thank you, sir, but on days which are not absolutely wretched, the walk will be good for Gordon—and me—for I will accompany him at least—until he is older."

Gordon frowned awfully at her, for making him look like a baby in front of Peter Dere, but she ignored him. "Yes, I and whoever else may care to join me, of a morning—we will ensure my brother's timely attendance."

Mrs. Dere struggled for words, torn equally between dread at having her drawing room constantly cluttered with Barstows and dread at the littlest Barstow having a carriage sent *daily* for him—what a burden upon the servants! How it would be gossiped about as a mark of favor! And into this breach Lord Dere said, "I approve heartily of fresh air and exercise, so I will not gainsay you, Miss Barstow, except to say the offer will stand, should you change your mind."

Adela made no reply except to smile at him and bow her head in acknowledgement.

"How—how Peter loves fresh air and exercise as well!" cried Mrs. Dere, determined to regain the upper hand. "We were just about to give the Barstows a tour of the gardens and park, Peter, which is why we came to fetch you."

"I've seen it a thousand times," he declared unhelpfully. But then he added, "But I'll come," for it occurred to him he should lay claim to it, lest the new boy think it available.

"I knew you would hate to miss it," replied his mother. "Mr. Weatherill, we will leave you to your preparations."

"Unless you would like to join us," said the baron. "It was too late for you so see the grounds when you arrived yesterday, and you might like to know your way around for your leisure hours."

Both Mrs. Dere and Adela had their reasons for preferring the tutor stay behind, Mrs. Dere because he looked so beggarly and Adela because she did not want him near while she sought to ingratiate herself, but neither of these things could be spoken aloud, and Mr. Weatherill agreed too promptly in any case.

Therefore it was a large and varied party which emerged onto the terrace a few minutes onward, only Sarah remaining within doors to watch over the napping Bash. Lord Dere offered one arm to Mrs. Barstow and the other to his niece, leaving Adela to claim the post on her mother's far side.

"Race you, Gordy," cried Maria, and the two children shot off at once, Peter hesitating a second before scampering after them.

"I hope they will all be friends," murmured Mrs. Barstow.

"Yes, indeed," agreed Adela absently, dismayed to see the graveled path ahead would accommodate a threesome at the most, and unless Adela was willing to tramp through the flowerbeds or clamber over the stone benches and urns which lined their way, she would be forced to fall back and pace beside Frances and Mr. Weatherill. Lord Dere delayed the separation when he halted to point out the statue of a cupid balanced atop a ball and they fanned out to hear him, but when the group resumed their walk, Adela was indeed shunted back.

Moreover, at the baron's age and encumbered as he was with two women, they did not advance quickly, and Frances soon lost patience. "I'll make sure Gordy and Maria don't do anything naughty," she told her sister, before skipping away.

Which left Adela beside the tutor.

Between the crunching of gravel underfoot and the softness of the baron's voice, it was impossible for the entire party to maintain one shared conversation, and Adela soon gave it up with a sigh.

"What's the matter?" asked Weatherill.

Adela glanced at him, her mouth twisting in rueful humor. What would he do if she were to tell him the truth? Suppose she were to say, "I am thwarted in my wish to seduce the baron, but I must make a start because my younger sister has eloped with a scoundrel, and when it is discovered, even our precarious new life may be in jeopardy." *Ludicrous!* She would have laughed if it were not so dire.

She contented herself with a morsel of the truth. "I had hoped to hear Lord Dere's descriptions."

"You are an enthusiast of gardens, then?"

Another bit of truth escaped. "I am an enthusiast of becoming better acquainted with someone who has been so good to my family."

He nodded at this. "Yes. As his employee, my position in relation to Lord Dere is by nature different from yours, Miss Barstow, but I too hope my situation at Perryfield will prove satisfactory."

Adela made another face under her bonnet brim. "If your position is different, sir, I would argue that it is preferable to ours."

"How so?"

"You offer Lord Dere a service: you teach his great-nephew and heir—not to mention his cousin's son—in return for a salary. But we Barstows...we are little more than parasites, I suppose. We take, giving nothing in return."

A more worldly man—a courtly man—would have spun her admission into flattery. He would have smiled lazily upon her and said something like, "A host of lovely ladies must be its own reward." But if Gerard Weatherill may have thought such a thing, he had not the experience to voice it.

Not at all.

Rather he said gruffly, "I suppose even the wealthy have their crosses to bear."

Crosses! Adela inhaled sharply, the fact that she had just implied as much herself, and the additional fact that it was the mere truth, doing nothing to soothe the sting of his words. In her chagrin her head dropped even lower, so that Weatherill could see nothing of her expression. But, as with her sigh, he heard her caught breath. And endured, as well, the heavy pause which followed.

They had reached the first corner of the gravel path, where marble benches were placed in an L, should anyone prefer to sit and take in the vista over the park, rolling away to woodland. Mrs. Markham Dere immediately plumped down with her back to the view, fanning herself and looking around for the children.

As much to get away from Mr. Weatherill as to seize the opportunity, Adela wandered up to her mother and Lord Dere.

"Are the woodlands part of Perryfield, sir?"

"They are. As I was telling Mrs. Barstow…"

She tried to listen, really she did, but her temper was still rising. *Crosses to bear, indeed!* No matter what he thought, on such minimal acquaintance he had no right to call the Barstows such a thing. No right at all. Even among friends it would hardly be excusable.

When Mrs. Dere was sufficiently recovered to take the baron's arm again, the party resumed its stroll, Weatherill trying without success to catch Adela's eye. He even offered an arm in its worn sleeve to support her, but if she saw, she disdained to make use of it.

Adela knew she should not return to the subject, if she spoke at all, but with the burning in her heart she could not help herself.

"Mr. Weatherill—" her voice was pitched low, to reach only his ears, and she swallowed hard to prevent it shaking. "You—agreed—that we Barstows—we—" (in frustration at her inarticulateness she pinched herself just above her glove). "That is—what would you do in our position, Mr. Weatherill? If you, too, found yourself someone else's cross to bear? A millstone around some unfortunate's neck? What would you advise?"

Gerard Weatherill might have little to no experience dealing with young ladies other than his late sister Susanna, but even he realized he had offended her. "Miss Barstow—I—my choice of words—"

"You are of course a *man*," Adela continued crisply, "which means you have more avenues to self-sufficiency than a household of *burdensome* women, but indulge me. What would you do if you did not have those avenues open to you?"

"A woman may teach," he said, as if determined to cut his own throat.

"So I might become a governess or teach in a school? Yes, yes, I might, and that would certainly spare my family—or I should say Lord Dere—the trouble of feeding and sheltering me," Adela rejoined. "I wonder I did not think of it."

"Miss Barstow, I am sure you *did* think of it."

She gave a brittle laugh. "Why, you are right! I *did* think of it. Ad infinitum, as you scholars would put it. Indeed, *ad nauseam.* More than once, that is to say, in the few months wherein my father declined and died, my brother having died in a short space before that. I thought, *Adela, you had better take yourself off at once and earn your keep. Never mind that Mama is bedridden with grief and Sarah little better, and Jane is—"* here she choked momentarily on a sob or gasp or simply from the rush of words spilling out pell mell, but she forced whatever it was back down and went on— *"that is, never mind, Adela, that you are the only one remaining to take the children in hand and come up with a plan—any plan—some sort of plan—for the future, now that you must get out of the only home you have ever known—"*

Mr. Weatherill had soon raised a hand to halt this speech, horrified at the Pandora's box he had opened, but Adela took no more notice of his hand than she had of his arm, and he was obliged to step swiftly in front of her, directly in her path, so that she must either stop or collide with him.

"Forgive me, Miss Barstow," he blurted, holding up one placating hand. "I misspoke. My suggestion was idiotic. Glib. Of course you, being an intelligent creature, considered the obvious possibilities."

Adela shut her eyes hard, feeling her face go all-over scarlet. Oh, heavens. Heavens, heavens, heavens. Why, she was a madwoman for such an outburst! What had come over her, to fire up at him like that? As if anything which had befallen the Barstows had a jot to do with Mr. Weatherill, whom she had only met *the day before,* for pity's sake. He certainly could not help being born a man. He could not help having more choice in life than she did.

Reluctantly, she opened her eyes again to find him watching her, brow knit in concern. To make matters worse, the sun sailed from behind a cloud as if in divine reproach, bathing Mr. Weatherill in its beams and displaying to disadvantage every ill-fitting seam and worn patch of his clothing.

He hasn't a penny more than you do, Adela Barstow, she imagined the sun chiding, clicking its fiery tongue, *yet you fly at him for taking you at your word. You fly at him because you are unhappy with yourself.*

"Mr. Weatherill," she murmured at last, seeing her mother glance back when the pair fell behind, "I am ashamed of myself. Thoroughly ashamed. I have behaved very badly, and it is you who must pardon me. What I said just now—my...unfortunate tirade—would have been better directed at—at Fate than at you, and for that I apologize."

But his thoughts had ranged quickly over what had passed, to determine his part in provoking her, and he replied with equal quietness, "In light of the painful circumstances pressing upon you all—which I cannot pretend ignorance of, after riding with you in the coach yesterday—I should not have called you 'crosses to bear.'"

"No, please do not attempt to excuse me," she sighed. "Where was the fault in your words, when I said as much myself? And in your further defense, at least you did not call us 'parasites,' as I did."

His mouth twitched. "If I had, I daresay you would have knocked me to the ground."

Her head whipping up at this, a pair of brown eyes searched him with a look so measuring that Weatherill's shrinking under it was only half in jest. But far from taking fire anew, Adela felt a curious little bubble rise in her chest, and she surprised both of them when it escaped in a giggle.

"Dear me, Mr. Weatherill. What a termagant you must think me. Thank you for taking my misconduct so graciously."

"It shall be buried in oblivion, Miss Barstow—at least on my part—and I hope you will excuse my own clumsiness. I...have no great experience with subtlety or the courtesies required by polite society."

Having forgotten his earlier vagueness about his own origins, the familiar shadow now falling across his countenance recalled it to her, and she heard herself say, "Haven't you? What...sort of pupils did you teach at your former school?"

Though he smiled, it did not reach his eyes, and she had the curious feeling he was withdrawing inside himself and closing the door behind him. "The poor sort, Miss Barstow," he answered. "The *burdensome* sort. You might even call it a case of the poor teaching the poor." With an inclination of his head toward Mrs. Markham Dere, he added, "I suspect if the lowly status of my students had been more clearly understood—"

He broke off, but Adela guessed the rest. If Mrs. Dere had known more of Mr. Weatherill's background or appearance, she might never have hired him as her son's tutor. Who knew, but that the worthy woman might still rouse herself to object and send him packing? Mr. Weatherill's position in the Perryfield orbit might be no more certain than the Barstows'.

"I understand you," Adela said simply. Much as she would like to satisfy her curiosity and ask another probing question or two, she wanted even more to see him brighten again. "Perhaps now, because we have mutually mistaken and mutually pardoned each other, we might make a new start."

Her words answered the purpose, and Mr. Weatherill emerged again, in a manner of speaking, to beam at her. He really had a very winning smile, with a dimple in one cheek so deep his mother must have loved to press her finger into it.

"Yes," he answered at once. "Let us shake hands mentally on our bargain, Miss Barstow. Nothing makes a better foundation for friendship than a breach which has been repaired."

By this time the group had nearly completed its circuit of the gardens, and had they parted there for the afternoon, Adela would have tripped away, congratulating herself on having made her first friend in Oxford-shire.

But, alas.

Just as they passed a second cupid balanced atop a second ball, this one smirking at its counterpart a hundred yards opposite, Mr. Weatherill said playfully, "You must admit, however, that there is one avenue open to penniless young ladies which is rarely, if ever, available to penniless young men."

"What one is that, sir?"

"The one your younger sister chose, whom you left behind in Twyford," he replied. "The avenue of marrying a *not*-so-penniless gentleman." Weatherill grinned at her, imagining this reminder of one sister provided for might please Miss Barstow, but instead of appearing gratified, confu-sion overtook her.

"Oh—indeed. Yes. I suppose so. Ha ha! Marriage. Yes. How right you are," Adela babbled, retreating a few steps into a patch of asters and then springing out of them as if they were molten lava. Mr. Weatherill's brows rose in amazement at her odd conduct, but fortunately Lord Dere and his two dangling matrons had reached the place where the path met the terrace steps, and Adela could leap to take Mrs. Barstow's arm. The children ran to join them, shouting of their discoveries, Frances trailing behind at a more dignified pace, while Sarah appeared at the French doors with Bash in her arms, the hubbub putting a decided end to any further tête-à-tête.

CHAPTER 6

**You are the only creature that I have made my confidante.
—Lady Mary Wortley Montagu, *Letter* of 5 September
(1709)**

"Mama," said Frances at breakfast a few days later, "Do you suppose Jane is married by now?"

Adela tried to kick her younger sister beneath the table but connected with poor Poppet instead, who had been lurking in hopes of falling tidbits. With a dramatic yelp, the lapdog was tossed against the nearby Outlaw and punished accordingly by the kitten with hisses and scratches. Maria and Gordon jumped up to separate the combatants, and peace was not restored for some minutes.

"Goodness!" said Mrs. Barstow, a hand to her brow, "I do hope those two become friends." But Adela saw the tears standing in her mother's eyes and knew Frances' question had distressed her.

Therefore, when it came time to walk with Gordon to Perryfield for his first lessons, Adela said, "Come along, Frances. It's a lovely day out."

"Pooh!" her sister replied. "I wanted to weave straw for a new bonnet. Take Sarah or Maria."

Before either of the latter could agree or refuse, Adela raised a warning brow which Frances knew from experience meant she had no choice in the matter. With a groan, she placed her basket of straw on a high shelf out of Outlaw's reach and stalked after Adela and the eager Gordon.

"I hope we don't see Mrs. Markham Dere," she complained as their brother dashed ahead to swing and jump from the branches of the great elm. "Why must we call on her or she call on us every single day? Already there is nothing new to say, and she looks at us like we aren't half good enough for her."

"Well, if that is how you feel, Frances, I am thankful you held your tongue when we have been with her."

"Pooh. I only feel how everyone else feels, secretly. And I'm fifteen—of course I can hold my tongue!"

Adela threw her a skeptical glance. "Indeed? Then I wish you wouldn't mention Jane to Mama."

"Why shouldn't I mention my own sister to Mama?"

"Because, you ninny, Mama is beside herself over Jane, and reminding her only pains her."

"If that is so, I warrant Mama thinks of Jane without my reminding her," retorted Frances. But then her nose wrinkled thoughtfully. "Poor Mama. Does this mean you *don't* think Jane is married yet, then, Della? I daresay she and Mr. Merritt could almost have walked to Gretna Green by now."

Adela heaved a sigh, debating inwardly whether Frances' vaunted fifteen was or was not old enough to understand the truth. But Frances guessed the trouble without being told because her eyes grew wide, and she flapped her hands in the air. "Della, you think something has gone wrong. You think—but—but you can't think Roger Merritt won't marry her after all!"

That being precisely what the elder Barstows did fear, Adela had no reply.

"Oh!" gasped Frances. "Oh, goodness! What will become of her, if he doesn't marry her? Our Jane will be a *fallen woman*! In that case, she had better leave him, wherever they are. Leave him. Run away and come to us here. Only—what would we tell everyone became of Mr. Merritt? Could we say that he is dead, like Sebastian and Papa? We should not have told the Deres his name. Do you think they will blame us?"

"Hush, Frances!" Adela urged, as her sister's voice rose in excitement. "Yes, of course they will blame us. Everyone will blame us. I wish the Deres did not know his name either because Mrs. Markham Dere will blame us the most of all, and she might even persuade Lord Dere that Gordy is not a fit companion for her son Peter."

"Not fit?" squeaked Frances. "You really think so, Della?"

"It's possible. It's all possible."

"That would be very awkward, since we live so near. And who would teach Gordy, then? You don't know any Latin or Greek. Perhaps we could ask Mr. Weatherill to teach him apart from Peter Dere."

"Don't be ridiculous," returned Adela. "We could not stay here, don't you see? Mrs. Dere would convince Lord Dere to send us away."

"But—but where would we go? To join Jane and Roger?"

Adela rolled her eyes. "In a word: no. We could not join Jane and Roger, if we even knew where they were. I have no idea what we would do or what would become of us if we were cast out." Unwillingly she recalled Mr. Weatherill's suggestion when they walked in the Perryfield gardens. "I would likely have to—to leave and become a governess. And Mama would have to find other lodgings for the rest of you. Smaller ones. Cheaper. Though I don't know how that could be done when Lord Dere lets Iffley Cottage to us for a pittance. She would probably have to take in a lodger as well. Shhhh! Don't shriek so, Frances! This is why you must talk of the matter to nobody but me. Do you understand? I don't want any of this to happen to us either, so I am—making a plan."

"You do have a plan, then? What sort of plan, Adela? Tell me, and I won't tell a soul," her sister begged. Having always been the middle child, neither included with the two eldest sisters nor willing to be counted with her younger siblings, Frances leapt at this chance to be Adela's chief stay. "Tell me your plan, and I will do all I can to forward it. I *will*. You may depend upon me."

How could Adela resist this plea? She, who had been laden with cares for months, from the time they first learned of Sebastian's death, after which one blow followed another. She and Sarah and Jane used to share confidences, but then Sarah had her own grief to bear, and Jane was distracted by the charms of Roger Merritt. And when Jane forsook them...

Clearly neither Mrs. Barstow nor Sarah could be confided in now—they would each be horrified by her decision to pursue Lord Dere and would try to prevent her, while having no better solution to offer. Poor Jane was gone heaven-knew-where, so that left Frances. Frances, who might be young and often still childish, but whose sincerity Adela did not doubt.

Frances it must be.

She took her sister's arm and pressed it. "Very well," she began, "I tell you in complete confidence that I think Lord Dere must be won to our side. We must gain greater influence over him than Mrs. Dere, so that if the truth becomes known, we will still be secure."

"Yes, yes," agreed Frances. "That makes sense. Do you mean we must discredit Mrs. Dere?"

Adela started. "What? No, nothing like that. I don't mean to make an enemy of her, if it can be helped. In fact, if we could manage to win over both Deres, why, we would be unassailable!"

"Oh." Frances sagged with disappointment. She would have liked to vex the woman a little. "Yes, I see. What then, Della?"

Taking a deep breath, Adela tightened her grip on her sister's arm. "Don't scream or make a noise, Frances, but I am thinking it would be best if I married Lord Dere. That is, if I can persuade him to offer for me."

Thank heavens she had the foresight to warn Frances because the girl's mouth fell open to its widest, and she actually halted to stand stock-still in the path.

"No screaming!" hissed Adela, tugging on her. "And come along, or Gordy will be late."

Like an automaton with a broken mechanism, Frances jolted into motion again, but it was some minutes before she could speak. Some minutes in which a series of emotions washed over Adela—embarrassment, shame, despair, resentment.

Then— "But why can't it be Mama who marries him?" asked Frances.

Adela felt a little of the tightness in her shoulders ease. Then her sister was not going to denounce her as unmaidenly? Could it be that Frances *understood*?

With the beginnings of a wavering smile she answered, "Darling, you know how Mama adored Papa. I do not suppose she will marry again, and even to broach the possibility with her now would outrage her."

"Yes, I see." Frances frowned meditatively. "I don't suppose we might persuade Sarah to do it, then? Little Bash needs a father."

"And our Gordon doesn't?" countered Adela, nodding her chin at their brother, who was balancing atop the stile before he leaped down. "Besides, how would throwing Sarah at him be any better? She already shares Sebastian's pension with the lot of us—we could not ask her to do more, even if she were not so recently widowed herself."

"Not to mention the contrast between Sebastian and Lord Dere. One so young and virile, and the other—the other—so—that is—"

"Indeed," said Adela, with a twist of her mouth.

"Oh, Della!" wailed Frances. "*Can* you do it? He is so old! Even though you haven't been married before and are not in love with somebody else." Another round of hushing her, followed by a squeeze to her arm, persuaded the girl to choke these sentiments down, but she made whimpering noises under her breath as they climbed over the stile.

"He is kind," Adela declared, her own voice unsteady now. "And I don't even know if I *can* do it—accomplish it, I mean. Make him offer for me. I'm sure other ladies have tried. He is rich, you know."

"And a peer, if one likes that sort of thing."

"Yes."

Frances smothered another whimper, but then she tried to get hold of herself. Throwing back her head to gaze at the approaching stone wall of Perryfield, she said, "All right, Della. If it must be you, it must. But—if you don't succeed—*I*—I will try my hand at him next."

Adela would have laughed at Frances' air of martyrdom if she weren't closer to crying. "Dear, dear Frances," she murmured, pressing a cheek to her sister's shoulder. "It will not come to that. If I fail, we will think of some other course. But perhaps I will not fail. I will have one advantage over anyone else who has tried her hand—I will be a great deal in Lord Dere's company, if I can manage it."

Relief washed over Frances' face to find her self-immolation refused, but she straightened and favored Adela with a stern look. "You mean to say, if *we* can manage it. Because tell me what I must do to help."

Seeing Gordon doubling back to join them, that he might not arrive at the house alone, Adela said quickly, "Only this for now: if you can be as charming as possible to Mrs. Dere. Talk to her. Listen to her. Distract her, so that she will be slower to notice or guess what I'm up to. Every minute I can spend studying Lord Dere and trying to commend myself to him, the better."

There was only time for Frances to give a solemn nod before Gordon rejoined them, disheveled, perspiring and full of chatter, and then the sisters must leave off their private scheming to put him to rights. But it was enough. Adela found her determination renewed and her thoughts buzzing and whirling.

I must work to discover his likes and dislikes. How can he have remained a bachelor for so long? If I cannot charm him, could he possibly be brought to adopt Gordon? Not as his heir, to be sure, but as a sort of surrogate second grandson?

Adela scrutinized her brother, trying to see him as a stranger would. But that was impossible. He was their Gordy—sunny, lively, winning. All of which might work against him, if Mrs. Dere or her son Peter chose to be jealous. She suppressed a sigh. Gordon might be another iron in the fire, but he equally might not. It all remained to be seen.

Having steeled herself for the first assault on Lord Dere's heart, Adela marched up to the great house ahead of her younger siblings, only to have the door swing open before she reached it. And instead of the footman Wood, the Barstows were presented with the tutor Mr. Weatherill.

"Oop!" he exclaimed as Adela stumbled in surprise, his hand shooting out to prevent her knocking her head against the door jamb, with the result that his fingers were crushed between those two articles.

"Mother of pearl!" uttered Mr. Weatherill before he could help it.

Gordon guffawed at this outburst, but Frances in her new role as Adela's right-hand man gave him a vicious pinch which silenced him. Manners prevailed thereafter, however, with both Adela and Weatherill pretending nothing had happened as they made their bows to each other. Though she kept the brim of her bonnet lowered, Adela feared Mr. Weatherill had seen her blush. Gracious—he would either think her hopelessly clumsy or that his appearance discomposed her. But surely the blood rushed to her cheeks out of embarrassment, and not because the unexpected sight of him had any effect on her.

Surely.

For, if she had Frances as an ally now, did she not also count Mr. Weatherill as one, after their last conversation? He should not then cause her any discomfiture. But he did, for whatever reason.

Mumbling a greeting, Adela wished she had warned Frances about the tutor. No, no—why should a warning be necessary? It was the tutor himself who had jokingly suggested Adela find a wealthy husband. But would he think it so amusing, if she did what he proposed and entrapped their mutual benefactor?

"I hope the walk from Iffley Cottage was pleasant," he said while these thoughts chased each other through her head.

"Very. What—er—brings you outside, sir?"

To her surprise, he straightened abruptly, swallowing and looking so conscious that she forgot her own unease. "Goodness!" she almost laughed. "How guilty you look. Have you murdered somebody and just returned from hiding the body?"

"I was—posting a letter at the Tree Inn," he answered reluctantly. "And having received one in return, I chose to read it before I entered the house."

Why, the man was as crimson as Adela had been a moment ago, and she felt her curiosity piqued, rather than satisfied. "Doesn't Wood collect the Perryfield letters?" she asked.

"He does. But—a walk is a pleasant thing."

A walk, and a correspondent he omitted to name.

Here they were again, on the shadowy edge of Mr. Weatherill's history, where all were discouraged from further encroachment. Did he write to a family member in London? Adela wondered. Someone from the charity school? Or a sweetheart?

As they entered the house, she considered ignoring his no-trespass signals, but before she could decide to forge ahead, there was Lord Dere, crossing the hall with a folded newspaper beneath his arm.

His appearance drove everything else from Adela's mind, and judging from the alarmed glance Frances threw her, she was not alone in her concern. Taking care to move sedately, Adela dropped a careful curtsey, struck by the contrast between the baron's silver, aging dignity and what Frances had called Mr. Weatherill's "youth and virility." Though Mr. Weatherill wore again his seedy, ill-fitting coat and rusty trousers, they somehow detracted less and less from the essential fineness of his form, in the same way a bright summer sun would eventually burn through obscuring clouds.

"Good morning, Miss Barstow, Miss Frances, Master Gordon," Lord Dere greeted them in his mild way. (Did his voice sound reedier than she remembered?)

With a great effort, she forced a smile to her lips and blinked at him in what she prayed was a beguiling manner, but Lord Dere didn't seem to notice. He turned instead to Gordon.

"Eager for your first lessons, my boy?"

"Yes, sir."

"Lead on then, young man. Unless you don't remember the way, and then Weatherill must do the honors."

"I know where it is!" declared Gordon. "It was only up the big stairs and then along the first floor to the stairs at the far end, and then there it was on the left at the top."

The boy sprang away, Lord Dere chuckling and murmuring, "Excellent," as he indicated for the others to follow.

"Perryfield is hardly *labyrinthine*," Frances muttered, disgusted by her little brother's boasting.

The baron heard her. "What a big word for such a young lady. Who has been in charge of *your* education, if I might ask?"

"My Papa was, and Papa's books," Frances answered. "He called me his—his little autodidact—" she broke off suddenly, a hand fluttering to her lips, and Adela knew why. Grief was like that—always in ambush. It was only that the Barstows had been so harried from pillar to post that they eluded its grasp so long. Reaching for Frances' restless hand, Adela clutched it and threaded her fingers through her sister's. In return, Frances bumped her shoulder against Adela's. Then the younger girl cleared her throat and resumed, "But now, with—Papa—and his library gone, I suppose Della is."

Lord Dere paused at the top of the grand staircase and just tapped Frances' elbow with his forefinger. "Miss Frances, I am certain Miss Barstow will prove an excellent instructor, but should you wish to feed your *autodidact* tendencies, you and your entire family have my permission to make full and free use of the Perryfield library. In fact, after we have deposited Gordon and Mr. Weatherill in the schoolroom, I will take you there for a detailed tour and to choose some books."

The sisters stole glances at each other before assuring him of their approval. Oh, yes! Books would be delightful, but even more so would be the opportunity to make inroads upon his affection.

"Sir," spoke up Mr. Weatherill, "I wonder if Peter and Gordon and I might join you for the detailed tour? I would encourage them in reading anything which might interest them, even if it is only the descriptions of illustrations."

Of course the baron agreed to this at once, and Adela pressed her lips together to hide her chagrin. But this was not all, for when they reached the second floor, Mrs. Markham Dere's voice carried to them out the open schoolroom door.

"—Shall be along presently, I daresay. Oh! There you are, Mr. Weatherill. And—my, my—and several Barstows, I see." The handsome lady stood by the window, arms crossed, and no sooner did she take in Adela's and Frances' presence than her gaze returned to the tutor. Evidently his worn apparel was not yet fading into the background for her, for she shut her eyes briefly and shuddered. And much as Adela would prefer not to have Mr. Weatherill around to witness her activities, nor did she want him to lose his position because of Mrs. Dere's displeasure. No gentleman would wish to appear as shabby as Mr. Weatherill if he could help it, which meant he could not help it.

"Good morning, Mrs. Dere," she hastened to say, therefore. "I hope you are well today."

"Very well, Miss Barstow. I enjoy excellent health. And your mother?"

"Also well. And we thank you for the jars of preserves and confits you sent to us."

"The peach is delicious!" cried Frances.

"Hmm." Mrs. Dere turned again to the tutor. "Well, here are the boys, so we will leave you in peace, Mr. Weatherill."

"Thank you, madam, but we have something of an expedition planned, to begin with."

Naturally, when the matter was explained Mrs. Dere joined their party and took it upon herself to lead them back down to the library. They had glimpsed it on their earlier tour, but now Lord Dere pointed out the system of classification his grandfather had used, and which his father and he had continued.

"Many of these books were gathered on their Grand Tours," he explained. "History, philosophy, art, plays, and so on. Weatherill, you will likely find this shelf helpful—sketches of ancient Greece and Rome. Travel here. Biography. Science. Religious works. Please, please—take them out and inspect them."

While the late Mr. Barstow amassed a respectable collection of three hundred volumes (all of which Adela had catalogued for the auction), the Dere collection numbered in the thousands, bound in tan or black or brown, the spines and covers embellished with gold lettering and leaf.

Adela waited for the others to scatter sufficiently about the room (Frances hovering a few feet from Mrs. Dere and pretending interest in the religious works) before wandering back to their host, her heart racing like a soldier's before a charge.

This was the moment, then.

Let the assault begin.

CHAPTER 7

Amavi ego a teneris annis studium Natura.
From my tender years I have loved the study of Nature.
—G. A. Scopoli, *Entomologia Carniolica* (1763)

D o you have personal favorites among all these, sir?" Adela asked
Lord Dere, a blush coming without effort.

"I do, which you would soon have discovered if you came upon any
of their dog-eared pages," he answered. "Shall I show one to you, Miss
Barstow?"

Blessing her luck—why, with a few hours spent in the library, pulling
each volume off the shelf to consider its condition, she might have a wealth
of subjects with which to fascinate him!—she nodded, fixing a look of glee
on her face and following him to the center bookcase. From the lowest shelf
he withdrew a modest volume and placed it lovingly in her hands.

Adela's expression slipped a little when she saw the title. "*Ento-mo-En-
tomologia C-Carniolica?*" she ventured.

He nodded, beaming. "Open it. Please."

As her sister Frances had pointed out earlier, Adela "had small Latin and
less Greek," but when she turned past the marbled endpapers to the title
page, there was no mistaking the word in large print: "*Insecta.*"

"Oh, I see," she breathed. "It is—a book about...bugs?"

The baron's smile widened. "Insects, yes. With more than forty plates of illustrations."

"Fancy that!" She gave an uneasy titter. "I'm afraid the Latin is sure to be beyond my understanding, though."

"Never mind the Latin, then," said Lord Dere kindly. "I can scarcely be bothered with it either, when the pictures are so fine. Do look at them."

Now, it must further be told that Adela Barstow, however courageous she was in every other aspect of her life, was, in the presence of insects, snails, and spiders, the most hen-hearted of cowards. Whenever any family member wanted to play a prank on her, he need only place one of these creatures upon her pillow or beside her plate or in her workbasket for Adela to be reduced to a squeaking, quivering jelly.

Feeling the blood drain from her upper half, she with trembling hand began to turn the pages of *Entomologia Carniolica*, the shaking only increasing as she began to see, over and over, the heading "Scarabæus." *Scarabæus dubius. Scarabæus fasciatus. Scarabæus cyatheger. Scarabæus adiaphorus.* It was like holding the lid down on a particularly terrifying jack-in-the-box, afraid of what would spring up if she let go. *Scarabæus sylvestris...*

And then there it was! The first illustration plate, composed of two facing pages of beetles, ten in all, the largest as big as her hand and real as life. With a yelp, Adela jumped and dropped the book as if all ten scarabs had leapt at her. She took a stumbling step backward, only to have her retreat at once thwarted by collision with the very solid person of Mr. Weatherill, whose resulting *whuff* of breath only drew wider attention to her panic.

"Miss Barstow!" he and Lord Dere said together.

"I am terribly sorry," Adela gulped, inwardly berating herself. She lunged to retrieve the fallen book just as the baron stepped forward to—what?—ensure she had not lost her senses? Whatever the reason, the unfortunate result of this second conjunction was that Adela's face came perilously close to the most inexpressible portion of Lord Dere's inexpressibles, an infinitely more humiliating impact avoided at the last instant only by her twisting to the side and falling to her knees.

Then all was noise and confusion. Adela found herself hauled up by Mr. Weatherill on one side and Frances on the other, to be deposited on a sofa, Frances and Lord Dere peppering her with questions.

"I'm sorry," Adela kept repeating. "I felt a little faint."

"I would offer you sal volatile, Miss Barstow, but there is none on hand," declared Mrs. Dere. "For *I* am never faint."

"It's a shameful weakness," agreed Adela to appease her, but this effort miscarried in that respect, for Lord Dere strode to the door and called for the nearest servant.

"A cup of tea and perhaps a buttered roll for Miss Barstow," he ordered. She demurred, of course, saying she had already breakfasted, but he waved this away. "You Barstows have been through a great deal in the past week, and if I am not wrong, you have been the manager of your removal and arrangements, Miss Barstow. It is no surprise at all that you should have overtaxed your strength. You rest here, while we continue to mill about. And would you like anything to peruse while you wait for your refreshment?"

Determined to throw the helve after the hatchet, Adela said distinctly, "Perhaps the insect book? I might then study those beautiful illustrations at my leisure."

"But Della, you hate b—" was as far as Gordy got before Frances shouted, "Gordon, you have something on your lip!" and clapped a hand to his mouth to wipe the imaginary speck away. When he wriggled and scowled in protest, she dragged him off to the farthest corner to "show him something marvelous."

"Yes—yes I do—er—hate *books*," Adela struck in wildly. "Books about things, that is. I mean, I hate them in comparison to the things themselves.

Things which can be observed and—er—touched and—er—experienced. How can books possibly compare?"

To her amazement, the baron met this gabbled pronouncement not only with credulity, but with inexplicable delight. "Can it be so, Miss Barstow?" he asked, swiftly retrieving *Entomologia Carniolica* for her and opening it again to the first plate.

Now that she was prepared for it (and safely seated), Adela managed to fix her eyes on the loathsome beetle portraits. It helped to cover them partially, on the pretense of tracing their outlines with her fingers. And to work at deciphering their Latin labels in their calligraphic script.

"This one I have," said Lord Dere, a hum of excitement in his voice. He pointed to easily the most hideous of them. "*Lucanus cervus.* Both male and female specimens. It is the male pictured here with the well-known stag horns, from which it derives its common name."

What else could poor Adela say? "H-have you? How—splendid. I would very much like to see them."

A snort was heard behind her, but when she whipped her head around it was Mr. Weatherill, sneezing multiple times in succession into his handkerchief. When she turned back, Lord Dere had already crossed the room to open a long, shallow drawer in one of the cabinets.

Mrs. Markham Dere was upon the baron in a flash. "My lord! What can those be? I beg you, put those hideous things away." But while her vehemence was enough to make him hesitate, he was the next moment swarmed by Peter and Gordon, and Mrs. Dere was compelled to give way. The tray of pinned beetles, male *Lucanus cervus* occupying pride of place in the exact center, was set with great ceremony on the table before Adela, and she must lean forward with every sign of apparent delight to inspect it.

Amidst the boys' clamor, Adela need not speak right away, a lucky thing, considering she was struggling against an inclination to gag. No, she need only smile, lips parted and eyes wide and awed. Lord Dere received this silent tribute with a twinkle in his own eyes, and it would have been an unqualified triumph, if not for Mr. Weatherill looming over the baron's shoulder, a skeptical eyebrow raised as he scrutinized not the beetles but Adela herself.

Confound the man! Why shouldn't she like insects, if she pleased?

"They're—marvelous," Adela breathed. "In such excellent condition, sir. One might imagine them caught just today or—or—or still alive."

Lord Dere swelled with satisfaction. "My collection has been the work of years, Miss Barstow, and I have many more examples for your viewing pleasure, but this magnificent fellow I found at least twenty years ago. I cannot tell you what gratification it gives me, to meet a young lady with an interest in the smallest members of our natural world."

"But, sir," uttered Gordon, glancing up from the tray to regard Lord Dere with incredulity, "Della has never—*ehrmmf!*"

"I missed a spot!" bellowed Frances, grabbing her brother's mouth and scrubbing her hand back and forth over his protests. When he kicked at her, she dragged him backward, hissing sternly in his ear.

"Heavens," Mr. Weatherill said mildly. "Remind me to keep my upper lip clean around Miss Frances."

"*What* have you never, Miss Barstow?" asked Peter, poking her. "What was Gordon going to say, before his lip got dirty?"

"Oh—I'm sure he was going to say that I have never—er—before been known to demonstrate a *strong* interest in such creatures." (Adela thought the nearer she held to the truth, the less there would be to explain later to Gordy.) "But goodness, aren't they something? So—so intricate, if one really looks at them." She did just that, forcing herself to sit forward on the sofa and to bend over the case, her eyes blinking rapidly. She could feel her palms break out in perspiration and her skin prickle as she imagined the repulsive little things crawling—scuttling—*springing*. Did beetles spring?

Dead beetles don't spring, at any rate, Adela scolded herself. *And this one has been dead twenty years.* Gripping *Entomologia Carniolica* to her chest as a shield, she hunched another inch closer, only to hear a rap on the case as the stag beetle flew at her!

With a shriek, Adela vaulted up, dropping her book shield and nearly knocking down small Peter Dere in her scramble, but the boy's yowl of surprise halted her flight.

"Miss Barstow!" Lord Dere and Mrs. Markham Dere gasped, the former concerned and the latter astounded at such a display.

"I—I—was startled," panted Adela. Her gaze flew to the tray of beetles, now lying innocently motionless atop the table.

"I *do* beg your pardon," said Mr. Weatherill, reaching down to rub his knee. "How clumsy of me to bump that."

"You did that?" she demanded with an accusing point of her finger. He had jolted the case on purpose—she could swear it!

The tutor shrank in mock alarm. "Yes—as I just confessed…"

Though she began to sputter, whatever regrettable words might then have issued forth were conveniently forestalled by the entrance of Wood with the requested tea and buttered roll.

"Ah," said Lord Dere, "just what our poor Miss Barstow requires. Come, my dear. You are not only tired, but you are set on edge. This will help."

She allowed him to return her to her seat, and despite her vexation at Mr. Weatherill's teasing trick she was wise enough to rein in her show of temper and even muster a smile for the baron. "How silly I've been! I'm sure you're right, sir. Please, everyone, pay me not one jot more attention."

"Madam," Wood addressed Mrs. Dere, "Cook asked if she might consult you about the menu again. Something about there not being enough cold pheasant for two pies."

"Nonsense! Cook simply has no idea of the proper way in which to pick the most meat from the bones," insisted Mrs. Dere. But she begged the Barstows to excuse her and marched after the footman.

"That reminds me," said Lord Dere, taking advantage of his niece's departure to settle into the armchair to Adela's right, "I meant to send Mrs. Barstow a note—or to call myself—asking that you might all dine at Perryfield with us any days you please. We must not stand on ceremony."

"Thank you, sir. I know my mother is occupied with settling into Iffley Cottage, but I am certain she will wish to accept your kind offer in future."

"Tomorrow, perhaps?" Humor glinted in his eye. "I do not dare ask you all to come today, if there is indeed a shortage of pheasant. Say tomorrow and again Sunday following church."

"I will ask her, sir." Color rose to her cheeks, and the irregular throb of her heart was not at all pretended. Could it be, despite her blunders, she was succeeding? Making progress?

"Splendid. Now, if you don't mind, I will move this out of your way..." He took up the case of beetles to replace it in the cabinet, the two boys following in hopes of further exciting treasures and Frances following Gordon to ensure he told no tales.

Which left Mr. Weatherill.

Adela seized upon the others' absence to throw him a half-wary, half-cross look, which he met serenely as he claimed the vacated armchair. If they were the tentative allies she thought they were after their garden talk, the man should not be playing brotherly pranks on her. Because unlike with an actual brother, Adela could neither lash out at him nor seek revenge.

With a nod toward the boys gathered about Lord Dere he said impassively, "Clearly my pupils share your zeal for the insect world, Miss Barstow." Seeing Adela's lips tighten, his own twitched. "Therefore, if you wouldn't mind, perhaps I will take *Entomologia Carniolica* off your hands and up to the schoolroom—that is, unless you wanted to pore over it further."

Swallowing a retort, Adela fairly tossed the book at him, but if she hoped to catch him off guard she was disappointed, for he caught it neatly.

"I see the refreshment has already done its work," Weatherill further observed. "A commendable throw. Do you prefer bowling over or around the wicket?"

"Why are you being so teasing, sir?" Adela snapped, goaded. "Shouldn't you gather Peter and Gordy now and get to work?"

"Get to work, so *you* might get to work?" he returned. He tapped his chin, adding thoughtfully, "Not that my presence has hindered you."

"I don't know what you mean."

"Don't you? You must have hit your head harder on the door jamb than I thought. Then again, my poor fingers likely did not cushion the blow as much as one would hope. In any event, I allude to our earlier conversation—to your efforts to work yourself into our benefactor's favor."

Adela stole a peek at Lord Dere and the children still occupied at the cabinet before she hissed, "Then if you remember that talk, and you remember why I seek his good-will, why should you throw it in my face now? You may be a salaried employee, sir, but you would do well to imitate me. We all of us hold our places solely by his grace and favor, so what can be wrong in working to win his good opinion?"

"What, indeed? No, no, Miss Barstow. I well recall our garden chat. But I never supposed, when I spoke in generalities of marrying for advancement—a suggestion which discomposed you at the time, I might add—that you would seize so rapidly upon the idea. Nor that you would take our benefactor as your object. If I am not mistaken, he must be at least five and thirty years your senior."

If the fire in her eyes could have found material form, he would have been incinerated on the spot. "How dare you. Who says I am—doing what you say I am doing?"

His eyebrows lifted, but he said nothing for a moment. Then he made her a half bow. "It seems I have been mistaken."

"Indeed you have," replied Adela, now avoiding his gaze. She picked up the breakfast roll and tore it into several pieces. Then she shifted the teacup and saucer to a new position on the tray.

Mr. Weatherill sighed and gave a shrug. "I daresay it's not the first time I have misread the evidence." Slapping his hands on his rusty trousers, he rose. "If you will excuse me, Miss Barstow. As you pointed out, it is high time I 'get to work.'"

Leaving her to her thoughts, he tucked *Entomologia Carniolica* under his arm and turned to call to his pupils.

CHAPTER 8

Believe it Sir, That clothes doe much upon the wit...and thence comes your proverbe, *The Taylor makes the man.* —**Ben Jonson, *Staple of Newes,* I.ii.111 (1631)**

P lease let your arms hang naturally, sir," the tailor instructed Weatherill, as he stretched the tape from one shoulder to the other.

Gerard had not imagined his arms could hang *un*naturally, but the afternoon had been full of surprises. Not two hours earlier, he had dismissed Peter and Gordon, shutting the door after them so no sound would carry to him while he set the schoolroom to rights, straightening the books on the shelf and wiping clean the blackboard.

It was when he was at his desk, purporting to plan the next day's lesson but in truth mulling over the same thoughts which had occupied him the past fortnight, that a knock came, followed by Mrs. Markham Dere's entrance.

"Ah, Mr. Weatherill. If you have a minute, there is something I would discuss with you," she said.

A dart of uneasiness pierced him.

She had not to this point sought him in his classroom, and as he had chosen to take his meals in his sitting room, he had encountered her far less than might be expected for two occupants of the same house, however large that house might be. Lord Dere he saw more frequently, crossing his path in the library or the gardens, and the baron never failed to stop and speak courteously with him, asking how Gerard was liking Oxfordshire and Perryfield in particular, or inquiring after the boys' progress. But Mrs. Markham never appeared to find pleasure in meeting him, a pained expression fleeting across her features before she could master it.

This occasion was no exception, a line appearing between her brows, to be smoothed away with an effort. Was he about to be dismissed? Had she somehow—learned something about him?

Bracing himself, Weatherill stood, palms upraised to indicate his readiness to listen.

Pinning a smile upon her handsome face, Mrs. Dere folded her hands and took a deep breath. "Mr. Weatherill, I am delighted to say my Peter tells me he enjoys his lessons with you. As does little Gordon, I believe."

He bowed his head in acknowledgement. "Thank you. I rejoice to hear it. They are both intelligent lads."

The line appeared again, and he wished she would waste no more time with preliminaries.

Mrs. Dere must have been of the same mind because she took one more deep breath and forged ahead. "Yes. Well. Lord Dere, too, shares my satisfaction with your early efforts. To the point that—in fact—he would like you to…feel yourself more a part of the—the family." Another grimace came and went. Clearly, whatever Lord Dere's opinion on the matter, Mrs. Dere did not share it.

"I have discussed it with him," she went on, "and understand him to mean that he would welcome your presence at—certain meals and in the drawing room in the evenings. Of course I explained to him that you surely would like to have time to call your own, so that you were not always at your employer's beck." (The emphasis on *employer* was faint but discernible.) "I also observed that we are raising Peter to be the gentleman his rank in life demands."

Weatherill might have turned to stone, so still did he hold himself. *Now for it*, he thought. *Now for it all.* Aloud he said, "I see. I am at his lordship's disposal."

"Mm."

If he had been less on edge he might have realized Mrs. Dere was feeling her way and trying to read him in turn.

"The fact is," she resumed, "not to mince matters, but if you do indeed choose to join us regularly—even in, or, shall I say, *especially* in company—I feel you might make a—a better presentation of yourself. Your outward self, that is. I do not imply that you do not have the manners and carriage of a gentleman—far from it! If that were the case, we should have sent you packing at once! Heh heh. But Peter is an impressionable young creature and the baron's heir, so you will understand why I wish him to appear in, and be shaped by, the best company. Lord Dere is not as scrupulous in these details as one might wish, issuing invitations to Perryfield willy-nilly—but—never mind. In short, Mr. Weatherill, I wonder if you might benefit from an advance on your salary."

"An advance on my salary?" he repeated, almost laughing in relief at the unexpected direction of her words. This was not about the Fleet and Rioting Rob, then—it was about her thinking him an aesthetic blight?

"Yes," she hurried on. "There is a very acceptable sort of tailor in Iffley who might assist you with some—additions—to your wardrobe at no great expense. I daresay ten pounds would suffice to fit you out, prices here being considerably cheaper than in town. If you were to go this afternoon, you might have something new by Sunday, both for church and for the rector and his wife, whom Lord Dere has invited for supper."

As a household dependent there was only one choice to be made, which was how Weatherill came to be in the village, having his measurements taken.

"Two coats, black and dark blue. Two pairs of trousers, buff. Four shirts. Four neckcloths. Socks." The tailor made notes in his book. "I may have a few items as soon as Friday afternoon, if you care to be fitted then, sir, and I will send the bill to Perryfield as you request." Spinning the book around on the counter, he tapped the box in which he had calculated the total, and Weatherill was pleased to see he had kept to the allowance. He might even purchase a new pair of boots. And however a village tailor might fall short of his smarter brethren in London, the new clothes could only be an improvement on the items Gerard had worn for the past three years, faded and ragged and ill-fitting as they had become. When he lived in the environs of the Fleet his shabbiness passed unnoticed, but here in Oxfordshire even the tradesman and laborers were better dressed.

Emerging from the narrow shop into the street, against his will he glanced up and down the length of it.

No sign of her.

Whether by luck or by effort, he and Miss Barstow had avoided the sight of each other since that day in the Perryfield library. Certainly Gerard had taken pains to keep clear of her. He had gone away that day nettled, his only comfort the satisfaction of having nettled her in return. But when that waned, his annoyance contrarily lingered.

Because she *did* hope to charm Lord Dere, whether she admitted it or not! It was disgusting, a young lady of her age seeking to entrap someone so much older, for the sake of security. Disgusting and designing and despicable. It was not the gap in age alone which made it so, nor the gap in rank or fortune. Her pursuit, undertaken without love, would be reprehensible in any circumstances.

Or so he told himself at first.

But Weatherill was a just person at heart, and before many days had passed he had to concede that, disgusting and designing and despicable as Miss Barstow's scheme might be, neither was it unusual. Quite the opposite, in fact. Similar plans were formed and similar matches made every day. Added to this, it just might be she would not even have considered Lord Dere in that light, if Gerard himself had not jokingly reminded her of the possibility of salvation through marriage. But he had never imagined she would consider marriage to *Lord Dere!*

From there it was a short step to ask himself why it should matter whom Miss Barstow chose to marry or why. Really, whom *anybody* chose to marry was none of his business, for he doubted he would ever have the means to do so himself. Perhaps if he waited until he was forty, after having saved every farthing, and if he chose a bride nearly as old, someone who by virtue of her age might present him with only five children, say, rather than fifteen.

No appearance of Miss Barstow disturbed his return to Perryfield this day, in any event, and he sought Mrs. Dere at her escritoire to make his report. The good lady nodded with approval, saying, "Excellent. Perhaps you might join us at dinner this Sunday, then, when Mr. and Mrs. Terry will be here? After which, when your wardrobe is complete, would you prefer to name regular days when we might expect you to dine, or would you rather only join us in company?"

Weatherill had considered the question, at first thinking he would only dine with the Deres in company, but if the company were lofty, would that not be awkward? Better to set a regular day as well, so that his presence would not be unusual. And that he might excuse himself from grander entertainments when he thought it fitting.

"Perhaps Wednesdays and in company on other occasions," he suggested.

"I will tell Lord Dere."

Peter Dere, for one, would likely be happy to see more of his tutor. Both he and Gordon had taken to tarrying in the schoolroom when lessons ended, only to have Weatherill shoo them out after a few minutes, lest Miss Barstow come in search of her brother. The fourth or fifth time they lingered, Weatherill said, "You mustn't keep your sister waiting, Gordon," only to have the boy reply, "Oh, but she doesn't fetch me anymore, Mr. Weatherill. She says I know the way now."

Weatherill stared. Had he been hiding on the second floor and avoiding Miss Barstow all this time for no purpose? "Does she still walk you over in the mornings?"

"Oh, yes, but that's because she is calling on Mrs. Dere."

Or calling on *Lord* Dere, more likely, Weatherill thought sourly, before repeating to himself, *None of my business.* Absolutely *none of my business.*

But whatever the progress of Miss Barstow's schemes, at least he need not witness her efforts in the afternoon and might have the freedom of the house again.

When the tailor delivered the first of his new wardrobe on the Saturday, Mrs. Dere told him by way of Wood the footman that the carriage for church would be called for at nine, and Weatherill "would be welcome to sit in the second Dere pew." His mouth twisted at the news—the Sunday before, he had attended the afternoon service with the servants and workingmen of the parish, who greeted him gruffly and uncomfortably, but now he was to be promoted to morning attendance with the "quality"?

Descending the stairs a few minutes ahead of the appointed time, he was reminded absurdly of the débutantes in novels, entering their first ballroom in full view of the critical public. For in the entrance hall stood Lord Dere, Mrs. Dere, Peter, and a few servants, all with faces upturned and eyes fixed on him.

The adults were too polite to remark, of course, though Mrs. Dere swelled with approval and gave one nod, but little Peter cried, "What have you done with your old patched coat?" He was silenced with a look, however, and the party proceeded to the waiting landau.

Set above the Thames, the old Norman church of St. Mary the Virgin with its beautifully ornamented façade and central bell tower dominated the village, and as Harker unfolded the steps for them to descend, Lord Dere murmured, "At some point, Weatherill, you must allow me or the rector to show you the carvings around the great west door. Very fine."

For the moment, however, they joined the parishioners milling in the church yard, who parted to permit the baron passage. Among them stood the many Barstows, and Weatherill thought it must have sent a thrill to the very core of Miss Barstow when Lord Dere smiled upon them and beckoned to her mother with a "Please join us in our pews." Shooting a glance at the young lady, however, he did not catch any delighted cunning on her face, nor was she even looking at the baron. Instead, her gaze of unaffected surprise, brown eyes wide, was all for *him!*

Oh, Gerard realized, that was right. His new clothing. Plainly he had indeed looked bad, then, and the young ladies had all noted it, for Miss Barstow was not the only one of them staring. (Wonder threatened to dislocate the lower jaws of Miss Frances and Miss Maria, so far did they hang open.) Self-consciousness made him color, unwittingly adding to his newly emphasized charms, and he drew back to let the Barstows precede him. Miss Barstow tore her eyes away, lowering her head as she passed by, so that he was presented with the familiar crown and brim of her bonnet.

The congregation entered by the south door, overlooked by a carved figure astride a lion, to follow Lord Dere up the aisle. The Dere pews were directly before the pulpit, and Weatherill filed into the second of them, where he found himself beside Miss Frances and behind Miss Barstow.

Let it not be assumed by the young man's inattention to the service that the reverend Mr. Terry was deficient as a priest. On the contrary, Mr. Terry was a pleasant, not unhandsome rector of middle age with the gift of making pithy, interesting sermons, during which even the children did not kick their legs or fidget overmuch. But others in attendance did not have Miss Barstow seated immediately in front of them and were thus not distracted by a slender neck rising from sloping shoulders encased in blue cambric muslin. It was the first time he had seen her wearing a color, with only black ribbons threaded through inserts in the sleeves to indicate her mourning. A few tendrils of dark hair slipped from beneath her chip bonnet to curl lovingly about that graceful neck, tendrils he found himself tracing in his mind, and altogether the sight held an inexplicable magnetism which made it impossible for him to pay Mr. Terry's words the slightest attention.

The unheard sermon was followed by prayers. The peace. The Eucharist. The offertory. Someone's banns were read.

At last, when the blessing was given and the service ended, the congregation again filed out, greeting the rector at the door, to walk home or to stand about in the churchyard until carriages were brought, Mrs. Markham Dere by Lord Dere's side and Weatherill standing a decorous few feet to the side and rear, determined not to stare at Miss Barstow. Instead, after bowing to her mother and sister-in-law, he trained his gaze on Peter and Gordon, who along with Mr. Terry's youngest pupil had gone to dart in and out among the leaning tombstones.

"—New tutor at Perryfield—"

"—Fine figure of a man—"

"—Somewhere in London—"

The chatter was impossible to ignore, though he was obligated to pretend he neither heard it nor was aware of heads turned his way.

"They all want to be introduced to you, I expect," said Miss Frances, appearing at his shoulder. "We've already met most of them because they called at the cottage or at the rectory when we were there too."

Her guess was correct, for, as if on an unseen signal, the parishioners bowing to Lord Dere and Mrs. Dere were soon being led by them to address him. As might be expected in a village so near to Oxford before term had begun, there were several dons and fellows and assorted university affiliates, along with a few wives and daughters.

"Mr. Weatherill came highly recommended by Mr. William Keele, formerly of Exeter College," Mrs. Dere announced with a complacent smile. "Not only was he taught by him, but he also served as his assistant master at a school in London."

"Keele!" exclaimed one with a wagging, goatish wisp of beard. "One of the finest scholars of ancient languages Exeter ever produced. A schoolmaster, you say? So that's what became of him. He was one so inflamed by Norden's *Travels in Egypt* that he vowed to see the ruins himself."

"He did see them," Weatherill replied carefully, "long ago, penetrating as far as the Second Nile Cataract. And he has ever since been at work on an account of his findings." It was the truth, if only a partial picture. But it would serve no good purpose for anyone to learn how William Keele lost both his archaeological treasures and his welcome in Egypt after an international squabble with the French comte de Volney over the riches buried beneath the sand. Keele returned a broken man, only to be further broken by the accumulated debts which landed him in the Fleet. In all the years Weatherill had known him, the fading adventurer would spread his sketches of Medinet Habu and Karnak across a shaky deal table and mull over the great work he would one day produce, one which would silence his doubters and perhaps even buy his freedom. Indeed, part of Weatherill's work for the man had been to summarize and organize the hundreds of scraps and transcriptions, the drawings and notes.

To Weatherill's relief, as the Oxford set crowded about him that morning, they were too busy talking over each other, sharing reminiscences of

Keele and opinions on Egyptian expeditions, as well as rehearsing a few related academic squabbles, to properly interrogate him.

"You must give Keele my regards," concluded Wisp of Beard, when the Dere carriage arrived and the flock began to disperse, "when next you write to him."

Weatherill bowed in vague acknowledgement but made no promises before he followed the Deres into the landau. Surely such men would let William Keele slip again from their minds, as they had let him slip for decades, and Mrs. Dere would have no further cause to bring him up again.

Indeed, Mrs. Dere had more pressing concerns as they drove away.

"Sir," she addressed the baron, "I did not realize you intended to ask the elder Barstows to dine, along with the Terrys."

"Yes. I suspected Mrs. Barstow would like to be hospitable to the rector and his wife, but with their limited resources and the fullness of Iffley Cottage, I thought this would be simpler. As it will just be the two Mrs. Barstows and Miss Barstow, I do not think it will incommode Cook much."

"Can't Gordy come too, Uncle?" asked Peter.

Lord Dere smiled at him. "He cannot, because you will not be here to host him. You see, Mrs. Barstow thought it would be a treat in turn for you to dine at Iffley Cottage. An exchange of sorts—the delightful younger Barstows in place of the strait-laced older folk. Unless you would prefer to be at table with the rector...?"

Peter gave a whoop in answer, his delight only increased when Lord Dere told him Harker would drive him and likely let him hold the ribbons for part of the way.

Mrs. Dere's faint frown remained, however, and though Weatherill was glad to know her displeasure was not directed at him on this occasion, it troubled him nonetheless when she said, "Sir, it is very kind of you to condescend to the Barstows, not only in letting the cottage to them and allowing Gordon to share in Mr. Weatherill's services, but do you not fear that…an excess of favor might…raise their hopes beyond what would be advisable?"

"How so, Mrs. Dere?"

Brushing an invisible speck from her dress, she smiled demurely. "I'm afraid there are *some*—and I do not say I know enough to include the Barstows among them—but indeed there are *some* who would seek to…profit from such a connection. It might become, 'When we dine at Perryfield,' or 'Our cousin Lord Dere says this and such,' or—or even expectations as to—to future emolument might grow! Sadly, sir, there are some who, as the proverb teaches, if given an inch will take an ell."

"Thank you, my dear," Lord Dere replied. "I will keep that in mind."

Weatherill ought to have felt thankful to Mrs. Dere as well, for certainly Miss Barstow intended to take an ell if she could manage it. But to his own amazement he was conscious of increasing vexation. Not only because the accusation was utterly unjust to the two Mrs. Barstows, but also because even Miss Barstow was a reluctant schemer. If she were not in such precarious circumstances, would she ever have considered trying to charm the baron?

He suppressed a sigh at his own weakness, his own eagerness to seek the best interpretation of matters. Perhaps all schemers were driven by precarious circumstances. A Miss Barstow might be explained, but she could hardly be defended.

So why should he wish he could?

The Perryfield
Library

Church of St.
Mary the Virgin

The Rectory

The Tree Inn

CHAPTER 9

Marriage is a desperate thing, the Frogs in Æsop...
would not leap into the Well,
because they could not get out again.
— R. Milward, *Selden's Table-talk 33* **(1689)**

I f Lord Dere took to heart the warnings of his tenants' possible machi-nations, no sign of it appeared when he welcomed his guests. Mrs. Barstow, Sarah and Adela arrived at the same time as the Terrys because the coach had been sent for the lot of them. Weatherill was already present in the drawing room when they arrived, preferring not to draw attention to himself by making an entrance, and from his position behind the Deres he had time to make one lightning survey before the guests acknowledged him.

Miss Barstow wore the same blue gown from the morning, minus the muslin tucker, as the September day had grown quite warm. Having also removed her bonnet, the dark hair which had fascinated him at church was revealed in all its luster. Straightening from her curtsey, she raised a glowing face to Lord Dere, only to jar to a halt, blinking, her gaze snagging on the tutor. This infinitesimal break went unnoticed by the others, Lord Dere having turned to address Mr. Terry, but Weatherill raised an arch brow. *Yes, here I am. Will that interfere with your evening's plans?*

It would. Absolutely it would.

It was not embarrassment or shame which caused the hitch in her movement, but something equally disturbing to Adela. For her first thought on recognizing him was, *Goodness, but Mr. Weatherill truly is handsome in his new clothing!*

As much as Weatherill had been avoiding her, Adela had been avoiding him in return. Why else would she confine her visits to the morning and let Gordy walk home alone from Perryfield? In the mornings there was less chance of Mr. Weatherill rattling about loose. Less chance of encountering his condemnatory gaze and feeling her shame rise up to choke her. For she *was* ashamed. Humiliated that her desperate scheme should be guessed at and censured. Humiliated that he thought ill of her as a result.

Added to these unhappy feelings, Adela fretted that her actions were transparent to all. For if Mr. Weatherill saw through her so easily, Mrs. Markham Dere would be the next. (It never occurred to Adela to think that Mr. Weatherill *scrutinized* her in a way Mrs. Dere did not.)

At church that morning, after her first amazement, Adela had been determined not to look again at her judge, and when Frances talked later of "Mr. Weatherill's new coat" and what everyone thought of it, Adela made an excuse to leave the room.

And now—here he was—unavoidable! Dressed like a county gentleman and standing in the drawing room as if he belonged there! The mocking look he gave her only added to her confusion, and for a moment she thought of postponing her wooing work to another day. But how could she, after the fortnight already lost to her cowardice? She was like a mason ordered to complete a brick wall by a certain date, but who was only allowed to lay one brick per day. One morning walk to Perryfield with Gordy and ten words spoken to Lord Dere: one brick. Lord Dere slowing his carriage in the village to greet her and Sarah as they returned from their call on the rector's wife: another brick. Another time accompanying Gordy, but only having Lord Dere wave to them as he rode over his grounds beside his steward: a fraction of a brick. At this creeping pace Adela could only say the baron seemed to like her as well as anyone else, no better and no worse, but that was a very long way from wanting to offer for her.

But this evening—this evening must be the start of a determined *campaign!* This evening she no longer had a choice but to build the wall as high and as hastily as she could, for she had finally, finally heard from her sister Jane. And far from reassuring her, Jane's letter so unsettled Adela that she had yet to share it with the family.

For the past fortnight Adela had made visits to the Tree Inn upon her return from Perryfield, becoming a familiar sight to the postmistress Mrs. Lamb and accepting with equal impassivity bills forwarded from Twyford and letters from past neighbors and parishioners. Therefore, when Mrs. Lamb placed in Adela's hands a letter with the direction written in a familiar, spiky script, Adela paid over the pennies without a tremble. There was trembling enough, however, after she stole away to Iffley Meadow to read its contents unwitnessed. The missive was long and crossed, and even in the bright sunlight Adela had to hold it close at times to decipher it. Or perhaps it was her tears which blurred the page.

> *Birdbury Inn*
> *Shropshire*
>
> *10 September 1800*
>
> *My dear Della,*
>
> *The coach for London leaves within the hour, but I scribble*

you this note because I know you have been waiting and waiting for word from me. Oh, how I wish I could see your sweet face, and Mama's and Frances' and Maria's and Gordy's and Sarah's and Bash's! You mustn't think I regret marrying my Roger—for we are *married, and you must tell Mama so she may cease to be anxious on that point. The journey to Scotland was long and arduous, though we went as quickly as it could be managed. I cried a great deal, I am afraid, and fretted Roger so, but I could not help it because I missed you all and thought how you would all cry yourselves to find me gone, and though I love Roger I did not like to be on the road with him before we were married, for fear of what everyone we met would think.*

I will say little of the ceremony itself, except that it was not at all like in the novels we read. It was raining and muddy, and our witness was cross with a toothache, but Roger says we will laugh about all that soon enough. We stayed only a night in Gretna Green before returning to Carlisle, where we spent two days because Roger wanted to inspect the garrison and castle, and I wanted to rest. Della, when I think I had never before been ten miles from Twyford! Now, to jaunt thus all over Britain—for we proceeded from Carlisle to Penrith, Penrith to Kendal, Kendal to Lancaster, Lancaster to Preston, Preston to Liverpool, Liverpool to Warrington, Warrington to Chester, Chester to Whitchurch, Whitchurch to Shrewsbury. I am exhausted anew just recording our journey. I did so try to be a good traveler, for Roger's sake, but I fear I got very homesick and had all I could do not to weep for weariness.

We had hoped, of course, that Shropshire would be the end of our wanderings. Roger went first and alone to see his aunt Merritt, thinking it better if she knew nothing of our marriage until he could prepare her, but our precautions were all for naught. Mrs. Merritt flew into a towering, unreasoning rage and said many terrible things about how Roger has proven unworthy to be her heir or even to claim the name of gentleman(!). She said she had been more than patient while he sowed his wild oats, but she could be patient no longer, not if he had been such a fool as to marry a "destitute green girl" who could do nothing for him, instead of a Miss Barker person who had always hoped to marry him and who boasts a fortune of fifteen thousand pounds. (When Roger related his interview to me, I did cry—I could not help it—to be the cause of his ruin and estrangement. He comforted me with kisses and assurances of his affection and declares if she continues thus he might refuse to know her, but how can these blows not diminish his love for me, eventually?) For there will be no army commission from Mrs. Merritt, she vows, nor even a continuance of his allowance, and we must make our own way in the world. I offered to meet her, to see if I could soften her obduracy, but Roger thought it unwise at present. He said perhaps later, if there were to be a child...His aunt had been very fond of him as a child.

You must tell Mama as much of this as you think best, Della, but we go to London now, where Roger hopes to find employment. I might also do some sewing or trimming of bonnets, though you know you and Frances and Sarah are better at such things than I. Again, you must not fear that I regret my elopement. It has not turned out as I imagined when he proposed to me, but it will come right in the end. When I think of how my absence lightens Mama's burden (for at least it stretches her money further), I take some comfort. And now that you can tell her I am indeed married, she will think it was the best course.

How I wish I knew where we would be, so that when we arrived there would be a letter from you! I miss and miss all of you and long to hear how you are liking the cottage and whether Lord Dere is a cross old bear who resents you or whether he loves you all already and does not begrudge a penny of the outlay. If the latter, perhaps he might be brought to recommend Roger for a post somewhere? Oh, may heaven forgive me for that last line. My dear, enterprising husband will manage it all.

There is the coachman calling, and I must go. A thousand kisses.

Your own affectionate sister,
Jane Merritt

If the paper Jane sent had not already been cockled with the new bride's own tears, the drops which fell from Adela's eyes upon reading it would have served the purpose. The heartening news that her sister was indeed married and not altogether ruined as the Barstows feared was swallowed up in all that followed, and it was hard to say which part of the rest was most distressing. Yes, the marriage was accomplished, but was it not a case of "out of the frying pan, into the fire"? Jane, crying! Lighthearted Jane, who always teased her sister into good humor. The contrast between this weeping, worried letter and the laughing, heedless note she left when she eloped! As much pain as Jane's actions had caused her family, Adela wept just as hard to learn of her sister's unhappiness, homesickness, and fears, which the sad little offer of learning to be a seamstress or milliner and the repetition of her trust in Roger Merritt only emphasized. What would become of her? How long would Jane's little purse keep them? *Could* Lord Dere be brought to do anything for them?

But to ask Lord Dere for assistance at this juncture might bring everything down about their ears. Without having gained his affection or his promised protection, Adela could only appeal to his pity and native kindness, while an outraged Mrs. Markham Dere could call upon Morality. Propriety. What Was Owed to His Heir. What Was Owed to the Dere Name. She would persuade him that poor relations were one thing, but black sheep must be driven off and penned elsewhere.

No. Adela had no alternative but to keep to her plan, Mr. Weatherill or no Mr. Weatherill.

This evening she would play and possibly sing for Lord Dere. Or partner him at cards. Or sit beside him in the drawing room after dinner. Or read to the company, if that was what he preferred. And she would agree on behalf of her family—over her mother's continued hesitations and demurrals—to the baron's repeated invitation to dine regularly at Perryfield, that more metaphorical bricks could be laid at speed. And somewhere in between all those activities, she would court Mrs. Markham Dere because Frances was not here to do so. (Not that Frances said much in Mrs. Dere's presence, but the very way she would sit quietly and admire the woman as if she were one of the wonders of the world, had not escaped Mrs. Dere's flattered notice.)

Yes. The work must go on, whether Mr. Weatherill were present or not, handsome or not.

Therefore, with a lift of her chin, Adela inwardly shoved her misgivings and dismay in an imaginary trunk and sat upon the lid. Giving Mr. Weatherill a tick of a nod, she proceeded to ignore him.

"Sir," Adela addressed Lord Dere at the first possible opportunity, when the weather, the ride over, the morning service, and Mrs. Dere's latest amendments to the drawing room had been thoroughly discussed. "I was in Iffley Meadow yesterday and was delighted to come upon an insect I hoped you might identify."

The baron's face brightened at once. "You don't say, my dear Miss Barstow! Did you capture it?"

(Adela had a brief memory of running her fingers through the plants along the riverbank as she mulled over Jane's letter, only to have a stem swing back like a trebuchet to fling the creature at her, from which she ran screeching.)

"Sadly, no," she answered. "But it was a beetle, a green one, and shiny like metal. And it was on a stalk of tansy."

Slapping his knees in delight he replied, "Why, you have named him yourself then, my young entomologist! It must have been a tansy beetle. *Chrysolina graminis.* Quite a beauty. I have one in my collection, which I will show you as confirmation of your discovery."

"Thank you, sir."

"Perhaps Miss Barstow might like to fetch the tray herself from the library cabinet," spoke up Mr. Weatherill.

Adela would gladly have thrown a cushion at him for this, but it was the rector who intervened. "Speaking of beetles, Weatherill, now that I have learned of your connection to Exeter's own William Keele... Do you know, long ago I once read a treatise of his on the Egyptian predilection for scarab beetles."

"*Scarabaeus sacer,*" supplied Lord Dere. "The Kheper, more familiarly known as the dung beetle."

Sudden scarlet washed over Mr. Weatherill's face, but before he could reply, Mrs. Dere intervened.

"Absolutely *no* beetles before dinner," she insisted. "And my dear uncle, I do wish you would indulge me. Let there be no exhibition of your specimens on this occasion. I had hopes of spending our time more decorously this evening. For while you love your insects, you also love music. When we have eaten, we shall have the Barstows and Mrs. Terry play for you."

The others politely (or happily) allowed the subject of beetles to drop, but Adela pondered the tutor's unexpected discomfiture at the rector's comment. Heaven knew Mr. Weatherill did not share her dread of insects, so was it the reference to his former mentor Mr. Keele or to Exeter or to Egypt which disturbed him? If, for whatever reason, the tutor was going to throw grenades at her, it would behoove Adela to arm herself in turn.

When Wood called them to dinner, Lord Dere led Mrs. Terry, followed by the rector and Mrs. Dere. Mr. Weatherill then offered his arm to Mrs. Barstow, leaving Sarah and Adela to bring up the rear.

With only eight at table and everyone seated by precedence, Adela found herself between the Terrys and directly across from Mr. Weatherill, which meant nothing she said would go unheard by him, unless Sarah or Mrs. Barstow chanced to engross him in private conversation. But with Jane's letter utmost in her thoughts, Adela would not be deterred.

"Well, Lord Dere, how do you like having young boys at Perryfield?" asked Mrs. Terry. "It has been a very long while—since Mrs. Markham Dere's husband was a boy, I imagine."

"I like it well. They are good lads."

"Sir, allow us to say again how grateful we are for Gordon to learn beside Peter. He loves his lessons—"

"Miss Barstow, if you will forgive me for interrupting you, I must beg you never to mention it again. It heartens me to see Peter with someone his age, for I am too old to frolic." This last was delivered with a benignant gleam in his eye. "But perhaps it is not me you should thank, for if Gordon were any trouble, it would be Weatherill who has 'borne the burden and the heat of the day.'"

All heads turned toward the tutor, who lay down his spoon. "They both have a great deal of energy, but if we break up the lessons with some active game or running about the grounds or up and down the stairs, I find them willing enough to apply themselves."

"Indeed?" responded the rector. "Perhaps I should try such things my-self with Wardour, my youngest pupil. For a boy of eight he is remarkably restless."

"More like a puppy," agreed his wife.

"Were the pupils at your former school so young, Weatherill?" Mr. Terry asked. "I suppose Keele gave you the younger ones, for he could hardly be expected to romp about or to apply the whip when necessary."

Again Adela noted how Mr. Weatherill's color came and went, but he said merely, "One or two of them were young."

"We have three pupils at the rectory now," rejoined Mrs. Terry. "Thomas Wardour the puppy, his older cousin, twelve-year-old Thomas Ellis (two Toms in one household! You will understand why we only refer to them by their surnames), and the son of a former pupil, one George Denver. Denver is just fifteen and might as well have 'Innocent as the Newborn Babe' branded on his forehead. In fact, I tell Mr. Terry Denver's education must be enlarged beyond the classics, history, geography, and mathematics, or what will become of him in that den of vice known as Oxford? He will fall at once into debt and drunkenness and heaven knows what else, out of sheer simplicity! I rather wish his parents had sent him to a school in London such as yours, Mr. Weatherill, for then his eyes would have been opened long ago, I daresay."

Though used to Mrs. Terry's outspokenness, Mrs. Markham Dere nonetheless took offense at this and gave a curt laugh. "My very dear Mrs.

Terry, what can you mean? Of course you cannot think I would entrust my Peter to a tutor who was not of the highest character and who did not demand the same of his charges, no matter the setting of the school. And while there are indeed some parts of town which no man might frequent without stain to his reputation, they are hardly places where schools are found!" With an air of having put Mrs. Terry firmly in her place, Mrs. Dere turned to regard Mr. Weatherill, fully expecting him to share her indignation and to come thundering in, righteous and wrathful.

"AUUUUUUGGGH!" roared Mr. Weatherill. "HAUUUGH! HAUGH!"

Everyone at the table jumped at this eruption, as did Wood and the other footman standing along the wall. Cries of "Gracious!" and "Mercy!" rang from Mrs. Terry and Mrs. Dere, but before anyone could do more than this, the tutor sprang up, napkin to his face, and bolted from the dining room.

"Follow him, Uncle!" Mrs. Dere commanded. "It's a fit of apoplexy!"

But Adela held up her hand. "No, no, madam—it's only that he choked on his soup, I believe. He will be better presently." And indeed, as they all listened, they could hear Weatherill in the passage, his wounded-rhinoceros barks diminishing ever so gradually to robust coughs interspersed with wheezing.

"Ah," said Mrs. Dere, simultaneously taken aback by such a performance and relieved it was not worse. "Wood—take Mr. Weatherill his glass of wine. Mrs. Terry, do tell us what you intend to do, for this young Mr. Denver's protection…"

The conversation and the meal moved on, Mr. Weatherill stealing back to his seat before many minutes had passed, but Adela studied him furtively, taking care to look elsewhere if he glanced at her.

She had found her weapon, she was certain. For there was some mystery here. Some secret. She had seen his jaw tighten with Mrs. Terry's reference to his London school, but it had been Mrs. Dere's fierce defense of his character which caused his unfortunate intake of breath and soup. *Had his former school failed in producing upright young men? Had Mr. Keele been some sort of reprobate? Or had Mr. Weatherill been dismissed from thence for some failure of character? Did he, as much as the Barstows, have a scandal to be hidden? Whether he did or no,* from the state of his original clothing she knew he was as poor or even poorer than they, and had therefore as much to lose.

As she ate her fish and what Mrs. Dere reported was the last of the grass lambs, Adela puzzled over the mystery, taking care still to smile when Lord Dere smiled and to toss in murmurs of approbation when he spoke. By the time the dishes were removed and the apricot tart placed on the table, only one thing was clear to her: Mr. Weatherill feared banishment from Perryfield as much as Adela did. But why then did he choose to judge her and pick at her? Could they somehow band together to achieve their aims?

She dismissed the idea soon enough. No—if Lord Dere and Mrs. Markham Dere could only be brought to tolerate one scandal, it had better be the Barstows'. Let Mr. Weatherill look to himself—a handsome young man would always land on his feet.

Even as she arrived at this conclusion, she lifted her eyes to him. Eyes which said, *Sir, you may have taken my measure, but now beware, for I have also taken yours.*

CHAPTER 10

Barren, barren, barren; beggars all, beggars all.
— Shakespeare, *Henry IV, Part II*, V.iii.3401 (c.1596)

Really, if one counted the tithes paid by the baron to the church, the entire company that night was dependent on Lord Dere's beneficence, and had his nature contained the least tyrannical streak, he could have made their lives unpleasant.

As it was, when they repaired to the drawing room, he allowed the ladies to choose their seats before settling on the sofa beside the rector and saying, "How shall we entertain ourselves? With reading, cards or music?"

"They all sound delightful," answered Mr. Terry, "but because Mrs. Terry and I have a house full of boys, I confess a leaning toward music. What do you say, my dear?"

"You speak for both of us, Mr. Terry," his wife agreed. "While Denver and Ellis have been learning the fiddle and Wardour the flute, it would be a stretch to call it music. Come, Mrs. Barstow. Let us hear your family's repertoires. It will all be new to us."

Sarah visibly shrank at this request, and both her mother- and sister-in-law knew how little she liked to perform for strangers. Therefore Mrs. Barstow turned to Adela, who rose at once to go to the instrument. Having no pianoforte in Iffley Cottage, it had been weeks since she played, and a rill of nerves rippled through her. But the thought of Jane bolstered her as she leafed through the sheet music, lighting on a piano sonata which had been part of their collection in Berkshire—one of her father's favorites, in fact.

Choosing it was a mistake, perhaps, for as soon as Adela played the opening bars, she heard a little *hmm* from her mother and felt her own throat constrict. *Oh, Papa! If you had lived, none of this would be necessary. None of this would have happened. If you had lived, we would still be secure in our happy Twyford home.*

But Adela had to concentrate her efforts, and she was rewarded by both the gradual easing of tightness in her person and by the baron bursting out with applause at the conclusion. "Brava, Miss Barstow! Now that I know you can play Haydn, you will find yourself obliged to do so with tedious regularity, I'm afraid."

Catching the raised eyebrow of Mr. Weatherill over Lord Dere's shoulder, Adela's answering flutter was not all assumed. "I am a little rusty and made more mistakes than I would have liked, but thank you, sir. To tell the truth, I only muddled my way through that one because we had that music in Twyford."

Perplexity fleeted across the baron's features before he snapped his fingers. "Ah—of course. You did not bring your instrument when you removed to Oxfordshire. I should have remembered that. What a shame. But Miss Barstow, you must come to Perryfield whenever you like to practice. Your sisters as well."

"Thank you, sir."

"And if it would not be too tiring for you now, would you play a little more?"

With a surge of satisfaction, Adela dutifully chose a second piece—an easier one—which met with equal delight from Lord Dere, but she demurred from the performance of a third because she noted the tightening of Mrs. Dere's lips.

"Mrs. Dere," she said impulsively, "now might we hear you play or sing? Just as Mrs. Terry craved novelty, so too do we Barstows."

It was the right thing to say, for Mrs. Dere required little coaxing to replace Adela at the instrument, and after a nod to Mrs. Terry to rise and assist in turning the pages, the good woman both played and sang. With the hostess occupied, Adela offered to make the tea when it was brought in, learning that Lord Dere liked his very milky but not sweet. (Whereas the rector preferred sweet but no milk, so Adela must take care not to confuse them.)

"May I make you a cup, Mr. Weatherill?" Adela asked him softly, when the others had been served and she could no longer avoid speaking to him.

He did not answer right away, though he looked at her, and she felt her color rise. "What?" she demanded, *sotto voce*.

"You have done well for yourself tonight. Earning admiration *all around*."

Her brows flew together at the light emphasis in his words, and she retaliated with a flick of the finger toward his new clothing. "I might say the same to you."

Straightening in his chair, his jaw hardened. "*These* are from an advance on my wages, that Mrs. Dere might be spared the pains of my shabbiness."

For no reason whatsoever, a spark of annoyance stung her. Mrs. Dere interested herself in the tutor's appearance? "How thoughtful of you to consider her feelings," said Adela.

"I mean that she requested I buy a new wardrobe," he clarified.

"Did she? What presumption! And I suppose you let her choose the colors for you?"

Her vexation was returned, it appeared, for he retorted, "I myself chose them. Because, I repeat, I paid for the clothing from my future earnings.

They were not charity. Not that you would balk at the latter, I suppose. I daresay if you asked for the gift of a pianoforte, Lord Dere would deliver one to the cottage by week's end."

"And if he did? Why would that be your concern? He would not need to rob your pocket to do so."

"I was not expressing concern. Merely making an observation. Calling a spade a spade."

"*What* spade?" she hissed. "There are no spades here, sir, requiring your identification."

"Oh no, Miss Barstow? If it were permissible to contradict a lady—"

But here Mrs. Dere's clear soprano and Mrs. Terry's accompaniment faded into applause, in which Adela and Mr. Weatherill quickly joined. The latter overdid his appreciation by raising his arms, however, which drew Mrs. Dere's eyes to him standing beside Adela. Adela stiffened, and it took everything in her to resist stepping away from him, which would only make her appear guilty.

"Did you say milk and two sugars?" she asked loudly.

"Just a touch of milk and only one sugar, thank you."

Adela escaped to prepare his tea, relieved to hear Mrs. Dere begin another song. And though it was petty of her, she ignored Weatherill's preferences and stirred in a half inch of milk and two sugars, as if she were preparing Gordy's childish cup. *I will give it to him without another word,* she decided. *Let him be Mrs. Dere's pet, and let me be Lord Dere's, and we will both have what we seek.* But she still dragged her feet as she approached.

He rose.

With her expression elaborately blank, she held the cup out.

But he did not take it from her.

His hazel eyes narrowed, fixed on hers. At this nearness she saw his irises were ringed in brown, with green and brown and golden shades radiating from the centers.

"Here," breathed Adela, as if he might somehow have overlooked the teacup.

The intensity of his gaze held her locked. "Admit—it," he bit out, his voice scarcely above a rumble.

"Admit what?" she returned, clenching her teeth to quash the shiver which went through her, tip to toe. She did not think any man had ever looked at her so hard.

"Admit that you're chasing him."

Anger flared, warring with shame, and she would have denied it again, but his gaze would not let her. "I—I—" The cup rattled in her grasp, and she set it down on the nearest table, the milky liquid slopping into the saucer.

"And if I am?" she croaked. "What business is it of yours? Why don't *you* admit you're just as eager to please Mrs. Dere because there's something you—you don't want her to know."

That served. His breath caught sharply, and it was he who faltered. The shadow she had seen before fell once more over his features, and though he did not stir a step, she was left with the sensation that he had withdrawn, retreated beyond her reach.

What more was there to be said? Adela turned on her heel and walked away, returning to the tea urn.

Then she had guessed right—that Mr. Weatherill, like she, kept some shameful secret which could jeopardize all. And now he knew that she knew of its existence. It hardly mattered that she did not know the details, any more than he knew about Jane. The mere mention of its reality was enough. He would leave her in peace now. She had fired her new weapon, as it were, and it had carried the day.

So why did she feel as if she had lost?

Drumming upon the last chord and following it with a playful trill, the rector's wife spun on the bench to curtsey alongside Mrs. Dere when their audience broke into renewed applause.

"Excellent, Mrs. Dere, Mrs. Terry," the baron praised them. "And now you must rest and enjoy your tea."

"Lord Dere," the rector's wife addressed him some minutes later, her blue eyes twinkling with mischief, "since I find you of such a musical mind, I have a little proposal to make you. I warn you: Mr. Terry has not given his approval, preferring to defer to you, but I assure you you will like it."

Mr. Terry shook his head fondly at his wife.

"What about me, Mrs. Terry?" interposed Mrs. Dere, indignant at not having been consulted. "Will *I* like this proposal?"

"Of course you will, madam," she replied with a laugh. "But first I must ask a question of the newest member of our community. Mrs. Barstow, are your family great dancers?"

Surprised to be addressed, Mrs. Barstow turned a faint pink. "We are all of us perfectly adequate, Mrs. Terry, though we have not done any dancing in months." Spreading her arms, she indicated the tokens of their mourning, but the rector's wife shook her head at this.

"I do not ask you to dance publicly, and therefore mourning makes not a jot of difference. Especially when your participation would be an act of charity. I have told you all of our innocent boy Denver. He simply must practice some dancing and social niceties before he is cast upon the wicked world. If you and your daughters are amenable, I pray the baron and Mrs. Dere would let us hold an informal little assembly here. A mere nothing, a children's ball. The young ones will stand up together, and we older people will teach them the figures. You have so many girls, Mrs. Barstow, and of such varying ages. It will be perfect."

Mrs. Dere made preliminary sounds which almost certainly would have developed into objections, had Lord Dere not struck across her with a decisive, "A splendid notion, Mrs. Terry. If Mrs. Barstow consents, Perryfield is at your disposal."

Raising helpless palms, Mrs. Barstow answered in her mild way that she would be content with whatever they should decide, and Mrs. Terry clapped her hands in satisfaction before turning back to the instrument to pound a few triumphant chords from Handel's *Rinaldo.* "It is decided! Denver shall be saved! Now, before the baron chooses a date, Mrs. Dere, won't you indulge us by letting us try a figure or two tonight? If I recall, you are an excellent dancer, and it has been too long since we have been treated to seeing you."

Adela had to admire the skill with which the lively, white-haired rector's wife flattered and managed Mrs. Dere, for their hostess blushed prettily and called at once for the footmen to roll back the carpet and push the furniture against the walls. Too bad Frances was not with them, to study Mrs. Terry's methods! Adela would have to study them for her.

"Who will be our three couples?" demanded Mrs. Terry briskly. "I must play, of course, and the baron, Mr. Terry, and Mr. Weatherill must be our gentlemen, but who besides Mrs. Dere will be our ladies?"

Both Mrs. Barstow and Sarah attempted to excuse themselves, which meant Sarah had to yield to her mother-in-law, but Adela naturally had no more choice in the matter than the gentlemen. And as the gentlemen courteously chose their partners by rank, she found a tight-lipped Mr. Weatherill asking her for the honor when Mrs. Terry called them to take their places.

"When we have all the children there will be enough for a good longways dance," she explained, "but with only three couples we had better keep to...let me see...Country Courtship and The Happy Couple." She waved the corresponding sheets of music. "Now, now, Mr. Terry—do not fret if you don't remember the steps, for I will play slowly and call them out."

Since Country Courtship was set to the Irish Washerwoman tune, it was long familiar to Adela, but never had she heard it played with Mrs. Terry's drawn-out deliberation. "Country Courtship! Now, then, first couple cast down and second lead up...First couple half figure eight down around third couple..."

The result of this pace was that, what would ordinarily be a touch and go, a turn and pass, a circle and wind, became something altogether different.

Adela and Mr. Weatherill took their places as the third couple in the set, but mercifully for the first part of the pattern they had only to stand there across from each other, not touching, attention fixed on Mrs. Terry at the pianoforte and the first and second couples. Mrs. Terry might have praised Mrs. Dere's dancing, but Adela thought the baron more deserving. For a man of his age he moved with grace and fluidity—far more so than the stumping, methodical Mr. Terry. As Lord Dere passed before her in the figure eight, he gave her a droll wink, and she smiled and blushed, though the blush was more for fear Mr. Weatherill saw the wink than otherwise.

At last she and the tutor entered the figures, passing back to back without a word before having to take each other's hands for the rights-and-lefts. Each grasp of the hand lasted as long as a handshake. Each turning in circle a season. Adela could not account for how she might take Lord Dere's hand or Mrs. Dere's with no more care than if they were strangers on the street, but Mr. Weatherill's—!

Why, Mr. Weatherill's bare hand was composed of electricity wrapped in velvet, and each time Adela lay her fingers across his palm, she felt the contact to every fiber-end of her person. Oh! If only she had replaced her gloves after playing the pianoforte! They would have offered some protection from this unnerving sensation.

Praying her treacherous weakness was known only to her, she kept her lashes lowered and forced herself to think of other things. Harmless things. Things which would prevent telltale blood from rushing to her face to betray her. She thought of boiled ham and brickbats. Bombazine and badgers. Bag bonnets and ballooning.

Nothing worked.

Adela grew pinker and pinker. Her palms began to sweat. When it came time for their two-hand turn (which they had to repeat over and over because Mr. Terry was bungling the rights-and-lefts below), meeting Mr. Weatherill's eyes could no longer be avoided. But she was afraid to. Would his hazel gaze fascinate her again, as a snake did its prey? Or—almost as alarming—would he still be withdrawn? Angry?

He was neither. He was...Adela didn't know. His color was high—as high as hers, she imagined—and she thought he appeared almost...sheepish?

"Mr. Weatherill—"

"Miss Barstow—"

He yielded to her, of course, and she heard herself say (underneath Mrs. Terry's insistent, "No, Mr. Terry! Clockwise!"), "Mr. Weatherill, what I said earlier—please pardon me—it sounded as if I wanted to threaten you. I do not. Nor do I mean to pry. Your business is your own, just as I hope my business is my own. I am not—seeking to make enemies."

His smile with its single dimple bloomed, and Adela's pulse sped for entirely other reasons. "Permit me to apologize in turn for my inexcusable efforts to provoke you, Miss Barstow. I have not the right. As we have acknowledged before, we are both of us in the unwanted and precarious position of dependent. No wonder it makes us...cross at times."

"Yes," she agreed with alacrity. "We lash out from dissatisfaction with our own...helplessness. Or that is a portion of it." His disapproval of her accounted for the other portion, Adela knew, but what could she do about that? She must do what she must do, and the devil take the hindmost.

As if following her train of thought he said, "While I am anxious to declare a truce, Miss Barstow, there is one thing I cannot understand."

"O-oh?"

"In the weeks you have been here, I would say your family have already become favorites. Is—more than that—necessary for your peace of mind?"

It was her turn to shrink away, which she did physically as well as inwardly, averting her head, lest he read the answer in her eyes. A truce was one thing—but confiding Jane's calamitous elopement another altogether.

For his part, had it been possible, Weatherill would have snatched the words back—anything to restore the amity they had been enjoying—but before he could think what to say, a jangle came from the instrument and Mrs. Terry cried, "That's right! You've got it now, my dear. First couple! Mr. Terry has mastered the rights-and-lefts at last. Miss Barstow, Mr. Weatherill, if you would go twice in circle yet again, please."

With a grimace at the timing of it, Weatherill held out both hands, and, after the briefest hesitation, Adela placed hers lightly within his clasp. She was trembling, and it might have been this which made him press them convulsively. As they whirled around, he bent his head to catch her eyes again.

Look at me.

But she would not. Adela was too occupied in willing her trembling to stop. Never mind that the electricity and velvet made nonsense of her thoughts, so much so that she botched the figure eight in her haste to put distance between herself and Mr. Weatherill. Let them all think her a blunderer, only never let them guess that she—that she—

Only later, as she lay beside the sleeping Sarah, did Adela have the courage to finish her thought. *Never let them guess how attractive I find him.*

It was only that, she told herself. Only an involuntary response to a young man's charm and good looks, nothing more. Knowing hardly anything of the man, how could it be more? Yes, yes, she supposed he could be kind, as well, and was already a great favorite with Gordy, but he was also penniless, mysterious, evasive. Sometimes antagonistic. Therefore what possible good could come of liking him? Even were she to indulge these budding feelings, and even were he to come to return them, they could lead nowhere. The two of them could never afford to marry, much less support her large family, and Adela would never abandon the other Barstows to deal with poverty and Jane's scandal on their own.

No. It was fortunate, merciful, that she recognized her...inclination before it could develop into something more dangerous. A mere "attraction" could be got over with diligent effort, which Adela fully intended on undertaking.

I won't dance with him again, if I can help it. Nor talk to him apart, she vowed sternly. *In fact, this is the last time I will let myself dwell on him at all. Tonight, and no more.*

Which might explain why it took Adela so very, very long to fall asleep.

CHAPTER 11

**We needs must take the seeming best of bad.
— Samuel Daniel, *The first fowre bookes of the civile warres
betweene the two houses of Lancaster and Yorke* (1595)**

One part of Adela's vow was easy to keep, for a few days later Mrs. Terry called to announce the Children's Ball must be postponed.

"You will never believe what Denver has done, Mrs. Barstow," the rector's wife sighed, even as she shook her head in amusement. "Our young man was walking in the meadow with his nose in a book, and he wandered too near the Thames."

"Did he fall in, Mrs. Terry?"

"Of course he fell in! But that would be nothing—a mere dunking. No, Mrs. Barstow. Denver not only fell in, but he caught his boot in a tree root as he fell, so that one limb was held fast while the rest of him ended in the river. In short, he has broken his ankle, and there will be no dancing for him until November or December, the doctor Mr. Travers tells us. Ridiculous boy. Denver, that is, not the doctor."

Without glancing up from her needlework and leaving the other Barstows to gasp and sympathize, Adela ignored the disappointment darting through her and thought, *Good. Very good. In that I am spared. Perhaps*

I might stay away from Perryfield for a few days altogether, until my feelings have...lessened.

She could not have everything her own way, however, for no sooner did Mrs. Terry depart than Mrs. Barstow turned from the window with a sigh.

"What is it, Mama?" asked Frances. "Were you so eager to see us all dance?"

"No, it is not that, though it would have given me pleasure, and I am sorry for poor Mr. Denver. No—it was that I wish we might hear from Jane. It has been weeks!"

Fifteen-year-old Frances inhaled swiftly and shot Adela a look which plainly said, *You* must *tell her, Della!*

Nor did the look escape their mother's notice. "What is it?" she demanded, her soft voice sharpening. "Do you know something?"

All eyes turned to Adela, even little Maria looking up from where she sat on the carpet, shaking a rattle for Bash.

Feeling her color drain, Adela tucked her needle in her sewing and smoothed it before laying it aside. "There was a letter, and I will show it to you, but I did not want to upset you. The good news—the very good news—is that they are indeed married. More worrying, however, was that Mr. Merritt's aunt was...not pleased to learn this. Not pleased at all. Jane reported that she and Mr. Merritt must think of other means to support themselves—"

Mrs. Barstow was already holding out an implacable hand for the letter, and, with a grimace, Adela produced it for her.

What a scene followed! Pained silence, exclamations, tears, questions, fruitless discussion. It was full half an hour before order was restored, and Adela feared the weariness and woe lining her mother's face would be even longer in the banishment.

"Can we—write to them, Adela, and tell them to come to us?" Mrs. Barstow suggested at last.

"We do not know where they are, Mama. We must wait to hear from them again."

"And where would we put them if they did come?" wondered Frances. "We are all of us on top of each other as it is. But perhaps Irving might build them some bunks, and they might sleep in the shed."

When Adela frowned at these unhelpful observations, her younger sister tried to make amends. "Or they might live at Perryfield! Lord Dere said he would be glad to host our guests."

"Frances," said Sarah, prodding Bash with the toe of her slipper to make him chuckle, "we could hardly expect Lord Dere to house *permanent* family members for us."

"True," Frances conceded, "and suppose Jane had a baby every year! Soon Perryfield would be fuller of Merritts than Deres."

Here Adela cleared her throat loudly and redoubled her frown, and Frances finally fell silent.

"Mama," Adela said, threading her way through the parlor furniture to put an arm about Mrs. Barstow's waist, "I fear that, even if Roger Merritt could submit to live as a mere adjunct to our family, dependent on Lord Dere and Perryfield for everything, Mrs. Markham Dere would never allow it."

For a moment Mrs. Barstow shut her eyes, her head lowering in defeat. "I know. You are right. A spirited man like Roger Merritt would never be persuaded; nor would Mrs. Dere ever permit it. But what will become of them? Could we ask Lord Dere for the loan of a sum to send them?"

Adela shrank from this suggestion. "Better just to call it a 'gift,' Mama, for who could say when or if it would ever be repaid? No doubt the baron would be willing, but there we find the same difficulties. For Lord Dere would have to keep it a secret from his niece, lest she object—vehemently—and I'm afraid it is Mrs. Dere who 'wears the breeches' at Perryfield."

None present bothered to argue the point with her, and they sat some minutes in miserable contemplation, with no other sound than Bash's mirth, as Poppet had wandered near enough to have his tail tugged.

When the silence was broken at last, it was little Maria who spoke. She had been sucking on her finger, which Outlaw had clawed, and petting the cat with her free hand, and she said idly, "Maybe Mr. Weatherill could help. Gordy says Mr. Weatherill is an excellent fellow."

"Mr. Weatherill's excellence is neither here nor there," returned Adela in a high voice. "For what could he do for us? He hasn't any money himself nor a home to offer them."

"He is from London, though," Sarah observed. "And because he has no money he might know of places where the poorer sort live or where they might seek work—"

"Yes! Yes!" cried Mrs. Barstow, seizing at this. "That is very true, Sarah. And what a clever proposal, my sweet Maria. Gordy does admire Mr. Weatherill, and so do I myself, I daresay, for he seems like a worthy young man. Surely we could ask him in deepest confidence...?"

"He would have no reason to betray us," continued Sarah. "And suppose, by some glorious coincidence, Mr. Weatherill's acquaintances *knew* of Roger Merritt! We lose nothing by asking, Mrs. Barstow."

Shaking free from Adela's arm, Mrs. Barstow went at once to the escritoire. "I will write a note to Mr. Weatherill asking him to call at his convenience, and you may give it to him when you fetch Gordon this afternoon, Della."

"But I don't fetch Gordon anymore," Adela protested feebly.

Her mother raised an eyebrow. "You may fetch him today. Perhaps, if he is not occupied, Mr. Weatherill might even return with you! Oh, Della, I know you think it unlikely we will learn much, but after weeks of being unable to do or say anything—"

"Yes, Mama," she said, resigning herself. "I will take it."

"I had better go with you," Frances announced when it was nearly two o'clock. "Not only to safeguard your reputation, but also to distract Mrs. Dere if she's lurking about."

And to keep me from having to speak to Mr. Weatherill alone, Adela added in her head as they tied on their bonnets. She had successfully avoided him since the Sunday dinner, though it meant she had seen little of Lord Dere either. The one morning she and Sarah came to practice on the pianoforte, Lord Dere had been meeting with his steward. The time lost! Each day, each hour which passed was squandered, Adela agonized for the hundredth time. She must, must overcome this unwanted, ridiculous *tendre* for Mr. Weatherill so that she might make the most of each opportunity. As it was, she had arrears of unfulfilled plans for pleasing the baron.

But luck was against Adela when Wood admitted them. Not only was there no sign of the baron, but there was Mrs. Dere crossing the entry hall like a watchdog, and Frances had to bounce in, calling, "How fortunate for me, Mrs. Dere! Della and I have come for Gordon, but I hoped I might see you and ask you to show me that new music you ordered, if you are not busy."

"I would be glad to. Come with me, Miss Frances. And Miss Barstow, if you would mention to Peter—and to Gordon, of course—that Cook has made his favorite treacle cake...?"

That left Adela to climb to the second floor alone, extracting her mother's note from her sleeve as she went.

The door to the schoolroom stood open, so that Gordon's voice carried to his sister's ears. "—Della's Mr. Liddell harped on him, that's all I know, but I'll still try him, if you like."

Her hand flying to her mouth, she halted, the note fluttering from her fingers.

"'Della's Mr. Liddell'?" repeated Mr. Weatherill. "*Has* Miss Barstow a Mr. Liddell?"

"Yes," answered Gordy stoutly. "Or she used to. Papa's old curate. Frances said he would marry Della, but he married someone else instead."

A pause followed in which Adela hardly dared to breathe, and then Mr. Weatherill rejoined, "That must have been a disappointment to you all."

"Nobody cried about it," the boy answered, doubtless with a shrug. "But then again Della never cries. The only time I've ever seen her cry was the morning we left Twyford, but that was because my sister J—"

"Gordy!" shrieked Adela, scrambling up the remaining steps, only to have to scramble back down to retrieve the fallen note. "Gordy, I'm here to fetch you!" Her panic was ridiculous, in retrospect, since she held in her hand the invitation to come and learn about Jane's elopement, but—oh!—far better that Mr. Weatherill hear it in Mrs. Barstow's appealing tones than that Gordy drop the news like a cannonball upon him.

The next moment Mr. Weatherill was in the doorway, regarding her with some amazement as she scrabbled at the step for the paper, cheeks pink and manner flustered. And every good vow Adela had made to herself fell to the ground like ripe fruit when the tree was shaken, for she gulped and gabbled and required three attempts to take the note securely in hand.

Gordon and Peter appeared to each side of their tutor, Gordon not looking at all conscious for having been speaking of his sister's failed *amours*.

"Oh, say, Della. What are you doing here? You haven't fetched me in ever so long."

"I'm fetching you today," she said lamely, glad to have someone to look at, so perhaps Mr. Weatherill might miraculously overlook her confusion. "Are the lessons not yet finished?"

"They are," Weatherill answered the top of her head, for Adela still hovered two steps below. If she had been able to meet his eyes, she would have remarked his own discomfiture—*Gracious, had Miss Barstow overheard him asking about her former beau?*

"Very well."

Adela would rather Peter Dere not know about Mrs. Barstow's note—only look how young boys could not be trusted to keep mum!—but neither did she want both boys to decamp at once, leaving her alone with Mr. Weatherill.

She compromised. "Er—Peter—Mrs. Dere asked me to say that Cook has something for you in the kitchen."

"Only for Peter?" protested Gordy, outraged. "Cook said I might come for a treat every day, if I liked!"

Adela stifled a groan. So much for that.

"Come on, then," Peter urged, and the boys bolted past Adela down the stairs, calling their good-byes to their tutor over their shoulders.

Clearing her throat, Adela gathered her courage in both hands and regarded Mr. Weatherill's left ear. Or more specifically at the waving lock of red-brown hair covering the top of his left ear. Really a lovely shade of hair. One a girl would sell her soul for.

Another throat clearing. "Right. Sir—my mother Mrs. Barstow has a message for you."

"A message for me?" he echoed. "From Mrs. Barstow?"

"Yes, and there you are." Adela thrust the paper at him as an assassin might thrust a dagger between his ribs, and his hand came up instinctively in defense. Which only led to her fingers colliding and tangling with his as the note crumpled between them.

Fearing she would combust with mortification at this latest awkwardness, Adela did not even attempt to apologize and simply fled.

Weatherill watched her go, uncertain if her retreating steps or his own hammering heart were responsible for the thumping in his ears. Either way, he waited for it to die away before sinking to sit on the landing.

"You idiot, Weatherill," he muttered. "Your own fault for asking about the faithless curate." He was almost positive Miss Barstow had heard him, judging by her unease and abruptness. What bad luck that she should be hovering within earshot! She, whom he had hardly seen since he had danced with her.

He deserved to be caught, he supposed, because it was not the first time he had encouraged Gordon to talk of his sister. Indeed, under the guise of lessons, he had gleaned a morsel here and a morsel there about Miss Barstow (and about the other Barstows and Mrs. Markham Dere, for that matter, but with *them* Weatherill admittedly did not mull over each titbit, wondering whether the information was truth or fancy). Collected discoveries included Miss Barstow's favorite color (blue); Miss Barstow's preferred biscuit (ginger); Miss Barstow's favorite musician (Haydn, or perhaps Pleyel); whether Miss Barstow rode (no); and whether Miss Barstow read aloud to the family (usually it was the younger Mrs. Barstow who read to them). Deeper questions required more maneuvering on Weatherill's part, and he had not been successful. Touching on the topic of how the Barstows liked Iffley, for example, yielded only: "Maria and I love it!" Nor had he asked questions about the lost Barstow men, not wanting to sadden Gordon, though he would have liked to know more there.

An honorable, disinterested man would have overlooked Gordon's mention of this Liddell person, but where Miss Barstow was concerned, Gerard seemed to be discovering more character flaws in himself every day.

A door opened further along the passage, and Weatherill rose hastily, nodding at the chambermaid who appeared before slipping back into the schoolroom. Going to the window, he smoothed out the crushed note and slid it open. The message was brief, cryptic. A simple request: if he would call on Mrs. Barstow at his convenience any time in the coming days, to be consulted on a confidential matter, she would be deeply appreciative.

Considering how Weatherill had been unable to banish Miss Barstow from his thoughts and how he had been grasping at petty scraps of knowledge about her, it was impossible that he should resist this summons. Why not now? *Now* was convenient, even if he arrived on Miss Barstow's and Gordon's heels.

He had not accounted, however, for Miss Barstow having to gather her brother from the kitchen and Miss Frances from the drawing room, so that, by the time Gerard straightened the schoolroom, clapped his hat upon his head, and hastened down the stairs, the Barstows were but fifty yards ahead of him down the drive.

At once Weatherill slowed his pace and was on the point of veering into the nearby trees when Gordy spied something and retraced his steps to inspect it more closely. The boy straightened and hallooed, waving. "Mr. Weatherill! Come look at this!"

There was nothing for it but to comply, and Weatherill advanced with as nonchalant air as he could muster.

"Good afternoon again," he said, adding a half bow toward Miss Frances. "I—thought I would walk into the village and perhaps call at the cottage."

The younger sister sucked in a breath and glanced at the older, but Miss Barstow gave only a nod. After a hesitation, Weatherill offered an arm to each lady, which Miss Frances took readily enough. Miss Barstow was about to refuse when Gordy said, "See what I found, Della! Do you want to keep it to show the baron?" Opening his hands, he revealed a green little meadow grasshopper, which instantly saw its chance for freedom and leaped—onto Miss Barstow's skirts. With a shrill which would have done credit to a banshee, Adela gave a corresponding leap backward, colliding forcefully with Weatherill's chest. Miss Frances' sympathetic screech drowned the *whoof!* compelled from him, and the threesome tumbled to the ground like so many ivory dominoes.

The grasshopper hopped away.

"Della! Look what you've done!" accused her brother, dancing off in vain pursuit.

"Yes, Della," grumbled Miss Frances, striving to untangle herself. "Look what you've done."

With Miss Barstow sprawled across him, bonnet askew and head resting on his shoulder, Weatherill could not resist: "Yes, Della—look what you've done."

"I-I beg your pardon," she panted, too horror-stricken to note his effrontery. Struggling up required pressing off of him with one merciless elbow while using her other hand to hold her short black lace cloak modestly in place.

"Say nothing of it," he coughed, sitting up and rubbing the diaphragm she had distended. "I know how your delight carries you away whenever you see an insect."

This, too, was allowed to pass without remark, though it must be said that Gordon stifled a giggle and even Frances pressed her lips together as the tutor assisted her up.

"Off we go now," announced Miss Barstow, not meeting anyone's eyes. Her voice was tight and businesslike, as if knocking people to the ground were one of those commonplace nuisances one must expect in man's fallen condition.

After that, Weatherill could not have offered his arm to her again without fairly galloping alongside, so astonishing a pace did she set, her siblings tearing after her, and he himself having to take long strides to keep up. Before they reached the Tree Inn, Gerard decided the more courteous thing to do would be to let the Barstows arrive at Iffley Cottage before he did, so he slowed accordingly.

"Mr. Weatherill is coming to call, Mama!" shouted Gordon, bursting through the cottage door.

"Goodness me, what noise," scolded the maid Reed. "Mrs. Markham Dere never let Peter roar like that." The Barstows were already too used to such observations to heed this one, however, and Reed soon had her hands full with the ladies' bonnets and with curtseying to the visitor coming up the walk.

It had been determined beforehand (and not entirely to everyone's satisfaction) that when Mr. Weatherill came to call, only Mrs. Barstow, Sarah, and Adela would be present. Therefore, with only the smallest pout, Frances took Bash from his mother's arms and herded Maria and Gordon to the back parlor for a game of Casino.

"Mr. Weatherill, thank you for coming," Mrs. Barstow greeted him, after Reed took his hat as well. "Won't you sit down? Would you like some tea? We have started a batch of elderberry wine, but I'm afraid it's not ready yet."

"Thank you, but no. I—er—hope the day finds you all well?"

Mrs. Barstow made the usual responses and asked the usual questions without paying much attention to them. Indeed, throughout this exchange of courtesies she mindlessly pulled her handkerchief through her hand over and over. Sarah was not much better, embroidering a leaf in the wrong place on Bash's gown which would have to be picked out later. And Adela—after what had already passed that afternoon, Adela would have gladly postponed this moment to another day.

But, no, here it was. And while her mother would begin the business, it was understood that Adela would be her lieutenant, taking over altogether if Mrs. Barstow faltered.

It had been weeks since the Barstows removed to Iffley. Weeks since they had seen Jane. And Adela was beginning to think she might soon have to compromise Lord Dere if she were going to make any progress in securing her family's situation. All she seemed to have accomplished in all these weeks was to develop an inconvenient—nay, *impossible*—liking for someone who could not help them at all.

Unless he could.

CHAPTER 12

**He's as true as Steell to his Word.
— John Dunton,** *The life and errors of John Dunton late citizen of London* **(1705)**

M r. Weatherill," said Adela, when her mother trailed into silence. "You will be wondering why we—why my mother—asked to speak with you."

"I am happy to call at Iffley Cottage in any event," he answered.

"Yes. Thank you. Well. We will not beat about the bush, sir, but come right to it." Here Adela looked at Mrs. Barstow, who gave her handkerchief another, harder, wring.

Weatherill did his best to appear expectant, rather than devoured by curiosity-tinged-with-dread. Were they not pleased with Gordon's progress? Had the boy let slip his tutor's unnatural inquisitiveness about—the family in general and Miss Barstow in particular?

"Mr. Weatherill," Mrs. Barstow began with a visible effort, "you will recall that I have one daughter whom you have not met."

"Yes, I do recall. Though I cannot remember her married name, I'm afraid."

"Mrs. Merritt," replied the older woman softly. "Her name is Mrs. Roger Merritt."

"Ah, yes."

Another pause followed. Another wring of the handkerchief. Another misplaced stitch.

"Have you—er—heard from Mrs. Merritt?" he asked, hoping to jog things along.

"Yes, we have. She is married now."

His brows lifted a trace at this repetition, and Mrs. Barstow threw a stricken look at her daughter. With a silent sigh, Adela braced herself, sitting forward in her chair.

"Jane is married," Adela took up the thread, "and we have learned she and Roger are living in London. Or planning to live in London." Intent on telling the whole sorry tale before her courage leaked away, Adela trained her gaze on the carved scroll of the armchair in which Mr. Weatherill sat and thus failed to notice how he stiffened at her words.

"I'm afraid she wrote to us without mentioning where we might direct our own letter when they reached town—most likely because they did not yet know themselves," Adela continued. "You see—they had hoped to live in Shropshire where Mr. Merritt has an aunt, but—that proved unfeasible. Mr. Weatherill, the fact is, they haven't much money—any money, really—and probably ought not to have married, but it is done, and they intend to make the best of it."

"You know young love," spoke up Mrs. Barstow, almost pleading. "How impatient and sometimes unmanageable it is."

Both Weatherill and Adela colored at this interposition and suddenly found various items in the surrounding furnishings worth inspecting. From her seat on the sofa, a sigh escaped Sarah as she traced her embroidery with a fingertip. Yes, that was exactly how her Sebastian had been when he courted her: impatient, ardent. His leave was only so long—why should they wait? But Sarah had not needed to "manage" him, being just as willing as he to hurl herself into marriage.

Fearing she had drawn attention, Sarah swallowed hard and glanced around, hoping her sigh had gone unremarked.

It had.

And judging by the look she caught fleeting across Adela's face—a look Sarah Barstow had certainly never seen there before—Sebastian Barstow's courtship style had been the furthest thing from her sister-in-law's mind.

"In any event," Adela resumed, "Jane and Roger were impatient and unmanageable, and the deed is done. To make a long story short, sir, they are poor, and we are...anxious for them."

"I see. But—if I might ask, why do you tell me these things?"

Mother and daughter shared a glance.

"Mr. Weatherill, I need hardly say we depend upon your confidence in this," Mrs. Barstow murmured, now winding her abused handkerchief about her hand as if she were bandaging it.

"You have it," he assured her at once.

Though they had not shared the shame of the elopement, they had told Mr. Weatherill the worst of what remained, and he had taken it as calmly as they could hope. Adela therefore plunged ahead. "It is this," she said. "We wondered if you, sir, having come from London and having London acquaintances and—and correspondents and so forth—if you might know of likely inns or places in town they might seek out, or people who might know where a penniless man might go to find work or—or amusement. Roger Merritt is—a lively sort."

Even as she spoke, that familiar shadow returned to his eyes, and although he did not stir, Adela sensed again his rapid inner retreat. As if to catch him before he escaped, she babbled on: "We might send a letter to the general post office, of course, but how likely would it be that Jane would go there to ask for it? Oh, Mr. Weatherill—we do not demand the names of your acquaintances or—or—or need to know why or how you would know certain places or such. We only ask that you...call upon your knowledge."

There was a long silence while Weatherill contemplated the carpet.

As it stretched, the ladies could hardly bear it. They had gone too far. Asked too much. Burdening him with their confidence and now reminding him of things he preferred, for whatever reasons, to forget.

Adela saw her mother's lips part, but she gave her a quick shake of the head. *No. Let him consider.*

It served, for at last Weatherill asked, "Do you wish to have them come to Iffley?"

Mrs. Barstow sagged with relief. "*I* do," she said. "But Della says Roger would never consent to it, and no doubt she is right."

"We wish them to know they are welcome, at least," Adela conceded. "Or—Jane is, if Roger refuses to come or if—he cannot support them both."

He seemed to understand what was unspoken—the flaws in Roger Merritt's character which caused the family such fear—because his mouth tightened, and he ran a rapid hand through the back of his hair. "I understand," he said. "Yes. I am...flattered you would consult me, and I am willing to write to my—acquaintances, though I should warn you they are not particularly numerous or—apt to get about much in town."

"Thank you! Thank you!" Mrs. Barstow cried, looking as if she wanted to hug him. And the tentative smile Adela gave him did much to smother his misgivings.

Weatherill could have kicked himself for spoiling it the next moment when he said, "But, if you will pardon me asking, have you thought to speak of this to the baron?"

Adela's smile vanished and she bristled. But it had been an honest, genuine question, and he held up his palms to indicate as much.

"Not yet," she admitted. "Because he has already...done so much for us, as you know."

And because you don't want to spoil your chances, he thought, bitterness rising. He was to jeopardize his position at Perryfield, so that she need not jeopardize her own? But this wasn't fair, he supposed. When Miss Barstow asked him to take pen in hand, she did not know the price of her request.

"But I would have asked Lord Dere," Adela insisted, hoping she was speaking the truth. She gripped the arms of her chair so tightly that her nails dug tiny crescents in the varnish. "*We* would have, if not for the likelihood that word of it would reach Mrs. Markham Dere. If Mrs. Dere were to learn of Jane's difficulties—" she broke off, making a helpless gesture of her own.

"Yes, of course," he agreed dryly. "I understand."

She softened another inch. "So you see why we would like to try this first. If the baron and Mrs. Dere must learn of Jane's trials, they must. But if it is at all possible to pursue this avenue discreetly..."

"I do indeed have a few acquaintances still in town," he replied, as if the majority of people he had known left London at the same time he did.

"Your former employer Mr. Keele?" Mrs. Barstow suggested.

"And perhaps families of your former pupils?" put in Sarah.

To this Weatherill made an indistinct sound in his throat which may or may not have been affirmative, and from sheer relief and gratitude Adela hurried to direct the conversation away from his no-thoroughfare. "We will appreciate any efforts you make, sir, and content ourselves with however much or little you learn. Thank you. And now, speaking of pupils, what did you think of Gordy's lines? He took pains to learn them."

A quarter of an hour later Weatherill took his leave, and the three women held a short conference before re-admitting the younger Barstows.

"Adela, why did you not let him tell us who he would write to?" asked her mother.

"Because he didn't want to tell us, Mama. Have you not seen? He always grows rather reserved when one refers to his London life or connections."

"If she did not notice," Sarah said slyly, "it might be because she has not spent as much time studying him."

Adela would have scoffed at this, except it proved impossible. "He is a new acquaintance," she said, stiff as stiff could be. "All new acquaintances are of interest."

Sarah smiled as she began to pull out the straying embroidery stitches. "Indeed. But few new acquaintances are of such interest as handsome young gentlemen."

"Sarah, don't tease," chided her mother-in-law, chuckling. But she ceased abruptly when she turned to share the joke with her daughter. "Why, Della! You're red as a poppy!"

"Pooh."

"But—can it be so?" breathed Mrs. Barstow. "Do you like the young man? He is amiable, courteous and—we hope—trustworthy—and certainly Gordy is already as fond of him as I could wish, but I don't believe he has a penny—"

"Pooh," said Adela again. "One may admire a young man for being handsome, especially now that he is more smartly dressed, without being in love with him."

"Too right," agreed Sarah. "But it is also true that one may admire a young man for being handsome *even more* when one is in love with him."

"Oh, dear," worried Mrs. Barstow. "Poor Della. First Mr. Liddell, and now this! But you have too good a head on your shoulders to lose your heart a second time to a man who cannot afford to marry."

"I didn't lose my heart to Mr. Liddell!" protested Adela. "I only thought I could like him, if I chose to."

"Then you admit you've lost your heart to Mr. Weatherill?" Sarah asked innocently.

"What? I—no! I admit nothing of the kind."

Mrs. Barstow was shaking her head mournfully. "Darling Della, I know you are no Jane, and that you would never consider—"

"I am no Jane, and I would never consider doing anything such as Jane did," interrupted Adela, raising a peremptory hand, though her voice shook a little. "In fact, quite the opposite. We have enough burdens, Mama. I do not intend to add to them."

She was swept into an embrace which would have been comforting, had Sarah not been looking on with a skeptical lift of one eyebrow and had not Adela herself felt contrarily low. It was not as if Mr. Weatherill were going to ask her to run away with him, or even that there was any danger of him returning her feelings. It was just that, even if were unexpectedly to do either of those things, Adela could not be Jane. *Jane* had been Jane, and it might yet break her family. Adela had no choice but to be Adela.

Sensible, dependable, resourceful Adela.

"A letter has come for you at last, Mr. Weatherill," said Mrs. Lamb when he poked his head in at the Tree Inn on his way back to Perryfield. "A pleasure, finally, to hear from your London friends."

"Mm. Thank you." He fished the necessary coins from his pocket and laid them on the counter, wishing the postmistress-tapstress might go back to cleaning the bar, but she continued to watch him eagerly through her spectacles.

He held up the missive as he backed away. "From my former employer. Thank you, again."

"Imagine coming from a place so big as London and getting so few letters! Why, the Barstows hail from piddling Twyford, and they hear from more people than you do, sir."

He fended this off with a forced laugh. "Charming ladies like the Barstows will always have more friends than a bachelor schoolmaster. Good day to you, Mrs. Lamb."

There was one benefit from the timing of Keele's letter, however, Gerard realized: when he sent his reply, Mrs. Lamb would think nothing of it. Whereas, if he had been the first to write, doubtless she would have peppered him with questions.

Keele's message was brief. He asked about Weatherill's new situation and followed with news of those who might interest him, their births, deaths, liberations from debtor's prison, unfortunate returns. He wrote of former pupils; Mrs. Bundicomb, who had looked after Susanna; newcomers to the Fleet—and Rioting Rob.

"The senior Mr. Weatherill has been unwell, I am sorry to say. Since your departure he has grown close and surly, displaying less and less of the good cheer which made him so popular a man. Others begin to avoid him because he grows violent on occasion, but, as you know, he can be generous in the taproom, and there are sadly always new souls to befriend. I tell you these things only for your knowledge, not to urge your return or even that you should write to him. We have discussed many times my feelings on the matter. It is past time that you live as the free man you are." The letter was signed, "With God's blessings, Wm Keele."

His father surly? Violent? Gerard could hardly believe it, Rob Weatherill being with others than his own family always loud, always robust, always hail fellow well met.

Keele anticipated his former pupil and assistant's response correctly, for Gerard's first instinct was to set out at once for London. Was his father changed because he had lost both his children?

But—going to London—how could he go to London, so soon after his removal to Oxfordshire? How would he possibly explain it to Mrs. Dere?

He could not. Perhaps if his father had been dying, but even that would lead to questions…and consequences.

Going to London now might mean giving up his new position. His new life. And Miss Barstow.

Weatherill's pace increased, but he veered off the lane into the adjoining field, where no one but a few sheep would bother him.

"Miss Barstow isn't yours to give up," he muttered, glaring at one of the sheep, who merely chewed and returned his gaze, unruffled. "She asks this favor of you out of desperation, not *adoration*."

"But she asks it of *me*, nevertheless," retorted some irrepressible imp in his head. "And not of the vaunted, wealthy, peerless peer Lord Dere."

"Lord Dere, whom she plans on marrying, if she can manage it."

"And suppose she can't?" asked the imp. "What will she do then? She lives buried in Iffley, portionless, encumbered with too many family members who all rely on her. Who is she to marry if she fails in her efforts to ensnare the baron? You might as well have her, then."

"Me? She may be portionless, but she is respectable."

"So were your grandparents. All respectable. Unexceptionable."

"Yes, they might have been, but my father is another story—! Would anyone stoop to marrying the son of a Fleet debtor?"

"You needn't mention that straight away, you fool. If ever. Why, the moment you confess that, you will lose your position, and then there will be no engagement, not even in ten years, when you can afford a hovel of your own."

Ten years!

"She is too lovely to be unclaimed all that time," he argued with himself. "Even if I could keep the truth from her so long. Too lovely and intelligent and courageous. You see how she is the rock of her family. And how she can play and dance! Many a man—any man—would overlook her lack of fortune."

"Stuff," said the imp. "You're just besotted. If you're so afraid she'll be snatched up, ask her for a long engagement."

Weatherill halted mid-stride, mindlessly crumpling and uncrumpling Keele's letter. Suppose he *were* to woo her? Once he presented her sister's whereabouts on a platter, to tears and acclaim, and her heart was softened by gratitude? Yes. He would write to Keele *and* to his father. He would tug two of the many strands which composed the spiderweb of the Fleet, setting the whole thing vibrating, each strand attached to countless other branches throughout the capital. Someone, somewhere would know of this Roger Merritt and his bride. There was no squalid quarter of the city which could not be touched in this way.

Unsettled by the man standing like a statue in their field, the sheep trotted away, but Weatherill hardly noticed.

Yes. He would write his letters that very afternoon—and commence his wooing. Not that he had any idea how to go about it.

"To begin with, stop teasing her about Lord Dere," advised the imp. "It only makes you look like a jealous fool."

"But I *am* a jealous fool," sighed Gerard. "Other than my youth and industry, the baron has far the better hand. A peerage, wealth—he's not even villainous, that I might despise him."

No imp was necessary, however, to counter these arguments. Weatherill remembered how others had responded at church, the first time he wore his new clothing. Their interest in him. Their willingness to accept him as one of their rank because he was good-looking and now decently dressed. He thought as well of Mrs. Markham Dere's sway at Perryfield. Her high-handed treatment of Lord Dere could not do otherwise than diminish him in the world's esteem. In Miss Barstow's esteem.

Could it be done? Could he make himself agreeable enough to her that she would give up her schemes? She did not want the Deres to know of her sister's difficulties, but if Gerard assisted the Barstows in hiding this, she might not be so desperate to secure their situation. She might then be willing to consider other qualities in a possible husband.

"What about that curate Liddell?" spoke up the imp.

But Weatherill frowned him down. "What about him? If he abandoned her to pursue someone else, he wasn't worthy of her. Moreover, if she is willing to sacrifice herself on the altar of family security, she is clearly not pining with love for the man."

Anyone who might have observed Gerard Weatherill muttering to himself that afternoon would surely have gone away convinced the new Perryfield tutor was mad, but had they been miraculously transported to the Fleet's flights, galleys, or racket-ground, they would have seen many, many others with the same habit. Men pacing up and down, consulting only themselves—a habit born of walls, worry, and wretchedness.

CHAPTER 13

The thick'nd Skie Like a dark Ceeling stood;
down rush'd the Rain Impetuous.
— Milton, *Paradise Lost*, xi.743 (1667)

Nature conspired against the best-laid plans of both Adela and Weatherill in the period which followed, for the heavens opened, pouring forth day after day of dreary rain. Rain which inspired Lord Dere to send the barouche for Gordon every morning, that he and his sisters be "spared the walk to Perryfield," and rain which kept everyone within doors.

"Mr. Weatherill would surely send a note or call upon us, if he had heard anything," Mrs. Barstow said to Sarah and Adela after breakfast. Her eyes turned to the streaming windowpanes, against which a branch full of blackening leaves lashed.

"I'm sure he would," Sarah reassured her. "I don't envy the post, driving in such weather. It's more like Shrovetide out there than Michaelmas!"

"He would need to write to whoever his correspondents are, and then they would need to make inquiries, perhaps, and then reply to him," Adela said, having thought it through a hundred times. "And Jane and Roger's whereabouts would not be a pressing matter to strangers, of course."

"It would all be nothing, if only Jane would write to us again," sighed her mother.

"I will walk to the Tree Inn and ask Mrs. Lamb if anything has come," Adela said.

"You'll be drenched and catch cold," spoke up Frances from where she was reading a book with her feet upon the fender. "And wouldn't Mrs. Lamb have sent word if there *were* something?"

"Still," insisted Adela. "It might have just arrived, and she may be too occupied to send word. I will wear my cloak and carry the umbrella."

Frances groaned. "I suppose that means I have to go, too. Can't you take Maria?"

"I don't want to go!" protested her younger sister. "Besides, Della set me at these writing exercises."

"No one needs to come with me," Adela said. "I could throw a rock at the Tree Inn from here. Though I may wander in the meadow to see how high the river is because I'm going mad with restlessness."

"Don't fall in like poor Denver," said Frances, going back to her book.

"But you'll come right back if there is a letter from Jane, won't you Della?" asked Mrs. Barstow.

"Certainly I will."

There was no letter from Jane.

"I would have sent my boy to the cottage if there had been," Mrs. Lamb told her. "But tell your mother not to fret. You know those new brides—heads too full of their husbands to remember their families. Wait a year, and she'll be writing to you all the time, I warrant."

Briefly Adela was tempted to ask if any letters had come for Mr. Weatherill. No doubt the chatty postmistress would tell her, but then Mrs. Lamb would also be just as certain to tell anyone else who cared to listen that Miss Barstow must have her eye on that Perryfield tutor, make no mistake, or why would she want to know if the handsome fellow had any London sweethearts writing to him?

No. Better not to ask. But what if any coveted replies had indeed arrived, and Mr. Weatherill did not come for them, preferring not to venture out in the muck? The Barstows would have to wait and wait, their nerves stretched thus.

Emerging from the inn, Adela opened her umbrella and squinted up at the low clouds still spilling their steady rain. No, he would not come in this weather.

With a sigh she turned aside from the road into Iffley Meadow, trudging through the squeaking and sucking grasses, the hem of her cloak darkening with the wet and dragging over the bent and defeated wildflowers. When she reached the river, she found it high and grey-brown after so many days of rain, the current running quickly. Her eyes traced its movement, charting its dilatory path in her mind and thinking of Jane somewhere near its end, where the Thames wound through the capital before spilling into the sea.

He was nearly upon her before she saw him.

"Mr. Weatherill!" gasped Adela, smothering a yelp of surprise. "Whatever are you doing here?"

"Is that you, Miss Barstow?" He made her a bow, letting the water stream from the brim of his hat. When he straightened, he was smiling, a smile she returned. "I am stretching my legs, as I like to do. Though conditions such as these make the Perryfield gallery more appealing. You were wiser than I, I see," he said, indicating her umbrella.

And he really did look quite forlorn because he had only his threadbare, shabby greatcoat, which might have shielded him in some places but which stuck damply to him in others.

"I went to the Tree Inn to see if Jane had written," Adela told him, reluctantly turning back toward the village. She could hardly stand in the rain in Iffley Meadow speaking to him. "But why aren't you teaching, sir?"

"You mean, why do I shirk my duties?" he asked, falling into step beside her.

Adela laughed. "Maybe that is indeed what I mean."

"Apparently some bigwig from the late Mr. Markham Dere's college at Oxford was calling upon the baron, and Mrs. Dere wanted him to sift poor Peter. Or, I should say, poor *me*, for I confess I had no desire to witness the result."

"If Peter is found wanting, you can hardly be to blame, sir," Adela defended him, "for it is only Michaelmas, which means you have had the teaching of him for scarcely six weeks."

"Thank you. Perhaps if I could trouble you to step over to Perryfield, you might say as much to this Head of House, or whoever he is?"

Raising her umbrella to look at him, Adela said boldly, "If I did, it would be only fair, considering the favor we Barstows asked of *you*. I—if you would permit me to ask, Mr. Weatherill, *were* you able to write to your friends in London?"

She thought if she surprised him she might slip under his guard, but he instantly drew himself up, his playful mood banished. "I did," he replied shortly. "And please assure Mrs. Barstow that, if I had received a response, I would have called at Iffley Cottage to make a report."

"Yes, so I told her," rejoined Adela meekly.

He grimaced, belatedly recalling his ten-year-engagement plan. If he wished to soften her, win her, he could not rebuff her whenever she asked quite natural questions, however uncomfortable they made him.

He tried again. "It was a delicate matter—making inquiries without...raising additional questions. Had I said anything like, 'Run out at once and ask every person you see about Roger and Jane Merritt,' then my—friends—might have had a greater sense of urgency, but they would also have...talked a great deal more, if that makes sense."

"It does," Adela answered, her brow clearing. "It does, truly. We did not think of that. Thank you, Mr. Weatherill, for your discretion. Your explanation will help us to be more patient."

Flushing, he said, "Patience is one of those qualities which can only be learned in the doing, I'm afraid. But—speaking as someone who has often had to wait for things, the waiting can seem more bearable depending on the reward."

"'Jacob served seven years for Rachel; and they seemed unto him but a few days, for the love he had to her,'" she murmured. But as soon as the words left her mouth she colored vividly. "That is, yes indeed. I'm sure you're right."

"Why are you blushing? I didn't know clergymen's daughters blushed over Biblical references."

"Then you know nothing about the Bible," she retorted. Lowering her umbrella, she gave it a twirl, sending out a spiral of drops. "What was your papa, Mr. Weatherill? Butcher, baker, candlestick maker? Or a schoolmaster like yourself?"

Though she kept her eyes on the umbrella, she noted the hesitation in his step before he plodged through a puddle. "He was—is—I suppose you might call him an adventurer."

This did not strike Adela as an actual profession one might claim, nor did it seem one Mr. Weatherill was inclined to expound upon. But she knew almost nothing of him and could only deny herself enough to shift her questioning a degree or two away. "You have the advantage of me," she said, "for, apart from Jane and her Roger, you met all the family I have in the world directly upon your arrival in Oxfordshire. You even met our family's pets, to your misfortune. But a man who travels alone may claim to be anyone and anything he pleases. Do *you* have siblings? Or—if that is too prying a question—I can ask instead if you had a pet of your own in your portmanteau."

She was teasing him, and Weatherill was torn between enjoying her interest and wishing himself very, very far away.

"No pets. But I—had a sister Susanna," he managed at last. "Younger by ten years. We were...very close. She died some months ago."

It was Adela's turn to plodge in a puddle as she halted. "Oh, dear me! Forgive me, Mr. Weatherill."

"What is there to forgive? I seem to remember blundering around the subject of your own late relations when we met."

They smiled ruefully at each other, and for a moment his hand lifted—to do what, he had no idea. Touch her hand? Her hair? Trace the line of her face? Press the firm rosiness of her lower lip?

"Still. I'm sorry," she said again. "Mr. Weatherill, one gets so very preoccupied with the difficulties in one's own life that one—that *I*, rather—forget that others too have their—their—"

His rueful smile metamorphosed into a wicked grin. "Their crosses to bear?"

He thought she would either laugh at this reminder of their earlier disagreement or smack him for it, and they frankly both sounded appealing. In both cases he knew what he would like to do in response: catch her by the shoulders and kiss her so hard she gasped for mercy.

Something of this must have shown in his eyes because her own widened, and she took a squelching step back.

"Goodness me," she whispered. Then, clearing her throat she said in a more normal voice, "How late it grows. My family will wonder what became of me. We are even to dine at Perryfield tonight, and just look at me!" Spreading her arms, she displayed her damp and muddy cloak.

"You look as if you were dragged up the Thames by a barge."

"And you, as if you were knocked into it by a passing post-chaise," she returned, both relieved and regretful to recover the easier tone of their conversation. This was why Mr. Weatherill was dangerous to be around. This was why he needed to be avoided.

"May I walk you back to Iffley Cottage?"

"No, thank you. If Mrs. Lamb were to see us, it would be all over the county by nightfall. But—perhaps we will see you at dinner, along with the daunting Oxford personage, if he stays that long?"

It was not Wednesday, but Gerard fully intended on appearing at table whenever the Barstows came. With another bow of acknowledgement and another humorous stream of rain tipping from his hat brim to the ground, he strode away.

The daunting Oxford personage turned out to be precisely that, being a tall man whose countenance was marked with a strong nose and penetrating dark gaze, but this gaze barely brushed over the Barstow ladies upon their arrival.

"Come, come, my dear Barstows," urged Lord Dere. "You must take the seats nearest the fire."

"Thank you, sir," Mrs. Barstow answered, "but your coachmen kept us quite warm and dry, and the rain is not as heavy as this morning."

"This is Mr. Eveleigh," Mrs. Dere announced, her handsome bosom swelling with satisfaction. "Provost of Oriel College and prebendary of Rochester Cathedral. His wife Dorothy was a school friend of mine. You find us discussing the academic standards at Oxford, which Mr. Eveleigh tells us are sadly lacking."

The introductions performed, the Barstows, which this evening included Mrs. Barstow, Sarah, Adela, and Frances, politely chose seats while Mr. Eveleigh took up the monologue their coming had interrupted. Pinning a pleasant expression to her face, Adela listened for a minute or two before seeing her participation would not be required and allowing her mind to wander free. But where her mind went, her eyes shortly followed, and she ventured a peep at Mr. Weatherill, who had chosen a chair where he might converse with the guest if called upon but otherwise not obtrude his presence on the company. Though the tutor was attending Eveleigh's speech, he must have felt Adela's glance, for his eyes flicked to meet hers, and a prickle ran through her. At once she returned her attention to the provost's soliloquy: "...Found that conversation improved in the Oriel common room," he intoned, "after the introduction of the tea-chest. Too many common rooms are mere excuses for excessive drinking, to my mind. Consider All Souls. They boast the best port in Oxford and toss off four bottles of it a day, but how this contributes to the advance of knowledge is anyone's guess..."

Mrs. Dere made affable murmurs of outrage and agreement, while Adela's mind and gaze drifted away once more. This time she looked toward the baron, silver-haired and sedate in his favorite armchair. She had not seen him in days and thought, with a little pang, that he appeared older than she remembered. Not unwell, but older. Could it be because her mind and eyes had been so full of Mr. Weatherill that the baron suffered by comparison? She could not, could not let things go on as they were. Suppose Mr. Weatherill's friends had no news to impart? Would Adela simply let matters drift, to land where and how they may? Nursing her useless, reprehensible *tendre,* instead of doing what she must to remedy matters? Here she had let days go by, all for a little rain. Yes, Lord Dere sending the coach had taken away walking Gordy to Perryfield, but she ought to have climbed into the carriage with him, on the excuse of going to practice her music!

You swear you have committed to this, Adela Barstow, but your actions say otherwise.

Perhaps it was the intensity of her regard which attracted the baron's notice because, like Mr. Weatherill, he too looked over, but the tremor which rippled through her then was altogether different from the one a few minutes earlier. This one, she guessed, was akin to what Poppet felt when discovered chewing Mrs. Barstow's slipper.

Whatever her expression, however, Lord Dere only gave his usual kindly smile, which Adela tried to return before tearing her eyes away once more and fixing them on Mr. Eveleigh's wagging chin.

"What say you, Mr. Weatherill?" the provost asked, turning for the first time to the tutor. "Mrs. Dere tells me you received a private education from an Oxford scholar but never yourself matriculated."

"That is true, sir. I was taught by Mr. William Keele of Exeter College." Perhaps it was the sheer repetition of it, but Weatherill thought this was the best he had done yet. He had neither fidgeted nor colored. But he hoped Eveleigh would not prove too inquisitive.

"Exeter, eh? Mr. Keele must have hailed from Devon or Cornwall, then."

"Devon, I believe."

"But his school is in London? Or perhaps I should say *was,* if he has retired."

Now Weatherill shifted in his seat and felt his face heating. He had congratulated himself too soon. "Yes," he replied quickly. "London. And—he has not retired. In any event, I daresay he would agree with your opinion about both the decline of academic standards and the excessive drinking at Oxford—or at Exeter College, at least."

The ruse succeeded, for Eveleigh was recalled at once to his hobby horse. Dropping the subject of Keele and the London school, he repeated a portion of what he had already said before questioning Weatherill on his teaching philosophy and methods with Peter and Gordon.

"Hm. Excellent. Very promising, young man. Mrs. Dere, allow me to commend your decision to educate your son privately. I cannot say I have been overmuch pleased with the pupils who come to us from the local schools. They might even be the most indolent and bibulous of the lot, having imbibed Oxford ways, so to speak, from their tender years."

Adela could not help grinning. "Sir, if you have met our rector's wife Mrs. Terry, you will find someone who shares your exact opinion. She speaks of Oxford as a hot-bed of mischief, when it comes to forming young men's characters."

Mrs. Markham Dere drew herself up at this interposition, not so much for the sentiment expressed, but rather because she thought it most forward of Miss Barstow to accost the provost when no one had been addressing her. Nor did her mother Mrs. Barstow rein her in with an arched brow or a touch of the hand—the widow actually smiled in agreement! *Hopeless.* If only the impertinent girl were more like her younger sister Frances, who sat primly, hands folded in her lap, as if butter wouldn't melt in her mouth. And see how Miss Frances had the grace to look embarrassed for her sister! Miss Frances threw Mrs. Dere a pained glance and then elbowed her older sister, both measures which did much to smooth the older woman's ruffled feathers.

As for Mr. Eveleigh, his umbrage equaled Mrs. Dere's, and after making no more response than a tight smile and vague sound in his throat, he turned pointedly to the baron. "One day I should like to meet the rector of St. Mary the Virgin. Terry...former fellow of Christ Church, was he not?"

Adela could have blessed Lord Dere when he replied, "Indeed, Christ Church. But Terry is a man of peace. I believe Miss Barstow is correct in calling Mrs. Terry your greater ally. If she were present, she would doubtless second many of your opinions on the decline of Oxford with a hearty 'hear him!' and perhaps a thump on the table."

With the baron taking Miss Barstow's side Eveleigh was obliged to retreat, but he fired a parting shot: "Dear me. Mrs. Terry must be quite the Amazon. As I often quote to my daughter Jane, 'A continual dropping in a very rainy day and a contentious woman are alike.'"

A trilling laugh from Mrs. Dere met this. "How very apt, sir, with the weather we are having! But surely your dear, dear Jane needs no such reminder. What a daughter to be proud of. If I had ever been blessed with a girl, I would have wanted her to be just like your Jane. Dorothy writes to me that she has never given her family a moment's distress. An 'angel dropped to earth,' she calls her."

Little Jane Eveleigh might never have given her parents a moment's distress, but her name and the insistence on her perfections had quite the opposite effect on the Barstows. Suddenly they were all to be found staring at the carpet or their hands or a corner of the room. Mrs. Barstow began to drag her handkerchief agitatedly through her clenched fist, and her daughter-in-law who sat beside her on the sofa edged an inch nearer.

"Wh-what is your opinion, Mr. Eveleigh," blurted Mr. Weatherill, "on the education of young ladies? Will Miss Eveleigh be sent to school?"

Thankfully the provost had firm opinions on this subject as he had the previous one, and the conversation moved into this safer channel.

Adela threw Mr. Weatherill a grateful glance, her lower lip trembling a little, and he gave the barest of nods. It was neither a glance so fleeting nor a nod so infinitesimal, however, that it escaped Mrs. Dere's notice, and she continued to study them quietly. What was this? What secret understanding was here? Good heavens—imagine if this insolent girl was to carry on some sort of *affaire* with Peter's tutor, right under their very noses! *O di immortales!* Wretched, wretched Miss Barstow, to prey upon the penniless Mr. Weatherill, when heaven knew nothing good could ever come of it and when Peter was so fond of him! Why should the minx be allowed to flirt for amusement, heedless of the consequences? Some girls simply could not keep themselves from coquetry, it seemed. It was the air they breathed, however inappropriate the object. But she, Mrs. Markham Dere, would see those parasitical Barstows detached and floated off before she would banish the tutor. Ah—what fools young men were, to be so easily caught!

For the present, however, Mrs. Dere confined herself to raising her head to issue a warning glare at Miss Barstow. *You will not have your way so easily, my girl.*

My eye is upon you.

CHAPTER 14

**Ev'ry Knight is proud to prove his Worth.
— Dryden, translation of Virgil, *Georgics,* iv (1697)**

The rain cleared, to be followed by autumn days which began frosty and crisp before mellowing into afternoon warmth. And true to her resolution, Adela resumed her morning walk to Perryfield with Gordy, usually accompanied by Frances. It must be admitted that, though the weather improved, spirits at Iffley Cottage contrarily sank lower and lower as each day passed with no word from Jane and no report from Mr. Weatherill's circle.

While Adela did not encounter the tutor again when calling at the Tree Inn for the post, he came every day or two to Iffley Cottage, ostensibly to deliver his no-news himself. The first time this happened, the sight of him coming up the walk threw the Barstows into a flurry which they could scarcely disguise when Reed announced him. Indeed, Gerard almost regretted coming when he admitted he had nothing to tell and saw the faces of the older Barstows fall. By the third visit he developed a routine: he shut the gate smartly to announce himself and then gave a decided shake of his head as he approached, knowing that whoever peeped out the window would tell the others, "It's Mr. Weatherill, but he hasn't heard anything."

"One—correspondent—did reply to say he...asked around," Weatherill reported at this third call as he chose the seat nearest Adela. "Unfortunately without success. But he said that was likely a good thing, as he—well—he lives and moves in a rather shabby part of town."

Mrs. Barstow murmured her understanding and tried to smile at this, but Weatherill could see his words did not comfort them.

"Is there more than one shabby part of town, Mr. Weatherill?" Adela asked. "That is, if Jane and Roger are not known in that particular part of London familiar to your friend, could that mean they might be doing...a little better for themselves?"

When she turned those lovely brown eyes upon him, he wished he could say things which brought the glow to them, but he was too incorrigibly honest. "Sad to say, Miss Barstow, but there are several poorer areas of town. Moreover, I—don't know anyone in the other parts."

"I understand," said Adela, but after a pause she could not help adding, "And it would be an expense and an inconvenience for your friend to venture all over London on an errand which means little to him. If only we might offer a reward!"

"I might sell my cameo brooch," offered Sarah at once, though it gave her an immediate pang, for it had been Sebastian's last gift to her.

"Nonsense, Sarah," declared Mrs. Barstow. "You have so few things to remember Sebastian by. I-I will sell my mother's pearls."

"I have *Bash* to remember Sebastian by," Sarah protested, "and you treasure your mother's pearls, Mrs. Barstow."

"That may be, Sarah, but I will point out that I do not wear my mother's pearls every day, as you do your cameo."

"We *all* have Bash to remember Sebastian by," pointed out Frances, "and you *do* treasure your mother's pearls, Mama, so clearly we should sell the amber cross Sebastian bought *me*."

"Sebastian gave me a locket," said Maria from the carpet, where she and Gordon were playing draughts. "Though I should be sorry to give it up. And Gordy, what about that penny whistle he gave you—"

"What a hurry you all are in, to give away Sebastian's gifts!" Adela interrupted, unable to repress a laugh. "You will make Mr. Weatherill think we did not love him a jot, when it is precisely the opposite. But all your self-sacrifice is neither here nor there because I don't suppose we can offer a reward. At least not discreetly."

"I fear Miss Barstow is right," put in Weatherill. "For one thing, you would have to go at least to Oxford to sell your possessions, but there is such close communication between Oxford and Iffley that it would be known in Iffley by nightfall. And, if I were to tell my correspondents of a new reward, it might indeed lead to greater motivation, but it would also lead to more talk and more questions."

"Too true," sighed Mrs. Barstow, sinking back in resignation. "You and Della are right. Of course we cannot trust everyone to be as trustworthy and confidential as you, Mr. Weatherill."

He colored under this praise and could not help glancing at Miss Barstow to see if she agreed with it, and the tender, rueful regard he met with nearly finished him. *Ten years*, he reminded himself. But heaven help him to refrain from speaking his feelings another ten *minutes*!

"Mr. Weatherill," Adela began abruptly, inching forward on her chair. She looked in turn at her mother, Sarah, and Frances, and Mrs. Barstow gave a quick nod. "There is something we have not told you. Something—additional—which makes your discretion—everyone's discretion—all the more vital."

The tutor straightened, perceiving the sudden tension in the room. Even the younger children sat up from their game.

"There is a reason our Jane has been so uncommunicative. It is not just that she is made conscious by the difficulties she and Roger face, though there is that." Adela's pleading look made Weatherill wish he could take her in his arms to reassure her. Whatever she had to say could not begin to compare with what he would ultimately have to confess to her, before he could ask her to be his wife. In fact, he realized with a thrill of eagerness, perhaps it might even lessen the horror of his own secrets.

Twisting her sewing in her hands in a manner which reminded Weatherill of Mrs. Barstow, Adela raised a level gaze. "You see, Jane and Roger did not simply marry out of Twyford before the rest of us removed to Iffley. They—eloped. For the longest time we did not even know if they *would* marry. We—did not even know if Roger Merritt were gentleman enough to make an honest wife of her. Such are the doubts we have had about his character."

"I see," he murmured, when she choked to a halt. Now every last Barstow fixed the same anguished look upon him, as if he were their judge and jury. But it was not condemnation of them which caused the glitter in his eye. It was indignation that any rogue might attach himself to such a family, might try to press his advantage against ones who had so little.

"Yes. You see why this is the very last thing we would ever want Mrs. Markham Dere to know," Adela hurried on. "She would certainly tell the baron he should not receive—much less house—such reprehensible connections. She would urge him to turn us out, if not for the sake of the Dere name then for the sake of his heir's character, Peter being at such a vulnerable age."

"I see," Weatherill repeated, his brow continuing to darken. Not only Adela, but every Barstow, assumed they were sinking—plummeting—in his estimation, when truly even Roger Merritt's knavery had now been displaced in his thoughts by another revelation altogether. *So this was why Miss Barstow was so desperate to catch Lord Dere!* Gerard had not understood why she should form so extreme a plan when the baron already freely welcomed her family and seemed disposed to be generous.

This was why.

And she was not wrong in thinking Mrs. Dere would do precisely what she feared, if ever she found out. After all, was that not the very reason why he himself kept his cards so close? For fear of dismissal and expulsion?

Ah…but what would this mean for his own suit? Were he to throw himself at Miss Barstow's feet now, even if her heart inclined to him (something of which Weatherill was not confident) and even if she were willing to entertain the preposterous idea of a ten-year engagement, she could not possibly choose him above her current plan, not when he was helpless to stave off the disaster which threatened her. Worse—when his own background only compounded the threat.

I need more time.

Indeed, his only hope lay in Lord Dere remaining oblivious to Miss Barstow's efforts. But how long could that last, especially if Miss Barstow multiplied her attempts? If his obliviousness gave place to awareness, then Weatherill's only hope would be reduced to Lord Dere gently, inexplicably resisting her appeal. That is, Lord Dere would need to prove insensible to youth, beauty, flattering helplessness, and the desire to play rescuer.

A grimace tugged at his lips. He himself could never do it. Resist her. If Miss Barstow came on her knees to him, pleading for him to save her, save her family—if she came, having only her lovely self to offer in the balance—she would not have time to frame her entreaty before Weatherill's kiss would devour the rest of her words.

It was Mrs. Barstow who broke the silence, her voice humbled. "Mr. Weatherill, I see we have shocked you. That you too, perhaps, wish yourself free of our acquaintance—"

"What?" His head came up suddenly, hardly understanding her because his thoughts had been so removed.

Adela too misread his scowl of perplexity, and seeing undeserved shame raise her mother's blush, indignation flooded her, driving her to her feet.

"We have taken enough of your time with our private problems, I daresay," she said coldly.

Leaping to his own feet from automatic courtesy, Weatherill sputtered, "No, indeed. That is—unless I have taken too much of *your* time, considering I had nothing of consequence to impart."

But Mrs. Barstow disapproved of her daughter's show of reserve, and she too stood, a placating hand extended toward the tutor. It was not Mr. Weatherill's fault, after all, that Jane might bring disgrace on the Barstows. If he shrunk at their confession, it was no more than the world would do. "Mr. Weatherill," she said in her soft manner, "you are always welcome at Iffley Cottage. We recognize that your assistance, though it has not yet yielded new knowledge of the Merritts, was nevertheless freely and kindly given."

Though Adela had stiffened, fearing he would hesitate to take her mother's hand, she was proven wrong at once in her suspicions, for Mr. Weatherill fairly lunged at it and bowed over it as if Mrs. Barstow were a duchess.

"Thank you, madam. And permit me to assure you again that what you have said to me today shall go no further. While I—agree with Miss Barstow that we had better not offer a reward, I will write again to my small circle and, as unconcernedly as I am able, renew my inquiries."

He was rewarded with smiles and pleasant leave-takings from all present save Miss Barstow. Even Miss Maria and Gordon crowded about him, entreating him to play draughts with them on his next call. But just when Gerard assumed Miss Barstow's frosty demeanor would continue, she alone accompanied him to the door to wait with him while Reed fetched his hat.

As her mother had a few minutes earlier, Adela extended a hand to him, her lowered lashes dark on her scarlet cheeks. "Mr. Weatherill, I would like to second what my mother said," she murmured. "You have indeed been a friend to us, despite knowing more to our detriment than anybody in Iffley."

While her motion and sentiments resembled Mrs. Barstow's, Weatherill seized her hand in an entirely different spirit from how he had taken her mother's. Adela wore no gloves, having been at her needlework, and Weatherill's grip was such that his skin might as well have been bare, such was the warmth which passed between them. It might have been ten seconds or ten minutes before Reed marched back into the passage holding Weatherill's hat, but either way they remained thus until they heard her steps. Then, dropping their clutch like a thief might his sack of ill-gotten goods, they mutually retreated a step.

Weatherill took his hat. Thanked Reed. Reed curtseyed and slowly departed.

But then, though each sorely regretted the maid's interruption, the moment could not be recaptured. Neither Weatherill nor Adela was able to think of a single thing to say to the other, though perhaps their eyes and discomfiture said enough.

No. Weatherill could only bow again and stumble out as best he might, leaving Adela to sigh and lean against the closed door. How many times they re-lived the scene afterward in their minds would not be an easy calculation to make, but suffice to say, each was to wonder later whether its intensity had been real or imagined. Shared or unequal. Was it, Weatherill asked himself, because he had grasped her slender fingers so ferociously? Or had it been, Adela worried, because she wound her fingers between his, in bold, unmaidenly fashion?

Mrs. Lamb had to call Weatherill's name twice before he remarked it.

"Ah, sir," she said from the Tree Inn doorway, "good afternoon. Come, come. A shame I call it. A disgrace."

His thoughts still full of Adela's difficulties, her choice of words stopped him on the spot. "Good afternoon, Mrs. Lamb. What can you be referring to?"

"I don't mean a 'what' at all, Mr. Weatherill. I mean a *who*. If you would wait one moment…" She vanished inside, returning shortly with a letter held high. "You see? That wretched boy Nick makes a habit of tossing the post bag between the chair legs in the bar-room. Lines the chairs up like a tunnel and then slings the bag like a curling stone across my polished floor! In any event," she hurried along, holding out the letter, "I found this later when I was sweeping. It's from your London friend."

With difficulty Weatherill restrained himself from snatching it, and after a minimum of vague chat in which the postmistress probed and he parried her curiosity, he got rid of her.

The Fleet
4 October 1800

Dear Gerard:

Forgive my long silence. I did not want to burden you with the expense of paying for letter after letter, if each one said little more than, "I have learned nothing." But at last I have a budget for you, little of it good, I'm afraid.

You asked me to be on the lookout for word of your new acquaintances' family members' whereabouts, that they might write to them. In my confined world I have little reach, as you are aware, though I sounded those with greater, when opportunity arose. But alas, Gerard, without assistance from anyone I can now report exactly where Roger and Jane Mer-

ritt may be found. Because they are here.

The tipstaff delivered Merritt yesterday to the warden, directly from Serjeant's Inn where the judge for Common Pleas sat, and the man is now to be detained in the Fleet "until the amount of the damages and costs in the action of Spacks against Merritt be fully paid and satisfied." It was a sorry sight, I assure you. Merritt was gay and defiant enough, a handsome rogue who puts me in mind of your father, but his little wife clung to him all in tears. At present all rooms on the Master's side are occupied, so the Merritts are tenants of old Eddings and his wife, but at least they were not reduced to the closets which pass for apartments on the Common side.

I do not envy you the task of telling the Merritts' family and will certainly write to you again if I learn of any improvement in their circumstances.

So much for the task you set me. Gerard, you will want to know if your father's health improves, but I cannot satisfy you there. He has lost weight and grown haggard, though that might be attributable to the long effects of drink. He will be Rioting Rob to the last, I fear.

There is one tiny atom of personal good news, and I have none save you who would understand or rejoice to hear it, but Antiquities of Egypt *is to be published at long last, and Murray has agreed to the anonymous authorship of "An Oxford Scholar." I insisted on this latter point, having so disgraced both my name and my college, but if* Antiquities *succeeds in finding enough readers, he will consider a second volume with additional plates! You know how long I have labored over this. Indeed, you were a fellow laborer in the vineyard. My dear boy, if there is a circulating library in Iffley, might you persuade them to purchase a copy?*

Your obliged and faithful friend,
Wm Keele

Weatherill had indeed spent many hours of his youth laboring alongside his teacher and mentor, organizing the unending stacks and sheafs of scrawls and sketches, ordering and summarizing. The announcement of *Antiquities of Egypt's* long-awaited (and long-doubted) debut would ordinarily have struck Gerard like a thunderbolt from a clear sky, but in the shadow of the Merritts' fate it hardly made any impression.

Roger Merritt arrested for debt and sent to the Fleet! He and his wife, the former Miss Jane Barstow, huddled in Eddings' room with however many others, until a private apartment should become available? Good heavens. This would *kill* the Barstows. Every detail of it. How could he possibly, possibly be the bearer of such ill tidings?

Despite his earlier assurances to them, Weatherill did not retrace his steps to Iffley Cottage. How could he, when he thought of Mrs. Barstow's kindness to him and Miss Barstow's warm hand in his?

No, no, thought the unwilling messenger. Let them have another day's peace before he crushed them with this news. To cast the Barstows into such a slough of despond without offering any hope for how they might eventually struggle out? They certainly had no money to pay Roger Merritts' debts, any more than Merritt himself did. And if Merritt had not been able to support himself and his wife while at liberty, the task became nigh impossible once he was imprisoned. Only see how many years Keele had taught the most promising prison children for pennies, without earning enough to purchase his freedom! Indeed, few could, after paying their expenses of food and lodging to the warden.

Slowly, despondently, Weatherill paced along Wallingford Way. When he came to the long wall of Perryfield, he paused at the open arch, hoisting himself into the stone frame of the glassless window where he might re-read Keele's letter, repeating over and over in his head, *What can be done? What can be done?*

The twentieth time he read the letter a possible answer finally came to him.

He has lost weight and grown haggard.

That was it! He would return to London, with the excuse of visiting his ailing father. And once there, he would see what, if anything, could be done for the Merritts. At the very least he could pass comforting words to Mrs. Roger Merritt of her family's continuing love, and carry back to the Barstows a firsthand report of their prodigal.

His meditative gaze wandered toward the great house. Mrs. Dere would not like him taking a leave of absence, that was certain. But at least he had been longer at his post now and hopefully earned more of her trust. And Weatherill was certain the baron would permit it. Besides, what choice did Weatherill have? He would far rather Mrs. Dere direct her disapproval at him, than at the poor Barstows. Imagine Mrs. Dere learning the Merritts had been arrested for debt and confined to the Fleet! She would send the Barstows packing before you could say Jack Robinson, and even the baron might not be able to hold his ground against the withering force of her condemnation.

With the memory of Miss Barstow's hand in his, Gerard hopped down from the arch, brushing himself off and tucking the letter away. Then he strode, jaw set and mind made up, home to Perryfield.

CHAPTER 15

**The parting of Friends and Lovers,
is like the parting of the Soul and Body,
always most easy when least warn'd of it.**
— Eliza Heywood, ***The Female Spectator*** **(1745)**

Adela learned of Mr. Weatherill's departure completely by accident, being sent by Mrs. Barstow to the rectory to deliver a bottle of the new elderberry wine.

"Miss Barstow," the maid greeted her upon opening the door. "They're in the parlor."

Assuming the servant referred to the Terrys and their cohort of pupils, including the clumsy and unlucky Denver, Adela followed her wordlessly along the stone passage which led from the older, Norman portion of the rectory to the "newer," more comfortable Tudor part, where the Terrys spent most of their time.

Exactly the group Adela pictured was ranged about the room, though no sooner was she announced and greetings exchanged than the two Tommies, Wardour and Ellis, slipped past her to freedom. Poor George Denver of the injured leg followed their departure with resigned eyes and shifted the cushion under that limb. But Adela had no time to pity Denver because she was contending with surprise at Mrs. Markham Dere's presence.

"Miss Barstow!" cried the good lady, appearing rather ruffled, "I intended to call at Iffley Cottage directly upon leaving here."

"I hope you will, madam," answered Adela, "for we have some of our elderberry wine for Perryfield as well."

When they were seated again and all waiting to see who should renew the conversation, Mrs. Terry leaped into the breach with her usual confidence. "Mrs. Dere has been making arrangements—successful arrangements—for the boys' education."

"Successful *temporary* arrangements," amended Mrs. Dere.

Adela's brow rose, and she glanced at Denver. "The 'boys'? Mr. Terry, do you seek a respite from teaching the Tommies and Denver?"

"Wouldn't that be delightful!" laughed the rector's wife. "We could take a little seaside holiday, my dear."

Mr. Terry chuckled at this. "I'm afraid not, Miss Barstow. It wasn't my boys Mrs. Dere referred to."

"Not a bit of it," Mrs. Dere said. "I meant Mr. Terry has kindly agreed to take on Peter and Gordon. I was going to call at Iffley Cottage next to inform your mother."

"But—why must Mr. Terry be encumbered with Peter and Gordy? They already have a tutor." Her heart had flown up to beat in her throat and choke her, it seemed, for this last emerged little better than a croak.

"Yes. Well. Mr. Weatherill has gone away," said Mrs. Dere with a wave of her hands.

It was fortunate here for Adela that Denver's cushion chose this moment to squirt from between his ankle and the ottoman, quite distracting everyone from noticing her gasp. And as she sat closest to the boy, she further hid her shock by bending to retrieve the item, making quite a business of securing it, as its satin cover made it as slippery as a fish.

"Please, Miss Barstow, do not trouble yourself," Mr. Terry urged, half rising. "Denver's injury is of such date that he likely need not elevate it any longer, but if he insists on it, he may hobble after his accoutrements himself."

Thrusting the cushion at Denver, Adela resumed her seat, hoping the flush of crimson staining her cheeks was attributed by all to her recent exertions. But the subject was too important to her for her to let it rest.

"Won't five pupils be too many for you, Mr. Terry?" she asked, so she need not come at the subject of Mr. Weatherill straight off.

It was Mrs. Terry who answered. "Five would be too many if Peter and Gordon were boarders, like the others, but as they will be day pupils, we will manage."

"Ah. I see. Well, thank you, sir, for taking them." She cleared her throat and strove for nonchalance. "You say the tutor has gone away, Mrs. Dere? Gordy made no mention of it."

"Gordon doesn't yet know of it. Harker and Ogle drove Mr. Weatherill to the Angel Inn only this morning, that he might find a seat on the London coach. There is only one departing on Saturdays, and he did not wish to wait until Monday."

"Why—why the rush?" What she would have liked to ask was, *How could this possibly be, when I saw him only yesterday, and he said nothing of it?*

"I'm afraid he received word that his father was unwell," explained Mrs. Dere, with a compression of her lips which perfectly expressed her opinion of fathers who inconveniently fell ill when their sons had jobs to do. "I thought he might like to wait for further details, or for his father to send for him—he admitted the man had not yet done so—but the baron insisted he go now. At once! Therefore who can say when he will return? Depending on what ails the elder Mr. Weatherill, it might be a week or a *month* before he either recovers enough for his son to feel comfortable leaving him or—or—"

"Or is carried off altogether by his ailment," supplied Mrs. Terry helpfully. Her husband had been a clergyman far too long for her to feel any squeamishness around the topic of death. She fished in her workbasket for her etui of needles. "But more troublesome than the senior Mr. Weatherill recovering his health after a period of time, or cleanly pitching over the post, would be for him to develop a chronic condition. Chronic conditions are so very unpredictable! The junior Mr. Weatherill would be obliged to fly up to town over and over in such a situation. Yes, Mrs. Dere, let us pray you are spared a chronic condition."

Mrs. Dere had known Mrs. Terry long enough to suspect she was being teased, and she drew herself up with injured pride. "I know I sound heartless," she admitted, "but Mr. Weatherill had never before mentioned his father or, indeed, *any* family, and I believe I may be excused for thinking him alone in the world. Moreover, if you were not so amenable, Mr. Terry, to letting Peter and Gordon join your pupils for an indefinite amount of time, I don't know what we would have done, being thus left in the lurch."

Snapping off her thread, Mrs. Terry only said, "What are neighbors for, Mrs. Dere? Though we may become a hair less neighborly if Mr. Weatherill Senior chooses to prolong his malady till Christmas. In the meantime, set your heart at rest. I, for one, see one cause for thankfulness: these two new students brought to sit at the feet of my Gamaliel are at least not named Tommy."

A quarter of an hour onward, Mrs. Dere and Adela took their leave, Mrs. Dere pulling on her gloves and accepting Ogle's assistance to mount. "Thank you for telling your mother and brother of Mr. Weatherill's absence, Miss Barstow, for the wind is picking up, and I will be glad to return to Perryfield. I wish I had taken the carriage. In any event, we will see you at church tomorrow, I expect. Good day."

Though the rectory stood a stone's throw from Iffley Cottage, Adela took her time returning home, her heart palpitating miserably. *Why had he said nothing?* The post arrived at the Tree Inn in the morning, so he would have known already of his father's condition before he called on them the day before. *Unless there is nothing wrong with his father, and he had other reason to go.* But, no, he had not seemed agitated when he called. He had not seemed to be turning over some scheme in his mind and hiding it from them. Could a courier have arrived at Perryfield the night before? Surely Mrs. Dere would have mentioned that. Adela had not wanted to pepper the woman with questions, however, for fear of arousing suspicion.

She sighed. Suspicion of what? Of Jane's scandal, or of the state of her own heart?

Why, why, why was she so foolish as to—love—Mr. Weatherill? A man of whom she knew almost nothing, except that he was poor and kind and intelligent and teasing and handsome and a good teacher and educated by an Oxford man. Oh—and she knew also that he disapproved of her hope to marry Lord Dere. (Another sigh.) And why shouldn't he disapprove? He would not be the only one to feel thus, if she succeeded, but somehow his disapproval weighed more heavily on Adela. Her family would be horrified but understanding. Mrs. Dere would be outraged but understanding. It was the way of the world, after all.

What does it matter what Mr. Weatherill would think? she told herself ruthlessly. *He has gone away without a word, without a note, as if he did not give a rap for the trust you had shown him. And who knows when, if ever, he will return?*

However harsh Adela was with herself, it still hurt to share the news with her family, for they had no compunction in voicing every question she would have liked to pose to Mrs. Dere.

"Gone away?" gasped Frances. "Just like that?"

"Why did he not mention it yesterday?" asked Mrs. Barstow.

"For how long?" Gordon demanded. "That's a rum go!"

"Don't use such language, Gordy," Frances scolded.

"Why shouldn't I? How else should I put it? To leave without even telling me or Peter!"

"He didn't tell any of us," put in Sarah. "Unless he told you, Della...?"

She shook her head and found herself having to defend the man. "He didn't know, I suppose. It must have been quite sudden. I don't know how long he will be away. Mrs. Dere didn't share any details, and I didn't like to ask."

"Why didn't you ask?" Gordon scowled. "I wish I had been there. I would have asked."

Adela wished her young brother *had* been there. He could have asked a hundred questions with Mrs. Dere thinking no more than that he was ill-mannered. "Perhaps you can ask Peter tomorrow at church or on Monday when you go to the rectory for your lessons."

"Why did he not tell us he had a father?" was little Maria's question.

"Everyone has a father, poppet."

"A *living* father," she clarified.

"Though possibly not for much longer," said Gordy, drawing the ire of his elders. "What? What? It's the truth. Unless it isn't, and Mr. Weatherill simply had enough of Iffley and wanted to make his escape."

"Della," began Sarah after a hesitation, "do you think it might be that Mr. Weatherill...had another reason for going?"

"What reason would that be?" Adela's voice was sharper than she would have liked, as she immediately pictured some bonny London sweetheart from whom Mr. Weatherill could no longer bear to be away. How the wretched girl would run to meet him, marveling over his new attire and the change chinking in his pockets.

"Why, to look about for Jane and Roger himself," Sarah proposed. "Perhaps our...dissatisfaction stirred him to making his own effort."

A little silence fell while each considered this possibility. Adela was conscious of momentary relief that her sister-in-law did not suggest the existence of the sweetheart in town, but this was soon swallowed in worry. A worry her mother shared.

"I hope not," said Mrs. Barstow. "That is, I hope Mr. Weatherill did not lie to the Deres for our sake. That would be very risky and foolish of him, and I would hate to think he was driven to it by our immoderate disappointment! Imagine if he thought us so ungrateful as to imply he should be doing *more* for us."

"Still, he might as well do some investigating while he's there," pointed out Frances, adding, when the others frowned at her, "What? Now I'm as bad as Gordy? I only mean that he might ask a question or two, or peep into an inn or two, when he isn't sitting at his father's bedside."

This seemed reasonable enough, they had to admit, though Mrs. Barstow said he might not have time, if his father were truly very ill, and for a minute they were heartened by the idea. But it was Frances again who said in her practical way, "If he does learn anything of Jane and Roger, however, we will be the last to know, for now we will have to wait until he comes back to tell us. *If* he comes back."

"He will come back," Sarah declared, "or at least he will write to Mrs. Dere to say that he will not be returning. He seems a responsible young man. And I am certain, madam," she said to Mrs. Barstow, "that if he learns anything at all of Jane, he will send you word. Or at the very least, he will positively insist upon Jane doing so herself!"

It was dark when the coach arrived in the narrow yard at the Bolt in Tun in Fleet Street, but there had been no danger of Weatherill dozing off en route. For one thing, he had spent the journey in an outside seat, clinging to the roof like a piece of baggage, without benefit of a strap to fasten him down. For another, there was the din and smell and dirt of London swallowing him whole the moment the coach jolted across Oxford Street. And for a third, there was the tautness of his nerves, stretched by the risk he was taking.

He had not guessed it would be so easy to detach himself from Perryfield, and perhaps it would not have been, except that the baron was present when Weatherill made the request of Mrs. Dere. It was Lord Dere who said in his mild way over his niece's sputtering, "Illness is illness, and family is family. Of course you must go, Weatherill, and never mind us. Your loyalty to your father reflects well on your character." That only made Weatherill feel worse, naturally, for Rioting Rob's health provoked more regret than concern. Regret for the father Robert Weatherill might have been, had he not been, in fact, Rob Weatherill. And his father's health formed only a portion—and a small one, at that—of his motivation in going.

Climbing down stiffly, he took no offense when the coachman flung his battered portmanteau at his feet. Indeed, unlike in Adela Barstow's imaginings, the Gerard Weatherill who returned to London was met by no one and was outwardly indistinguishable from the young nobody who departed from the same inn in August. He wore his shabby clothing again; he carried his shabby bag.

The brief five-minute walk from the Bolt in Tun to the Fleet could have been accomplished at once, despite the street being still full of hackney coaches, carts and foot-walkers, but he knew the prison gates would soon be shut. His errand would have to wait for the following day. After securing the smallest room at the coaching inn and depositing his bag, however, he decided on a short stroll to stretch his legs. (A very short stroll, however, lest he meet with misfortune or violence.) Perhaps just to the bridge to look over the dark waters. What a contrast London was to the sheep-fields of Iffley and its sparsely populated lanes! Weatherill was half amused how unused he had grown to the whirl of town, and he kept to the wall to avoid being driven into the road. But once he stood on Blackfriars Bridge, the nearness of the Fleet beckoned, and he could not resist. With dragging feet he retraced his steps, not approaching the gate but rather standing back across Fleet Market while the memories flooded him.

Susanna.

Keele.

The school.

All those years.

And, of course, his father.

The exodus of the last visitors and the clanging of the bolts awakened him from his reverie, and he gave himself a shake.

Whatever the past was, those walls now enclosed his unknown future. For within those walls Jane Merritt waited, and her rescue was the task Gerard had set himself, in order to win the heart of her sister.

The following morning, after attending the service at St. Bride's, Weatherill walked again to the prison, following Ludgate along one edge of the Liberty of the Fleet.

Soon enough he stood before the open gate, only long enough to draw a deep breath, steeling himself, before he entered. With a turn to the left, he passed through the door into the corridor which led to the heavy, foreboding inner gate, by which a burly turnkey stood guard.

"Is that you, young Weatherill?" growled the man, squinting at him. Though it was day, the sky was overcast, and even in the brightest sun it was shadowy within the prison. "What are you doing back here, when you went off to see the wide world?" Grabbing Gerard's shoulder with a beefy hand, he groaned. "No—have you gone and bankrupted yourself? Did you learn nothing?"

"No, Quint. If I had bankrupted myself, I would be in someone's custody," Weatherill returned reasonably. "I am here on a visit, my good man. Keele wrote to me to say my father was unwell."

The turnkey snorted. "Unwell is he? Begging your pardon, but what else would you expect after a decade of being a five-bottle man?"

"Still drinking everyone under the table, I take it?" sighed Weatherill.

"And why not? It's how he makes half his rent, and you know as well as I that there's always new blood to try it on. King of the taproom is old Rioting Rob. Do you mean to lodge with him? Because he's had a—tenant—for some time."

By "tenant," Gerard knew that meant a disreputable woman, and he shook his head. "No, thank you. I'll sojourn with Keele if he'll have me."

"Can't with Keele," said Quint stoutly, marching ahead of him down the dirty, stone-paved gallery.

"What do you mean I can't?"

Halting before the damp and gloomy staircase leading to the hall flight, Quint peered at him. "He's gone, he is."

"Gone!" exclaimed Weatherill. "But I just had a letter from him! Do you mean he has—died?"

Whooping, the turnkey smacked the greasy stones of the wall. "Bless you, Weatherill. I don't mean he's dead. I mean he paid his debts and got his freedom." Weatherill's stare made him chuckle as he nodded. "That's right. That's what we all thought. Not a soul expected it. But it turned out those heaps and bags and files of worthless papers were worth something to somebody after all."

"*Antiquities of Egypt*," breathed Weatherill. "Upon my word." So much for staying with his old mentor. Who knew where the man had gone now, after living so many years a prisoner? Keele had likely written to him of his new address, but that letter would sit under Mrs. Lamb's eye at the Tree Inn until Weatherill returned. He would have to inquire at the publisher Murray's, if he stayed that long. He huffed out a resigned breath. Either his stay in town would be briefer than he intended, or he must make other arrangements. Perhaps two birds with one stone...?

"Who do you know with a spare bed, Quint? Perhaps Eddings?"

Old Quint stared to hear the young man name such a squalid "land-lord," but there was no denying that, to judge by his appearance, wherever young Weatherill had been, he had failed to get any richer. Therefore the turnkey shrugged. "You can ask," he said and led on.

As they penetrated further into the prison, the galleries and staircases grew more crowded, and Weatherill recognized with a heavy heart the blank looks and listlessness, the degrees of shabbiness. Oh, heavens, how he had wanted to put all this behind him! But for Miss Barstow's sake he went on. It did him good to think of her, however. Just picturing her in his mind, with her glowing brown eyes and rosy color livened him. Warmed him.

And then something miraculous happened.

Just beyond Quint's meaty shoulder, leaning against the open doorway in the dimness of the gallery, she stood. As if he had conjured her.

His voice emerged husky and barely audible.

"Can it be? Miss Barstow?"

CHAPTER 16

She was a Phantom of delight
When first she gleam'd upon my sight.
— Wordsworth, *Poems,* vol. I.14 (1807)

Of course it was not she.

As soon as his eyes adjusted to the murkiness he realized his mistake, for this young lady, though she too had dark hair, was thinner and paler than Miss Barstow, and her eyes were more hazel than brown. And when she abruptly straightened at being addressed, he found she was also taller than his beloved.

"Who are you?" she demanded, in a voice which nevertheless caused him a pang. This *had* to be Jane Merritt. The resemblance would be incredible otherwise.

Quint the turnkey looked from one to the other, and Weatherill raised a hand. "Pardon me. I misspoke. For surely you must be Mrs. Roger Merritt."

She shrank back, gathering her shawl about her, as if she would retreat from the corridor.

"The turnkey will vouch for me," he added quickly. "I am Gerard Weatherill, an acquaintance of your family in Iffley. In fact, I tutor your young brother."

"Y-You know Gordy?" she whispered.

"I do. Gordon, the two Mrs. Barstows, Miss Barstow, Miss Frances, Miss Maria. Even the baby Sebastian. I know them all. I was with them only Friday."

Tears welled in her eyes which were so like her sister's, and she mouthed, *Oh.* For a second Gerard thought she might throw herself in his arms and cry like a child, and he braced himself for it, but instead she gulped noisily and dashed at her eyes with her sleeve.

"Would you introduce me to Mr. Merritt?" he asked gently.

At the mention of her husband, her demeanor became flat. "Roger? You may find him yourself in the tap-room, if you care to. If he is not there, he might be playing billiards."

"It can wait. Perhaps then there is somewhere we might speak?" He allowed a pair of men to shuffle by, his indignation flaring when one of them looked Mrs. Merritt's person up and down.

She was too dulled to remark it, however, and when Weatherill added, "My old friend Quint here may serve as chaperone, if you haven't anybody else," she only shrugged. Things were worse than he had supposed. Another week here and she would be as hollow-eyed as the prison veterans.

Weatherill led the way back to the graveled racket ground, surrounded by its high brick walls. It was crowded with people like shades, pacing up and down, but few of them gave the trio a second glance, being too occupied with their own unhappiness. The fresher air revived his companion, however, and she soon urged in a trembling voice, "Tell me about my family. How are they? How I miss them and long for them. Are they well? Is my mother well? Did they send you to me? But how could they, if they did not know where I was?"

"Shhh...I will tell you all, if you will allow me," he soothed. "They are all in good health. Excellent health. And would have no care in the world, if not for their concerns for you, Mrs. Merritt."

"I know it!" she cried, covering her face with her hands, so that her words emerged muffled. "I never meant to worry them. And I was going to write to them again, the moment we were settled in—a pleasant place. But there was never any pleasant place."

It was all Weatherill could do not to pat the girl's shoulder, and he saw even the hulking Quint biting his lower lip—Quint, who had seen the worst of everything passing through the gates of the Fleet!

"They do not know you and Mr. Merritt are here," he continued. "I discovered it only because a—friend—told me. You see, knowing I came from London, your family asked if I might learn your whereabouts by asking among my acquaintance. When I did learn, I came at once, without even telling them where I was going."

Lifting her eyes, she plucked at his sleeve. "Did you? You must be...dear to them, for them to confide in you thus."

Dear to the Barstows? To *Miss* Barstow, in particular? How he hoped so!

She saw his color change, a muscle twitching in his jaw, and his consciousness distracted her from her own woes for the first time, long enough to inspect him curiously.

"The Barstows and I...we are all newcomers to Iffley," he hurried on. "In fact, we arrived the very same day. And we are all Lord Dere's dependents, in one fashion or another, so it is—quite natural—that we should become friends."

"Quite natural," agreed Mrs. Merritt, still regarding him in that acute way which reminded him unsettlingly of her older sister. But then her cares pressed upon her again and she sighed. "I thank you for your friendship to them, Mr. Weatherill. You did say your name was Weatherill?"

There was a hitch in Gerard's step at the question, though he gave a nod. The Fleet held perhaps three hundred prisoners at any given time, besides the workers who ran it and the visitors like himself who came and went. Surely a young lady like she could have no knowledge of his disreputable father Rob Weatherill! She had only been a denizen of the place a week, after all, and he doubted Mrs. Merritt even knew where to find the tap-room. The same could not be said for her husband Roger Merritt, however, and a man who would not keep close guard on his wife in a place like this very well might know Rioting Rob. Had Merritt mentioned Gerard's father to his wife? Seeing a faint line appear between his companion's brows, Weatherill was in two minds whether to tell Mrs. Merritt what he had as yet told no one beyond these walls. But before he could make up his mind to do so, she shook off her thoughts and the moment passed.

"Well, sir, if you are my family's friend, you are mine as well," she said at last. "And now that you have found me in this shameful place, in these shameful circumstances, what will you tell them?"

He had given this much thought as he clung to the coach roof all those hours, and he made his proposal now. "Mrs. Merritt, what if you were to tell them yourself, whatever *you* would like to tell them?"

"Do you mean write to them? Send a note back with you?"

"Better than a note or letter," he replied. "What if you were to send yourself? *Go* yourself? There is a respectable old woman who lives just outside the Liberty of the Fleet. I could ask her to accompany you to Oxfordshire."

But Mrs. Merritt was already backing away, shaking her head. "Leave Roger? How could I? However unfortunately this has all turned out, he is still my husband. I cannot simply...abandon him here." Her voice rose, and she fanned a hand before her face in distress. "I thought—I thought—Roger would take better care of me. I—believed everything he said. I—thought by now I would be writing to my mother from Shropshire to say all was well. I thought we might even send *them* some money, but—but—"

"Listen to me," he insisted. "I cannot suppose Mr. Merritt is any happier with how things have fallen out, but seeing you in these conditions and knowing that he himself is responsible for it will only add to his suffering. If you were to return to your family, he would be saved the expense of your keeping here, and he would have the additional comfort of knowing you were safe and cared for."

"I—but I—I am going to find work as a seamstress or milliner," she protested, dashing away her tears angrily. "And how would Mama keep me, when she hasn't any more money than Roger?"

"You may work as a seamstress or hat-trimmer in Iffley, if you insist, but I believe the combination of the baron's generosity and your family's small income will stretch to support you. They are not wealthy by any means, but they have enough for now. And certainly Lord Dere expected you to be one of the party at the outset, so there will be no problem there."

"But what would I say happened to Roger?" she persisted. "Do the Deres not know I am married?"

"They do know it," Weatherill admitted. "Your family had to explain your absence, you see. But the Deres do not know you and Mr. Merritt—er—eloped. Your mother and Miss Barstow thought it best to keep that detail quiet. Nor do the Deres know how difficult things have been for you since your marriage. You might say anything to them at this juncture. That town is so expensive, say, and it was easier for him to find lodging for a single person, but that you will rejoin him when things are more settled."

She was wavering. He could see it. Indeed, it would have been unthinkable that she did not waver. Only look at her life here, weighed against the tug of family and quiet and peace! Weatherill himself did not know how he had borne his time here so long. But he had had Susanna, and poor Jane Merritt had nothing but her shiftless husband.

"Only say the word," he murmured, "and I will arrange it. You might be in Oxford as soon as tomorrow evening and in your family's embrace but one hour later."

"Oh," she moaned, hanging her head. "By tomorrow! I want to so badly, may heaven forgive me. But how can I? You think Roger would be glad to think me safe, away from here, but—but you don't know him. I suspect he would think I had no confidence in him."

Have you any? he wanted to ask, but he managed to smother the question.

"I cannot go," she sighed, so low he had to bend to catch her words. "I am his wife, for better or worse. He will have no one to care for him if I were to leave. Already he—drinks too much. If I went, he would despair. It would hasten his ruin."

Though he had never met this Roger Merritt, Weatherill was beginning to think the man had no redeeming qualities. With his wife in such a place, how could the rogue waste their little money drowning his sorrows with spiritous liquor? Gerard could not be blamed for feeling this way—any child of Rioting Rob would, who had seen his father go down the same path Roger Merritt now trod.

He had but one more card to play, then, if he was to persuade her.

"Mrs. Merritt," he said slowly, "it is entirely possible that your husband will choose to drink whether you are with him or not. Whether he can afford such a pernicious habit or not. He may also resent your going, even if it meant you might be able to pay his debts and buy his freedom the sooner. But you *must* go. For your own health and safety, and for the sake of your family."

She looked sharply at him when he spoke this last. "How so? How could it possibly benefit my family, for me to bring my shame home for them to bear, when it has been all my own doing?"

"Because, Mrs. Merritt, if it is discovered that your husband has been imprisoned here for debt, the scandal may jeopardize your family's situation." Briefly he explained the existence and character of Mrs. Markham Dere, concluding with, "I would not even want Mrs. Dere to know of my visit here, for I do not doubt it would cost me my position if she learned of it. How much more your family's welfare? If you go yourself, you and you alone will determine the narrative, rather than letting the story reach Iffley through whatever channels, a story I think you must agree is shocking enough, even before gossip supplies its common exaggerations."

His speech was not without effect, and for a moment he thought, in her burdened, weakened state, it required only this touch to make her crumble. Her silent tears flowed, driving both Weatherill and Quint to dig in their pockets for a handkerchief to offer, but Quint rejected his as too grimy and applied it therefore to his own eyes, and before Weatherill could draw his out, Mrs. Merritt had thrown herself against his chest to sob into his travel-stained, threadbare coat.

"Don't tempt me, sir!" she cried. "I can't leave here, I tell you! Don't, *don't* tempt me!"

Surprise paralyzed him for an instant, and then, before he could work his arms loose from her grasp to pat her or stand her upright again, the next thing Gerard knew, he was taken by the collar and hurled to the gravel.

"That'll teach you to lay hands on my wife! Tempt my wife!" came a slurring roar, followed by a kick to Weatherill's backside which might have done him great injury, had it been administered by a sober man. As it was, the boot struck him such a glancing blow that it slid straight off, carrying its owner off his own feet and landing him flat on the gravel beside his victim.

"Roger!" shrieked his wife, flying to kneel beside him. "Have you hurt yourself?"

"Let's have no more of that, you," barked Quint, the brawny turnkey stabbing a thick finger in Merritt's face.

Humiliated, Merritt jerked his head away from the reprimand and glared at his better half. "Push off, you deceitful hussy!" This, as he began to struggle to a sitting position by pulling himself up her arm hand over hand.

"Oh, Roger," wailed Mrs. Merritt, tipping over atop him. "How *could* you speak to me that way? Why, why, must you drink?"

By this point Quint had assisted Weatherill to his feet, and the tutor stood dusting himself off and eyeing with dismay the rent in the knee of his trousers. He had a strong desire to return Merritt's attentions in kind, a desire not lessened by hearing the manner in which the drunkard addressed his poor spouse.

"—Listening to s-scoundrel's s-speeches! Throwing yourself at strange men like a common strumpet when my back is turned—"

"I have done nothing to deserve that name, and neither has he," she insisted as they grappled and grumbled up. "And how could I help being distraught when Mr. Weatherill brought me news of my family? For he has seen them, Roger! Mr. Weatherill *knows* them—Mama and Della and Sarah and Frances and Maria and Gor—"

"Weatherill?" he bellowed. "Did you say '*Weatherill*'?"

"If you had not thrown me to the ground, sir, I would have introduced myself," said Gerard stiffly.

"Yes, Roger," Mrs. Merritt resumed, "Mr. Gerard Weatherill—he knows them all, and I was so overcome by missing them that—"

"I would have guessed it soon enough," growled the worthy Merritt, paying his wife no heed. "You have the look of him about you."

There was no need for Gerard to ask whom Merritt referred to; nor was he likely to find the remark flattering. But Mrs. Merritt fell silent, the line appearing again between her brows. She raised her head and tapped her husband's chest. "Who does Mr. Weatherill look like, Roger?"

"Who?" he snapped. "Who else? Like Weatherill *Senior*! Like Rioting Rob himself!"

"I don't understand," she said faintly, now frowning at Gerard.

Ah.

Here it was.

The truth he would have kept from the outside world, if he could have. Would she now tell it to her family, if he could convince her to leave her husband?

After a long breath he said, "I'm the son of Robert Weatherill. Better known within these walls as Rioting Rob."

Her hazel eyes, shaped like her beloved sister's, grew wide, and Gerard wondered if Miss Barstow's would be so round and horror-struck when she too learned his secret. He had little time to ponder this, however, before Merritt was upon him again, wrenching free of his wife's supporting arm to fling himself at Gerard's throat. "And just like that one," he roared, "you mean to come between me and what's mine."

Before his assailant's fingers did more than brush Weatherill's neckcloth, Quint had him in hand. "I said that's enough out of you, Merritt," he chided, giving him a shake. "You need your head under the pump and then a visit to the warden."

The turnkey marched him away, calling back to Weatherill, "Better be on your way for today, sir. This will need a little straightening, and the warden will likely call your father in as well. Come back tomorrow and see him then."

He needed no further convincing, for Mrs. Merritt prepared to follow Quint and her husband, her shoulders slumping and arms wrapped about herself. But after a few steps she turned and darted back to him.

"I should apologize for my husband," she blurted, stopping several feet away. "I suppose appearances were deceiving. And I don't know what he meant about your father coming between Roger and me because I've never met the senior Mr. Weatherill to speak of him. I've only heard of him from Roger and—and by reputation."

Gerard's bow of acknowledgement was ironic. Yes, the biggest thing about Rioting Rob Weatherill was his reputation. And the bellicose Roger Merritt was likely not the only person in the world who believed that even being related to such a fellow warranted punishment. Take Mrs. Markham Dere: should she ever learn the truth, Gerard didn't doubt she would metaphorically try to level him.

"Mrs. Merritt, only tell me if you will continue to think on what I said. You can see this is no place for you."

But she backed away again, shaking her head. "How could I? You would not know it, because of the...condition he was in, but this is no place for Roger, either. We must—we must pray that no one else learns of my sad situation. You have my family's confidence, sir, and now you will have mine. Please. I ask you to continue to keep my secret from them."

Weatherill ran a distressed hand through his hair. "Could we speak further tomorrow, Mrs. Merritt? I could bring the older woman I spoke of."

"I don't know. Perhaps we had better not."

But he was not above the use of cunning. Carefully he said, "I could tell you more of your family."

She turned anguished eyes on him at this, her hands clenching and unclenching. Then, with a short nod: "If you come early enough, before noon, say, my husband will still be abed. I can often be found in the chapel."

Then she was gone.

Only hours later, after another walk and another cheap meal in a chop house, as he lay in his tiny, noisy room at the Bolt in Tun, did Gerard return in thought to Merritt's curious accusation. If it was not Jane Merritt whom Rob Weatherill purported to steal from Roger Merritt, who or what was it?

CHAPTER 17

But he was at home there, he myght speake his will.
Every cocke is proude on his owne dunghill.
— John Heywood, *A dialogue conteinyng the nomber in*
***effect of all the proverbes in the englishe tongue* (1546)**

Despite the unpromising end to his conference with Mrs. Merritt, Weatherill thought it advisable to make further preparations for her deliverance, and the morning found him in Gough Square, knocking at the door of a timber-framed brick townhouse.

"It is I, Gerard Weatherill, Mrs. Bundicomb," he said in response to the timid "Who's that?" Relief filled him to hear her voice, for he had no idea whether the old woman was still living, much less keeping her boarding-house. It was here he and Susanna had lived, when Gerard saved enough of his pittance from Keele to afford lodgings separate from their father's in the Fleet.

Glancing up at the spiked iron bar over the fanlight which discouraged burglars, he heard her unfastening the corkscrew latch and chain, and the next minute he was giving the ill-fitting door a bump with his shoulder to help her get it open.

"Master Gerard!" cried tiny Mrs. Bundicomb, peering up at him. "I never thought to see you again."

"Nor I you," he answered honestly. "May I come in?"

"Of course you may. Come, come. Do you need a room again, sir? No? Though my niece and her husband have taken your former one, and I have two other lodgers—you remember old Mrs. Turpin and Mr. Gust? Oh, not Mr. Gust? That's right—he came in September, so of course you would not. In any case, another lodger is always welcome and can be squeezed in somewhere because it is quite something, to make both ends meet! And I had to have Meggy—that's my niece—and Tom her husband because I am getting old myself, you know, and must have some help, though they are not here at the moment. Meg has gone to the market, and Tom delivers coal in the mornings. But, yes, more lodgers can always be accommodated, sir, if you change your mind, especially any old friends."

Mrs. Bundicomb's chatter was as familiar to Weatherill as the dark wood panelling and creaking floorboards, and when she led him into the parlor he almost smiled to see the smoke-grimed portrait of her long-dead husband over the fireplace. He and Susanna used to call him Mr. Bunvictim because it was a sad truth that Mrs. Bundicomb would have made a better brickmaker than baker, so hard were the buns, biscuits and rolls produced by her.

"Have you breakfasted yet?" she smiled at him, indicating a tray of just such delights on a table at his elbow. "You must share mine."

It was easier to accept than to refuse, but Gerard took care to chip fragments from his bun and dip them hastily in the tea before attempting to chew them. Fortunately, Mrs. Bundicomb had much to tell him while he forced his food down: neighborhood gossip, the doings of each of her lodgers, changes since his departure, the everlasting struggle to keep one's head above water. Given what he intended to ask of her, he was not altogether sorry to hear how desperately she could use additional money, though his mouth twisted ruefully. *Silver and gold have I nearly none, but such as I have give I thee...*

"But how do you like your new position in Oxfordshire, Master Gerard? You have not lost it, have you?" She asked at length, when she had wound up her lengthy speech. Her gaze traveled doubtfully over Gerard's worn clothing—the same clothing he had worn when she last saw him a few months earlier—lingering on the wretched knee patch he had fashioned for his trousers the night before from a piece of his coat's inner lining.

"Not yet," he replied lightly. "I am back in town because I heard from my old schoolmaster Mr. Keele that my father was declining."

"And is he? How do you find him?"

"I don't know yet," he admitted. "I hope to see him when I go from here today, but it is in regard to another matter that I have called on you, Mrs. Bundicomb, remembering how faithfully you tended Susanna."

Her watery blue eyes widened. "Oh? What matter is that?"

Setting down the unfinished portion of his breakfast bun, he wiped his fingers on his handkerchief. "Mrs. Bundicomb, I have learned of a debtor only recently confined to the Fleet who is—known—to some of my new friends in Oxfordshire. These friends are as yet unaware, and I have no desire to explain to them my long and personal connection to the place. As you will understand, in order to keep my tutoring position, I thought it best to conceal the particulars of my father's unfortunate history. When I learned of this person's fate, I did want to help these friends, but in order to do so, I would need *your* help. Your help and your discretion. It would require two days of your time, but I am able to pay a small allowance for the inconvenience."

This combination of significance, secrecy, and silver was too much for the good woman. Though she remained seated, she fairly danced with anticipation, beating a tattoo with her feet on the carpet and gripping her own breakfast bun so tightly it shattered. "Indeed? Do you hope to...liberate this person and hide him here? I am ordinarily a God-fearing, law-abiding person, but for you, Master Gerard, I could—"

"Heavens, no, Mrs. Bundicomb, nothing like that," he laughed in spite of himself. "It is not the debtor I plan to rescue, but rather the debtor's wife."

"Oh," she sagged a little. "Well. That is better, I suppose. Meggy and Tom wouldn't like me to harbor fugitives."

"Nor would I," he rejoined dryly. "No, Mrs. Bundicomb, I do not know for certain if it will come about, or the timing of it all, but my scheme would involve a little journey for you..."

An hour later, with the good woman's assurances secured, Weatherill presented himself once more at the Fleet's inner gate. There was no Quint this time but rather a new turnkey whom he did not recognize, who merely shrugged when he admitted him and said loudly, "Weatherill to see Weatherill, is it? I'm guessing you need no guide, then."

Nor did he. Still, he said, "Same room?"

"As when?" was the surprising response.

"As three months ago. First gallery, over the coffee-room."

The man chewed the nothing in his mouth, screwing up his eyes as if he were trying to picture the plan of the prison. "Ayuh, no. He hasn't been there for weeks."

Gerard frowned. Was his father in truth unwell? Had all the stairs become too much for him? Or was it the cost? "Where, then?"

The turnkey whistled, and a bony, scraggy lad shuffled over. "Potts, show this person here where Rioting Rob can be found, though you take your life in your hands, mister, to be knocking 'im up before two."

The unprepossessing Potts sniffed and jerked a shoulder, to indicate Weatherill should follow, and the latter did, stifling a sigh as he dug in a pocket for a tip. Between the expenses of coach fares, the Bolt in Tun, and hiring Mrs. Bundicomb, the remnants of Mrs. Dere's initial advance were nearly exhausted. He had thought Keele might lodge him, but alas.

Not eager for more witnesses than necessary, Weatherill paid off Potts and began the long process of waking up his father. First the soft knock. Then the soft, steady drumbeat. Then the sharp rap. Then the woodpecker-like tattoo, accompanied by the rattling of the door handle. Throughout, Gerard periodically called Rob Weatherill's name through the crack where the door did not sit squarely in its frame.

At last, a roar was heard, followed by a thumping and the clatter of flimsy furniture being kicked aside. Then the door flew open to a volley of curses which died abruptly in the older man's throat.

"You!"

Slipping inside, Gerard shut the door behind him, despite the stuffy, unpleasant closeness of the room. If room it could be called. It fit only a narrow bed, a washstand, and a dilapidated wardrobe missing one door. In Gerard's time it had belonged to an old shoemaker who plied his trade from a bench squeezed alongside.

Thank goodness there's at least no "companion" to deal with, he thought.

Rob Weatherill tumbled back onto the unmade bed. "What are you doing here?" he mumbled. "Never thought...to see you again."

"Mr. Keele wrote to me to say you were unwell."

His father waved a dismissive hand. "A touch of fever at the turn of the season." And indeed, to the indifferent observer Robert Weatherill might appear unchanged, but the keener scrutiny of a son discovered his weight a touch lighter, perhaps, and the lines marking his handsome face somewhat deeper. As if guessing at these discoveries and resenting them, the father said with a sneer, "Never say you have already lost your position?"

Gerard rolled his eyes. Why did everyone assume he could not keep a respectable post, when the only thing jeopardizing it were the very things he could not control? The very things attributable to the man who sat before him!

"I am still employed," he said shortly.

"Well, then? You see I am in no imminent danger of popping off, so you may tell Keele to mind his own business, and *you* may take yourself off again." But when his son didn't move, Rob Weatherill eyed him warily. "I see they haven't been paying you much, wherever you have gone."

With a sigh, Gerard sank down to sit beside his father, the bed giving a fearful creak under their combined weight. "I have nothing to complain of there, sir. I even have a couple new suits of clothing, but I thought it better to appear here as I was."

"You always were too proud for this place."

That elicited an exasperated laugh. "Father. The Fleet is a *prison*. To land here is nothing to boast of, and to grow up here is a hardship to be overcome. When did you decide this was enough for you?" A growl met this, but no words, and after a minute Gerard went on. "Now that I am grown, would you tell me the size of the debt which has kept you here all these years?"

His father shook his head.

"Don't worry, I'm not going to offer to pay it," Gerard said dryly. "I think I have but four shillings left to my name. I only mean to say you must have *some* income—you have been paying for your room and board and...sundry other expenses for decades now. Though you seem to have economized somewhat—" he indicated the cramped chamber "—since I last saw you."

"Had to pay the doctor's bills," grumbled his father, "or he said he wouldn't come back a second time."

Gerard merely cocked an eyebrow at him.

"I won't tell you," Rob Weatherill said. "You're not the only one with pride. I don't need my own son telling me I could give up drinking and gaming and roistering and be out of here in time, if I only chose to. I *don't* choose to. I choose to live my life how I choose to live my life, and no one will tell me otherwise."

Briefly Gerard debated arguing with the man. It would be fruitless in the end, he knew, but he would have done his duty.

As if he read his mind, Rob Weatherill said, "You think your old man is a disgrace and a stubborn fool, I warrant, but I tell you that in here I am king. If I were to leave now or in a few years, having paid my debts, what would I be but a broken old man with nothing in the world and no time to make anything of it? Here I am housed and fed. I rule over my little domain, and no one will take it from me."

Robert Weatherill, king of the Fleet taproom. Duke of the Fleet billiard-room. What did that make Gerard? What honorary titles might be conferred on him? One princedom, to be sure. And the courtesy title of Marquess of Weatherill.

If it all weren't so pitiable, Gerard might have grinned. He almost did. After all, what was Lord Dere's barony, in comparison?

"All right, father."

Then Rob Weatherill looked directly at his son. "I don't want you coming back here again, Gerard. Not even if you hear I'm dying. I don't imagine I will go slowly and quietly at any rate. No. You go and live your life now and leave me to mine. With my blessing, for what it's worth."

"Sir." He was chagrined by the tightening of his throat. So this was how it would end? This would be the last time they saw each other?

His father pushed to his feet and began his ablutions at the washstand, though the room was so confined that Gerard felt some of the drops of water strike him. Uncertainly he stood up himself, being careful not to knock into the bed or his father, but there would be no getting to the door until Rob Weatherill moved. Not that he wanted to escape. If this would be the last time they talked, Gerard somehow wanted *more* from him. In truth, he had always wanted more from his father and had always told himself there was no more to be had. No more that Rioting Rob Weatherill would or could give.

But still he stood there.

Scrubbing at his face with the tattered towel, Rob finally emerged ruddy and guarded. It seemed he was as surprised as Gerard to find the younger man holding out. And the surprise shifted something in the older one. His guard unexpectedly lowered. "Wait, boy. Before you go—tell me a little about your new place. Are you—contented—there?"

Gerard felt a flush burn his cheeks. How long had it been since his father asked him about himself? He could not think of a time. Remember a time.

Swallowing, he said carefully, "I like it well. Very well. I have two agreeable young pupils, comfortable lodgings, a generous stipend."

"Not so generous that you can pay off your father's sins, though, eh? Ah, don't look like that, boy! Do you not know a joke when you hear one? Well, we can't all be world conquerors. So will this be the rest of your life? Tutor, tutor, tutor?"

Later he could not explain to himself why he said it, but he did: "Perhaps in several years I will marry and have a family."

Immediately he regretted sharing this, and he grimaced, half expecting another mocking remark. But fleeting across his father's features was an expression Gerard had not seen before. (Had Adela been present, she would have recognized it as "the shadow," and noted the resemblance between father and son.) But Gerard, having no conception of what he looked like when his own "shadow" came on, struggled to interpret it. Thoughtfulness? Wistfulness? *Nostalgia?*

"Your mother," Rob Weatherill began, studying the towel he still held, "was a woman worth waiting for."

"Did you...wait for her, sir?" Gerard had only the vaguest memories of a quiet, sad-eyed woman. One time she was humming as she sewed, another time rocking an infant Susanna.

"Four years. I waited four years." His father folded the towel in half precisely and laid it on the edge of the basin. "She...deserved a better life. A longer one, certainly." Raising his head, his gaze met his son's. "If she had lived, well..." He shrugged. "Well, then I suppose I would not be the monarch of all I survey. I hope you and your lady fare better."

Such a confession from his father forced more unwilling words from him. "Thank you, sir. I hope so too."

"Then there *is* already a young lady?"

Gerard's silence and renewed color was answer enough, even if he had not muttered, "There is. At least, I want to marry her. She doesn't know it yet."

"A good girl? Kind? Gentle?"

"Everything," Gerard whispered. "The best girl. Delightful. Spirited. Lovely. The anchor of her family."

Rioting Rob sighed heavily, his hand lifting for a moment as if he would place it upon his son's shoulders, but he was not quite that courageous, and it dropped back to his side. Still, he said in a quiet voice, "Whoever she is, I wish you the winning of her. May she be...worthy of you, my son."

Something large and unswallowable lodged in Gerard's throat. He nodded. And to make his feet move, he told himself that this need not be the last time. His father was a prisoner! Whether Gerard ever came again or not was not Rob Weatherill's decision to make.

Reaching out, he did place his hand briefly on his father's shoulder. And then he edged around him, stopping just before he opened the door. "Goodbye for the present, Father. Oh, and perhaps I should mention, look out for one Roger Merritt. He has some grudge against you. He mentioned his wife."

His father only chuckled. "The fool. I have no designs on his wife, though she's a pretty thing whom he doesn't deserve."

Perhaps it was the after-effect of their unexpected moment of rapport, but Gerard heard himself blurt, "She's—Mrs. Merritt, that is—it so happens that she's sister to the...one I told you about."

"Is she indeed?" The older Weatherill's eyes lit with something of their old sparkle.

"Yes. That is the other reason I am here again—to see if anything might be done there, to help."

"Gerard Weatherill, white knight." His father's words were mocking, but the son might almost have called the smile which accompanied them *fond*. "Well, you go and rescue Mrs. Merritt, son, and deposit her at your lady's feet. After all, 'faint hearts never won etc. etc.' And never mind about Merritt bearing a grudge against me. I won a little money from him. He thought it personal, but I was only collecting the taxes due on his folly. Nothing to do with the young lady at all." Rob Weatherill scratched his head thoughtfully and then shrugged. "I suppose I did unwittingly cross him in regard to *another* lady friend, but could I help it if she preferred me? Nah, forget about him."

Descending the dark staircase from the first gallery to the hall gallery, Weatherill faintly heard Great Tom from St. Paul's striking the hour, and he could only hope Mrs. Merritt would still be found in the chapel.

The square and spare chapel was not entered from the noisy and dirty galleries but from the outer courtyard or racquet ground, and he picked his way to the door, through the usual crowd of unfortunates of every description, paying no attention to the two hulking men with caps pulled low, one bearded and one not, loitering by the entrance. The Fleet was full of loiterers, after all, hulking and otherwise.

"That the one?" said the first.

"Aye, that's him," answered the second.

Light slanted through the three windows in the chapel's left wall, the center one arched as a decorative concession, and when his eyes adjusted he inspected the few people scattered in the pews. It was impossible to pick her out from the back, so Weatherill walked slowly up the short aisle, glancing left and right, and it was she who spied him first, half raising a gloved hand to signal to him.

"I feared you would not come after all," she whispered, when Weatherill was sitting in the pew before her. "But I waited because—I have decided I will go. Not right away, but on Thursday morning because Wednesday is my husband's birthday. I told him I would only be gone for a time and that I would find work when I was in Oxfordshire, however I could, to help pay our debts."

"And did he agree to these measures?" Gerard asked, his voice barely above a rumble.

She was silent. Long enough that he peered over his shoulder to ensure she was still there.

"He was not pleased," she admitted. "He was so displeased and so...intoxicated yesterday that I did not dare mention it until he had slept for some hours. Not that the delay made him more amenable. It was more that *I* had time to think about it, and I have decided it will be for the best. For Roger, for my family, and—for me."

Weatherill's relief betrayed itself with a smile, and then he did turn to look at her, but she gave a sharp shake of her head. "No, please—we must not know each other. Roger is not usually a suspicious person, but it is another regrettable effect of the gin. How I hate gin with all my soul! Therefore I pray you will forgive him and make allowances for him. But we had better not be seen talking, and certainly not traveling together!"

"I understand, Mrs. Merritt. Have no fear. I have made the arrangements, and my old friend and landlady Mrs. Bundicomb will be prepared to meet you at the gate, so that you may catch the early coach. I have a note here which I will leave on the bench, enclosing the coach fare and indeed a little extra to hire the Angel Inn's cart to take you from Oxford on to Iffley."

"Should I write to my mother, that she might expect me?"

"Let us save them the pennies of postage," he answered, "for it is likely I will reach Oxfordshire before you, though if my remaining errand in town delays me until Thursday, I will take an outside seat, and we need not acknowledge each other. In fact, if I might ask you, Mrs. Merritt—would you not mention my part in all this, if you can help it? You might merely say you met with a...benefactor. I will certainly tell your family myself at the appropriate time, but for the sake of my position I would rather the Deres knew nothing of my being here."

"Of course," she promised. "That makes perfect sense, and I would hate to do you an ill turn, after all your kindness to us. To me and to my family."

"Farewell, then. And we will meet again in Iffley."

Rising, he slipped from the pew, and with a quick glance to make sure she was not observed, Jane snatched up the folded note left behind.

He emerged into the racquet ground, not ten yards from the chapel steps, when iron arms seized him from behind, wrestling him back into the narrow gallery passage, one grimy hand pressed to his mouth to muffle his protests.

CHAPTER 18

**For nothing is secret, that shall not be made manifest; neither
any thing hid, that shall not be known
and come abroad.
— Luke 8:17, *The Authorized Version* (1611)**

The village of Iffley was too small for a circulating library, so it was
not until the Sunday after Mr. Weatherill's departure that Adela first
heard of the book which dropped from a clear sky like a cannonball, rolling
for several days before its explosion threatened to demolish the Barstows'
carefully constructed new life.

"There isn't a copy to be had in all Oxford," a parishioner with a goatish
wisp of beard declared to the usual clutch of dons, fellows, and university
affiliates in the churchyard of St. Mary the Virgin after the service. "I looked
in Donwell's, Clairworth's, and even that old stand by Nixon's. With
Napoleon's army occupying Egypt, this may be the closest any Englishman
comes to seeing the place for himself, so, as one of the booksellers phrased
it, the books have wings and move as fast as he can stack 'em."

"What book would that be, Dr. Lane?" asked the rector.

"*Antiquities of Egypt* by an Anonymous Oxford Scholar."

"It must be a hoax," said Mrs. Terry at her husband's side, "for I never heard of any Oxford scholar willing to publish his findings anonymously, lest someone else take the credit. 'Anonymous' will probably turn out to be some imaginative Welsh blacksmith who has never gone beyond the Severn River, much less set foot in Egypt."

Unsurprisingly, several of the Oxford scholars surrounding her took umbrage at her joke, and an awkward pause followed.

"Della," spoke up Mrs. Barstow, hoping to get them over the difficulty, "speaking of Welshmen, what was that book your father was reading, before his health made it too difficult for him? Wasn't that set in Wales? We never did finish it."

"Yes, it was a story which took place in Caernarvon," answered Adela, "A novel. But I think the author was neither Welsh nor a blacksmith because her name was Emily Clark. Papa said it was full of the gothic and exotic, and I remember him rather enjoying the book. I wonder what happened to it."

"That settles it," pronounced Mrs. Terry. "Mrs. Emily Clark may not be a blacksmith, but if she prefers the gothic and exotic, she has now turned her attentions to Egypt."

Reluctant chuckles met this, but Mr. Furnival wagged a finger. "Now, Mrs. Terry, we know you love a good joke, but by all reports this work of scholarship is the genuine article, neither a fiction nor a mere restatement of Pococke's *Description of the East* or Norden's *Travels in Egypt and Nubia*. Indeed, if you ask me, I think we can all guess who wrote it."

Furnival waited until he had everyone's attention before announcing, "Why, William Keele, of course. It has to be. Weatherill said he did in fact travel in Egypt, digging in the sand and sketching whatever he unearthed. The only question was whether he could ever make anything of the years of notes he gathered. *Antiquities* must be Keele's masterwork, completed at long last."

This guess produced a miniature uproar amongst his auditors, but finally one piped above the clamor: "Ask Weatherill! He will know. Lord Dere, where is your tutor? He must settle the question."

"Unfortunately Mr. Weatherill was called to town to visit his ailing father," Mrs. Markham Dere struck in before the baron could answer.

"Rotten luck," said Furnival.

"Rotten luck about Mr. Weatherill senior, indeed," agreed Mrs. Terry with a mischievous smile, "but we are rather enjoying having a house full of boys at lesson time, aren't we, Mr. Terry? Mr. Terry has taken on Peter Dere and Gordon Barstow in the tutor's absence, you see."

"What is the name of this coveted book again, Lane?" asked her husband. "If it contains any plates or maps, I imagine my pupils would enjoy it."

"Pooh!" laughed Mrs. Terry. "If ever we manage to secure a copy, I suspect your pupils will never get a chance to look at it because *you* will be so busy poring over it!"

"I've got it!" exclaimed Dr. Lane, snapping his fingers and turning to the baron's niece. "Mrs. Dere, if you are corresponding with Weatherill, might you ask him to fetch a copy or two? He might even get Keele to sign the title page, if the man will own it."

Mrs. Dere frowned, more in doubt than in anger, and she glanced at her uncle. "I'm afraid I don't know where he may be reached. Did he leave a direction with you, sir?"

"None at all," admitted Lord Dere. "An oversight. He was in such a hurry, though, that I did not like to burden him with writing to us. He is a responsible young man. I am certain that he will either return shortly, or he will write to us unbidden, to let us know the state of affairs. Then I assure you we will make your request, Dr. Lane, Mr. Terry."

Dr. Lane bowed, his whisp wagging. "Ah, well. One doesn't like to trouble a man when his father is unwell. Ten to one he will not even see

Keele while he is in London. We will have to wait, like every other would-be Egyptian scholar in England."

Had the matter ended there, Adela would have forgotten all about it, except to speculate with the rest of them when Mr. Weatherill would return to Iffley. There, she was on tenterhooks, wondering with each passing day if the Deres had heard from him. She even considered asking the postmistress Mrs. Lamb, before deciding arousing the woman's curiosity was more trouble than it was worth. Surely if the baron or Mrs. Dere received a letter from Mr. Weatherill, Mrs. Lamb would mention it unprompted.

On Thursday, however, Adela did at last learn something of the absent tutor, and well might she have wished it unlearned. She was with her mother and Sarah in the kitchen, pickling the last of the season's grapes, when the manservant Irving appeared with a bundle in his hands.

"Mrs. Lamb sent this with her boy Nick, madam," he explained, "because she said Miss Barstow did not go for the post this morning."

"Heavens! What can it be?" asked Mrs. Barstow, wiping her hands on her apron.

The package was soon freed from its wrapping of brown paper and sheets of newspaper to reveal two leatherbound volumes comprising *Ianthe, or the flower of Caernarvon* by Emily Clark.

"It's from the baron," Sarah read the accompanying card from Donwell's bookshop in Oxford. "Isn't that just like his thoughtfulness, to remember you mentioning Mr. Barstow's book?"

Mrs. Barstow gave a rueful smile, running her finger across the title. "How kind of him. We will take turns reading it, and if we think Lord Dere might enjoy it, we will read it to him as well. What do you say, Adela?"

But Adela was staring openmouthed at the crumpled newspaper in her hands.

"What is it, Della?" asked her mother. "Bad news? Does it say something about Jane—or Roger?"

"No, no," Adela reassured her hastily, squeezing her arm. Something terrible indeed would have had to happen to the Merritts, to get them written up in the *Morning Post*. But this might hardly be better!

Without a word she pushed aside the stone jars and grape pickle ingredients to spread the newspaper across the table. Then she indicated a column with her finger.

"'Author of *Antiquities of Egypt* revealed,'" read Sarah. "Oh! Look—Dr. Lane guessed correctly. It was indeed Mr. William Keele, formerly of Oxford University and—and—" Breaking off, her fingers flew to her lips, and she gaped at Adela.

"And what?" cried Mrs. Barstow, looking from one to the other before leaning over the newspaper to learn for herself. "...So so so...'Mr. William Keele, formerly of Oxford University and, unknown to the scholarly world, more recently the inhabitant of a far less prestigious institution. To wit, the Fleet Prison.' What? The Fleet *Prison*? Impossible!"

"Impossible," echoed her daughter-in-law. "Utter nonsense. If his mentor had been imprisoned for debt, how would Mr. Weatherill then have even known him?"

"Exactly," agreed Mrs. Barstow briskly. "Mr. Weatherill said Mr. Keele was a London schoolmaster! What rubbish they print nowadays. Why, anyone might say anything now, about anybody!"

"But Mr. Weatherill did not say *where* in town the school was," whispered Adela.

Mrs. Barstow and Sarah regarded her reproachfully, knowing Adela's opinion would carry weight and perhaps force them to change their minds.

As one, the three bent their heads to read on.

And there it was in black and white. Mr. Keele—Mr. Weatherill's Mr. Keele—had been imprisoned for debt in the Fleet for twenty years, where he had "taught fellow prisoners' children for pence while working endlessly on his magnum opus, the newly published *Antiquities of Egypt*, the advance for which had finally allowed him to pay his longstanding debts." There was more: the nature of Keele's debts, the rapid sales of the first volume and clamor for the second, how the author's chequered history had first come to light, and so forth, but when Adela's eye reached the bottom of the column with no mention of Mr. Weatherill, she allowed her whirling thoughts to spin off.

"But if Mr. Keele's school was for 'fellow prisoners' children,'" Sarah puzzled, "how did Mr. Weatherill come to teach there?"

"Mr. Keele was also his teacher, according to Mr. Weatherill," Adela said dully.

"It could be that the school took additional charity students from the general London poor," suggested Mrs. Barstow. "Those who were not children of prisoners, I mean."

"It could be," her daughter replied, the doubt in her voice undeniable. "But what shame would there have been, had he merely been poor, Mama? Everyone could see he was poor. Before he got his new clothing he might as well have carried a signboard advertising the fact. But there was always something...else there, that he did not like to talk about."

"Della," said Sarah, "can you possibly be saying you think Mr. Weatherill himself was once a debtor, imprisoned in the Fleet?"

"That doesn't make any sense," Mrs. Barstow objected. "If he was taught by this Keele, he might have been Gordy's age. How would someone Gordy's age be arrested for debt?"

"It had to be his father," Adela frowned. "Mr. Weatherill must have—grown up in the Fleet! Where he was taught in Mr. Keele's school and eventually came to teach himself."

"Yes, that fits," Sarah agreed. "Only—why do you suppose he stayed so long, if he himself had his freedom? I would guess he is nearly five and twenty."

"He had a younger sister," Adela murmured. "Who died. He must have stayed until she was—no longer there to care for."

For a minute the Barstow women were silent, each marveling or fretting over such a revelation, until at last Mrs. Barstow began to clear away the books and their wrappings and Sarah to help her. But Adela sat on a stool, her arms wrapped about her middle.

"How can he possibly return to Iffley?" she asked them. "You know Mrs. Dere will be fit to murder him when she learns this. When she learns he has hidden such a thing. That he presumed, with such a history, to teach the heir to Perryfield! It need hardly be said that he will be dismissed. Disgraced. Turned out, without a character or a penny."

Her companions said nothing, their pursed lips and creased brows admitting their agreement. Yes, Mrs. Dere would do all those things.

Sarah stirred the grape pickle with distressful vigor, clicking her tongue, while Mrs. Barstow folded the offending newspaper over and over until it was too thick to continue. Then she set it aside, where the tight folds instantly sprang apart, so that it blossomed like a poisonous flower.

"Poor Mr. Weatherill," Mrs. Barstow sighed, shuddering when she saw the "Author of *Antiquities*" headline again. "He was so very kind to us regarding Jane, even if nothing came of it. And Gordy will be sorry to see him go."

"Do you suppose, if Mr. Weatherill's father was truly ailing, that he is even now visiting him *there*?" Sarah wondered.

Another silence.

Then Adela leaped from the stool and began untying her apron. "Where is Frances? I must go at once to Perryfield."

"Perryfield?" echoed her mother. "Do *you* intend to break the news, Della?"

"Don't you see? We must—*I* must—get to Lord Dere before anyone else. If Mrs. Dere reaches him first, she will have her way. She will convince him to—to ruin Mr. Weatherill! I must get there first. Sarah, get me a bottle of the elderberry wine to bring them."

"But we already sent Mrs. Dere some," Sarah reminded her, disappearing into the pantry nonetheless.

"That's right. Never mind it, then." Adela snapped her fingers. "Mama, quickly—write a note thanking him for the books, and I will deliver that instead."

"But what can you possibly say to him, Della, that would prevail over Mrs. Dere?" Mrs. Barstow asked, even as she scrambled to obey. "I am sorry to say that, while I do not believe she should be vindictive, I imagine most employers in her place would dismiss him as well."

"Oh, Mama, this is no time to be *reasonable*," wailed Adela. "If we do not stand up for our friends, who will stand up for *us* when our own troubles are discovered? When they learn about Jane's elopement and disgrace?"

"Very well, very well, if you think it will do any good. Heaven knows I like the young man very much, and one can hardly blame him for wanting to escape blame for the sins of his father."

Though Mrs. Barstow usually prided herself on her elegant penmanship, on this occasion, with her oldest daughter in such a nettle and Frances soon complaining and running about and Maria asking questions and the baby starting to cry because of the uproar, only a scrawled couple lines could be managed before her girls were out the door.

"But what is happening, Della?" Frances panted, one hand on her bonnet while she sped to keep up.

"I will tell you, but we can't stop to talk about it," her sister replied maddeningly. Not that her warning did any good, for it seemed Frances must come to a complete halt as each detail was shared and ask a thousand questions, until Adela had to seize her by the hand and *pull* to keep them moving. But at last, when they reached the arch in the Perryfield wall, and everything had been explained and understood and sufficiently marveled at, Frances' new question became, "But what do you mean to *do* about it, Della?"

Then it was Adela's turn to stop, so suddenly that Frances stumbled to avoid colliding with her. Her color was high, whether with exertion or from other causes. "I mean to outwit Mrs. Dere."

"Yes, of course, but *how*?"

"You know how."

Frances' mouth popped open. "You mean—you still intend to marry Lord Dere?"

"Hush!" hissed her sister as she glanced around.

"There's nobody here," said Frances stoutly. "No one could possibly have maintained the pace you set. I must say I thought you had given up your plan. You are always amiable around the baron, and he seems to like you as well as he likes any of the rest of us, but no more than that."

Adela groaned. "Frances, I know I have been half-hearted about winning Lord Dere," she conceded. "That is—I know I have not accomplished much beyond making myself generally agreeable. But it does not therefore follow that I have given it up. In fact, I am grateful you were so diligent in doing *your* assigned task, for I think it plain that Mrs. Dere likes you the best of any of us."

Pleased by this praise, Frances plumed herself a little. "She does prefer me, doesn't she? It wasn't very delightful work, I assure you. I had always to smile until my face hurt and to agree with every opinion she shared, even if I didn't agree one bit. I was going to ask you soon if I could leave off, but it seems I can't?"

With a vehement shake of her head, Adela said, "No. I'm afraid not. Please! Although I have left it so long and not worked as hard at it as you, today I must bring it to a head. A crisis."

"But why today, of all days, Della? What has changed? Why should learning Mr. Weatherill's secret make you so determined?"

Why indeed.

Adela wrung her hands, having no desire to bare her innermost heart to Frances' scrutiny. "Look here," she said, in the steadiest voice she could command, "Mr. Weatherill has been a friend to us, and the idea that I might use any sway I have for his benefit certainly plays a part, but only a part. It served as a prompt—a reminder. A nudge to act."

"So what will you do? And what am I to do, while you are doing it?"

"We must find Lord Dere, wherever he may be this morning, and then, Frances, if Mrs. Dere is there, you must get her away and keep her away."

"Are you going to propose to him?" squeaked her younger sister, giving a little hop and clapping her gloved hands.

"I don't know yet, you wretched girl! A young lady can't very well propose to a gentleman."

"But will you throw yourself at his feet?" Frances persisted. "Oh, how I wish I could watch! If Mrs. Dere is from home, may I?"

"No! I don't think I could bear it. I couldn't bear anyone being there. I can hardly bear the thought of Lord Dere being there! But come, we had better move along, or my courage will altogether fail."

In truth, it was already failing. *Should* she throw herself at the baron's feet? She would have to give some reason for doing so, but if she confessed her family's failings, and he did not respond by raising her up and throwing the cloak of his name about the Barstows, then what would happen? The best she could hope for would be that he might still overrule Mrs. Dere's objections to his cousin's family out of pity, suffering them to continue, reduced and humiliated, in Iffley Cottage, but how then could Adela ever hold up her head again? How could she live the rest of her days seeing the baron two or three times per week, having tried and failed to win him?

But ready or not, the moment was upon her, for as the sisters turned in at the gate, there stood the baron Lord Ranulph Dere on the lawn, the great house of Perryfield gleaming behind him in the oblique autumn sun.

CHAPTER 19

I must dissemble,

And speak a language foreign to my heart.

— Joseph Addison, *Cato*, I.ii (1713)

G ood afternoon, Lord Dere," Adela called, striding forward to meet the crisis, heart pounding.

"Miss Barstow, Miss Frances. What a pleasure." Removing his hat, he bent his still-slender person in a gracious bow.

"Taking a walk, I see," Adela said lamely.

"Very fine day for one," croaked Frances in support. "I am amazed Mrs. Dere does not join you."

Chuckling, he replied, "It is just as well because she would scold me for 'rooting in the grass for insects.'" Gently he tapped a pocket in his greatcoat and winked at them.

Oh, mercy, thought Frances, *he's got one in there, and Della is going to jump and screech, and this will all go off.*

But there Frances underestimated her sister, for Adela searched her soul and found that, in such an emergency, insects counted for nothing. Indeed, with a magnificent toss of her head worthy of Saint George charging the dragon, Adela said, "What luck, sir! We came to thank you for the books you sent to my mother—indeed, I bear a note from her to that effect—"

(in her agitation she thrust it at him ungracefully, as a creditor might an overdue bill) "—but now, if you might spare a moment, how I would *love* to see what you have found and—and how you might classify it in your collection."

Delight lit his features. "Would you, Miss Barstow? Then do come along with me to the library, and I will show you."

Frances' hand stole into her sister's to comfort her as they followed the baron into the house, but Adela only shook it off and wriggled her fingers, mouthing, *Play the pianoforte.*

"Lord Dere!" bellowed Frances instantly. "If you would excuse me, I would like to practice on the instrument a little while. Unless I see Mrs. Dere, that is. In fact—if *you* see Mrs. Dere, sir, could you send her to me in the drawing room?"

"A little music would be just the thing, Miss Frances. The house has been so quiet with the boys gone to the rectory."

With one last encouraging look, Frances retreated to the drawing room, leaving Adela and Lord Dere to continue to the library.

And Adela could not help herself: "Have you...heard anything from Mr. Weatherill?"

"Not a word, I'm afraid." He drew out one of his hideous specimen trays and inspected it. "Would you put this on the table, my dear, while I fetch the pins?"

Accepting the tray of horrors, Adela beamed down upon them as if she had never been entrusted with anything so charming. "Gordy likes Mr. Terry well enough," she ventured, "but he doesn't come home bubbling over with what he has learned. There is no 'Mr. Terry said this' and 'Mr. Terry told us that,' as there so often was with Mr. Weatherill."

"Little Peter misses him too," he agreed, as the sound of scales carried to their ears. "And I know my niece regrets his absence. I will tell you a little secret, Miss Barstow, which will certainly get me into trouble, should Mrs. Dere learn of it."

"S-secret?" Heavens! Had he already learnt of Mr. Weatherill's scandalous origins? And if he had and made no objection to them, might she be excused from the task she had set herself?

He held the box of pins to his ear and shook it as he joined Adela at the table. "I gave him an advance on his wages," said the baron with a mischievous grin.

"Oh." Was that all? Adela almost sagged with disappointment.

"You disapprove? I know Mrs. Dere will. She will say, 'Uncle, that is the second advance the man has received in only two months' work, and now goodness knows when he will ever return!' She gave him a little shortly after he came, you see, because she wanted him to make a more worthy appearance," he added, when Adela said nothing. "My niece has firm opinions—*very* firm opinions—on the honor due to a baron's family, and poor Mr. Weatherill's shabbiness quite offended her. And I have learned it is easier to keep the peace than to make a fuss. But how I rattle on! We had a task before us. Let us see to this little fellow I pocketed."

Adela could have shouted, *Confound the little fellow you pocketed!* but she fixed the imitation of a smile to her face as one might nail a sign to a post, while the kindly baron proceeded to go on and on about how one might easily mistake *Elasmucha grisea* for *Elasmostethus interstinctus*, and see how he already had several birch shield bugs, male and female, here and here, but this was the first 'parent bug' he had caught in all these years, just imagine!

She could wait no longer.

What more confirmation of her course did she need? Lord Dere had as much as stated that Mrs. Dere ruled the roost at Perryfield, and each passing second brought the doom of both the Barstows and Mr. Weatherill nearer!

"Sir," she blurted, just as he expertly pierced the unfortunate *Elasmucha grisea* through its thorax, slightly to the right of center. "Words fail to express how dependent so many less fortunate ones are on your unstinting kindness. Your generosity. Your willingness to—"

In alarm at this unexpected broadside of gratitude, Lord Dere wheeled back, bending the pin in his grip.

"Oh, dear!" cried Adela, springing forward with outstretched hand. She nearly, nearly touched the impaled insect, only to recoil at the last instant, but fortunately the baron was too occupied in trying to straighten the pin to notice.

"Miss Barstow," he addressed his tray of the family Acanthosomatidae, "I believe I asked you not to refer again to your supposed debts to me. Your mother is my cousin, and your family has brought a welcome liveliness to Iffley and Perryfield, so there is no need for these continuing thanks—"

But Adela could not risk being silenced. "Yes, I know you don't like it, sir, but if you knew how easily we might have slipped into the abyss of poverty and disgrace—how easily we *still* might slip, you would understand why—"

"What do you mean, 'still'?" he interrupted, looking up at last, his mild blue eyes sharpening. "Is there some need of your family's going unmet? Some lurking threat you and your mother have not shared with me?"

"Not a money need, no—I refer to—that is—the unmet need I referred to was only—a-a-a-a need of—the heart," stammered Adela.

It was impossible to turn any more scarlet than she now turned, without actually bursting into flame, and Adela half wished it would happen. For if she combusted, though she might leave burn marks on the carpet, she and Lord Dere would be miraculously delivered from this mortifying situation.

He clearly was not the least bit in love with her, nor did her hint appear to fill him with anything save dismay. Indeed, the man stared at her as if she had run mad. Slowly, slowly, he released the pin between his fingers and pushed the tray some inches away. Adela noted dimly that Frances had stopped playing. Was that because Mrs. Dere had come into the drawing room, or was her sister simply choosing her next piece of music?

In any event, she was running out of time. It was no difficulty to let tears well up, distressed as she was, and to let those tears then spill over was as easy as falling down the stairs.

"Miss Barstow," he breathed, when he managed to get his voice working, "I have been a fortunate man. Which means I have never experienced desperation, as you Barstows seem to have, with your painful losses and your—financial woes. I am glad—even grateful—myself, that I could be useful to you all. But you must not mistake gratitude for—for—er—ahem!" With a bark he succeeded in clearing some obstruction from his throat. "That is to say—let us speak no more of it—any of it—from this hour onward."

"Oh, Lord Dere, if only that were possible," Adela wailed. "If only my heart had not been so affected by...what has transpired that I feel—I feel—I feel—I feel all might still be lost to me if-if-ifeverIwerepartedfromyou." This last came out in a rush, like the eruption of rock fragments with which Mount Vesuvius had bombarded unfortunates below, when Adela was Frances' age. And like those ill-fated victims must have, the baron threw up his arms in horror.

"Miss Barstow!"

"Because—what if we—what if *I*, that is—were to lose your favor?" she hurried onward. "What would become of my—heart?"

"You surely can't mean that you—you—"

"I do mean it, sir! That I—I—*oh*!" Being unable or unwilling to say precisely what she meant (or didn't mean), Adela took a deep breath, like a diver preparing to plunge into icy waters far below. She screwed up her features, clenched her fists, and *flung* herself at him.

Having never in all his years been pursued with such violence, the baron was wholly unprepared for Adela's assault, and when he shrank aside, instinctively hunching over his precious specimen tray, it was not a deliberate lapse in chivalry on his part. That is, Lord Dere did not choose for Adela to fly through the space between them with no waiting arms to receive her. He did not choose for her to crumple in a heap at his feet; it was simply what happened.

But once she was on the actual floor, a loosened comb slipping from her hair and her fingers scrabbling at his boots in an attempt to drag herself up, he did what any man similarly circumstanced would do, dumbstruck or not: he bent down to assist her. Grasping her by the upper arms, he tried to lift the flailing girl up, and had he been twenty or thirty years younger, the effort would not have gone amiss, but as it was, amiss was precisely where it went. Over they pitched, Adela landing flat on her backside and Lord Dere atop her.

For one wretched sliver of eternity they lay there, aghast, and so deep was their humiliation that they might have gone on thus to the last trumpet, if the more familiar sounds of voices and footsteps in the passage had not reached their ears.

Madly and silently, both Adela and the baron scrambled to untangle themselves, with the unlucky consequence that she kneed him in a vulnerable location and reduced him to moaning immobility.

The door opened.

"I thought they were here," Frances Barstow's puzzled voice floated above them. "Lord Dere was going to add an insect to his collection."

"There is the tray on the table, indeed," came Gerard Weatherill's reply.

Mr. Weatherill? *Mr. Weatherill!*

Adela's eyes sought the baron's. *I'm sorry*, she mouthed. *Please forgive me.*

Grimly, he gave her a nod, before slowly and carefully extricating himself to rise to his feet and face the newcomers. "Here I am," he said.

"Uncle!" shrieked Mrs. Dere, hastening toward him, "Did you fall? Or have a fit?" The question was hardly out of her mouth before it was swallowed in a second shriek when she saw Adela pushing herself to a sitting position. "Miss Barstow! What on earth?"

A half century later, Adela would tell a favorite granddaughter the story of that afternoon with tears of laughter in her eyes, but as it was unfolding there was nothing remotely amusing about the incident. Nothing remotely amusing about standing up to face a shocked Mrs. Dere and a returned Mr. Weatherill. A patch covered one of his eyes and his old clothing looked, if possible, worse than she had ever seen it, being now mended and patched in several places with mismatched cloth. But it was his pallor and the accusation in his remaining eye which turned her to stone and sewed shut her lips.

"Miss Barstow fell down," said Lord Dere, as if such acts of clumsiness were everyday occurrences for her. "You are welcome back to Perryfield, Mr. Weatherill. I hope your father has made a thorough recovery."

The tutor's lips parted, but no reply emerged. He gave a short nod.

Of them all, Frances was the only one who did not gawp as if she had been clouted over the head. Indeed, she raised her eyebrows wonderingly at her sister, as if to say, *Well done, you!*

Mrs. Dere gave an audible swallow. "But—how did *you* come to be on the floor, sir? Did she trip you?"

His answering chuckle sounded only slightly forced. "Nothing of the kind. It was my own awkwardness." Briefly he shut his eyes, and Adela saw his chest rise and fall in a noiseless sigh. Then he said ever so calmly, "It has been many years, and I suppose I was out of practice in expressing my ardor."

"Your...*ardor*?" Mrs. Dere made another unladylike gulp.

"Yes." Another of those stilted chuckles. "But I hope you will congratulate us. Miss Barstow and me, that is to say. She has just accepted me and made me the happiest of men."

The next thing she knew, Adela was lying on the library sofa, opening her eyes to the coffered ceiling while Frances and one of the footmen leaned over her.

"This can't become a habit," she muttered. But then another part of her muzzy head observed, "This is only the *second* time in your life you've fainted, Adela Barstow, and even your enemies would agree that, on both occasions, the circumstances were most trying."

"Ah," came the baron's voice. The footman's head receded, to be replaced by that of Lord Dere. "Some cordial for Miss Barstow and my niece, Wood."

"Did I...imagine it?" whispered Adela in her sister's ear as Frances helped her to sit up.

"I'm afraid not," Frances hissed back.

No, she had not. For there sprawled Mrs. Markham Dere in the armchair opposite, only herself coming to, while another footman fanned her. And there stood Mr. Weatherill, like one turned to stone, looking at the tray of shield bugs on the table. Looking at nothing.

"Please, Weatherill," says Lord Dere, "be seated. That was a little to-do, but now that the ladies are reviving, we may sit and talk like well-mannered people."

"Sir." With unwilling steps, Weatherill chose a chair, running a finger along the ugly seams of the patch at his knee.

The baron lowered himself beside Adela on the sofa. Not so near that he touched her, or even her skirts, but beside her all the same. *Well,* she reproved herself, *wasn't this what you wanted? And just in the nick of time, for here is Mr. Weatherill's secret about to be blazoned. They had better keep the fan handy for Mrs. Dere.*

"You must distract us for a few minutes," Lord Dere commanded affably. "You say your father is doing better, Mr. Weatherill, but, if you will pardon me for saying so, you seem to be somewhat the worse for wear."

"Yes," rejoined Frances. "Whatever happened to your eye, Mr. Weatherill? I hope it is...still there, under your patch?"

"It is. I—ran into something. The patch is merely to spare all of you the colorful consequences."

His answer made something flare inside Adela, and with incredulity she identified it as anger.

Anger?

Anger! Here she had literally thrown herself at Lord Dere in order to save Mr. Weatherill, and instead of feeling relief that he could no longer be harmed by the revelation of his scandalous history, she felt resentment. It was contrary; it was nonsensical; but there it was. *Because he continues to hedge and dodge and hide! What in heaven's name did he run into, that it blacked his eye and tore his trousers?*

Her new betrothed therefore pleased her unwittingly when he said, "Weatherill, I believe I speak for all present when I say we are glad to see you again for another reason: you may settle a question which has absorbed Iffley in your absence. Do you happen to know whether your former mentor is the 'anonymous Oxford scholar' who authored the wildly popular new book *Antiquities of Egypt*?"

"Your Mr. Keele," said Adela, addressing his scuffed boots. (She need not have bothered, for he had not looked in her direction since the baron made his announcement.)

Weatherill's straightened, his visible eye flicking between the baron and Mrs. Dere. "It is," he answered warily. "I did not see him while I was in London, but a mutual acquaintance said as much."

"Too bad about not seeing him," said Lord Dere with a smile. "As soon as the Oxford set in Iffley made the connection, they asked us to use our connection with you to secure a coveted copy. Alas. But good for Keele, and good for you, Weatherill."

As quickly as it had come, Adela's anger left her, pushed aside by alarm on Mr. Weatherill's behalf. He didn't yet know! He had no idea he stood on the edge of a precipice. How could she begrudge him his evasiveness, when so soon he would be exposed?

Mrs. Dere, at least, had other fish to fry. Pushing aside the footman with the fan and refusing Wood's proffered lemonade with a vehement shake of the head, she addressed her uncle in trembling tones. "Uncle, this chit-chat is all very well, and I am as glad to have Peter's tutor back as any, but I must insist we return to your astonishing announcement."

"If you like, Alice," he said gently. "I thought it best to let the notion sink in your mind first."

"That will certainly take some time, sir," his niece allowed. "Not that I count it a marvel, that any lady you apply to would be greatly flattered, but—I had thought you content to remain a bachelor—"

"If you will excuse me," Weatherill muttered, rising, "I will unpack and make myself presentable."

"And Frances and I will go now," said Adela, shooting to her feet. "I would like to be the one to tell Mama and my siblings, sir, of our—our—ahem—our engagement." (Adela nearly choked on the word).

"Of course, Miss Barstow." He did not look eager to be left alone to face his niece, but Adela was too flustered herself for surplus sympathy, and with a jerk of a curtsy she made her escape, Frances and Weatherill not far behind.

CHAPTER 20

I give away my selfe for you,
and doate upon the exchange.
— Shakespeare, *Much Ado about Nothing*, II.i.290 (1600)

He wanted, more than anything in the entire world, to be alone. To slap his hat on his head, don his greatcoat, and walk for days and days and days.

For weeks, even.

Or months.

He could walk to Scotland. Or the Arctic. Let the mud and rain and ice be what they were. He would walk anywhere where he would never have to speak to anyone again, never see anyone again. Never mind that the person he wanted least to speak to or to see, ever, ever again, was even now beckoning to him.

"Mr. Weatherill, if I might have a short word," murmured Miss Barstow, making the tiniest come-with-me motion again with her hand. "I know you have things to do, but if I might have just the one word with you—preferably out of doors. It's terribly important, I'm afraid."

Of course it was.

Would it be, *I know you are surprised, but you have known almost from the beginning what I planned to do.* Or was it, *I don't know why you won't look at me—I thought we were friends.*

Without a word, he followed, the blasted eye patch making the passage dim enough that he had to take care. Merritt's ruffians had managed to black his eye and plant numerous blows to his midsection and kicks to his legs before the racket of furniture being knocked about, combined with his own struggles and shouts, brought others to investigate.

"Get you gone," snarled Ruffian Number One as Gerard panted and nursed his jaw, "or more of the same will come to you."

"And don't ever talk to or come near or even look sidewise at Mrs. Merritt again, if you know what's good for you," put in Ruffian Number Two, pounding his fist into his open palm in a manner at which Gerard would have rolled his eyes, if the movement had not been made painfully inadvisable.

Like a fool, he slurred through his aching jaw, "Hope Merritt hasn't promised you payment for your efforts because you can go whistle for it. He hasn't a penny he doesn't spend on drink."

The ruffians roared (in vexed recognition, Gerard hoped), each sending home a parting blow before racing away. It was Quint who got him on his feet a few minutes later, when one of the idle onlookers mentioned the row to the turnkey at the gate.

"That Merritt will come to no good end," he grumbled, letting Weatherill lean against him as he escorted him down the steps and past the warden's house. "Been here so short a time, and he's already made the most worthless friends possible. I pity his poor wife."

Merritt's poor wife was the reason Weatherill had to follow the two Misses Barstow now, rather than stalking away to the hinterlands straight off, as his heart desired. But the moment they stood safely upon the lawn which rolled away before Perryfield, he said without preamble, "You will find Mrs. Merritt at Iffley Cottage when you return."

This entirely unexpected announcement staggered his two companions, and whatever speech of her own Miss Barstow had planned melted into the air.

"*Jane?*" she gasped. "Can you mean my sister Jane?"

"Jane is home?" yelped Miss Frances.

"How do you know this?" "Is Roger with her?" "Is this your doing, sir?"

It was childish, but Weatherill addressed his answers to Miss Frances and to the crown of Miss Barstow's bonnet. "Yes, I refer to your sister Mrs. Roger Merritt. She is in Iffley. Because the same coach which carried me from town brought her as well."

But this only led to a new spate of questions, and in spite of himself it moved him to hear the emotion in Miss Barstow's voice.

But she would not be Miss Barstow for much longer. She was now the future baroness Lady Dere, and how such a lofty creature felt about this or that was no longer any of his business.

Perhaps it never had been.

"No, Mr. Merritt is not with her," he said shortly. "I will explain how it all came about at some later date, but now I am sure you would like to hurry back to Iffley Cottage to share in the reunion. If you will excuse me..."

He managed to retreat some five yards before Miss Barstow gave a squeak. "Oh! Do wait, Mr. Weatherill—I quite forgot! The mention of Jane drove everything from my head. Frances, you go along, and I will catch up with you."

It was rather hard on Frances (or at least Frances thought so) that Della must always be dismissing her when very, very interesting conversations were taking place, but in this instance, the desire to see her second sister again (and before Della did!) took away the sting, and she trotted away directly.

"I am sorry about your eye," said Miss Barstow, when her sister was gone. "Does it still hurt?"

"It improves daily," he answered, hardening his heart against her. "What was it you wished to tell me?"

She made a little sound in her throat and looked down at the grass, drawing the toe of her boot back and forth, as if marking the gap which now separated them. "Yes. I will be quick. In short, as the baron told you, there was a great deal of interest in Mr. Keele's book while you were away. And then today by chance I saw something in the *Oxford Journal* about that same Mr. Keele, the author of *Antiquities of Egypt*. It said—it said that he had been for years...a prisoner in the Fleet."

Weatherill might have been carved from the same block of marble as Perryfield's cupid statues, so still did he hold, his gaze fixed on the flattened grass in the lawn where they had passed. She must have been holding her breath as well, for there was a long spell so quiet that he caught the clatter of something metal from the distant kitchens.

Then she expelled a shaky breath and said, "Mr. Weatherill, because I fear it will be a matter for general inquiry very soon, if not already, tell me—did you know Mr. Keele from his time in the Fleet?"

Like one preparing to peel back a bandage which should have been changed or removed long since, he shut his eyes. Every nerve stretched in preparation for the worst.

"I did."

"Ah." There was neither surprise nor triumph in the little sound. If anything, there was a note of...disappointment?

Then he could resist no longer, and he raised his eyes to her face. Her lovely, beloved face. So it had been disappointment he heard, for her lip trembled.

"Exactly," he said. "You understand now why I would prefer such a fact buried in obscurity. Who would enlist such a person to teach his children?"

"Was it your own debt that put you there?" she asked earnestly. "It cannot have been. You do not seem the profligate sort. The sort who would live beyond his means or try to elude creditors, so that they would be forced to bring a suit."

"It was not my own debt," he admitted. His gaze drifted away again, following his thoughts into the past. "It was my father's. He was imprisoned when I was very young so that I hardly remember any other...home. And Susanna, my sister, was born within the walls of the Fleet. It was only when I was old enough to assist Keele and earn modest wages that Susanna and I found our own lodgings outside the gate."

"And...your mother?"

"She died ten years ago, of the same illness which took Susanna."

There, he thought wryly. He had confessed more about himself in two minutes than he had in the whole course of his life. Not simply because it could no longer be concealed—then he might have said as little as he had to Miss Barstow's sister Mrs. Merritt—but because now, though it could avail him nothing, he wanted her to know him. He wanted to be *seen*.

"I am sorry for it," she said, lifting her palms to acknowledge the inadequacy of her words. "For...all of it."

"Yes. Thank you." His voice was rough, and he had to clear his throat. Having so long feared the blistering judgment of the world, he was wholly unprepared for—was undone by—the balm of understanding. The comfort of sympathy. To have warm brown eyes turned on him over the wreckage and to hear a sweet voice say, *I am sorry for it.*

Unable to put into words all that flooded him, his hand reached for hers.

But Miss Barstow failed to see the motion, for she was wrapping her arms about herself and lifting her chin with a new resolve.

"And I am sorry you did not feel you could speak of it, any of it," she went on, in a stronger voice. "Though of course you could not, any more than I could speak of my sister's trials. And I want you to know, Mr.

Weatherill, that now you are safe. I mean to say, you need not fear losing your post over this."

If he had been on the point of drawing her into his arms, her last words overthrew the impulse. Nay, they operated like the wave of a fairy wand or a muttered abracadabra—banishing the fragile closeness Gerard had imagined between them.

His hand dropped.

"My post?" he echoed.

"Mrs. Markham Dere will make a great fuss, I do not doubt, but she will have to give way to me now. I will see to that."

Something was rising, unfolding, biting in his chest, and it had nothing to do with the bruises he had sustained from Merritt's bullies. "Ah yes," he said coldly, "you have achieved your aims. You have caught the baron and placed yourself out of harm's way. You and any whom you choose to protect."

Flushing scarlet at his tone, she retreated a step, and Weatherill had to stuff down a bullying instinct of his own, for he wanted to close the gap, seize her by the shoulders, and shake her till her hair tumbled down and her red lips begged for mercy.

"Yes," she said, scarcely audible. "I do not deny that I hoped to win Lord Dere's protection. You know I did. And why I did. We have argued about it before. But—he is a good man. A kind and generous one. And...women have chosen far worse husbands for far worse reasons. Therefore, be assured. In my friendship for you, I will make certain you keep your post."

"My post," he repeated derisively. "You think I still want this post? It was a stepping stone. And now if every last man Jack will know my disgraceful story, he will at least know as well my connection to the glorious William Keele, and perhaps celebrity will outweigh infamy. No, Miss Barstow. You and your intended husband and your intended niece-in-law may fill your precious post with the most spotless man in Christendom. As for me, I will advertise. I will go among new people without subterfuge."

"But—but surely we know you and will make allowances for you," she protested, her face falling. "And haven't you found Iffley and its inhabitants to your liking? Wouldn't you be sorry to leave it now, to begin all over again?"

The corners of his mouth turned down, twisting in bitterness. "Sometimes, Miss Barstow, a liar longs to breathe the air of truth. Or at least this liar does. There have been too many falsehoods told here, not all of them my own. If you will pardon me, I wish you a pleasant reunion with your sister."

Turning on his heel, he strode away.

But once he regained the house, after a nod to the footman, he took the stairs two at a time, as if pursued by hounds. No doubt Lord Dere still had his hands full explaining his engagement to Mrs. Dere, and Weatherill's presence was not yet required.

On the second floor he burst into his room to find a fire already lit and his bag carried up. He would unpack, though who could say how much longer he would be at Perryfield. He would draft his advertisement. He would write to Keele to congratulate him, in care of the publisher Murray. He would don his newer clothing again and toss these ones in the fire.

And yet the minutes passed, and Gerard did none of these things. Instead he leaned his elbow on the casement and stared out over the Perryfield grounds. Over the gravel paths of the gardens and the cupid statues and the flowerbeds.

Oh, Lord, what a fool he was. With his quixotic notion of rescuing Jane Merritt and returning to Iffley to be crowned with laurels by a blushing, grateful Miss Barstow. And then, after Miss Barstow covered him in kisses, to fall upon one knee and ask for her hand to be awarded to him *in ten years?*

Fool, fool, fool.

When he had dashed off on his quest, he had not suspected Miss Barstow would pursue her own so vigorously in his absence.

Well, they had both succeeded. Or both lost. It was hard to tell the difference.

It was a very long time—long enough to require the lighting of the candles—before he seated himself at his writing table to draw up his advertisement.

And longer still before the words would come.

She hated him!

When Weatherill left Adela on the Perryfield lawn, marching away without a backward glance, hurt and astonishment rooted her to the spot for a full minute. It was only the appearance of a face in one of the windows—a curious footman or maid peeping out at her, wondering why she stood alone, stock-still—which restored her power of motion. And then what motion! If Frances had not had the head start of several minutes, Adela would have soon left her behind, for fury lent her wings.

She had given him sympathy. She had not censured him for what he could not help. Not held his past against him. But he had not shown her the same grace. Not a bit of it. Instead he had condemned her. Judged her.

She had used a woman's weapons with Lord Dere, yes, but what other means had she, to fight for her family? She could not pack up and leave, as Mr. Weatherill could. She could not pass herself off as a person with no past, as he had done. And he dared to judge her?

But what hurt Adela most of all was the knowledge that even her family's compounding perils had not been enough to force her hand with the baron. Still she had delayed; still she had dragged her feet.

No. In the end it had been for love of *him*, for Weatherill, that she acted so impetuously. For fear of harm coming to *him* that she at last took the irrevocable plunge.

And this was her thanks.

He showed her no gratitude. He offered her no understanding. Only harsh words and condescension. Her sacrifice tossed aside, unwanted and unvalued. And now here was Jane, home safely without Roger. And here *she* was, engaged to the baron!

Bending to pick up a clod of dirt, Adela hurled it with all her force at the stones of the Perryfield wall, wishing it was the back of horrible Mr. Weatherill's head.

Then she turned to demand of a trio of nearby sheep, "What are *you* looking at?"

The sheep wisely kept their counsel, maddeningly indifferent to her fury. One even cropped a mouthful of grass, of which half fell out as it chewed. But for some reason, the prosaic sight steadied her. She almost even laughed, though it was half a sob.

The world falls apart, but the sheep graze on.

Yes. The sheep grazed, the planet kept turning, and life must and would go on. Moreover, Jane waited for her at home. The thought of her sister came as a relief from her own unhappiness. Against all hope, Jane was somehow restored to them, and the Barstows would be all together again, as they had not been since the day before her sister's elopement.

Squaring her shoulders, Adela mentally shoved Mr. Weatherill and Lord Dere from her mind to be dealt with later. From habit the baron went easily enough; indeed, he was left behind before she had gone ten yards, their new engagement notwithstanding.

But Mr. Weatherill was another story. Somehow, in both her mind and—worse—her heart, Mr. Weatherill clung like a burr. Somehow, in both places, he had made himself quite at home.

CHAPTER 21

Why have you stol'n upon us thus! You come not
Like Caesar's sister: the wife of Antony
Should have an army for an usher, and
The neighs of horse to tell of her approach
Long ere she did appear.
— Shakespeare, *Antony and Cleopatra*, III.vi.1869 (c.1606)

Jane!" The sisters fell into each other's arms, laughing and crying at the same time while the rest of the Barstows crowded about them, the younger ones jumping up and down and clapping with excitement and their mother openly weeping. Even Baby Bash bounced in his mother's arms, shaking plump fists. Only the flurry of the prodigal daughter's return could have made Mrs. Barstow and Sarah forget to ask Adela how she succeeded at Perryfield in her errand, but forget they did. Entirely.

"We told Jane not to tell us a single thing until you were home," crowed Maria over Poppet's wild barking. She was dancing around the pair of them as if they were a maypole.

"And *I* have not told a single thing either," said Frances archly.

"Then let us go inside now and hear it all," Mrs. Barstow commanded. "And Jane must eat and eat. She is far too thin."

Much as the two servants would have liked to hover about, once Jane's trunk and a mattress from the shed were stuffed into the blue-papered bedroom and a heaping tray of tea, biscuits, and sandwiches prepared, Reed and Irving were dismissed. For once the cramped parlor felt the perfect size, as Jane sat on the sofa with Outlaw on her lap, Gordon and Maria to either side and her mother directly across, keeping her teacup brimming. The others pulled their chairs near so as not to lose a word.

"Why did you not write to us, darling, to tell us you were coming?" asked her mother. "I am sure the baron would have let us send a carriage to the Angel Inn to fetch you. He is everything that is helpful."

Frances here gave a low cough, eyeing Adela, but her oldest sister pressed her lips together and gave the barest shake of her head. *Wait. Later.*

"I did not know I was coming myself, Mama, until it was too late to write. I thought Roger would like it best if I was there for his birthday on Wednesday, and I did not want to...ask permission too soon because—because one never knows what might come up. But a very kind old lady accompanied me down."

"And where has she gone? Why did you not invite her to stay with us?"

"She said she must return this very evening to London because she owns a lodging house."

"Is that where you are living in town? With this kind old lady?"

"Oh—no. Er—elsewhere."

"Well, never mind, then," Mrs. Barstow waved this away. "I wish her a pleasant return journey with all my heart. But did Roger stay in London because of his work?"

"He—er—he—" Jane stammered, her face flooding with color.

"What is it, my dear? Is he unwell?"

At that, Jane's face crumpled, and she buried her face in Outlaw's fur, much to the wriggling kitten's annoyance. It bolted away, leaving her to transfer all her wailing to a cushion Maria handed her, while the rest of the family writhed with helplessness.

"He's not unwell as you understand it," she cried, raising her blotched countenance at last. "You mean *is he sick*, Mama, and had he been, in the ordinary sense, I would never have left him. But it's—something else. It's that—he's *drinking*. Far too much, and all the time, and with money we do not have. Drinking and gambling and—and consorting with the worst sorts!"

She could not have astonished them more if she had announced Roger Merritt had taken to the high seas as a pirate. It was not that the Barstows drank no intoxicating liquors (both the Mrs. Barstows and Adela were passable brewers and winemakers), but they had little experience with anyone who drank for drinking's sake or who gambled for more than pin money at a card party. And while the Roger Merritt they had known had been more daring and dashing than others of their acquaintance, they had not dreamed he would come to *this*.

Had Mrs. Barstow not been so perplexed, she surely would have sent Maria and Gordon out of the room, but as it was she scarcely remembered they existed, and they were wise enough to shrink down and keep mum.

"He can't have squandered it all, in any event," she said uncertainly, "if there was money to spare for your coach fare."

Heaving a sigh, Jane shook her head. "No, Mama. There was no money, even for the coach fare. I had managed to put a little aside—I hid it in the mattress—but Roger found it. I had only pennies."

"Then however did you come?" wondered Sarah. "Did you borrow it?"

"I—did not borrow it, though I will repay the sum, if it is ever within my means, for I suspect my...benefactor...could ill spare the sum himself."

"A benefactor!"

Jane blushed. "Yes. A friend to both Roger and me whom we met in London. That is—he is a friend to Roger though Roger does not yet appreciate it."

"See?" said Mrs. Barstow. "All hope is not lost if, among Roger's new companions can be found this worthy benefactor. Excellent person, to give us back our Jane!" She poured her daughter a little more tea and pushed the sandwich plate toward her. "You must not yet despair over Roger, darling," she urged. "We must all make allowances, I suppose, for the disappointment he feels. Such a spirited young man, encountering his first true difficulties in life. His aunt's objections to your marriage must have quite overset him, and thus he gives vent to his feelings in this fashion. Though these are not—the means we would choose—perhaps when more time passes he will put these distractions aside."

Her daughter nodded miserably. "So I thought—so I *hoped* at first. And I did so want to be an encouraging, comforting sort of wife, like you always were to Papa, Mama, when he was ill and heavy-hearted. But when I tried to show sympathy to Roger, it only seemed to...irk him. *I* irked him. After a time it was impossible not to think he regretted marrying me."

"But...you cannot mean you have left him for good, my dear?"

"I don't know," answered Jane, her lip trembling. "Certainly I will return, if he wants me to, or if—you cannot afford to keep me."

"Of course we can afford to keep you," insisted Mrs. Barstow, for all the world as if they had been living high in Iffley with an army of servants and a wing of the cottage allocated to each of them. "You may stay as long as you like. As long as your sense of duty will allow. And Roger may join us, too, if he would prefer."

Adela could not smother a little squeak at this generous offer, but for the first time that day she almost laughed. Well, and why not? If Lord Dere must be made to bear his intended bride's eloping sister and the household tutor's imprisoned father, what more would one drunken, gambling, rowdy brother-in-law be? Good heavens.

"Roger will not join us," choked Jane.

Her mother regarded her with raised brows. "How certain you sound! Is it because his work will not permit his absence?"

"He has no work, Mama. How can he, as I have described him?"

"Then why do you say he will not join you, my dearest?"

Another, longer sigh escaped Jane, and she hung her head, hands clutched and uneasy. When she spoke again they had to bend to hear her. "He will not join me. He will not leave London. He *cannot* leave London, you see. Because—I'm afraid—he has been imprisoned."

"Imprisoned?" gasped Mrs. Barstow.

"F-For debt. He is in the Fleet."

A shriek escaped Frances at this revelation, and she clapped her hands to her mouth, goggling at Adela. No one but Adela took any notice of the girl's dramatic manner, however, because the rest of them were too horror-struck themselves. When Frances' shout faded away, a silence hung in the parlor, but only briefly. Then, like a soap bubble popping, it gave way to a din of questions and protests and more crying (from Jane and Mrs. Barstow). Poppet even woke from his nap to race around the room, barking.

Only Adela was silent. She could not have spoken to save her life because her throat was filled with a wild flutter. If she had not already been seated she would have collapsed.

The Fleet?

The Fleet *Prison*, in London?

Mr. Merritt now imprisoned where Mr. Weatherill had spent so much of his life?

And who was this "benefactor" Jane had referred to, one who could ill afford to share his funds with them?

It could not be.

And yet it surely *must*. Else why would Mr. Weatherill ride back to Oxfordshire in the same London coach? That could not have been mere chance, could it?

If he was the benefactor, how wretched I was to him! No, no—he was wretched to me. I did what I did to protect him, to be his benefactor, and he sneered at me. He called me a liar, in so many words, for catching at the baron. Desperately, Adela tried to hold on to her anger, but the more she grappled with it, the more it eluded her.

"—But tell us what it was like, Jane," Gordy was urging his sister, "living inside a prison!"

"Gordon Walter Barstow," his mother reprimanded him, "don't you see your sister is distressed?"

"I'm sorry, Jane," the boy said. "I don't mean to upset you. I only wondered—"

"Was it a Mr. Weatherill who helped you leave London?" Adela cut across her brother, her color high. "Jane, was a Mr. Weatherill your bene-factor?"

Belatedly Mrs. Barstow and Sarah Barstow remembered the poor tutor's welfare, and Adela could almost hear the *click* in their brains when the same pieces fell into place and the same conclusions were drawn.

As for Jane, she inhaled so sharply she coughed, and the alarmed round-ness of her tear-reddened eyes answered Adela's question even before she could reply. "He—ahem! ahem! He did not want it to be known directly. But yes, he said his name was Gerard Weatherill and that he was acquainted with my family and tutored Gordy. It was he who asked me to refer to him simply as a benefactor. He said he would tell you all himself be-cause—well—I suspect for the same reason I did not like to tell you about Roger. For the shame of it. As it is, now he will think I could not be trusted with a confidence."

"We will not press you for details, then," her mother assured her, though Adela wanted nothing more in all her young life than to press Jane for details. What if Mr. Weatherill would not trouble to explain himself now, now that he and Adela had fallen out?

If he will not, I will tell him I will pump Jane for information, Adela vowed inwardly. *Because if I do not learn all, I will* scream. *Gordy's curiosity will be nothing, in comparison to mine.*

"But oh, how very kind of Mr. Weatherill, to help you and Roger, Jane," Sarah spoke up. "He has been more than an acquaintance to us, because we applied to him when we learned you were in London. We asked him to ask his friends there if they had word of you..."

She trailed off, but Adela took up the thread at once. "We learned already, Jane—or at least we deduced it—that Mr. Weatherill must himself be—er—familiar with the Fleet." In as few words as she could, she explained his connection to William Keele and Mr. Keele's recent fame. "So you see you needn't fear exposing Mr. Weatherill. The deed is already done, and not by you."

"Yes, yes, Adela," cried Mrs. Barstow. "And how ungrateful I have been, forgetting him in the midst of this! What a very good young man, to seek you out, Jane, when he went up to visit his father. Dear me—Della, Mr. Weatherill's father must still be a prisoner in the Fleet, if he met Jane and Roger by chance there."

Adela regarded Jane closely. "Is he, Jane? Did you ever hear of another Weatherill there? It is no violation of Mr. Gerard Weatherill's confidence to tell us because we have guessed all his story ourselves."

But it was not fear of being thought a babbler which made Jane hesitate. No, it was the apprehension she always felt when her husband's purported enemy was named.

"Yes," she confessed, shrinking. "Yes, there is a Robert Weatherill there."

Gordon whistled in awe. "My own tutor with a father in debtor's prison!" he exclaimed. "Wait till I tell Peter and Wardour and Ellis and Denver!"

"Gordon!" his older womenfolk turned on him as one.

"You mustn't!"

"Don't you dare say a word!"

"Gordy, I will snap you in two if you gossip about Mr. Weatherill," Frances threatened.

"All right, all right," he said, raising his hands in surrender. "Though if Weatherill's Mr. Keele really *is* in the newspaper, everyone at the rectory will know soon enough. Say, Mama, do you suppose Mr. Terry will have to teach Peter and me forever now, because I think it would be great larks to have a tutor who lived in the Fleet!"

Mrs. Barstow shook her head mournfully. "You're right, Gordy. Everyone will know soon enough about Mr. Weatherill. And though I think my cousin Lord Dere a good-hearted sort, I doubt Mr. Weatherill will remain your tutor. Will he, Della? Did you manage to see the baron when you and Frances called at Perryfield earlier?"

Before Adela could think of answering, Jane blurted, "Oh, no, Mama! Do you really think Lord Dere will dismiss Mr. Weatherill? Would he be so cruel? Mr. Weatherill cannot help where he grew up! He cannot help having had a father such as Rob Weatherill."

"Is that his name, dear?" asked her mother. "No, poor Mr. Gerard Weatherill cannot justly be blamed for what was outside his control, but the world *will* blame him nonetheless. And my cousin must think of the duty owed his family and his name."

"If that is so, Mama," said Jane slowly, "then it is not only Mr. Weatherill who will be censured. I should not have come to Iffley. How will it be any more acceptable for the baron to house the wife of a Fleet debtor than the son of one?" Her gaze swept the beloved faces gathered around her. "I will go back," she declared. "No one need know anything. Mr. Weatherill will not expose me. I could not bear it if you had to leave here, leave this charming situation, and it was my fault! Oh, Mama, how selfish—how blind I've been!"

Throwing herself at Mrs. Barstow, she was at once wrapped in her mother's arms, with all manner of assurances and vows murmured over her, while everyone else gave way to varying levels of tears, and they were all as miserable as they had been happy such a short time ago.

Everyone except Adela.

She dashed from her lashes the few drops which threatened to fall and rose to her feet.

The moment was upon her.

Frances saw it immediately and left off her own sobs to take her oldest sister's hand. She squeezed it in what she meant to be a comforting manner, but in truth her grip was painfully tight.

"Don't cry, Jane, Mama," Adela said loudly, glad to find her voice so steady. "All of you—don't cry. Jane will not have to go anywhere, and neither will we."

As always, Adela's words carried weight with her family, and they fell quiet, but doubt mixed with their hopeful attention. Seeing the questions rising to their lips, she went on.

"I *did* speak to Lord Dere this afternoon," she began carefully, "though I had no opportunity to mention Mr. Weatherill. In any case, Mr. Weatherill has come back to Perryfield himself. He arrived just as Frances and I were about to take our leave."

"Did the baron or Mrs. Dere know yet about—what we saw in the paper?" asked Sarah.

"They did not seem to. Yet." Adela balled her fists. "Mr. Weatherill will tell them himself, I daresay. You see, Lord Dere and I had no time to talk of Mr. Weatherill because—because there was something else to discuss first."

How Adela could dance with impatience when people beat about the bush; yet here she was, doing precisely that! *Go on, then, you coward! It's not going to say itself.*

It might not say itself, but nearly as effective was a fifteen-year-old sister to say it for you.

"Della and Lord Dere are engaged!" cried Frances.

Glaring at the girl, Adela braced for a hurricane of noise to break out, but there was only disbelief and perplexity. And then Gordon laughed. "What stuff, Frances! Della and that old fellow." The others joined in, chuckling with relief, only to die out, one by one, in the face of Adela's sternness.

Sarah was the first to find her voice. "You can't mean it."

"It's true," said Adela, her chin lifting. "He—Lord Dere—announced it to Mrs. Dere and Mr. Weatherill and—and to Frances. It's true. It's done."

Having never seen nor met Lord Dere, Jane could only look at each of them in turn, from her mother's silently working mouth to Sarah's dismay to the younger children's frank puzzlement.

Gordon frowned, working it out. "Will you be Peter's great-aunt, then, Della? Step-great-aunt?"

"Hush," hissed Frances, releasing Adela's hand so she could dash over and shake a menacing finger in his face.

Pale and dazed, Mrs. Barstow got to her feet and took Frances' place, even clutching the same sore hand. "I did not know he thought of proposing to you," she said simply.

Adela reddened at that, knowing full well Lord Dere had not, in fact, thought of it. She gave an awkward shrug. "I suspect it will be a surprise to most."

"Tell me you love him, and I will give you my blessing," said Mrs. Barstow.

At this solemn adjuration Adela flinched. But screwing up her courage (or at least her best imitation of it), she replied, "I *will* love him, Mama.

Eventually. I am determined. And for the present I esteem him greatly. Indeed, apart from his age, I see nothing anyone you could object to. I do not doubt many will call me very, very fortunate."

But rather than appearing reassured by this speech, Mrs. Barstow shook her head sadly. "Oh, my Adela."

"So you see," Adela continued stoutly, "neither we nor Jane need go anywhere. I will speak to—the baron—and he will understand that Jane must be welcomed. It will be a case of 'love me, love my dog.'"

She had not expected any of her family to rejoice at her news, but the general glumness which met her announcement was worse than she imagined.

Sarah lowered Bash to the carpet, propping him carefully upright, like a plump little pyramid. Instantly his auntie Maria sprang from her seat to sit behind her nephew in case he overbalanced, while Sarah opened her workbasket to pull out one of Bash's gowns.

"And what of Mr. Weatherill?" Sarah asked, mild as milk. She drew the needle from where it had been tucked in the cotton and resumed her line of minute stitches. "Will he be another dog for the baron to love?"

Adela's lips parted, but no sound emerged.

Looking up from her sewing, Sarah's gaze sliced neatly through her. She said nothing, one eyebrow lifting just a hair.

Oh, heavens. Adela had the curious feeling that Sarah had opened a door to her heart and was inspecting its contents. *Heavens, heavens,* thought Adela. *She* knows.

CHAPTER 22

Who hath believed our report? and to whom is the arm of the Lord revealed?
— Isaiah 53:1, *The Authorized Version* (1611)

The rector's wife Mrs. Terry was the first to descend on Perryfield. Not from any malicious intent—indeed, she quite liked the tutor Mr. Weatherill—but rather to give warning.

Wood admitted her, his ordinarily expressionless face uncharacteristically expression-full, but Mrs. Terry paid no heed and even hurried ahead of him to the drawing room. And there she found Mrs. Markham Dere, not even standing to receive her. Indeed, the woman looked like she had suffered a blow to the head, for she sprawled—there was no other possible word for it—in an armchair, no work in her hands and her composure in pieces.

"Mrs. Dere!" cried the rector's wife, going to her side at once. "Are you quite all right? Shall Wood here fetch you a glass of wine?"

She didn't move. "Go away, Wood," came the dull response. And then, raising empty eyes to her visitor: "You've heard, I gather? I suspect it's all over the kingdom by now."

"For mercy's sake," clucked Mrs. Terry, contrarily inclined to make light of the situation, if Mrs. Dere were going to be so melodramatic. She plopped into the nearest chair and arranged her skirts. "Hiring any person, unless you know him beforehand or know and trust his family beforehand, involves risk, Mrs. Dere. I allow that you have discovered more than the usual amount of...unfortunate information, but nobody will blame you for it. We were all taken in."

Mrs. Dere's handsome face creased in puzzlement. "What on earth are you talking about, Mrs. Terry?"

Mrs. Terry's rosebud mouth popped open, awareness dawning on her that she had put her foot in it again, and Mr. Terry would have something to say about it. But the lot was cast now, at any rate, so she might as well forge ahead.

"Forgive me, Alice. I was referring to what is apparently in all the papers. That the Mr. Keele who authored *Antiquities of Egypt*—the same Mr. Keele who figured so largely in the life of your tutor Mr. Gerard Weatherill—"

"Yes, yes, what of him? Honestly, Mrs. Terry, I have much on my mind at present and don't want to hear another word about that worthless book everyone wants."

"You will want to hear this," returned Mrs. Terry equably. "That same Mr. Keele is discovered to have spent some fifteen years locked up in the Fleet, imprisoned for debts he was unable to repay until the publication of his 'worthless' book."

Sitting bolt upright, it was Mrs. Dere's turn to stare, astonishment warring with skepticism. "This is...in the papers?"

"Both the *Oxford Journal* and the *Morning Chronicle*, I'm afraid. Now, I know your Mr. Weatherill has gone to London—"

"He has returned. This very afternoon."

"Oh! My goodness. And he made no mention of Keele to you or...how Keele's circumstances might have intersected with his own?"

To Mrs. Terry's surprise, Mrs. Dere colored and looked away toward the modest fire. "There was no time. Other matters pressed. But you can be sure I will get to the bottom of the question as soon as I see him." The idea of this confrontation seemed to hearten her, for she drew a deep breath and recovered some of her usual air. Rising, she began to pace the room. "If it is true—why, the audacity of the man! To come among respectable people, posing as a respectable character!"

"In his defense, Mrs. Dere, Mr. Weatherill made no secret of having been educated by Mr. Keele or of later teaching under him."

"And why should he?" the baron's niece retorted. She pressed a hand to her bosom. "*We* have no acquaintance with those who have been in-carcerated! *We,* in our innocence, could have no objection to him being connected with a hundred Mr. Keeles! Lord have mercy! To think I was so taken in by his learned and intelligent reply to my advertisement! To think we have been sheltering a confederate of criminals, if not a criminal himself, under the very roof of Perryfield!"

"Now, now, Mrs. Dere," began the rector's wife, seeing her companion working herself into a state. "I would not call a debtor a *criminal,* per se."

"What else could one call someone who does not pay his creditors, Mrs. Terry? Is it not a form of thievery?"

"According to that definition, madam, I daresay there are many, many thieves at large in England, in every class of people."

"That may be," Mrs. Dere replied coldly, "but such persons will not be tolerated at Perryfield. *Mr. Weatherill* will not be tolerated at Perryfield. Such a person, to be entrusted with the heir to the Dere barony? I thank you for coming to inform me, Mrs. Terry. It was a true, neighborly act."

"Do you mean to dismiss him, then?"

"Of course I mean to dismiss him! And the sooner, the better."

"Mrs. Dere, do not be overhasty," the rector's wife advised. "While it is true Mr. Weatherill was not...open with you, and while it is also true there will be a great deal of talk and—I suppose—scandal, the fact still remains he was a good teacher and popular with your Peter and with Gordon Barstow.

Mr. Terry is always telling me how often they mention him. To dismiss him at once might appear...vindictive."

"How can it be vindictive?" demanded Mrs. Dere. "Do you know the man owes *us* money, Mrs. Terry? For both I and Lord Dere have each of us given him advances on his salary (Lord Dere over my objections). But, once a debtor, always a debtor, I imagine."

Mrs. Terry in fairness could not let this pass. "Now, Mrs. Dere, if Mr. Weatherill has spent time in the Fleet—and it seems we must assume this of him—it cannot have been for his own debts, for he would have been little older than Peter when he went in!"

But the baron's niece merely shrugged. "That may be, but whether it was Mr. Weatherill's own debts which landed him in the Fleet with this Keele person, or whether the debts belonged to his father, the two of them must be as alike as two peas. No. I wash my hands of Mr. Weatherill. But to show you I am not vindictive, we will not call in the debt. Right away, at least."

"There's a mercy," Mrs. Terry sighed. "I always did think it silly, to put someone in prison for debt and expect them somehow to clear themselves, when they were no longer at liberty to work. Well. I am sorry how this has all fallen out. No one will think less of you for having been taken in, Mrs. Dere, for I confess we all found him agreeable enough. I hope he might go on and live honestly and prosper."

The rector's wife had reached the drawing room door before she turned back, her head cocked in curiosity. "By the way, Mrs. Dere, when I arrived, did you think I came to tell you other news? You seemed unlike yourself."

As robust as it had been a moment earlier, Mrs. Dere's self-assurance faltered. "Oh—er—nothing. That is, the baron has...made some decisions affecting the family, which I will leave him to explain. They took me by surprise, is all. Good afternoon, Mrs. Terry. And, if you please, I hope Peter and Gordon may continue a little longer at the rectory with your good husband?"

With a bow of her head, Mrs. Terry withdrew.

Later that evening, a messenger skipped over from Perryfield with a note informing them that Gordon's lessons would continue at the rectory for the time being.

"But why," the boy protested, "if Mr. Weatherill has returned?"

"He injured his eye in some fashion and needs time to recover," explained Adela. It was cowardly, but she did not think she could bear to elucidate. If Mr. Weatherill chose to abandon his post, let *him* explain to his pupils.

After such a day, the family retired earlier than usual, but of course Adela could not sleep. She lay as still and quietly as she could in the bed she shared with her sister-in-law, however, absolutely determined that she would not cry and wake Sarah or Bash.

But when the house was at last utterly still, Adela felt a single, obstinate tear leak from her eye, and her hand stole up to blot it. At once Sarah rolled toward her and whispered, "I hoped you were awake, Della. If you were asleep I think I would have woken you."

"I'm awake."

"Then Della, I will tell you something," said Sarah softly, propping herself on her elbow. "I did not want to say it in front of everyone else, but I must now, or it will be on my conscience."

"Dear me," murmured Adela, striving for lightness. "Were you too a prisoner in the Fleet, before you met Sebastian?"

"I am quite serious, Della, and you must be serious too."

"All right," answered her sister-in-law meekly, but she could not help shrinking in trepidation. "Say away."

She heard Sarah take a deep breath.

"It's this, Della: I don't think you should marry Lord Dere until you are certain you can love him. I know he's a good man and so forth, but he must be older than Mrs. Barstow and at least thirty years older than you! Think, Della. Think what your life will be, if you do not love him."

With a groan, Della folded her pillow over her head, wishing she could bellow, "Get thee behind me, Satan!"

"I know why you're doing it," Sarah went on, still audible through the pillow. "To protect us. But Della, we would do better to tell Lord Dere the whole truth about Jane and trust to his native kindness."

"You forget Mrs. Markham Dere," growled Adela. She could have argued with Sarah's interpretation of affairs, but she knew it would be wasted breath. "We could never prevail over Mrs. Dere because *he* could never."

Sarah fell back against her own pillow with a sigh, and the room was silent, apart from the occasional rattle of the window or creak of the cottage. When several minutes passed, Adela thought she had won the battle, though she was aware of a contrary twinge of disappointment that both her mother and Sarah yielded so easily. Would there be no one, then, to save her from her self-appointed fate?

But her sister-in-law had only been thinking. Because she rolled onto her side once more and thrust a hand from under the covers. "Give me your hand, Della."

"Why? The room is cold."

"Give it to me. I want to ask you something, and I need to feel your pulse when I do."

"What sort of interrogation will this be?" Adela asked warily. "You're making me apprehensive, and my pulse has already jumped as a result." She obeyed, however, and felt Sarah press a finger to her wrist.

"Darling Adela, what are you so afraid I will ask, that your pulse speeds like this?"

"Whatever it is, get it over with," Adela replied. "This has been a trying day."

"Very well," agreed Sarah. "I will come to the point. My question is only this: ought you to marry the baron, when it is Mr. Weatherill you care for?"

She had no chance to measure the great leap in Adela's pulse which followed, unfortunately, for the simple reason that Adela snatched her hand back as if from a glowing stove.

"And there is my answer," murmured Sarah dryly.

"How did you know?" Adela hissed. "How could you possibly have guessed?"

"I've got eyes, haven't I?" Sarah answered with a rueful chuckle. "Or call it a suspicious nature. It was not so long ago that your brother won my heart, so I still recognize the symptoms."

"But I've told no one! *You* must tell no one! Not a soul, Sarah Barstow, do you hear me?"

"Who would I tell?" Sarah fluttered her fingers through the bar of moonlight falling across their beds. "But listen to me, Della. It is one thing to marry Lord Dere when your heart is your own, and another altogether to do it when you no longer have a heart to give."

"Certainly I have a heart to give," insisted Adela stubbornly. "Nobody else wants it. Nobody else claims it."

"That doesn't mean it's still in your possession," her sister-in-law sighed. "Your brother is lost to me now, but I still love him. My heart's gone missing, though Sebastian will never claim it again."

Sarah's voice cracked, and Adela felt her own throat tighten. *Ah, Sebastian.*

Quietly, Sarah cleared her throat, and when she spoke again her voice was steadier. "Have you said anything to Mr. Weatherill?"

"Are you mad? Of *course* I haven't!"

"Nor he to you?"

Adela gasped so sharply she choked and had to muffle her coughs in her pillow. "What would he say to me?" she croaked. "Do you think he might—like me a little too?"

"I have not seen him so many times as you," hedged Sarah, not wanting to raise Adela's hopes. "But I do not think him indifferent."

"And yet…" Woefully Adela recalled her last conversation with Mr. Weatherill. He had not sounded a bit like a man in love with her. Not that she knew what a man in love with her would sound like. If anything, the curate Mr. Liddell, whom she had once thought herself attached to, had sounded far friendlier than Mr. Weatherill. Not just *sounded* friendlier—Mr. Liddell had *been* friendlier. Adela could not remember arguing with him even once; whereas she and Mr. Weatherill argued with some frequency.

But Mr. Liddell gave you no chance *to argue. He simply defected.*

So there was that.

"What would you do in my place, Sarah?" asked Adela. "Let my family leave Iffley, to go heaven knows where? Were I to give up Lord Dere, doing so would not therefore gain me Mr. Weatherill."

"Perhaps not," returned Sarah, "but marrying Lord Dere will most definitely place Mr. Weatherill forever out of reach."

"It doesn't matter, Sarah," Adela said fiercely, her fists knotting. "He told me this afternoon he was going in any case."

"Going away!" echoed Sarah, more loudly. In his cradle Bash stirred and smacked his lips, and his mother lowered her voice. "Because he is afraid of Mrs. Dere?"

"I thought so—and I told him I would speak to the baron for him—but he wouldn't hear of it. He says that, now his secrets are known, he wants to make a new start somewhere else. I didn't say anything earlier because I didn't have the heart to tell Gordy straight off."

"But it cannot be so!" Sarah protested. "Where could he possibly go? Without a friend in the world, and with his father still in prison?"

"He says he will advertise for a new post."

"Mr. Weatherill may speak of wanting to make a new beginning, but with such a thunder-cloud forever hovering over him, who will make allowance for it, if not us?"

Adela huffed out a breath. "It is no use saying such things to me, Sarah, for I already agree with you whole-heartedly. But he was quite obstinate about it. And it's no use thinking what you had with Sebastian was something everyone might have, therefore. So you must leave me be, do you understand? Don't tell me to—to throw myself at Mr. Weatherill, or anything of that nature, because I tell you I can't do it."

Or, at least, she couldn't do it for a second time. Was it not humiliating enough that both her knees and her self-esteem were still bruised by having done so with the baron?

She could not see her sister-in-law's face in the darkness, but she imagined the wistful, resigned expression it must bear, for Sarah said nothing. She only stretched her hand out again, patting the coverlet until she found Adela's arm and pressed it lovingly. Then, with a whisper of a sigh, Sarah rolled to face Bash's cradle, laying her same palm against the wicker to feel the warmth imparted by his little flannel-swaddled body.

She would say she is lucky, Adela thought, *always to have this piece of Sebastian to love and keep by her. And maybe she is.*

It was more than Adela would have.

CHAPTER 23

Loud shrieks the soaring Hern.
— James Thomson, *The Seasons* (1744)

Adela woke early the following morning (if she had slept at all), drawn and tired.

What did one do, when one became engaged to a baron? On the one hand, she was dying to know what was happening at Perryfield, and, on the other, she never wanted to go near Perryfield again. Surely she must let Lord Dere choose how and when and where they would next see each other. After what had passed between them, Adela thought appearing unbidden again at the Great House would *finish* her.

A peek through the shutters showed her only the faintest brightening on the eastern horizon. Still early. Only Irving and Reed were up, the manservant fetching wood and Reed banging around in the kitchen, and Adela quickly decided she would don her cloak and heavy boots and go for a walk in Iffley Meadow before breakfast, following the winding Thames.

The morning was cold but not frosty and bid fair to be sunny by afternoon. Adela slipped through the turn-wicket, feeling her spirits lift as she tramped through the damp grasses. The hay-mowers had been through in August, of course, but closer to the river the untouched sward brushed her knees. While the walk could change nothing in her circumstances, the fresh, sweet air, combined with the exercise, restored her color and even a touch of her youthful optimism.

What if she were to tell the baron she did not wish to be married for at least a year? Anything might happen in a year, and by then even Jane's scandal would have been discussed to death. Jane might be pointed at and whispered about as a caution to other young ladies, but surely even Mrs. Markham Dere would be resigned to her ongoing residence at Iffley Cottage.

Yes, she would ask him for time. Would it be better to ask for the whole year at once, or to put Lord Dere off by snatches?

Before Adela could decide, a shout rent the morning peace, followed by muffled cursing. Oh, dear—how near that sounded! The sun was just beginning to clear the horizon, shooting forth rays of pink and peach, but among the trees by the river the shadows were still thick. Adela's heart thumped, and she glanced about in vain for a stick or other possible weapon she might wield. Unless she were to clamber over the wall at some farther point and take the long way back to the cottage, she must pass the person on her return. Well, for an unaccompanied young lady there was no choice in the matter, and she had crept some yards away from the voice before her conscience stopped her. Suppose the person had injured himself?

With a sigh she turned back, emerging from the tree-lined riverbank and treading the damp grass again toward the turn-wicket.

In half a minute she saw him.

"Mr. Weatherill?" she breathed.

Later she would think it must be an effect of love, that she would be able to recognize him from behind, in dim light, at a distance of over a hundred yards. For he was hunched awkwardly, tugging at something.

Though she had not spoken loudly, sound carried in the morning hush, and his head turned at once, revealing the eye patch, if she needed further confirmation. "Miss Barstow?"

"What are you doing here, sir?" she asked, rushing forward as quickly as uneven ground, wet grass, and patches of mud would allow. "Are you hurt?"

"I was walking, waiting until a decent hour to post my letters with Mrs. Lamb, and I seem to have stepped into a badger's hole. My boot is caught in something—let us pray it is not the badger's teeth—so that I can't free myself."

"Let me help you," Adela said, bending immediately to tug at his boot.

"Miss Barstow," he protested, "you will get muddy."

"A little mud is nothing," she panted, gritting her teeth and tugging harder. "I am just relieved you are not a highwayman or a vagrant. Are you pulling, Mr. Weatherill?"

"Of course I'm pulling, can't you tell?"

She could, in fact, tell. Adela Barstow had never clutched a young man's leg (or any man's leg, as far as she knew), and even through the leather of his boot she could feel the living, tensing hardness of it, a realization which brought the crimson to her cheeks.

"Well, that isn't working—perhaps if you were to relax your—your—*limb* instead...?"

Relaxing proved no more effective, however, and Adela soon released him and straightened to catch her breath. "Heavens. I don't know what you were doing, to get so stuck. I know I've stepped in a badger hole before and just stepped right out again."

He gave a rueful grin. "I would guess I'm at least three or four stone heavier than you, Miss Barstow, which makes a difference when stamping around in meadows."

"So it seems." Tapping her chin, she assumed her best older-sister voice. "If pulling on your foot failed, I suppose next we must pull on *you*."

"Who is 'we'?"

But Adela was already behind him. Shutting her eyes briefly for courage, she flung her arms about his waist and *hauled*.

Shlo-o-o-o-o-pwop!

At one go, the badger hole relinquished Mr. Weatherill (who roared with the wrench to his ankle), sending him tumbling backward against Adela, who tumbled in turn to the wet grass, Mr. Weatherill sprawled atop her so that they looked like a stack of overturned crabs.

"Adela!" he cried, scrambling up (and accidentally elbowing her in the ribs so that she yelped). "Blast! Have I injured you?"

Slowly, she rose to her feet and took stock. Her bonnet hung by its ribbons; her hair was half fallen; her leather gloves were streaked with dirt; her cloak was wet, with so many blades of marsh grass stuck to it that it might have been an embroidery pattern. But it was Mr. Weatherill's appearance which made Adela catch her breath, only to release it the next second in a whoop of laughter.

For he stood there, equally mud-spattered, one boot on and one boot off. The bootless foot was encased only in a much-darned stocking, and Mr. Weatherill seemed reluctant to put it down, leaving him posed like a species of heron.

"Dear me," laughed Adela. "At least here is proof the badger did not bite off your toes." Extracting the boot from the burrow was a simpler procedure when it was empty, and when she had done so, she held it out to him.

"Thank you." He debated whether to pull it back on by balancing on one foot, or to flounce down on his backside in the grass, but the first option would likely involve undignified hopping about and the second would soil his greatcoat.

"You had better hold on to me," said Adela, guessing his thoughts.

After the slightest hesitation, he did so, his hand descending on her shoulder. He meant just to rest it there—applying only the minimum pressure to stay upright—but he had not counted on the unevenness of the marshy ground, nor the pain which shot through his ankle when he pointed his foot to insert it in the boot.

"Fire and brimstone!" cursed Weatherill, clenching Adela's shoulder until she squeaked and twisted away. With the loss of his buttress, over he toppled again, landing hard on his side, one bruised rib meeting squarely with a large clod of dirt.

"Mercy!" cried Adela, as further oaths rained down on her. "What a morning! I am so terribly sorry, Mr. Weatherill, but your fingers dug in so hard I thought they would break the skin."

"No," he said faintly. "Please—forgive my language. It's my fault. I must have sprained my ankle in the confounded badger hole. That hurt like the dickens. And I have a few lingering aches in my side from—er—when I hurt my eye."

Remembering her earlier resentment of his vague account, she regarded him sternly. "That's right. You said you 'ran into something.' Something which blackened your eye and tore the knee out of your—inexpressibles—and, apparently, made you sore about the ribcage. What an extraordinary 'something' that must have been."

Since he was already on the ground, he set his jaw and pulled his boot back on, inch by painful inch, and when she saw him blanch and wince, Adela relented. "I'm sorry again, Mr. Weatherill. It's none of my business, I suppose."

But he surprised her. "I will tell you now. Why not? You know the worst. I did not, in fact, run into anything, apart from a couple of charming miscreants in my visit to the Fleet," he sighed, rising first to his knees and then to his good leg, with only the toe of his injured foot touching the ground.

"Is it truly so rough there?" marveled Adela.

A humorless smile. "Not in the way you mean. It's entirely possible to go for years in the Fleet without a violent hand being laid on one, though there are assaults of other kinds." He made a bow. "Witness my ungentlemanlike expletives. I imagine in a swearing match I could hold my own against any man in England, simply from having heard abundant and various imprecations all my days." Slapping at his coat to dislodge the looser dirt, he shook his head. "You see, Miss Barstow, perhaps I really am not the sort of person one wants around young boys with unformed character."

"Nonsense!" she blurted, her earlier displeasure with him entirely forgotten in the face of this self-directed attack. "I have never heard you use improper language before, and when pain is involved, every man deserves leniency."

"Thank you," he said quietly. "You are gracious."

This made her color, for she knew very well all the ungracious thoughts she had had for him the day before. Apologetic words rose to her lips, but he anticipated her.

"Miss Barstow, I hope your grace will extend yet further, because I would like to beg your pardon for how I spoke yesterday. When you said you would defend me to the baron, I mean. Instead of recognizing your offer as an act of friendship, I was too preoccupied with my own...discomfiture to recognize it as such. Nor was it my place to...denigrate your engagement to Lord Dere."

Adela had lifted a hand to forestall him, but she withdrew it again at this. "Please, Mr. Weatherill. I confess I was resentful of your remarks, but it is *I* who should beg pardon. I should not have assumed you would welcome any interference with Mrs. Dere. After all, your life is your story to tell, not mine."

This drew a rueful laugh. "But that's just it, isn't it? My life story has always been something I wanted *no one* to tell, not even myself. But now it is told, whether I like it or not. And Mrs. Dere has asked me—quite politely and reasonably, in all consideration—to move on from Perryfield."

"Oh!" she gasped. "So soon? But who told her? She doesn't read the papers. I thought it would not be until Sunday at church that she learned."

"Mrs. Terry brought the news, according to Mrs. Dere, but you mustn't think ill of her for it. Apparently she preached forbearance, to Mrs. Dere's indignation. It makes no difference in the end. I have here in my pocket my advertisement to send to several newspapers, as well as—word to my father."

"Do you mean to go back to London, then?" asked Adela, hoping he didn't hear the forlorn note in her voice. How much longer would he remain in Iffley? A fortnight? A week?

"It is the only other place I have acquaintances," he answered. "But, Miss Barstow, despite all the mishaps of the morning, I am glad I met you here. That is, I am glad for this chance to say...good-bye."

Adela clutched at her cloak, suddenly breathless, as if a great serpent had streaked unseen through the vegetation to coil about her. "Good-bye?" she squeaked. "Surely Mrs. Dere does not turn you out immediately?"

The sun had risen above the horizon now, however, and he turned to regard her thoughtfully. Seeing his uncovered eye narrow against the light, Adela thought he must be remembering his unpleasant confrontation with Mrs. Markham Dere, but in truth he was only thinking of how the rosy light played across Adela's features and wondering if this was the last time he would ever see her. Though he had not come into Iffley Meadow expecting to encounter her that morning, he knew she occasionally walked there, and he had hoped it. One thing was certain: he would never have left without one final glimpse, one final attempt to restore friendship between them, so they might always remember each other without hostility.

"In so many words, she does not," he admitted. "But I can hardly continue lurking on the second floor and eating the baron's bread when I have no right to it."

"Oh, Mr. Weatherill! Are you absolutely certain you don't want me to speak to him? Even now I know I can prevail, if only you wish it."

"But I do not wish it," he said lightly, still watching the glow of her brown eyes as she entreated him. What—stay on and torture himself? Stay on, knowing he was there on sufferance, because the woman he loved begged for it? Begged for it and was granted it, because she asked it of her fond betrothed.

Never.

She gave one dip of chin in acceptance, her lashes lowered and her nails digging into her palms through her gloves to keep herself from shedding tears. It was a long moment before she could trust herself to speak again.

"Very well. Then, yes, I too am glad we are reconciled before you—go. Only—how will you live, until you have found a new position? Mr. Weatherill—as a last act of friendship, for all your kindness to—us—to all the Barstows, won't you let us give you a little...gift to smooth your way?"

Gerard would have laughed at this, if he weren't closer to crying. "A gift from the Barstows, out of their vast wealth?" he teased. "Thank you, but I tell you there is no need. The ever-generous Lord Dere pressed a parting sum into my hands, as if I did not already owe him money (which I have sworn to repay). Pressed it on me, even as he peeped in fright over his shoulder, lest Mrs. Dere catch him distributing largesse."

"Did he really?" cried Adela, raising delighted eyes to him, and tears sparkled on her lashes in spite of herself. "How good and kind and generous he is!"

This spontaneous praise of his rival infuriated him, as did his awareness of his own ingratitude toward the baron, and he wished he held the sum in his hands that very instant so he could hurl it across the Thames. *Confound the man, and confound his goodness, kindness and generosity!*

But with no sack of treasure ready to hand, Weatherill did the next best thing in his rage: he seized Adela by both shoulders and crushed her to him, his mouth coming down hard on hers so that their teeth knocked together. She would have shrieked with surprise, if it had been possible, but his lips pressed so hungrily to hers that it was *not* possible, especially since Adela found herself kissing him back with all her might.

Gerard didn't even feel his bruised ribs, though she strained so tightly against him, but when her arms flew up to circle his neck, he tried to steady them by putting down his bad foot. Pain shot up his leg, eliciting a groan from him as it crumpled beneath their combined weight.

"Mr. Weatherill!" she panted atop his chest, as she tried to slide off. "I've hurt you again. I forgot—your ankle—"

"Never mind it," he growled, pulling her back against him, careless of the damp grass cold against his back. "Kiss me, Adela."

She obeyed.

In all her life she had never so abandoned restraint. Her weight on him, the cold, the dank air, the public setting—all went for nothing as they lay in the meadow together, his person pressed to hers, his mouth pressed to hers, his breath mingling with hers. Adela felt his fingers winding in her hair, heard him murmuring unintelligible endearments—or was that her?

It was madness.

Sweet madness.

The sound of a coach rattling down Wallingford Way jolted them to awareness. Though they could not see it, the rhythm of the horses' hooves and the blast of the coachman's horn carried easily to their ears.

"It's the mail," Weatherill said, rolling her gently to his side and struggling to rise.

"Your eye patch," said Adela, scrambling up herself to retrieve it. "Ah, poor darling, look at it." She traced one gentle finger over the discoloration, and he caught her hand to kiss her palm.

"Marry me, Adela," he urged.

Her mouth fell open in astonishment, and he could not resist bending to kiss her again, but this time she drew back. "What are we doing? Don't—we can't."

"I know we can't marry now. Not yet. I have no position, no money, no home to offer you, my dearest—"

But she was already shaking her head vehemently, sanity returning like a dousing of icy water. "No. *No.* What was I thinking? What was I doing? I must go now. We will be seen together." Even as she spoke she was pinning her hair up and shaking out her cloak and looking every direction in trepidation.

"Adela, listen to me—" he grasped her wrist to still it. "I know it will be years before we can marry, but I will work so hard for you. I will—"

"Stop, Mr. Weatherill, I beg you!" she pleaded, wrenching from his hold. "It cannot be. You know it cannot. I am already engaged, and I must stay engaged. I must think of my family. I should not have—kissed you like that. It was dishonest. It was wrong."

"It was the truest thing you've done since you came to Iffley."

"Don't, Gerard. *Don't.* Please. You know everything must stay as it is. You and I cannot marry—we cannot afford to. Nor can my family afford to be driven away, as you have been. I was wrong to kiss you."

"You kissed me because you love me, Adela, as I love you."

But she was tying her bonnet strings and backing away. "It can't be. It can't be. I'm so sorry. Forgive my—my—unconstraint. My foolishness. Mr. Weatherill, I wish you all joy. I will—I will never forget you."

And then, with one last, longing look at him, the back of her hand to her lips to stop further speech, she turned and fled for the turn-wicket.

CHAPTER 24

From the Year are all its Honours fled,
And dull November rears his gloomy Head.
— Thomas Fitzgerald, *Poems on several occasions* (1781)

In later years, Adela would think of the weeks which saw October turn to November, and then the days of November ticking by, one by one, as the longest of her life.

"Certainly I will not press you for an early date, if you do not wish it, Adela," said the baron with courtly courtesy as he sat with her in the parlor of Iffley Cottage on the afternoon of the badger-hole incident, "but as to keeping the engagement quiet, I'm afraid it's too late for that. While I have not spoken to anyone beyond my niece about the matter, the servants at Perryfield—er—witnessed things, you will recall..."

"Of course. The servants." She twisted her handkerchief in her lap. "The news is likely all over the county by now, then."

"I confess I was congratulated by both servants and sundry people whom I passed in walking here."

Adela smothered a sigh and tried to appear shyly pleased, rather than despondent. When she had stolen home from her unexpected meeting in the meadow, there was no privacy available at Iffley Cottage, so she had taken it upon herself to spend hours in the kitchen pickling onions, that she might slice and slice and weep and weep, with no one the wiser. (Or so she imagined. If she had really given any thought to it, she would have noticed what a wide berth her family gave her and how Mrs. Barstow and Sarah conspired to intercept anyone who might interrupt.)

Now she sat, puffy-eyed, outwardly placid, and smelling faintly of vinegar, to receive her exalted beau.

"Has Mrs. Dere...recovered from her surprise?" she asked.

The baron's face gave him away, but he quickly smoothed his features. "Naturally she will need time to adjust, though she has only been mistress of Perryfield a few months. She would not be blamed for thinking it unlikely she would be supplanted. I have been a bachelor so long, you know."

In spite of her woes, curiosity stirred. "Did you never think of marrying when you were younger, sir?"

"Oh, naturally. But the girl I thought of thought of someone else in turn. And old story, I wager. And then the years passed, and somehow I never came so near again."

Regarding him, Adela wondered again that, in all those years, no girl ever set her cap for him, eligible as he still was, and with a flicker of her usual humor she said, "If only they had known the softness of your heart, sir, and how, when bidden at last to think of marriage, you did not show much resistance."

But he shook his head, smiling. "You must not underrate yourself, my dear Adela, simply because my thoughts did not tend that way until you...urged them to. I certainly was already disposed in your favor, being very pleased with all my new tenants at Iffley Cottage. And I have greatly enjoyed our conversations about music and entomology."

And there will be many more of those, I warrant. A lifetime of them.

"Moreover," he continued, "seeing how your family relies on you and looks to you, I can imagine how your presence would greatly add to a man's happiness and the happiness of his home."

Whatever Lord Dere's feelings toward her had been before she compromised him, in any event, he seemed resigned to his fate now, and Adela forced an answering smile.

Be fair, she chided herself. *Before you kissed Mr. Weatherill, you told anyone who asked that you* could *and* would *learn to love the baron. Lord Dere is still the same kind, generous old man you admired, and it is certainly not his fault you did what you did, or that Mr. Weatherill did what he did or said what he said.*

Though what was done could not be undone, it could be pushed from her mind, Adela vowed. Forgotten. Uphill work, yes, work which might require years to complete, but she was resolved.

Or would be resolved. Soon. When she was done bursting into secret tears.

Around the edge of the door Adela spied a dark hazel eye and eyebrow belonging to her sister Jane. The eye blinked; the eyebrow rose. Then both vanished.

That was right. When Irving had scuttled in to announce the baron's barouche approaching, every Barstow scrambled to escape the parlor, save Outlaw, who was curled up on a cushion asleep. Jane alone ran back, but only to hiss, "*Please* tell him about Roger being in the Fleet, Della, so we may know our doom as soon as possible!" And then she was gone again before Adela could even agree.

But such a devastating announcement could hardly be dropped on Lord Dere in the first moments of greeting him, even if Adela were not still flustered from kissing Mr. Weatherill. Indeed, the sight of her official betrothed—neat, silver-haired, quiet, slender, *old*—only made the morning memory more vivid by contrast, and, astonishingly, Adela soon forgot all about her sister's scandal.

Until now.

To give herself something else to look at, Adela picked up the slumbering Outlaw and transferred her to her lap, a disturbance the cat resented at once. With ears pointing angrily backward, Outlaw carelessly extended her claws a fraction of an inch and hopped down.

Fine, Adela resolved. *I cannot even make a cat do what I want. My engagement served no purpose with Mr. Weatherill, but at least let it help Jane.*

"Lord Dere," Adela began, "I thank you for such kind words. That is, I know you don't like me thanking you over and over, but I can't seem to help it. Especially since it always seems to be *you* doing us good, instead of the other way around." When she saw he was on the point of making his usual protests, Adela hurried on. "And I'm afraid there's one more thing I must tell you, sir. Something which doubtless not only Mrs. Dere but also *you* will find...shocking."

He waited attentively but said nothing.

"It—concerns my sister Mrs. Merritt, who I will introduce to you shortly, if you are willing to meet her."

"Why would I not be willing to meet any sister of yours, Adela?"

"Because, you see—Jane—she is not simply here on a visit."

"Is she here permanently, then?" he asked gently. "Do you hesitate because she will be one more person stuffed into Iffley Cottage?"

"No. Nothing like that. Sir, it pains me to tell you that Jane and—Mr. Merritt—her husband—will be living separately for the foreseeable future. Because—because—because—"

"Because the marriage was not a happy one?" he suggested.

"That's right. It wasn't happy." Without Outlaw to occupy her, Adela was thrown back on twisting her hands in her lap. "It wasn't happy because Mr. Merritt...took up some regrettable habits and—and—I'm afraid to tell you, he has been arrested for debt."

Whatever confession the baron had braced himself for, this surpassed it, and he held so still and stared so positively that Adela feared he would suffer a fit, and, not knowing what else to do, she plunged onward, the whole story pouring from her. The elopement. Mr. Merritt's aunt. His allowance cut off. Jane's inadequate pittance. The move to London. The accumulating debts. The suit. The arrest. The Fleet. The conditions therein. Mr. Weatherill discovering their fate, unbeknownst to the Barstows. Mr. Weatherill finding Jane when he went to see his father. Mr. Weatherill arranging for Jane's return.

When all was said, Adela fell silent, her breath coming quickly because all those mentions of Mr. Weatherill had wounded her like so many slashes of a knife. And each slash reminded her that the baron was not the only good, kind, and generous man of Adela's acquaintance.

No. There was another.

But he was gone forever.

Indeed, Mr. Weatherill's departure had been on the baron's tongue when he entered. "Harker set me down here," Lord Dere explained, "before driving poor Weatherill to Oxford, to catch the evening post-coach."

This matter-of-fact announcement took her breath away, and it was all Adela could do not to run to the window for one last, one very last glimpse of him. But she had just enough control of herself to refrain, instead rubbing her eyes briefly and saying something muddled about the onion pickle.

Fond as he was of onion pickle, Lord Dere's thoughts were still on the tutor. "Yes, what a worthy young man that Mr. Weatherill was, despite—or perhaps because of—his painful history. I regret that my niece saw fit to dismiss him, but Peter is her son, after all."

"Yes," murmured Adela.

"Besides which, he did not seem heartbroken by her decision. Indeed, he struck me as anxious to go."

"Oh?"

With a shake of her head to dismiss these thoughts, Adela returned to the present moment, relieved to see the baron had begun to absorb her shocking confession about the Merritts and was now breathing again. A twinge of pity even surprised her. Poor Lord Dere! How the women in his life did threaten his peace! First Mrs. Markham Dere, and now Adela herself.

Rousing himself, the baron drew a deep breath and took her hand in his.

After her engagement, it had been impossible for Adela not to wonder if or when Lord Dere might touch her or try to kiss her. And after kissing Mr. Weatherill, it had been impossible not to dread the event. But the manner in which he held her hand now was not at all horrifying. If anything, she found it contrarily comforting.

"Thank you, Adela, for telling me Mrs. Merritt's sad story," he said in his usual calm voice. "While I do not condemn her for it—she is very young—neither do I believe it needs to be more widely known. There will be food for talk enough, I daresay, if we put it about that the match was not successful. And I think we may trust that Mr. Weatherill will say nothing."

Adela nodded at that. No, Mr. Weatherill would not say anything. It was not Mr. Weatherill she feared, in this instance.

Clutching the baron's hand, she said, "But, sir,—considering how...strongly Mrs. Markham Dere felt about Mr. Weatherill's past, she will surely take great umbrage with Jane's."

To her dismay, her betrothed shrank, the glow of his gallantry fading visibly, and Adela could read clearly how he dreaded facing his commanding niece.

"Yes, yes," Lord Dere muttered. "Alice will have a great deal to say on the subject."

She knew he was picturing Mrs. Dere glaring coldly at him at every meal, stalking after him from room to room, wearing him down with her displeasure.

A tremble went through Adela. Would her great gamble be for naught?

She could not let it be so! If the baron would not fight for her, she must do so herself.

"Sir, shall *I* speak with Mrs. Dere?" she proposed. "I am…your intended wife, after all, and surely she will understand that—that—dreadful as it all is—you could hardly now turn your back on my family."

He nodded, but his color did not improve. Their hands clung together as drowning sailors might grasp at the same inadequate spar.

"Miss Barstow," he croaked, his confident use of her Christian name forgotten, "what would you say if we held your strategy in reserve? That is, suppose we were to keep Mrs. Dere in ignorance of your sister's troubles for as long as possible? She will have enough to say upon learning of the Merritts' separation, I well know. Therefore, let her accustom herself to the idea of our engagement and the enduring connection it will form with your entire family. Let her even become fond of Mrs. Merritt, if that is possible. (I know Miss Frances is a great favorite of hers.) And then, if further details later come to light, you and I will both be in a stronger position to—withstand her."

"Yes, yes," Adela was quick to agree. "There is great wisdom in your plan, sir. Let us do exactly as you propose."

The conspirators' handclasp became a handshake, and they shared rueful smiles before Adela carried his hand to her cheek in gratitude.

Then she rose to call in her family.

As if he had not already done more for them than could be repaid, Mr. Weatherill's final service to the Barstows was the coincidence of his exposure and departure with Jane's return. For Iffley and the Oxford set were far too eager to discuss the tutor's shocking secret, especially in light of his mentor Keele's newfound fame, to spare much attention to the more commonplace tale of a marriage encountering difficulties. Some might declare it was Mrs. Merritt's duty to return to her husband (as Mrs. Dere did *sotto voce* to Mrs. Terry), so long as Merritt did not beat or otherwise abuse her, but this minority was not passionate enough to press the opinion home.

No, Jane was soon permitted to take her place as just another of those attractive Barstow ladies who lived in the baron's cottage, largely at the baron's expense. What a burden so many poor, hapless relations would be, they all agreed, if not for Lord Dere's deep pockets! If that fortunate and wily Adela Barstow knew what was good for her, she would set a date and secure him for once and all. What was the girl waiting for?

Even Mrs. Markham Dere wondered at Adela's delay. While she never spoke the words aloud, she shared the opinion of Adela's great good fortune and cunning, and even marveled inwardly that the girl had been shrewd enough to feign interest in the tutor, to cover her deeper machinations. So why now did she hesitate on the brink? If Mrs. Markham Dere had been in her place, she would have fetched the baron to the altar at once, the sooner to produce the heir who would supplant little Peter Dere! What, indeed, was the girl waiting for?

The girl was waiting for her heart to heal.

As October dribbled into November, as the Barstow lives settled into new routines after the upheavals, as Adela herself sewed and baked and read aloud and attended church and made social calls and admired insects and played music for and occasionally held hands with Lord Dere, she waited. Waited for the memory of Mr. Weatherill to fade. Waited for his face to blur in her mind and his words to require effort to recall. Waited for the dreams, in which he seized her and planted those hard, burning kisses on her lips, to stop altogether.

She waited and waited.

"If this is love," Adela told herself as she walked the Upper Field or the Grove (she had not ventured into the meadows since the fateful morning—she could not bear to), "it is just as well that I do *not* learn to love the baron. I don't think I could stand it."

She was glad to have Jane back, however. Jane, who would walk quietly beside her wherever and however long Adela wished, each sister too absorbed in her own cares to break the silence.

It helped a little when the furore over Mr. Weatherill died down and she did not hear him mentioned at every turn. By All Souls Day Adela congratulated herself that she had not heard Mr. Weatherill's name for an entire week, but her rejoicing was premature, for that very day she suffered through a great, if final, outburst after the church service.

"Gentlemen," the baron addressed the usual gathering outside the west door of St. Mary the Virgin, "if anyone finally cares to peruse the much talked-of *Antiquities of Egypt,* you are welcome to call at Perryfield this week." Holding up his hands as questions flew, he explained, "It arrived in the post, courtesy of Mr. William Keele, and he thanked me for releasing Weatherill from his post here—that was how he put it—because then the young man was at liberty to assist him in the preparation of the second volume. Sadly I could not respond because Keele gave no address, but I have decided I will send my note to the publisher in London."

Adela's heart pounded at this news, and she pressed a fist to her breast, unaware of Sarah putting a hand to the small of her back. Mr. Weatherill working once again with Mr. Keele? Ah, she was glad to know he had found a place of some sort, and surely Mr. Keele could now pay him more than pennies. Perhaps Mr. Weatherill even lodged with the scholar, wherever he was.

She swallowed a growing lump in her throat. The sending of the books must have been at Mr. Weatherill's suggestion. He had done so, knowing the baron would talk about it, and Adela would hear. *Why did he not send his address? There was no need to hide his whereabouts. I can neither write to him nor seek him, and it would have given me comfort to know where he was.*

But no. Her sole comfort must be to know that he was all right. It was, she supposed, a way of saying, *Do not fear for me. Life goes on. My life, and your life.*

That was a day both comforting and wretched for her.

She looked at the volumes the next day at Perryfield—of course she did, with Gordon over her shoulder, but though the plates were beautifully engraved and the scope of the work vast, Adela did not find what she was looking for. There was no inscription, no handwritten marginalia. No private, coded messages.

It was later that same day when she quietly told Lord Dere she thought she was ready now to marry him. "But—must we have the banns read, sir? Though we know every last person at St. Mary the Virgin, somehow I shrink from Mr. Terry announcing it so publicly."

"What would you say, then, to a quiet ceremony?" he suggested. "Terry can recommend us to the bishop for a license, and then we may be married any morning you like, as your fancy takes you."

"Yes, sir. Let us do that. Thank you."

Another fortnight passed. The temperature dropped further, and Irving had to break the ice on the water bucket in the mornings. The Barstows knit woolen stockings, mended the lining of their spencers, and trimmed their black velvet bonnets anew.

As December drew nearer, Mrs. Terry proposed a new date for the children's ball. "Mr. Travers at last declares himself satisfied with Denver's ankle and has given permission for him to put full weight upon it once more," she announced after a dinner at Perryfield. "So what would you say to next Saturday, Lord Dere? I thought we might make it a party for the young people. They could dance and have lemonade and cakes."

The rector's wife thought it delicate to put the question to Lord Dere alone, rather than offend either the current mistress of Perryfield or its future mistress, but that only threw the dilemma upon the baron, and he glanced uneasily from niece to betrothed. Mrs. Dere began at once to swell with preparatory indignation, despite the youngest children cheering the idea, and Adela said quickly, "What would you advise, Mrs. Dere? We Barstows would be happy to assist in any way, whether to bake cakes or accompany the children or dance with them, but you must decide, because much of the onus of a ball falls upon the host."

Mollified by Adela's deference, Mrs. Dere soon condescended to approve the plan, and the days which followed brought a pleasant, distracting bustle. Mrs. Barstow and Sarah sewed Gordon a new coat and breeches; Reed and Jane baked spice and fruit cakes; and Adela and Frances spent several afternoons at Perryfield practicing on the pianoforte, the baron sometimes sitting quietly with a book and listening.

But in the end Mrs. Terry's fond project was not to be. For the very morning of the children's ball, an express came from London for Jane. While Sarah sought for coins to pay the messenger, Jane took one look at the direction of it and turned white as a ghost.

"You read it, Della, please," she whispered.

With shaking hands, Adela unfolded the single sheet.

25 November 1800
The Fleet, London

Dear Mrs. Merit:

Come at once. Your husband has sufferd a bad nock to the head and we feer for his life.

Your umble servant,
Ann Eddings

CHAPTER 25

I was in prison, and ye came unto me.
— Matthew 25:36, *The Authorized Version* (1611)

Though the yellow post chaise which carried them to the Old Bell in Holborn was not as elegant as Lord Dere's private coach, it was a great deal faster and more comfortable than the stagecoaches which had brought the Barstows to Oxford from Twyford. And what ease to have a man accompany them, overseeing the changing of horses and postilions and ensuring Adela and Jane lacked for nothing! In other circumstances, Adela might have enjoyed herself—nay, she *would have* enjoyed herself—for she had not been to London since she was a girl.

But these were not other circumstances. Adela sat snugly between Lord Dere and Jane, neither of whom had much to say, the baron because he was a quiet man and Jane because she was miserable and could not speak of her misery in the baron's presence. He knew the reason for their errand, of course. With Jane's permission, Adela had shown her intended husband the summons and accepted gratefully his offer of aid. The morning coaches had already departed, and the baron advised against the evening one because it was slower and would only have them arrive "tired and bewildered," so the Barstows must wait through the agonizing hours.

"Suppose Roger were to die before we reached him?" whispered Jane, when she crept to her sister's bedside in the darkness. "And I abandoned him?"

Adela whispered back in her ear, so they would not waken Sarah or Bash, "He will not, and you did not, dearest." Adela had a worse fear, however: suppose Roger Merritt were not himself and required nursing the rest of his life? How would she keep Jane from returning to him, or how would his care be paid for? Another burden to throw upon the baron, poor man.

I will repay Lord Dere with love and gratitude, if it takes my whole life to manage! she swore to herself.

The Old Bell was a timber-framed, galleried inn built around a courtyard, one of many coaching inns along Holborn. Lord Dere soon secured the girls a room on the first floor, at the greatest distance possible from the noise of the street and coffee room, and though it was already dark, Jane was most anxious to proceed to the Fleet.

"My poor Mrs. Merritt," the baron told her regretfully, "I'm afraid I would not advise walking these streets at night, and I daresay they will be locking the gates soon. We will go directly tomorrow. You have my word."

What could Jane do but give way? Adela embraced her and murmured encouragement, but she too was uneasy. Added to her concern for her sister, she was vexed with herself, for she could not help thinking of Mr. Weatherill. He had grown up so near here, perhaps walking these streets hundreds of times, where the shabby attire she had first seen him wear would pass all unnoticed. Indeed, she found her pulse speeding whenever any man remotely his size or coloring caught her eye. More reprehensibly, when Adela perused *Antiquities of Egypt*, she had noted the publisher Murray was to be found at Number 32, Fleet Street, and, still more reprehensibly, she had consulted a map and discovered Number 32 stood by Falcon Court, not a stone's throw from the Old Bell.

What is the purpose of knowing this? she demanded of herself. *It is not as if Mr. Weatherill will be sitting in Mr. Keele's publisher's office, and if Mr. Weatherill wanted you to know where he might be found, he could have supplied that information at any time in the last month!*

Therefore Adela made no mention of her knowledge, and, if it might have passed unnoticed, she would have given herself a ruthless pinch every time she turned to scrutinize some man who was absolutely *not* Mr. Weatherill.

The following morning, after a hasty breakfast which Jane hardly touched, they set out.

There was no need for a hackney coach, for the walk was short, though vehicles clogged Holborn and Fleet Market, and some of the passersby were rough. The girls clung to either arm of Lord Dere, Jane trembling and Adela all eyes. (She glanced at a heavy fellow who was at least five stone heavier than Mr. Weatherill and who had an enormous carbuncle by his left eye. This was becoming *ridiculous*.)

And then the outer gate of the Fleet stood open before them.

"Courage, my dears," urged Lord Dere, though Jane could not help herself and was trying not to tug them forward.

When they reached the inner gate, the burly turnkey surprised them by addressing Jane. "Why, it's you again, ain't it, Mrs. Merritt? Thought we saw the last of you and good luck to you, I said. I'm Quint, if you don't recall."

"I remember you," said Jane softly. "Mrs. Eddings wrote to me to say my husband was...unwell."

Quint gave a grim nod. "That's right, ma'am."

"But he's—he's still alive, isn't he? I'm not too late?"

"He's alive," said Quint doubtfully.

"Take us to him at once, my good man," urged the baron, feeling Mrs. Merritt sway against him.

Even if Mr. Weatherill had indeed been present and walking within the prison yard, Adela would not have been able to pick him out among all the wandering souls within the walls of the Fleet, male and female, young and old. The prisoners' expressions struck her as either vacant or cunning, and she leaned closer to Lord Dere as well. This *was the place Mr. Weatherill had known from his earliest years?*

"Surely the prison does not hold so many," ventured the baron to their escort.

Quint glanced about, as if surprised by the remark. Then he shrugged. "There are visitors, like yourselves, but this isn't so many. Those who have the means choose to live out in the rules, and when the court sits, others pay their five shillings to leave for the day. Warden wants security for that, though, in case they think to take themselves off permanent-like."

"Five shillings!" marveled Lord Dere. "They must have important business to transact, to pay so much for a day's leave. If they were to do it often, I wonder how they might repay their original debt."

Another shrug, as he led them up the steps. "Not all hope to walk out of here." With a sidelong glance at Jane he added, "Some are content enough to make their mischief here for a few shillings a week."

Adela too stole a look at her sister, but Jane was pale and withdrawn. The Barstows had never asked the amount of Roger's debts, but even if they were repaid, was Roger one of those "content enough" to make his mischief *here* for the rest of his life?

The wretchedness of the place proved effective in driving Mr. Weatherill from her immediate thoughts, and Adela wondered if she would ever forget the close quarters, the smells, the eyes which followed their progress. Bodies spilled from the tap-room (at this hour!), singing or quarreling with each other. Shouts and curses carried through the passages. Idlers infested the stairs.

Keeping her gaze lowered and staying as close as possible to Lord Dere, she failed to notice the hard look one of the idlers gave the group as he emerged from the billiard room, his eyes traveling from Adela to Jane and back.

At one of the open doors in the gallery, Quint halted and knocked on the jamb. "Eddings? Oh, it's you, Mrs. E. How's your patient today? Got visitors for 'im." With an ungainly half-bow, he touched his hat and backed away, leaving them there.

"Come in," called a woman's voice as she bustled up to meet them. "Mrs. Merritt! You've come back, have you? Just in time, I say, 'cause he's fearful bad."

Adela could have shaken the woman for this bluntness, for Jane gasped and slipped across the stifling room, weaving between the furniture to kneel beside her husband's narrow bed.

"Roger? Roger, can you hear me? It's Jane. I'm here. I've come back."

"He hasn't spoken since he broke his head," the withered Mrs. Eddings informed them with barely disguised eagerness. "And Eddings and I've paid fifteen shillings out of our own pockets for his nursing, we have."

From earlier practice Jane was able to stop her ears to her former hostess, but Adela and the baron did not share this skill, and they fairly dragged Mrs. Eddings into the passage, Lord Dere pressing a banknote into her grasping hands and Adela saying, "Please tell us what happened. What was the nature of the accident?"

"He was roaring drunk, of course," answered the good lady complacently (after which Adela snapped the door shut behind her, to spare Jane). "'Twas Monday after the wine club met. Must have been two in the morning, but he goes after Rioting Rob again out in the racket ground—bad blood between those two, you know, because of Merritt's louts beating Rob's son. I wasn't there, sadly, and most of the witnesses were likely little better off than Merritt himself, but the word is he took a swing at Rioting

Rob, and the man fell over, but Merritt was so muzzy himself he went right over too, and *crack!* he knocks his head on the stones, and there you have it. He can't last much longer. He hasn't eaten a thing nor taken any water besides what the nurse tried to dribble in his mouth."

Most of this was Greek to Adela, but she grasped enough to know that Roger Merritt had apparently made an ignominious end to his ignominious career, and she would have pitied him if she were not so furious. What a waste of a life! For *this* Jane had nearly ruined herself and her family?

"For someone who was not an eyewitness," came a voice from the gloom of the passage, "you've made a fine job of your account, Mrs. Eddings. I have but one correction." The voice took bodily form beside them in the figure of a tall man, shabby but somehow elegant, his dark hair only grey at the temples and sparkling in stubble along his jaw. Extending a hand, he plucked the baron's banknote from Mrs. Eddings' stunned fingers and returned it to Lord Dere. "This won't be necessary, for I paid the nurse's wages myself, as Mrs. Eddings seems to have forgotten in the fervor of the moment."

"Rioting Rob!" squeaked the woman.

Having spent much of the morning imagining Mr. Gerard Weatherill in every man she saw, no matter how dissimilar or unlikely, Adela hardly knew what to do when confronted with this particular man. She stared at him, speechless.

He met her gaze, if not squarely, at least with a touch of defiance.

Lord Dere took a step forward, tucking Adela behind him. "Do we know you, sir?"

"That's the Rioting Rob I mentioned," spoke up Mrs. Eddings, as if they had not just heard her say his name. "The one Merritt knocked himself out attacking! Attacked father and son both, on separate occasions, didn't he? Didn't his ruffians send your son away, Rob, with missing teeth and broken ribs and one eye put out?"

"If it was as bad as all that, I'll go in and finish Merritt myself," growled the man, reaching for the door handle.

"It wasn't—sir," blurted Adela, peeking around the baron. "As bad as that, I mean. If you are—if it is, by chance, a Gerard Weatherill you refer to."

Lord Dere twisted to give her a questioning look, but Adela was watching Rioting Rob's face for her answer, and when she saw it, she said, "His eye was blacked, but it was still there, and he could see out of it, and he complained of bruises, but nothing broken, nor any teeth missing."

"Thank you."

With the eyes of her betrothed still upon her, Adela realized all she had betrayed, and she added in confusion, "Of course, I—we—have not seen him for a month. Since he left Iffley. Have we, sir?"

This clumsy attempt to draw the baron into the conversation only made matters more awkward, but Lord Dere drew her hand through his arm and said with his usual calm, "At least a month, my dear. Which means he likely has made a complete recovery by now. I take it you are Mr. Gerard Weatherill's father? Your son was a splendid fellow, an excellent tutor to my great-nephew and Miss Barstow's younger brother, and we were sorry to see him go. I am Lord Dere, and this is my intended bride Miss Barstow, sister-in-law to the unfortunate man who lies within there."

He nodded toward the door Mrs. Eddings blocked, but Rob Weatherill had straightened at his speech and didn't care a straw for the unfortunate man indicated.

"Intended bride!" he repeated.

Although they owed no explanation of the situation to this person they did not know, both the baron and Adela colored. And while a gentleman would have caught himself and made haste to remedy the uneasiness he had created, Rioting Rob was, clearly, no gentleman.

"Well, well, well," he murmured with a bow that mocked them in its precision. "I have been shut away from the world a very long time, but I see it goes on as it always has."

Shrinking in embarrassment, Adela retreated behind the baron, and had she been less mortified, she would have spared some admiration for the way the slender old man swelled with dignity. Dignity and chivalry.

"Thank you for making yourself known," Lord Dere said coolly. "And now, if you will pardon us..." He extended a hand toward the Eddings' door, Mrs. Eddings responding at once to his manner and scooting away obligingly.

But Rob Weatherill had no intention of being dismissed, and he stepped forward himself. "Miss Barstow, is this what you mean to do?" he demanded. "Marry some ancient lord for his name and money?"

Adela gasped, her hand flying to cover her mouth.

"Sirrah!" exclaimed the baron, swelling even further. "You will kindly—"

"What about my boy? You heard the old man—my son the 'splendid fellow'? No money and no name—he's got me to thank for both those things—but he has his pride. More pride than you have!"

They might all have ended in being hauled before a constable, Adela would think later, for the next instant, the mild-mannered baron—who hardly dared to say boo to his niece—raised both arms to—do what? Assume a fighting stance? Give Rob Weatherill an almighty shove? Seize him around the neck?

But whatever Lord Dere intended in his displeasure, it would never come to fruition, for just then the door flung open to reveal a tearful Jane Merritt crying, "Della—he's gone!"

All was commotion.

They spilled again into the Eddings' chambers, Adela bumping against some of the narrow bedsteads because Jane was hanging about her neck, and the baron striding around them, pulling off his gloves to take up Roger Merritt's wrist and put a finger to it.

After a minute, he hung his head and replaced the man's arm upon the ragged coverlet. "Yes. He's dead, I'm afraid."

Mrs. Eddings screeched in the baron's ear as if, in harvesting Roger Merritt's soul, the reaper had nicked her own toe with his scythe. "Oh, Lord! In my own room! Death! Death! Oh, heavens! Oh, mercy!"

"Gracious, Mrs. Eddings, be silent," urged Lord Dere, even as running footsteps were heard and new faces appeared in the doorway. Grimy hats and caps were removed as the morbid and the curious crowded in, and when Mrs. Eddings made her explanations over and over, Jane must suffer the mumbled condolences of strangers. Not that Jane said anything. She kept her face buried in Adela's neck (which must have been quite uncomfortable, since she was a few inches taller), and it was Adela who had to nod and grimace in approximated smiles, again and again.

Such was the crowd and confusion that it was some minutes before Adela realized that Rob Weatherill was no longer among them.

Like his son, after having visited turmoil and confusion upon Adela's feelings, he was gone.

Lord Dere summoned a hackney coach for the return to the Old Bell.

"You and Mrs. Merritt rest here," he instructed Adela in low tones when he saw them back to their room. "When someone dies there are formalities to be gone through, and I will see to them."

"You are going back to the Fleet, sir?"

"I am. If you need anything, simply call the maid. Food, tea. A meal might be restorative for your sister."

"Oh, sir—how can we ever thank you enough—what would we have done without you—"

But he was already turning away, waving a hand. "Now, now, dear girl, you know I don't like that. You rest. It has been a trying day."

"Yes, but—" she caught at his sleeve. "Lord Dere—sir—at least let me say I am sorry for...the senior Mr. Weatherill's conduct..."

This too he met with a shake of his head, detaching himself gently from her grip. "Never mind it, Adela. Never mind *him*. There is always a certain amount of unpleasant raillery a man of my age must endure, I suppose, when he chooses to marry. Good afternoon, my dear."

But when he was gone and Adela curled in the armchair by the fire, absently thinking how luxurious the Old Bell was, compared to Mrs. Eddings' quarters, it was not Mr. Rob Weatherill's mockery she remembered. Rather, she thought of her own words and what they had revealed. That she knew the details and extent of Gerard Weatherill's injuries—even to the state of his teeth! (Thinking of Mr. Weatherill's teeth of course made Adela think of kissing him, and she hid her flaming face in her knees.) Her admission meant she had spoken to him of such things, of such relative intimacies! And then to say how long he had been gone, as if she had been counting the days. It all pointed glaringly to her affections for him, she was afraid, and what if the baron noticed? What if he asked her for an account of her behavior?

But *why* had Rob Weatherill made the biting remarks he did? What did he care, if an old lord should marry a young lady?

There must be some secret injury in his own past, she mused. Perhaps he had loved a young lady once, but she had refused him in favor of someone grander.

Because it could not possibly be that he minded *this particular* old lord marrying *this particular* young lady, could it? They were nobody to him, after all. Absolutely nobody.

There was only one person in the entire world who could have told Rioting Rob Weatherill anything about her, and he never would have, would he?

CHAPTER 26

When I sawe tyme I went to Sapience,
Shewyng to her with all my diligence
Howe that my hart by Venus was trapt,
With a snare of love so prively bewrapt.
— Stephen Hawes, *The pastime of pleasure* (1509)

Whatever misgivings Adela's rash words gave rise to in Lord Dere's bosom, he did not speak of them. Indeed, the following day he urged the two young ladies to visit the draper's.

"You will need fabric for a full mourning dress, Mrs. Merritt," he told them over breakfast. "A fair amount of bombazine and crape, I daresay. While you Barstows already wear crape bands and bonnets and such for the late Mr. Barstow, you might like to refurbish your trappings. Therefore, you had better visit Wilding & Kent at Grafton House and instruct them to send the bill to me. No, no, let us not argue about it. Some things simply must be done."

"But sir," ventured Adela, when she learned where Grafton House was, "surely we might find a closer draper and one...less expensive?"

"I must go," he announced, ignoring her question and setting a stack of gleaming coins on the table. "More arrangements regarding Mr. Merritt and other business I must transact, I am so rarely in town. We will meet again at supper."

What was there to do but obey?

And Adela saw the wisdom in his commands, for having a task set before them roused Jane from her sadness, and the possession of both credit and actual money in this shopper's paradise could not fail to inspire. Even the trip in the coach along Holborn to Oxford Street and thence turning down New Bond Street delighted. Here were fine shops and hotels, fashionably dressed ladies in carriages and lounging gentlemen entering eating places or emerging from lodgings. The girls could not look enough directions in their amazement, though when they descended from the coach they took care to wipe such provincial awe from their faces.

The wait to be served at Wilding & Kent was very long, but there was so much to observe that Adela and Jane hardly noticed. So many fabrics and colors! Such elegant customers! It was a shame they were there for black bombazine and Norwich crape, and that Lord Dere's money could not be spent instead on sarsenet and pink silk and clouded satin flounces.

When their purchases were made and the parcels directed to the inn, the girls indulged in shop-gazing for another hour. But when they grew hungry, they were too timid to enter the dining room of Long's, much less Steven's hotel, with its officers and men about town spilling out, and thus they returned to the modest, noisy Old Bell. As he predicted, the baron had not yet returned, and, after composing and posting a letter to Mrs. Barstow, the sisters borrowed a workbasket from the innkeeper's wife and settled down to sew.

"My crape bands will serve, for the present," said Adela. "It's you we must fit out first."

Jane made no protest, stitching away quietly at the lengths Adela cut for her, though after a time she broke the silence to say, "Della, do you think me wicked?"

"Wicked? Why would I think that?"

"Because—because part of me is *relieved* Roger is no more!" Jane confessed, head bent. "I loved him so much when I married him—or when I eloped with him, rather—but everything seemed to go wrong for us. And the more wrong it went, the less happy he became—we both became, I mean to say. It wasn't long before I knew he wished he had never made me his wife. If not for me, he would have gone on enjoying his aunt's favor and the allowance she afforded him. Oh, Della! Do you suppose I must write to her of his death? She hates me, or at least she hates the idea of me."

"Well, she need never hear from nor think of you again, after this," replied Adela grimly. "And I don't know if you're wicked for thinking what you think about Roger, darling. Or, if you *are* wicked, you're no more wicked than I, for I admit having much the same feeling, and likely sooner than you did."

Jane sighed. "If he had not died, I do not know what would have become of him or of us."

"No."

"I did not think he could possibly live to old age, because he lived so *hard*, but I supposed it would be years and years. I thought I might eventually pay his debts and free him, but then what would have happened? I could not picture him living quietly at Iffley Cottage with us."

"No," said Adela again.

Her sister dashed a hand at her eyes but then resumed stitching even more diligently. "And there's more, Della."

"More wickedness?" Adela asked. She meant to sound teasing, but sudden wariness gripped her. More news? Oh, goodness! Why had she not thought of it? Was Jane...in the family way?

But, no.

"More wickedness," answered Jane. "Because I find I...envy you, Della."

"Envy me?"

"Envy you your engagement," her sister added in a rush. "Because you chose such a kind and eminently respectable husband."

Adela blanched. "Lord Dere, you mean?"

"Of course, Lord Dere! Are you engaged to someone else I don't know about?" Jane almost laughed. "The baron may be much older than you, but he would not in a million years leave you circumstanced as I have been."

"That's true."

"I do wish, however, in his gentleness, he would not be so henpecked by Mrs. Markham Dere," Jane continued with a frown. "Will she and Peter continue to live at Perryfield when you are mistress of it?"

"I—don't know. Lord Dere and I have not discussed it."

"Haven't discussed it! But you said he went to see Mr. Terry and the bishop about a license."

"Yes. But we haven't discussed it, all the same. And Mrs. Dere certainly hasn't said anything about it to me," Adela said, "though she might still be in shock."

Holding up the panels she had stitched together, Jane smoothed them and set them aside before reaching for the next. "I don't blame her. You know, don't you, Della, that if you have a son, he will supplant Peter as the heir?"

Adela's hand fluttered to her throat, but she made no answer. Of course she knew that, but what was the use in saying that becoming the mother of a future baron never figured into her calculations when she threw herself at Lord Dere? If the law only allowed it, Peter Dere would be forever welcome to the title!

But the law did not allow it, so naturally Mrs. Dere had cause for resentment.

A scratch at the door was heard, and when Adela bid the person enter, the maid poked her head inside.

"Message for Miss Barstow."

"I am Miss Barstow."

"Lord Dere would like to speak with you in the coffee room."

The sisters glanced at each other. "Please tell him he may come up to our room," said Adela.

"Begging your pardon, ma'am, but he suspifically requested your presence downstairs."

Biting her lip, Jane crushed her sewing to her chest. "He's learned something else horrible about Roger, Della, I just know it! And he doesn't want me to hear it. Promise me you'll tell me what it is!"

Adela sighed heavily. "I promise, and I will tell him at once that I promised, so he can keep his confidence, if he prefers. I think it more likely that he has had to lay out even more money than he has already spent on us."

Pressing a kiss to her sister's hair, Adela followed the maid down to the coffee room, where the girl led her past the bustling tables to one of the private sitting rooms, opening the door to reveal a cozy parlor with four armchairs grouped about a low table before a fire. An untouched tea tray heaped with sandwiches and tarts sat upon the table, but Adela overlooked this bounty altogether, her eye being instantly drawn to the room's occupant, who had risen upon the door handle turning.

"Where is Lord Dere?" Adela and the man demanded in unison.

The maid scratched her head and shrugged. "Stepped out for a minute, I reckon."

And deeming her answer sufficient, she withdrew, leaving Adela alone to face the man. That is, to face Mr. Gerard Weatherill.

He bowed.

She curtseyed.

Each thought the other appeared thinner. Paler. Beautiful.

"Your black eye is gone," she said inadequately. "And the patch." (What a witless remark! If he no longer had a black eye, of course he no longer needed a patch!)

He nodded, equally at a loss, a muscle in his jaw working.

To keep herself from watching that muscle, she forced herself further into the parlor, choosing the chair diagonal from the one he had occupied.

"Please, Miss Barstow," he uttered, "would you rather not be closer to the fire? I—can move, if you prefer. That is—" (he turned a violent crimson) "that is—pardon me, if I should have called you Lady Dere."

"Lady Dere!" gasped Adela. "Oh—no—I am yet Miss Barstow. And this chair is perfectly satisfactory."

There followed a little dance of politeness, with Adela continuing to demur and Weatherill insisting, until they exchanged places and were both seated. Then a fatal silence fell. She wanted to ask, *What are you doing here?* but that seemed too bald.

He answered her question in any case, after another hesitation. "So," he began, "here you are in London. I was not aware—I received a letter from Lord Dere yesterday asking me to call here at this time but not stating the purpose of his request."

"Yes." She folded her hands in her lap, then saw how white her bare knuckles were and in a flurried manner began to pour a cup of tea. "How—how did you like your tea again?"

"A touch of milk and one sugar, please. If—you are not yet married, are you—in town to shop for your wedding clothes?"

Adela felt her cheeks burn. The teaspoon clanked against the rim of the cup. "N-No. Far from it. That is, the baron and I are here in town along with my sister Jane, because we received word Mr. Merritt had been injured." Her eyes flitted to his and away again. Did he know his father's part in the fracas?

"Injured? I am sorry to hear it."

"It gets worse," she said, dropping another lump of sugar in his cup in her agitation and then another. "We went to the Fleet yesterday, and we were just in time because—because Mr. Merritt died only minutes after Jane reached his side."

Weatherill made an indistinct sound in his throat, his brow sorrowful. Adela held out his teacup to him, but when his fingers brushed hers she nearly dropped it. He bumbled to steady it, and tea splashed to the table between them. More apologies and mutterings. Adela seized upon the nearest sandwich to occupy herself, while Weatherill took refuge in a gulp of tea, only to choke on the over-sweet beverage.

The minutes are racing past! Adela fretted, politely ignoring Mr. Weatherill's coughs and gazing at the tasteless sandwich in her hand. *And there is so much I want to know and to tell him before Lord Dere returns!*

She replaced the sandwich on the tray. Heaven knew, this moment alone with him was a gift, when she thought she would never see him again, and she was not going to squander it.

"Tell me—how you have been. Mr. Keele sent the baron a copy of *Antiquities of Egypt* and said you would be assisting him with the second volume. Are—are—are you enjoying that work? And—living here in London? I assume you live here. That is, I suppose Lord Dere must have gone to Mr. Keele's publisher to inquire—to find where he might write to you, I mean."

If he noticed her limping speech, he gave no sign, and, indeed, his reply was scarcely more fluent. "Yes. Here I have been. *We*—Keele and I—have been, though I think the air is not good for him at his age. The air and the memories. Moreover, the money would stretch further elsewhere."

"Where will you go?" Adela breathed. At least now in London she was able to picture him when she thought of him, but if he wandered far away, beyond her experience...? *There is a war. He cannot go very far, thank God.*

"We haven't decided yet. Though there is...nothing to keep us here."

She raised wild eyes to his. "What about—the publisher? And—and—and—doesn't Mr. Keele want to speak to the London societies? And what about—your father?" It was on the tip of her tongue to say she had met his father, but her courage failed her. It would be like throwing his past in his face. And Mr. Rob Weatherill had been so prickly, so cutting...

"Don't you understand? How can you not?" Weatherill demanded suddenly, making her jump. "Don't press me, as if you don't. Don't look at me, as if you don't." He set down his cup with a bang, and more liquid spilled over the lip. Springing to his feet he began to prowl back and forth like a menagerie tiger. "It isn't just Keele or his health which drives me—" he lashed her with narrowed eyes. "It's—I want to—that is—I—confound it all! I *need* to—get away from *you*."

It was strange, Adela thought, unaccountable, that she could shrink from the vehemence of his words, even while it felt like everything within her was expanding, warming, *glowing* like a sunrise.

He still loves me?

He still loves me!

Like a pasteboard puppet whose wires had been inexpertly manipulated, Adela rose unsteadily, gripping the back of the armchair to stay upright.

"Don't," he said.

She only looked at him, swaying, her lips parting.

"*Don't*, Adela."

"But—" She took an uncertain step toward him.

For an instant he leaned toward her, naked yearning in his eyes, but then he gave a fierce shake of his head.

"Adela Barstow, are you still going to marry the baron?"

His question hit her like a slap, and she blinked at him as if awakened from a trance. Raising helpless palms she answered, "I have to. I have said so. He has already obtained the license from Mr. Terry and the bishop. And he saved my family, you understand. You cannot think how much we owe him, in—in favors and—in money, frankly.”

"I know it," he said dully. "No one better than I."

"Gerard—"

He flinched at the sound of his name on her lips. But Adela, perhaps inspired by her sister's earlier confessions, had determined on utter honesty, no matter what he might think of her. If she was never to see him again, nevermore to indulge in memories of him, she would speak her mind—and heart—first.

First and last.

"Mr. Weatherill, if you are to go away," she began again, "and I am…to marry, there is something I must confess to you."

He said nothing. The muscle in his jaw tightened again.

"I know you have always thought me wrong to engage myself to Lord Dere," she whispered, "and likely you are right in your opinion, though I intend to be a dutiful and—and—affectionate wife to him, with God's help. But before I…redeem myself thus, I would just like to say that—that—when I kissed you in Iffley Meadow, it was as true a thing as I ever did in my life. And I ought to be sorry for it and ashamed of it, but I am not…yet. Another instance of my wickedness, I daresay."

The silence which followed this admission lasted even longer.

Adela smothered a sigh. She had been so quick to sympathize with Jane's confessions, but Mr. Weatherill stood there like a block, as if he thought the worse of her for them.

"Have you nothing to say in response?" she pleaded.

He looked down at the tray of food, his spilt tea and her discarded sandwich. "I do not see how saying anything will help," he answered at last. "But—I thank you for your honesty. And—I think I had better go. I will send my apologies to Lord Dere for not waiting."

"No—*I* will go," insisted Adela, "for he may talk to me anytime, after all, whereas you—" Flapping her hands, she tucked her hair behind her ears and smoothed her dress. "Yes. I will go. And—again—I—wish you every blessing and happiness, sir."

And before she could change her mind or he could prevent her, she darted at him and pressed a kiss to his cheek. It was meant to be a farewell, and not even a lingering one, for she was embarrassed of her forwardness as soon as her lips touched his flesh, but before she could withdraw, his head whipped around and his mouth was on hers, pressing as hard as ever she remembered. And she was kissing him back, their arms tangling in their struggle to pull each other closer.

They were out of their minds! To do this *here,* under these circumstances, when anyone in the world might walk in, including the good man they were both wronging! But though each thought so, a fiery haze enwrapped them, in which there was only him and only her and only their fever.

It was not until the door handle gave a preliminary rattle and began turning slowly downward that Adela and Weatherill released each other. She dropped breathlessly into the nearest armchair to fiddle with the tea tray, while he gained the fireplace in one long stride, propping an elbow upon the mantel to prevent his own collapse.

"Here's his lordship," announced the maid, her lip curling as she added inwardly, *and not a moment too soon, if you was to ask me!*

"Ah!" gasped Adela, trying not to pant. "Good afternoon, sir. I was just going to—to carry Jane a little snack, so I do hope whatever you wanted to speak to me about might be postponed a little while."

"Of course, my dear. I am sorry to have kept you waiting," the baron replied with his usual courtesy. "However, if *you* are at liberty to stay another minute or two, Weatherill, I will be quick. It is a pleasure to see you again."

Adela slipped past him, carrying a random assortment of her half-eaten sandwich, a tart, and Mr. Weatherill's sugar-laden teacup, but Lord Dere made no remark; nor did he glance behind him when she hesitated at the door to throw Weatherill one last, anguished look, her bruised lips just moving, mouthing a final message: *Good-bye.*

Iffley Meadow

The Old Bell, Holborn

Fleet Street Obelisk

St. James Piccadilly

CHAPTER 27

He that hath the bride, is the bridegroom; but the friend of the bridegroom, which standeth and heareth him, rejoiceth greatly. This my joy therefore is fulfilled.
— John 3:20, quoted by Beilby Porteus, *Lecture III* (1798)

The Right Reverend Beilby Porteus, Doctor of Divinity and Bishop of London, considered the letter from Baron Ranulph Dere, enclosing its sizeable donation to the Society for Missions to Africa and the East.

"Wilberforce would be glad of this money," he told his secretary. "And to be plain, so would I."

"Everything appears to be in order, my lord," said Quarrington. "The license from Bishop Randolph, the recommendation from the priest. There's something about a name change, but I suspect it would be a speedy business."

Lord Porteus thought of the number of missionaries Lord Dere's bank draft would underwrite, and the decision was soon made. "Let him come, then. All for the greater good, you know, Quarrington."

"Yes, my lord."

Mr. Roger Merritt was buried at St. Bride's, the brief service beside the grave attended by his widow, her sister, and Lord Dere. Poor Jane Merritt appeared paler than ever in her new mourning dress and short cape, but even in a blue kerseymere spencer (with new crape bands), the almost equally pallid Adela might have been mistaken for another intimate of the deceased.

She had waited for the baron to explain why he wanted to speak with Mr. Weatherill, but he did not, and when Adela could stand it no longer she introduced the subject herself the following morning at breakfast.

"Just a little business to transact," he answered pleasantly. "I made Mr. Weatherill an advance when he left Iffley, you know, with the agreement that he would begin to repay me in the new year, but as I found myself in London I thought it worthwhile to seek him out and sift his progress. Did you have an opportunity to chat with him before I came?"

"A brief one." Her smile was rueful. "We are *all* so in your debt, sir."

How different debts were, though, between gentlemen! By applying his shoulder to the wheel, Mr. Weatherill could and would in time pay off what he owed to the baron, but Adela had no means to cancel hers except to surrender herself, whether Lord Dere wanted her or not, much as the Iffley doctor Mr. Travers was sometimes obliged to accept livestock or crops in lieu of payment.

"It is natural to be out of spirits, after what you have experienced," the baron said when they stood in Fleet Street again following Roger Merritt's interment. He had to raise his voice to be heard over the din of vehicles, horses, and passersby. "And I would be remiss if I did not try to remedy that before we returned to Iffley."

Having been four days in London by this point, however, the return to Iffley was uppermost in the girls' minds, for they wanted nothing more than the comfort of their mother and siblings after their trials. But of course it was impossible to say they wanted no amusements but only to go home. Therefore they smiled (or, at least, Adela smiled—smiles were not yet expected from the bereaved Jane) and said, "What do you propose, sir?"

"I propose an M and an M," he declared. "A millinery and a mansion. What do you say?"

Even young ladies who wanted to go home would find a visit to a milliner difficult to object to, though Adela winced to think of *adding* to what they owed the baron, and they greeted this suggestion with proper eagerness.

The hackney coach stand was a few steps away at New Bridge Street in sight of the obelisk, and the threesome was soon rattling west toward St. James, the baron pointing out the offices of various newspapers, Somerset Palace, the figure of King Charles on horseback by Hubert le Sueur, and the columns of Carlton House.

"Is Carlton House the mansion we will see?" asked Jane when they alighted near St. James and Lord Dere paid the two-shilling fare.

"No, no," he answered. "A house owned by quite a different sort of person than the prince. That is, not so grand a house but nearly as grand a host. Now come, my dear girls. You must choose bonnets worthy of being seen by a mitre, if not a monarch."

Adela and Jane exchanged perplexed glances, but their companion beamed with mischief and joy and showed no sign of wanting to enlighten them. With Adela on one arm and Jane on the other, he led them up Pall Mall to the charming shop belonging to the Misses Allen.

As modestly and simply dressed as the sisters were, they warranted little attention from the modistes or their assistants until Jane was overheard whispering, "Yes, Lord Dere, that one is very pretty, but I would hate to cover it in crape." The word "lord" proved the key to the lock, and thereafter the trio received enough notice to please the vainest of princesses. Jane was coaxed into a black satin bonnet trimmed with blue-black ribbon, the flower garland at the crown removed and wrapped up in paper, to be replaced with a more sober rosette of ribbon. Adela would have chosen a lilac crape with a black straw brim attached, but the baron shook his head.

"No, no, I'm afraid that won't do at all, Adela," he admonished.

"You think I also should choose a completely black one?"

"I don't think you should wear black at all. Not today, at least. Not on such a beautiful day."

She glanced doubtfully at the lowering sky outside the bow window, but Lord Dere continued to beam at her. "Yes, indeed. A beautiful day. Wouldn't you say, Adela, that it is be a lovely day to be married?"

"Married?" she echoed wonderingly, while Jane stared and the shop assistants squealed with real or assumed joy.

"Married," he repeated with decision.

"Is your lordship engaged to this young lady?" the younger Miss Allen asked, clapping her hands and nodding to one of her assistants to fetch the more expensive designs.

"I am," he said briefly before turning back to Adela. "What do you say, my girl? Shall we go from here to the bishop's house in St. James Square?"

Adela sank to one of the padded stools, feeling the blood drain from her. "The bishop's house! The—bishop of *London*? But—but, sir, I thought we would be married in Iffley when we returned. We—discussed it, and you said you had spoken with Mr. Terry and applied to the bishop of Oxford."

"So I did, but all this gloom surrounding poor Mr. Merritt has me wanting to restore some light to these eyes! Don't you agree, Mrs. Merritt? Wouldn't it hearten you to see your sister married today, or at the very latest tomorrow? I've heard Lord Porteus has very fine gardens at Fulham Palace, so it is a shame it is not high summer, that we might call on him there, but Saint James Square is quite elegant and worth seeing."

But noting Adela's pallor, Jane was quick to say, "Oh, sir, I will leave the choice to Della. You mustn't think of me a bit. Whatever makes Della happy will serve for me."

"I—I—"

"Now, my dear girl," he coaxed, taking her nerveless hand between his own and patting it. "I've taken you by surprise, I know, but I had better confess that I was so confident I could persuade you that I have already applied to the bishop and accompanied my application with a donation to one of his favorite causes, the sending of missionaries to Africa."

Words were impossible. Refusal was impossible. *Escape* was impossible. Just as the word "lord" operated magically upon the Misses Allen, the word "donation" was like a prison gate slamming shut upon Adela. She owed him so much, had already leaned so much upon his grace and favor. She could not possibly object. Who knew how much he had spent on this trip alone?

And what did it matter, finally, whether she be married in London or Iffley? By the bishop or by Mr. Terry? Before a few witnesses in a strange chapel or in the eyes of the whole congregation of St. Mary the Virgin?

No matter the time or circumstances, she would become the wife of Lord Dere, and not the wife of...the other one.

So let it be. Sooner was better than later, even.

Yes.

And if she married him now, she need not see the worldly-wise understanding in the eyes of all those present, the nods which indicated, *She knew which side her bread was buttered on. What a catch for a girl of no fortune or connection!*

All this passed through her mind in a flash, so that when she lifted her chin and replied, "Yes, sir, it's a lovely day for a wedding," none was any the wiser, or so Adela thought.

From the Misses Allen's millinery, a three-minute walk brought them to the bishop's yellow-brick, three-storey residence beside Norfolk House.

"Isn't this delightful?" the baron asked, gesturing at the spacious square, laid out with greenery and flower beds, bordered by fashionable residences.

"Quite peaceful, despite its proximity to the hurly-burly of Pall Mall and Charing Cross! And so near the king, when his majesty requires spiritual aid! And then, when summer heat presses, my lord bishop floats up the river to Fulham. Charming, charming." Consulting his pocket-watch, he glanced about.

"Are we expected at a certain time, sir?" asked Adela timidly.

"I believe *now* will be just right. Shall we?"

The door opened at once, and the baron said in lofty tones Adela had not heard from him before, "Baron Dere, Miss Barstow, and Mrs. Merritt to see the bishop."

"Yes, my lord," intoned the footman, favoring them with such a supercilious look that Adela and Jane were glad of their new bonnets.

"Have the...witnesses...arrived yet?" asked Lord Dere, as the servant led them through the large entrance hall and up an imposing stone staircase.

"There are no other callers at present, my lord."

"Witnesses?" whispered Adela. "Will not Jane and—and a servant suffice?"

In answer he merely gave her arm a pat, and there was no time for more because the footman threw open the drawing-room door and bellowed their names.

Though her father had been a vicar, Twyford had been a modest parish, and Adela had never been in the presence of any clergyman higher than an archdeacon. Therefore she half expected someone so exalted as a bishop to parade about in mitre, ecclesiastical robe and stole, even in the privacy of his home. Apart from wearing a wig, however, the bishop of London dressed like any other (sober, fashionable) gentleman of a certain age, and his features, though stark and distinguished, were softened by a certain compassion. She would later learn he was an ally of William Wilberforce and, from the bishop's bench in the House of Lords, campaigned ceaselessly for the abolition of the slave trade.

At this precise moment in time, however, rising from her curtsey, she could only think, *Don't stand on your hem, Adela Barstow! And don't stare. And make certain your mouth doesn't hang open. If only I could hide behind Lord Dere! Let us pray Lord Porteus does not speak to me.*

"Ah, the bride," said the bishop.

"Yes, my lord," croaked Adela.

"Please—call me Bishop."

"Yes, Bishop."

"And you have the license from Bishop Randolph, Lord Dere?"

"Yes, Bishop."

"This is most irregular, you know, but you knew how to play your cards. I commend you for your generous donation to the Society for Missions to Africa and the East."

"I'm afraid matters are about to become even more irregular, Bishop," the baron replied, "but I would like to assure you I have long admired your writings and your concerns."

The bishop received this praise with a brief bow of his head. "Well, then. What is this irregularity you refer to? You said something about a name change?"

"Yes, Bishop. To speak plainly, a substitution."

"Impossible. Randolph's license is based on this Mr. Terry's recommendation of Lord Ranulph Dere of Perryfield and Miss Adela Barstow of Iffley. If either of these parties abstains, the license is null and void. All depends on this recommendation from Mr. Terry, you see."

"I do see, Bishop," replied the baron, beginning to slap at his pockets, "but I assure you Mr. Terry knows the substituted party as well and has sent a revised recommendation at my request."

The bishop clicked his tongue, his gaze shifting to take in Jane. "*Most* irregular. Surely you do not refer to a substitution for the bride, unless you have neglected to inform Miss Barstow."

"What *do* you mean, sir?" hissed Adela, inching nearer to him and trying to speak without moving her lips.

"No, not a substitution for the bride," Lord Dere said pleasantly, discovering the folded paper he sought and extending it to Lord Porteus. "Though you do remind me, Bishop, I have not, in fact, consulted her."

"Sir, please, what *can* you mean?" Adela asked again, unable to keep her voice from rising. "I beg you to consult me now!"

"Inclined as I am to be flexible in assisting you, Lord Dere," said the bishop dryly, without unfolding the sheet in his hand, "and even if the documents are in order, I can hardly marry parties *in absentia*."

"Yes," sighed the baron, pulling his watch out and shaking his head. "Very reasonable of you, Bishop. Of course, I set this by St. Dunstan-in-the-West as we passed, but perhaps they used St. James Garlickhythe."

Before Adela could forget herself so far as to *shake* the baron in her impatience, the drawing room door flung open once more, and the haughty footman roared, "Mr. William Keele and Mr. Gerard Weatherill!"

Had the servant announced the entrance of their majesties the king and queen, Adela could not have been more astounded. She gawped. She gulped. She trembled.

"Gracious me," said Lord Porteus, when the newcomers straightened from their bows. "Can this be the Mr. William Keele who authored *Antiquities of Egypt*?"

"The same, my lord," answered the dry, elderly man, running a hand over a wisp of unruly white hair in an attempt to flatten it. "I am honored you have heard of it."

"Heard of it! Why I have read a fair portion of it," the bishop declared, "as my time allows, and found much to marvel over. Not least marvelous, sir, if you will pardon me for mentioning it, is how you succeeded in producing such a monument to scholarship in your lamentable circumstances."

Mr. Keele shuffled his feet on the carpet. "Mr. Weatherill here was instrumental in gathering, organizing, and summarizing my materials, and we hope to produce a second volume."

"I rejoice to hear it." With an effort, the bishop tore his admiring eyes from Keele to consider Weatherill, his gaze narrowing as his mind worked through all that Keele's pronouncement implied.

"You, too…resided in the Fleet, Mr. Weatherill?" he questioned.

It took two tries for the young man to produce a sound, but he then managed, "Yes, my lord. Not in the Fleet proper, when I was old enough to earn money of my own, but hard by. Mr. Keele educated me and other children in the prison."

The bishop digested the implications of this as well, rubbing his chin thoughtfully.

Trying to be unobtrusive, Adela sank onto the nearest chair. She did not know if it was unseemly to sit if the bishop stood, but it was either sit down or fall down.

Her movement succeeded in recalling Lord Porteus to the matter at hand, however, for he glanced at Lord Dere. "Ah. Ahem. In any event, I presume one of these gentlemen is the proposed *substitute*, Lord Dere?"

"It had better be up to the lady," answered the baron mildly. "As she has kindly reminded me, I failed to consult her in the matter. Bishop, may I propose either we or they withdraw for a few minutes? You might, perhaps, ask Mr. Keele further questions about his work."

With eagerness belying his years, Lord Porteus snapped his fingers. "A capital suggestion. Come, whoever cares to. Join me in my library. My secretary Quarrington will wish to be included as well. Miss Barstow, Mr. Weatherill, we leave you two to sort this out."

Jane peeped at her sister, hoping Adela's eyes would beg her to remain, rather than go with such an august company, but Adela was staring at her hands and looking like she wished she might crawl under the furniture and hide. Jane would have to go. And then—great merciful heavens!—there was the bishop of London beside her, offering his arm to lead her from the room. Poor Jane touched feather-light fingers to the venerable man's sleeve and prayed with all her might he would not ask her anything about Roger.

When the others were gone, Adela lifted her head timidly. "I—don't understand what is happening."

"Whether it happens or not is entirely yours to decide, my love," he murmured, not stirring a step.

"I may—choose to marry *you*, instead of the baron?"

"If you will have me, Adela."

"But—but—I'm engaged to Lord Dere."

A slow smile curled his lips. "It seems he's trying to foist you upon me."

But this was too serious a matter for Adela to return his smile. "No," she said, her word wiping the mirth instantly from his face.

Weatherill inhaled sharply. "No?"

"No—I mean, you must explain it to me first," pleaded Adela. "If you knew the turmoil in my breast, you would not torture me, Gerard. You would explain all."

At her use of his Christian name, his smile returned, wider than before. "Very well," he agreed. "I will. But you must lay your stake upon the table before I hazard such odds. Suppose I were to make my lengthy explanation, and you then told me, 'Upon consideration, I'm afraid I must refuse'? Then I would have got nothing for my pains and patience."

"What shall I stake, then?" she asked, rising.

But she saw the answer plainly in his eyes.

CHAPTER 28

They literally lowered mountains, they raised valleys, they cut down woods, they removed all obstacles, they cleared away all roughnesses and inequalities, and made everything smooth and plain and commodious.
—Beilby Porteus, *Lecture III* (1798)

In a stride he was across the room, and she was in his arms, breathless kisses stealing all thought away.

"Adela, my Adela," he murmured against her mouth and neck, one hand going to the ribbons at her chin. The next moment her new bonnet, so carefully chosen with the aid of the baron and the Misses Allen, tumbled to the floor, and his fingers were twined in her lustrous hair. Her own hands explored the wondrous new territory of broad shoulders and the arms which enclosed her like iron bands, and she found herself breathing his name in return.

In short, they forgot themselves, and it was likely a blessing in disguise that no one had told the footman to give them privacy. As it was, he banged in again with the tea tray, and only his fixed attention on the full urn, delicately placed cups, saucers, milk jug, sugar bowl, teaspoons, tongs, and seed biscuits prevented him seeing the lovers' embrace, the ardor of which would certainly have been the most shocking sight in his ten years' service of the bishop. Weatherill and Adela sprang apart before they could be discovered, however, and with only a bow in their rumpled direction, the footman once again withdrew.

"That was a near thing," said Weatherill, suppressing a laugh.

"Too near," Adela answered, scarlet. But her own lips twitched. Reading that as an invitation, Weatherill reached for her again, only to have her raise a commanding finger and escape to one of the Venetian windows overlooking the square. "Go on then, sir," she said as she began to tidy her hair. "I have done as you asked, and now you must do as *I* asked, and quickly, before they return."

With a mock sigh, he spread his hands, palm upward. "Cruel mistress. Where would you have me begin?"

"At the beginning, of course, sir."

"What? 'Sir'? Sir me no sirs, Adela."

"*Gerard,* then," she relented. "But pass me my bonnet, please."

"A very fetching bonnet, I must say."

"Thank you. It was a gift from my former betrothed."

"Wretch!"

But she blew him a kiss, and he smiled. "Let me see...begin at the beginning? Well, that would be the day I arrived at the Angel Inn in Oxford, and an adorable creature—an angel herself—entered the coffee room..."

"Hush!" she scolded. "I am very interested in that part of the story, but we haven't time before the bishop reappears and I must give my answer. Skip to the point where you and Lord Dere came to agree on this mad scheme, if you please. Did you know of it when I last saw you at the Old Bell?"

"I did not. I had only discovered that very morning that Lord Dere was in London, having received a note from my father to that effect—"

"We met him when we arrived at the Fleet to see Roger Merritt," Adela interrupted. "Met Mr. Robert Weatherill, I mean, and I knew him at once for your father. He shares your proportions and—your handsomeness."

He grinned at her. "Oh, dear. Should I be concerned that you thought him handsome? I know how your taste runs to much older men."

"You!" She cast about for something to toss at him, but as everything belonged to the bishop and looked fearfully expensive, she settled for darting over and flicking a finger at his waistcoat. Which earned her a kiss in retaliation.

But this was getting them nowhere. Adela retreated again, taking a seat at some distance and determined to stay away until she knew everything.

With a sigh, Weatherill chose his own chair at a decorous remove. "Let me see...my father sent his note which was instantly followed by a letter from Lord Dere himself, forwarded by Keele's publisher. In it, the baron asked me to attend him at the Old Bell in regard to the advance he had made me. My heart should have sunk—I had only a few loose shillings I could safely spare him—but I was so hungry for news of *you* that I hastened over. Instead of the baron, however, the door opened, and you appeared. Oh, Adela, when I saw you there, after thinking I never would again..."

"I know it," she whispered. "I felt the same."

He cleared his throat. "Well. What happened next you will remember, I daresay."

"If I did not, today would have jogged my memory," she murmured with a glint of mischief.

Chuckling, his eyes fell briefly to her swollen lips. But he persevered. "To resume: following a sufficiently tumultuous encounter with you, Lord Dere at last made his appearance, and you slipped away. I thought when you left the room you were going out of my life forever, and I did not think I could bear that a second time. Adela, I nearly threw my shillings down to pursue you, but the baron must have guessed it because he leaned against the closed door. He was merciful, however. That is, he told me straight away that he had not summoned me to talk of money at all, but rather to put me to the test. To put *us* to the test."

"Test? What test?"

"He said he had for some time suspected I had feelings for you and—you for me. And he thought, if he threw us together, he would...see what happened."

Adela put her hands to her suddenly burning cheeks. "I do not doubt, when he saw my embarrassment and distress and how I fled the room, he needed no further evidence of my feelings."

"Say it, then, my darling," he urged, drawing his chair nearer. "I want to hear it. I told you I loved you in Iffley Meadow; now do you tell me."

What could poor Adela do when so bid, entreated by his glowing eyes, his voice sending shivers through her? She obeyed, but so quietly he must take his satisfaction more in reading her lips than in hearing her.

But it was enough. Contenting himself with drawing a fingertip along the length of her arm, he took up his account again. "You cannot take all the credit for persuading him. When you left the little parlor, I could scarcely string words together. I thrust the shillings at him and said I was sorry, but I must go, and I would pay him more as I was able, but he said I might be quit of the debt altogether, if I were willing to do him one service."

"You mean, if you were to marry me, in his stead?" she breathed.

"Precisely." Weatherill shook his head, smiling, and reached to take her hands in his. "He said, fond as he was of you, he suspected *I* was fonder. And fond as *you* were of him, he suspected you were fonder still of me. Therefore, having devoted much thought to it, he decided it would be better for all, including himself, if he remained a bachelor, and *I* took his place. Would I consider it? 'Miss Barstow has no portion to speak of,' he told me, 'but if you will agree to this more comfortable arrangement,

Weatherill, I believe it would be possible to provide a little wedding gift of sorts.'"

Her eyes filling, Adela cried, "Ah, he is too kind! When I think of all my family has cost him and how gracious he has been to us. This trip alone, for Jane's sake—"

"Softly..." Weatherill chuckled, "lest you decide you *do*, in fact, prefer him." He tugged on her hands and patted his lap, but she withstood his invitation, hissing, "The bishop, my dear! They will return at any moment, before the tea grows cold."

And indeed, the door to the drawing room opened once more, gently this time. Adela and Weatherill shot to their feet, their radiance evoking a gentle "I think we have our answer, bishop" from Lord Dere. Then they were swept up; Weatherill's hand was shaken and Adela's cheek was kissed, and the bishop's secretary Quarrington presented their marriage license to them.

"I thought eight in the morning tomorrow at St. James Piccadilly for the ceremony," said the baron.

"Tomorrow?" Adela and her sister asked in unison.

"It's too late for today, unfortunately," said Lord Porteus with a smile. "I'm afraid all marriages must take place between eight and noon, even those approved and licensed by the bishop of London."

"And if you are married early," continued the baron, "there would still be time for a post chaise to carry us back to Oxford by evening."

"But—will Della remain in London with Mr. Weatherill after she is married?" Jane asked in an unsteady voice.

"Another choice she must make," answered Lord Dere. "Weatherill, did you tell her of the little school?"

"There was no opportunity," answered Weatherill, having the grace to blush, for there would have been plenty of time to tell his bride of the little school if they hadn't spent so many minutes kissing each other. Turning to her now, he said, "By his grace and favor, Lord Dere has offered to me—to *us*—the lease of a building in Oxford, in Cornmarket Street beside the town hall. There Keele and I might keep a school, in addition to working on the next volume of *Antiquities*."

"I thought we might call it 'School for Scandal,' Miss Barstow," interposed the old scholar with a wink, "but Weatherill here preferred 'Keele's.'"

"If you liked, Adela, we might return with your sister and the baron to Iffley at once," her intended continued, "and stay either at Iffley Cottage or—"

"Yes!" cried Adela before he could finish his sentence. "Oh, yes, let us do that!"

He laughed, swinging her hands in his. "I was going to say, or we might stay here in town at my lodging house and show you more of London."

"Home again to Iffley Cottage, if you please," insisted Adela, laughing with him. "The only question is, where on earth will we put you?"

The following morning Mr. Parker of St. James Piccadilly joined Mr. Gerard Weatherill and Miss Adela Barstow in holy matrimony, with Lord Dere, Mr. William Keele, and Mrs. Roger Merritt bearing witness. Adela would remember ever after the sun peeping from behind the clouds to illuminate the gilded trim of the church interior and the airy, graceful carvings of fruit and flowers and symbols above the altar. The rector was quite proud of his church and would have given them a detailed tour after they signed the register, but when Mr. Parker spent ten minutes on Grinling Gibbons' baptismal font alone, the baron thanked him graciously, pressing a generous fee into his hands and allowing them to escape to breakfast.

And just as the baron planned, they were on the road before noon, rolling and rattling over the turnpike roads, Adela's arm wound comfortably through that of her dozing husband.

There was so much to be thought of, so much to be decided! How many pupils could the school take, and what was required for their room and board? *I will talk to Mrs. Terry. She will know about such things. Ah, but the rector receives his tithes in addition to the boys' fees. Will we have enough?* Might Gordy and Peter Dere be counted on as day pupils? If the baron already had his coachmen taking Peter to the rectory every day, might he not consider driving him instead—and Gordy too—to Oxford? Adela suspected the baron would authorize it, if she asked him, but heaven knew he had already done so much!

He has been an angel, she thought, lifting her eyes to him on the opposite seat where he gazed out the window. Jane had collapsed against him in sleep and would doubtless be mortified when she awoke, but he bore this, as he did most things, with his usual calm.

I dread to think what he has already spent on my family since we came to Iffley, Adela's thoughts raced on, *and now, having just lived down the scandal of engaging himself to me, he must announce that I have jilted him for the disreputable tutor! Poor, poor Lord Dere!*

Despite her pity, her lips twitched, and a giggle escaped her. The baron glanced over at once, raising a questioning brow.

"I was thinking what burdens I have placed upon you, sir," she whispered, "financial and otherwise. And how you will have still more to bear when we are home. Gossip and wonder and such. I am so, so sorry. You have only ever repaid me with kindness. Will you forgive me?"

He met this with a dismissive wave and a shake of the head. "If it relieves you, Adela, I will say so. But whatever I may have spent or endured," he replied, "I believe I will be rewarded with greater peace and harmony at Perryfield."

"How so, sir?"

"You're an intelligent girl, so I think you will understand when I say that, no matter the awkward way in which our engagement ended, Mrs. Markham Dere will take enormous comfort in remaining the mistress of Perryfield. I would venture to guess, in fact, that she will never utter a syllable of reproach regarding any of this. Rather, she will likely make life at Perryfield as pleasant as can be for me from now on, lest I ever frighten her again with another engagement."

Though his tone was teasing, Adela said dolefully, "You would never have frightened her with *this* engagement, sir, if I had not forced you into it. Oh, *do* say you forgive me!"

"Hush, my dear," he soothed. "I only wish you had felt easy enough to confide your cares in me, that we might have arrived at a solution together. Such desperate measures you took! You will have some neighborhood chatter of your own to bear in the coming weeks."

But he beamed as he spoke, and Adela was too happy in any case to fear further scandal. Now that she was married to her beloved Gerard, never to be separated again, the rest of the world might say what they liked and think what they liked and do what they liked, with her blessing.

Thus with a lighter conscience and a contented smile, Adela rested her head against her husband's shoulder and at last shut her eyes.

The End

The Barstow adventures
continue in *Mrs. Merritt's
Remorse*, the second book
of the Lord Dere's
Dependents series.

THE HAPGOODS OF BRAMLEIGH

The Naturalist
A Very Plain Young Man
School for Love
Matchless Margaret
The Purloined Portrait
A Fickle Fortune

THE ELLSWORTH ASSORTMENT

Tempted by Folly
The Belle of Winchester
Minta in Spite of Herself
A Scholarly Pursuit
Miranda at Heart
A Capital Arrangement

PRIDE AND PRESTON LIN

www.christinadudley.com

www.ingramcontent.com/pod-product-compliance
Lightning Source LLC
Chambersburg PA
CBHW061117310726

48974CB00002B/575